THE FOUNDATION

✶✶✶✶✶✶

W. MICHAEL GEAR
AND
KATHLEEN O'NEAL GEAR

WOLFPACK
PUBLISHING
— EST 2013 —

WOLFPACK
PUBLISHING
— EST 2012 —

Published by Wolfpack Publishing
5130 S. Fort Apache Road, 215-380
Las Vegas, NV 89148

Hardcover ISBN: 978-1-63977-007-6
Paperback IBSN 978-1-64734-649-2
eBook ISBN 978-1-64734-648-5
LCCN: 2021939555

THE FOUNDATION

******

TO

CHARLES CURLEY

WHO WILL RICHLY APPRECIATE
THE IRONY
OF THE FOUNDATION

CASTEL SANT'ANGELO, ROME. MARCH 15, 1946

***

JUSTICE IS A LIE.

Jack Simond studied Domenico Zaga's 1545 fresco known as *The Angel of Justice*. The art dominated one wall in the Hall of Justice—a vaulted room high in the Castel Sant'Angelo's warren-like maze. The painting flickered in the candlelight, its celestial figures soft and golden-hued.

The electricity had gone out, not an unusual occurrence in post-war Rome. The room had been pitched into blackness until a priest appeared with candles and an old kerosene lamp that swung from one hand.

Justice?

Whose? God's? Man's? Or was it all some insane human delusion? Hitler had cried for it. Tojo and Kenda had demanded it. What had begun as a crusade for justice, first in Manchuria, and later in the Sudetenland, had unleashed an insane rage that consumed the globe for eight long years. When it had finally burned down into smoldering embers, a third of the world lay desolate.

Was that Justice?

Simond considered the angel's intricately painted details and placed his hand against the wall. A chill leached from the underlying stone. Cold. Foreboding. Over the centuries, thousands had been judged in this very room—then brutally executed.

Do these walls weep with a million prayers, or only the heartbroken tears of the wrongfully dead?

The cold hinted of the wounded world that lay beyond the Castel Sant'Angelo's forbidding mass: Berlin, Dresden, Hamburg, Tokyo, Hiroshima and Nagasaki. So much lay in devastated ruin.

Sixty million dead?

How did a man comprehend—let alone quantify—the slaughter of that many men, women, and children?

The cold wall seemed to ache beneath his touch.

Justice was a lie.

He started when a soft voice spoke behind him, "Hello, old friend."

Jack turned, long coattails swirling around his legs. The newcomer stood in the doorway, his face candlelit. Yes, it was the same, but older, lined. Something terrible glittered behind the man's weary blue eyes. He removed a scuffed hat to expose red-blond hair trimmed close to the scalp, and his broad shoulders filled an old wool coat badly in need of patching.

Jack strode forward, calling, "Heinrich?" only to stop as the man's hand flew up, palm out.

"*Nein!* I am Gerhardt Wiesse."

"Ah. I see." Jack clasped the man to his breast. "Dear God! I'm so glad to see you alive! Helga sends her love. We have three girls now...your nieces!"

"Thank God." Gerhardt closed his eyes in relief.

"And Inga? Willy and Klara?"

The man who called himself Gerhardt pushed away. "They..." He gestured patience as he struggled for words. "You have to understand. The Wehrmacht and SS did terrible things in Russia and the East. Inhuman brutalities that exceed the imagination. After years of Nazi atrocities, the Red Army stormed into Prussia looking for justice."

His voice broke. "They were like mad dogs. Enraged. Women and girls were stripped bare. Thrown down in the snow and raped...and raped. And then..." He seemed to choke on the words. "They were cut apart as they screamed. Or perhaps nailed alive and left to hang from walls and barn doors. And what they did to children—"

"For God's sake, why didn't you get Inga and the kids out?"

Tears glinted in Gerhardt's eyes. "The Gauleiter there, Erich Koch, labeled any evacuation "defeatist". He made leaving a crime. A neighbor who managed to evade capture saw my Inga's naked corpse. She was frozen in the snow beside the road. My son and daughter were... were..." He waved it away. "Forgive me. As much as I loved her, she was also your sister. The children your niece and nephew."

Jack stared with dull disbelief. Inga dead? He'd so feared it—

refused to believe that Heinrich, with his connections, would have permitted it. "Why did you stay as long as you did?"

"I'm the richest man in Germany." He lifted his threadbare coat sleeve to wipe his eyes. "Though today my papers say I am an escaped and penniless Jew following the Rat Line out of Austria. An ultimate irony, yes?"

"Rich? They've seized all your assets."

"I left barely enough in the Deutsche Bank for appearances. The real wealth, my gold, the dollars, lira, and pounds sterling, is in Switzerland, New York, and London."

"Nevertheless, they must know you were the financial genius behind Krupp, Siemens, BASF, Junkers, Messerschmitt, and the rest. They won't stop hunting—"

"Heinrich Wulf is dead. I let Speer take the credit while I stayed in the shadows. Believe me, my friend, around a man like Hitler, the shadows are the safest place to be. Besides, most of the records have been destroyed. Blown apart by American bombs or burned by British incendiaries." He laughed. "I've heard that thousands of Nazi files are being used by Red Army troops as toilet paper. Fitting for Hitler's legacy, wouldn't you say?"

"Germany will be rebuilt. You can start over."

Gerhardt stepped close, his extended index finger trembling in emphasis. "The world is *changed*, Jack. America and the Soviets are poised to collide, and the ruination of Germany is nothing, *nothing* compared to what these new bombs can do."

Jack bowed his head. "They're working on even more terrifying weapons. The scraps of information I've heard make my blood run cold."

"There will always be new bombs. Better bombs that kill more and more people." Gerhardt placed his hands on Simond's shoulders, his keen blue eyes searching Jack's. "I need your help."

"We are family. Just ask."

"Think about this first. You've done very well with Boeing, General Motors, Martin, General Electric, Remington, and the rest. But another Hitler is inevitable."

"That's out of our hands, old friend."

Gerhardt smiled thinly, a thousand-yard stare behind his eyes.

"That's the old way of thinking."

"What are you getting at?"

"The political and military monsters will propel us to the brink again. Next time it won't just be Europe and Japan. They will destroy the entire world."

"Maybe, but what can we—"

"Look at me! But for you and Helga, everyone I love is *dead*! All of my family. My beloved Inga... My *children!*" He struggled for control. "The things I've seen! Until you've lived that kind of horror..." He shook his head. "My brain still cannot comprehend."

"I've seen the pictures."

Gerhardt's wounded eyes searched his. "What's the point of being the richest man in the world—of even surviving—if all that remains is an irradiated ruin?"

Jack softly asked, "What do you intend to do about it?"

Gerhardt stared coldly into Jack Simond's eyes. "I want to lay a new foundation. Reshape the very world. But it will mean secrecy. Cunning. Forging a different morality and power based only on survival."

From Jack's imagination, his sister's eyes, half-lidded in a pale and dead face, stared in horror. He tried not to think of what they'd done to her, how she had ended. Sprawled. Naked. Raped by how many filthy men? Frozen, with snow blowing over her brutalized body.

When his vision finally found its focus, he saw Gerhardt's questioning look, and over the man's shoulder, the Angel of Justice stared down in all her splendor.

Was it possible? Could they actually do it? He fought the urge to break into insane laughter. "A new foundation? When the only alternative is madness and rage? Just how do you plan to achieve this goal?"

ORIGINS

***

THE EARLIEST MENTION OF THE FOUNDATION APPEARS IN A REPORT GENERATED BY THE FBI in 1947. At the time Gerhardt Wiesse (GW) was traveling on a Swiss passport. He was flagged as having been in Moscow the week before. The stated purpose of his visit was to conduct business with various New York banking and investment firms, including First National City Bank of New York, the Chase Manhattan Bank, and Manufacturers Hanover Trust. GW did indeed conduct high-level meetings with principals of those organizations concurrent with the movement of large amounts of money through the ten regional Deutsche Banks (as established under the breakup of Deutsche Bank by the Allied occupation).

At the time GW was of personal interest to J. Edgar Hoover, then director of the FBI. A check of files indicates that GW was first noticed in January 1946. Claiming to be of Jewish descent, he first arrived in the US traveling on a Red Cross Displaced Person passport with identity papers issued by the Vatican Refugee Organization.

At the time FBI suspected GW to be Heinrich Wulf, a prominent member of the Nazi Party who had disappeared during the last days of the war. Wulf was suspected to have escaped Germany by the Brenner Pass route, through one of the Vatican 'ratlines'. Hoover's agents began building a case to prove that GW was indeed Heinrich Wulf.

It was during the 1947 surveillance that an agent overheard GW mention "The Foundation" while GW was having supper with Simon Thadeus Benton (STB) at the Waldorf Astoria. During the war years STB oversaw the transfer of funds from Nazi Germany to IBM, Ford Motor Company, and major American banks, especially Chase, through two of I. G. Farben's subsidiaries: American I. G. Chemical

Corporation and General Aniline and Film, head quartered in New Jersey. Note: Before the war Heinrich Wulf, (suspected to be GW) sat on the boards of Chase, Deutsche Bank, I. G. Farben, Standard Oil, and International Business Machine, all of which had substantial financial ties to Nazi Germany.

FBI surveillance of GW was summarily canceled a week later after GW was followed to Washington D.C., and observed having supper with Allen Dulles and John Foster Dulles at the Washington Hotel. (See note from Allen Dulles to J. Edgar Hoover specifically requesting that all surveillance on GW be dropped by FBI.)

A search of CIA files and records shows no record of any official meeting between the Dulles brothers and GW in February of 1947. Nor is there any record of GW in any Central Intelligence Agency personnel files, or any other record of his relationship with the agency.

—Paragraph 7, The Helen Rudy Report.

AFGHANISTAN, AUGUST 2020.

***

COLONEL BILL SOLACE WAS GIVING CAPTAIN BRENDA PEPPER THAT FAMILIAR MEASURING glance. She could read his worried expression like words on a page. Brenda kept rocking her jaw back and forth, trying to relieve the ringing in her ears. Flexing and stretching her muscles eased the quivering sensation that lingered in her bones. She'd thrown herself into the ditch at the last instant and covered her head as waves of concussion hammered her body and stunned her soul.

That had been twelve hours ago, and she was still rattled.

She gazed out at the cratered ruins of the village once known as Maluf. The Afghan midsummer sun, bright and relentless, cast shadows in the hard lines etched into Solace's face.

A knowing smile thinned his lips. "You got him, Captain."

Brenda stared at him unblinking, so tired she could barely feel her body.

Solace said, "Wake up. You look like you're asleep on your feet."

Brenda took a deep breath. "I'm more awake than I have ever been."

Bill had become more than Brenda's mentor and superior officer. Somewhere in the midst of what seemed to be the endless chaos of war, they'd developed an uncanny intimacy—as if two ancient souls had fitted themselves into a perfect match. He understood her horror as though it were his own.

"My God, I hate these savages," Bill said. "And Alahiri was one of the worst. Still can't believe we're holding peace talks with these animals."

Brenda ran a hand through her short black hair and let her gaze drift over the destroyed village. The torn bodies of several children lay in the dirt. From somewhere deep down inside her, she heard a little girl crying. Strange. Brenda tried to recall the event. What memory was that? When had she ever wept like that?

"Savages, Bill? Come on, if Americans had to live in squalor like this, we—"

"You're insane. For God's sake, we're a civilized people. These are mad dogs. Can you imagine an American family choosing to hide terrorists in their homes? With their children? We told them what would happen! *Stupid* savages. Pure and simple."

Brenda swayed on her feet. The dead children's faces were coated with dust. Many of them had their mouths open in silent cries. The "terrorists" had been their neighbors, their friends. They'd probably known those men since they were boys. It seemed so clear to her. "If I'd known so many children were inside, I..." the words trailed away.

Bill gave her a hard stare. "What do you think we're doing here, Captain? Saving the world?"

Brenda shook her head and looked away. By God, she wanted to save the world. She had dedicated her life to protecting her country, her people. And now—somehow oddly compressed and distorted—the narrow confines of her universe had boiled down to a focused realization: she'd become nothing more than a hollow-eyed monster. A cold weapon.

Maluf was only the latest proof of her talents.

Beyond the devastated village, the valley rose tan and dusty to the rocky gray slopes of the mountains. High peaks chewed at the sere sky like ragged teeth. The earth had devoured the heavens when the hellfire missiles consumed Maluf.

Torn rags of clothing flapped in the breeze. Cups, plastic containers, broken crockery, and dented cooking pots were strewn in confusion. Shattered stones from houses that had once cradled lives and dreams lay tumbled across the soil. Twenty feet to her right, the broken corpse of a little boy sprawled where the detonation had thrown him. Facedown in a pool of sun-blackened blood, the deformed skull was a magnet for an angry column of flies.

Surely she'd seen the kid. Disguised in a burqa, she'd walked down Maluf's narrow street the evening before. She fought to remember. Had she seen that boy playing in the street?

A dull emptiness filled her. As though her soul had crossed the river to the Land of the Dead, but her body had remained behind.

She said, "You shouldn't be here, Bill. The area's not secure."

"You got Alahiri. I wanted to see it myself." He paused, crows' feet deepening as he studied the dead, the blasted hovels. "Besides, Jim Alexander's people secured the perimeter."

"Glad you trust him." Brenda didn't. The guy was a West Point REMF. But she didn't trust anybody. Except Bill Solace.

She turned her attention to the rocky terraces that rose behind the waiting helicopter, whose rotors were turning slowly. She could sense the pilot's worry, feel the threat in the air she breathed.

She made herself look at the village again. Too many women and children. A broken and naked little girl—her dress ripped from her body by concussion—had been blown to one side by the detonating AGM-114s. The breeze seemed to toy with her dark curls, as if in some heartless jest.

Solace gave Brenda that cutting sidelong glance again. A faint and sympathetic smile bent his lips. "Back to the chopper, Captain. You did a great job here."

"Yeah."

Maluf and its luckless inhabitants were now merely statistics in the endless battle between abstract concepts of right and wrong.

Solace ground his teeth before saying, "Buck up, Captain. You know the kind of man Alahiri was. The atrocities he committed and planned to commit in the future. You should be proud."

Brenda blinked. Searched. Couldn't find even a hint of pride inside. Her thoughts drifted to her father. Colonel Harold "Leather Guts" Pepper had been the most important man in her world until Bill Solace had come along. She suspected that if her father could see Maluf, he'd purse his lips and give that short "it had to be done" nod that she'd hated and admired since she was little.

In a voice that sounded leaden even to her own ears, she said, "Give me something to believe in, Bill. Something to fight for."

"You just took out one of the worst of the bad guys. What are you talking—"

"And I killed almost a hundred women and children. Peace talks? The worst part is that we're leaving, pulling out with the job half finished. Five Alahiris will rise in this one's place. If I have to do shit like this, I want it to mean something. I fucking want *something* to live for."

Bill whispered, "Something to live for?"

She let Solace take her arm and turn her toward the waiting Blackhawk. Again, her gaze went to the terraces. That's where she'd set up her ambush last night, positioned her snipers. The shooting angles had provided an excellent field of fire, the dry drainages allowing for easy exfiltration.

Like a programmed robot, she took one step after another toward the helo.

"Maybe when we get back..." From his tone, she knew that Bill Solace had crossed some long-held line. "We've both got leave coming."

Throughout the two years they'd been working together, the attraction had grown. In off moments she'd allow herself to fantasize. A future without Bill Solace had become unimaginable.

Somehow, they had remained professional—though he crept into her dreams at night, the fantasy of his warm body comforting hers.

"I could go for a week in the Florida Keys," she heard herself say. "Someplace crazy like Key West."

"Never been there."

She turned to look up at him. If they did this it would be like pulling the pin on a hand grenade. Nothing would be the same again. "Are you sure?"

"Hell, yes, Captain."

The wind shifted, and the stench of torn intestines blew around them.

They were steps from the Blackhawk, and a corporal was crouching on the deck and extended a hand to help her up. "Glad you made it back, Captain. Colonel."

Brenda grabbed his hand, felt the pain in her bruised shoulder as she was pulled in.

Bill Solace was a half-step behind her. With a loud *pock-snap* and supersonic crack, a bullet blew his head apart. She saw it, a half-image at the corner of her eye: the exploding of his head, the spray. So quick and Bill was gone, dropped senseless below the helo's deck.

"*Go, go, go!*" the corporal yelled to the pilot. He dragged Brenda inside, and the helicopter lunged into the air.

"No!" Brenda shouted. "Bill's down! What if he's not dead? We have to go back! *Turn around!*"

"He's dead, Captain!" the corporal shouted over the roar. "Look at me! He's dead."

Brenda scrambled across the deck on her belly to reach the door and look down.

In the swirling dust, she saw him.

Broken.

Sprawled.

Bloody.

She saw him.

CHAPTER ONE

***

JACKSON HOLE ECONOMIC POLICY SYMPOSIUM, JACKSON, WYOMING.

Brenda Pepper jerked awake in the darkness.

Her body shook.

"Damn it."

She pushed sweat-damp sheets back and swung her feet to the floor. Leaning forward on the edge of the bed, she dropped her head between her knees and just breathed.

Afghanistan was far behind her. Bill Solace long laid to rest in Arlington. Just another in a long row among endless rows of heroes, a monotonous white marker at his head.

Behind her closed eyes, the image remained as clear as if she were seeing it for the first time: Solace, the back of his head blown off, facedown in the dust.

Brenda fought the shakes as she rose to her feet and started swinging her arms to burn off the adrenaline.

"You're in Jackson, Wyoming. You have your own security firm. You're keeping a woman alive. Chantel Simond. That's your job now. You're not a soldier."

I'll always be a soldier.

As images from the dream faded, her heart rate slowed, and the hotel room swam back into focus. She was head of Chantel Simond's security detail.

Bill came.

She knew why, of course. She'd been getting sloppy. Letting things slide because for the most part the job was meaningless. She despised the usual clients who hired her for personal protection. For the past two years she'd ensured that spoiled rich kids stayed out of their parents' way, and done her best to keep over-paid asshole celebrities out of jail and cleaned up their messes.

The Chantel Simond contract had come out of the blue. She'd been hired by an over-dressed blond guy named Poul Hammond in New York. It was a last-minute, rush-to-get-it-done, money-is-no-object assignment and looked simple enough.

But Bill didn't come to her unless something was about to go terribly wrong.

Unnerved, she pulled on her clothing, clawed her hair back, and forced herself to walk steadily to the door.

"That's it, Brenda. Make sure the night detail is still frosty and doing its job."

Stepping out into the hotel's hallway, she glanced to where one of her hired agents cradled a cup of coffee. He rose and signaled the all clear.

She nodded but needed to verify that herself. Just to be sure.

Flashback! So powerful it almost staggered her: Solace. His glance pierced her soul as he said, *"What do you think we're doing here, Captain?"*

She propped a hand against the wall and took a few moments to shake off the eerie tingling in her guts.

"I'm not trying to save the world, Bill," she whispered to her ghostly guardian. "Just one woman. I have to figure it out. If I were trying to kill Chantel Simond, how would I do it?"

That's how Brenda Pepper would keep Simond safe.

SIMOND

***

JOHN QUINTON SIMOND, AKA "JACK" (JQS) WAS BORN IN 1915 AT THE FAMILY ESTATE outside of Saratoga, New York, to Prescot and Althea Simond. JQS was the first of three children: Inga, born a year later (and later married to Heinrich Wulf; died 1945) and Terese born in 1920 (married Thomas Paul Heston; four children; died 2001).

Prescot Simond (PS) was well known for his financial interests in several of the larger New York banking institutions, having been integral in the formation of the Federal Reserve Banking system. An intimate of Paul Warburg and Avery Rockefeller, and E. Rolland Harriman, Prescot Simond sat on the boards of National City Bank, United Banking Corporation, Chase, and Manufacturers and Hanover. PS was integral to the formation of the Council on Foreign Relations in 1921.

JQS received the finest education, culminating in a bachelor's degree from Yale, where he graduated *summa cum laude* in International Law. He shared a room with Heinrich Wulf, whose acquaintance he had made as a boy while traveling with his father on business in Germany. Both were initiates in the notorious Order of Skull and Bones, and—as often happens among the order's initiates—ended up marrying each other's sisters. (JQS married Helga Wulf in 1938.)

While varying estimates are made of JQS's net worth, his international holdings made him one of the richest men in the world. In 1952 he acquired dual citizenship in Switzerland, and subsequently bought an island estate in the Caribbean to which he retired to raise his family: Felicia, Inga, Fallon, and Renaud. Though removed from public life, JQS was suspected of considerable influence on the international stage and is thought to be the American impetus for the founding of the "Bilderberg Group" along with Dutch Prince

Bernhard, Dr. Joseph Retinger, and Lord Victor Rothschild. Since its founding, the "Bilderberg Group" has been a shadowy orchestrating body behind the birth of the modern European Union culminating in the Maastricht Treaty in 1992.

Nor did JQS's influence stop there. He was thought to be a major player behind the scenes in the formation of the Trilateral Commission in 1972, and while he wasn't in the first meeting, the word is that he monitored the proceedings from an adjoining room.

—Paragraph 5, The Helen Rudy Report

CHAPTER TWO

***

"YOU BITCH! YOU STINKING, FILTHY BITCH! YOU TOLD!" THE WORDS WERE FORCED FROM A rage-constricted throat. Chantel cringed as the black apparition lashed out. With each strike she quivered, reliving the sting, horror, and blood.

"Gonna kill you, you fucking cunt!" The black wraith struck again, and again. Slicing, cutting, and stinging as blood ran warm and sticky. He loomed over her, slinging blood with each movement of his scythe-shaped hands. Red and hot, it spattered on her face, matted her hair, and spotted her body with starburst patterns.

Terror and pain.

She huddled down in the darkness. Fragments of her soul shattered and fled. Each burst with a hollow pop. Bits of her were blowing apart, flying off. Vanishing. Even the last whimpering essence would splinter into a numb infinity.

And then nothingness.

She screamed...

"Chantel?" a soft voice intruded on the horror. "It's just a dream."

Chantel flinched in anticipation of another strike and rending of her flesh, only to jerk awake in a dark room.

Her pulse raced, breath tearing past her lips. Her skin had gone clammy with sweat.

Sitting up, she pushed the sheet down and gasped the cool air. She was in a bedroom. A hotel. The room was illuminated by the dim light of the bedside clock and the glowing electronics. In Jackson, the economic summit.

"You alright?" Janeesh's voice asked from the door.

"Just a nightmare." Chantel pulled her hair back and tried to still her fevered body. "Go back to bed."

"Yes, ma'am." The door closed.

The dream came and went in patterns she hadn't quite deciphered, but usually in spring. On the anniversary. Though, like tonight, it would come surging up from the subconscious to remind her that terror and pain lurked just past the thin illusion of security and safety.

"It's just a dream, Chantel."

Throwing the covers aside, she swung her feet to the floor, turned on the bedside light, and stood. Years of experience had taught her the self-delusion of lying in bed, trying to sleep. The markets had been open for hours in Europe. She could get four hours of work in before the rest of her team would be up and on the job.

Padding over to her clothes, she pulled off her sleep shirt, and froze. In the full-length mirror, her body looked lean and graceful with long legs. A narrow waist accented her hips and flat belly. Her breasts were high and proportionate to broad shoulders. The kind of woman's body Hollywood would salivate over.

She couldn't stop herself. As if caressing the forbidden, she ran fingertips down the long lines of scars that disfigured her otherwise flawless skin. As if she needed a physical reminder that she lived a cursed and lonely existence.

CHAPTER THREE

***

FOR TAYLOR AND HIS SPOTTER BENNIE, THIS WAS THE BIG ONE. MOST OF THEIR WORK consisted of eliminating drug lords, aspiring political rivals, business competitors, or the occasional government official. They didn't come cheap. Their base fee for a job was two million Euros, even for a simple third-world elimination without complications. From there the price went up.

They had no shortage of clients. In the high-stakes game of business, shelling out four or five million to remove a pesky bureaucrat who'd been building a case that might deny a permit, or impose fines, was cheaper than tens of millions in lost revenue and penalties. More than one third-world dictator had called upon their services when rising political opponents threatened long-held power. In the calculation of cost-benefit ratios, a few million spent on Taylor and Bennie might be enough incentive for a rival cartel to abandon even a most lucrative "pharmaceutical" market. Often it didn't even entail taking out a kingpin. Sometimes just taking out a wife or child would do the trick.

Prior to the client's phone call, Taylor had never heard of Chantel Simond. He still wasn't sure why she was important. Some sort of investment banker? What did matter was that someone was willing to pay ten million Euros to have her killed in a most public way. This meant that a great deal more than that stood to be either gained or lost.

For Taylor, it would be the score of a lifetime. He didn't just live for his record—he *was* his record. One shot. That's all he had ever needed over the years.

But more than that, with this job he'd finally have enough to buy his island: a beautiful Aegean gem off Naxos. Owned by a Greek transportation magnate, and on the market for years, it was now within Taylor's reach. Finally. After years of saving.

One more shot, and it would be his.

Taylor, always the consummate professional, looked like a tourist. The blue jeans, flannel shirt, hiking boots, and sunglasses—along with a scruffy five-day beard—gave him an outdoorsy look that fit right in with the rugged Jackson Hole image.

Now he stood on the southwest corner of Cache and Broadway with Jackson's world-famous town square across from him. He raised a camera to his eye, adjusting the telephoto lens as he studied the Wort Hotel a half-block to the west. One by one he checked the windows on the top floor. The blinds had been drawn on each.

Earlier he had cut through the lobby and into the Silver Dollar Bar, unsurprised to find the place crawling with security. Access to the upper floors was strictly monitored.

Chantel Simond's new protection—being run by a recently hired woman—was turning out to be top notch. Taylor had never liked the idea of women butting into men's jobs. Putting this one in her place would be a pleasure.

"What do you think?" Bennie stopped beside Taylor just as the light changed and traffic began to accelerate.

Taylor lowered his camera. "They had a man on the roof using binoculars to sweep the surrounding buildings. The target's in the master suite. They're keeping the drapes pulled. If we try to set up for a shot, they'll spot us before we have the opportunity to take it."

Benny grunted, rubbing the stubble on his chin. "I've done a circuit of the hotel. Assuming they bring her out the front door, we'll have to be close. No good shooting angles with enough distance to allow us to extract."

"Nope." Taylor narrowed his eyes, ignoring the passing pedestrians. "Chantel Simond is proving to be one tough target."

Taylor gave Bennie a sidelong glance. "The client said she'd have average security. Some executive protection firm from New York used to catering to spoiled movie stars and rich executives."

Bennie sucked absently at his lips, then nodded. "I don't care what the client said. We don't have a shot. Can you trust this guy 'Flapjack' to give us a heads up when they evacuate her?"

"He comes well recommended."

"Then it's off to Plan B. If you can't hunt..."

"Ambush," Taylor finished their private joke.

Chantel Simond wasn't leaving Wyoming alive. The record demanded nothing less, not to mention the island.

"A WORLD-WIDE WEB"

***

THE QUESTION OF JUST WHAT THE FOUNDATION IS STILL REMAINS. IS IT SIMPLY A FAMILY business consortium? It appears so on the surface. Gerhardt Wiesse and Jack Simond ruthlessly and relentlessly built a global empire. In doing so, they used money and power, and did not hesitate to stoop to assassination, bribery, extortion, and blackmail. They also showed remarkable acumen in the investments they made and the industries they gained control of. The difference seems to be in their long-term goals. Whereas most entrepreneures are focused on profit and wealth, The Foundation has, since its beginning, set its sights on control.

Implicit in the notion of control is an understanding of the fundamentals of economy: food production, mining, manufacturing, finance, medicine, distribution, energy, and communication. In each of these areas, either Wiesse and Simond had firmly established themselves, or they created strategic alliances and elbowed their way in. This is best illustrated by the marriages of their children to prominent leaders of the various industries and regions across the globe that they considered critical to the achievement of their goals. In that way, The Foundation is much like a medieval monarchy.

—Paragraph 18, The Helen Rudy Report.

CHAPTER FOUR

***

OHIO'S JUNIOR SENATOR THOMAS JESSE ORTEGA HAD BEEN ALL OVER THE WORLD—mostly compliments of the United States Navy and Special Operations Command—but he'd never been to the heart of Wyoming's Rockies. He hadn't been prepared for the magnificent sight of the snow-capped Tetons.

Nor was the scenery the only thing that absorbed him. Tom Ortega had spent the last three days picking up the equivalent of a shock course in economics. Though the COVID precautions had sucked, he'd had meetings with the chairman of the Federal Reserve, joined the head of the Securities Exchange Commission for cocktails, met and listened to some of the richest and most successful magnates from Wall Street, and shared breakfast coffee with some of the movers and shakers in the banking world.

Most of the financial masters from the real world were polite, if not mildly condescending, acting as if a mere senator should be tolerated, and definitely kept at arm's length. Nevertheless, because he was willing to listen and learn rather than throw his political weight around, Ortega had begun to catch glimmerings of what concerned both bankers and traders. On the whole, they were anxious.

The world economy, he'd learned, hung by a thread, top-heavy with debt that couldn't be repaid without rabid devaluation of currency. And COVID, with its trillion-dollar rescue plans, had been the final straw. Nor could the Fed allow an increase in interest rates, or the debt would balloon, which in turn would crater lending and suffocate both investment and capital formation.

Speculation was rampant about the new Russian leader, Leon Platnikov, and what his policies meant for a teetering world economy.

And the cognoscenti uniformly condemned the recently introduced "Banking Reform Act", Senate bill 107.

Tom was sipping morning coffee on a deck at the Snow King Resort. Across the table from him sat Treasury Secretary Timothy Johnson, a cup in his hand as he looked up at the ski slope, green now, with hikers climbing the trail. That's when Tom's aide, Trevor Hughes, stepped out the sliding glass door bearing a piece of paper.

"A woman named Chantel Simond, from Simond International Holdings, would like to have a face-to-face with you this afternoon at three. In *her* hotel room if you can believe it. Just thought I'd check before sending your most sincere apologies."

Setting his coffee down, Johnson cried, "Chantel Simond wants to see *you*?"

"Gee, Tim. You make it sound like I'm dirt on someone's shoe. I've never heard of Simond International Holdings. I should drop everything? Go to *her* hotel? She can schedule with my office if—"

"Take the meeting." Johnson stabbed a finger at him. "No, you haven't heard of Simond International Holdings. They like it that way."

"Who are they?"

"Only the biggest players in international finance. You've met the CEOs of Citi, Bank of America, RBS, Deutsche Bank? Credit Suisse? The ECB? If something's important, those guys don't tie their shoes without an okay from Simond International. Simond is John Galt. The people behind the curtain." He made a face. "Hell, I'm the Secretary of the Treasury, and I've never even *seen* the head of Simond International Holdings, let alone been invited to a meeting."

"And what does this Chantel do for Simond?"

"She's the new queen. Young. Just took over the reins from old Fallon Simond, her uncle. Word is the guy keeled over from a heart attack a couple of months back. Not much gets past their firewall, but I heard Chantel came out on top after a nasty power struggle to take his place. Nobody had ever heard of her up until a couple of months ago."

"So, what does Chantel Simond want with me?"

Johnson leaned back, expression pensive. "Maybe she's taking this 'Ortega for President' chatter seriously. This could be the most important meeting of your life."

Something about the look in Johnson's eyes set alarm bells ringing.

CHAPTER FIVE

***

AT FIVE TO THREE THAT AFTERNOON, THOMAS ORTEGA CROSSED THE LOBBY OF THE WORT Hotel and climbed the steps to the top floor. He was met by a competent security detail that took his name, checked his ID, and actually looked up his picture on the Capitol website.

"Ms. Simond will see you now, Senator," the detail leader, a woman, told him. She was trim, fit, and oozing competence. Ex-military. Tom could see it in her walk, the way she led him to the suite door, and called, "Senator Ortega, ma'am."

"Send him in."

Tom straightened his cuffs and strode through the door. Whatever he expected, it wasn't to see a flurry of activity as staff people watched monitors, tapped on keyboards, and talked on cell phones.

And there, behind the desk, sat a very attractive redhead. Ortega judged her to be in her early thirties. Cool green eyes set in a delicately formed face were taking his measure. Her hair was pulled back in a serviceable ponytail that hung over a tailored gray wool suit. A very expensive suit, he realized.

"Senator?" she stood, offering her hand. Her grip was professional, her gaze searching his.

"My pleasure, Ms. Simond."

"Have a seat." She waved to the chair beside the desk. "Janeesh, I believe the senator prefers an Americano with two extra shots. As I recall we have some Vienna Roast in the command center." She glanced at Ortega. "Is that agreeable?"

Tom asked warily, "How did you know that?"

"We make a habit of impeccable research, Senator. How is your daughter Jessie doing? Osteoarthropathy, isn't it?" Her smile barely registered on un-glossed lips. Up close, her only recourse to makeup consisted of mascara. The fact was she had the kind of complexion that didn't need any help.

"She's not well. But thank you for asking. It's a rare bone disease. They're trying everything they can."

Simond nodded, as if she already knew that. Her assertive calm left him feeling even more uncomfortable. Not that his daughter was any secret—she'd been featured during the campaign.

"Your election upset a lot of people, Senator. On both sides of the aisle." She gave him a faint smile as coffee was delivered by an aide. "Any thoughts as to why you appeal to voters? Is it just that you are a war hero?"

He took the coffee, sipped, found it delicious. "After the latest presidential implosion, the country's in chaos. Political double-speak has become the art of saying nothing until the polls come out and the potential benefits, pros and cons, are weighed against campaign contributions. The people aren't fools, and they're exhausted by the partisan bullshit. I just tell it like I see it."

"May I ask how you are leaning on S-107?"

Now we get to the heart of the matter. He took another sip of coffee before he answered, "The Korkoran-Hardy bill is interesting."

She raised a challenging eyebrow. "I call that political double-speak, Senator."

"A lot of people are worried about big banks getting bigger and bigger. That's a lot of money centralized in a few, very elite institutions. I'm uncomfortable with 'too big to fail'. Especially given government debt after the COVID relief borrowing and the fast and loose way we've heard derivatives are being handled. And I'm even more uncomfortable with the information coming out about irregularities with international lending. My take is that we didn't learn anything from the 2008 crash."

"Do you understand the significance of the LIBOR?" she asked, sipping at her own cup of coffee.

"The London Interbank Offered Rate, yes. It's the interest rate that international banks charge each other when they borrow money back and forth. I know there's some kind of problem, but no one's talking much."

"The problem is in London. A fellow by the name of Colin Penwick.

It's a complicated and clever scheme, but essentially he's been making a killing manipulating the rates." She paused, a line forming in her brow. "The debt crisis is real. When the next crash comes, there will be no bailouts. Global banking will be destroyed overnight." She paused. "And with regard to S-107, I'd like to ask you a favor."

He set his cup of coffee on the desk and folded his hands in his lap. *Here it comes.* "And that is?"

"You are probably aware that they put you on the Banking Committee because Korkoran figured you'd suck up to his power and experience and vote as you were directed. Your vote on the Senate banking committee is key. I'm asking you to put a hold on the bill for a couple of months."

"Why would I do that?"

Her cool gaze seemed to peer into his soul. "First, because we need a couple of months to deal with Penwick and the derivative problem. You are correct to be concerned, but we'd like a chance to handle it in-house. Keep an eye on the financial news, and you'll know when we've cleaned it up. Second, have you actually read the Korkoran-Hardy bill?"

Tom winced. "I've started it. It's an understatement to call it tough going."

"Fifteen hundred and sixty pages. All carefully crafted over the years by Senator Korkoran's dedicated staff. Hardy introduced the House version as a means of milking campaign donations, and it makes good populist press for his re-election."

She steepled her fingers. "Did you know that Korkoran's senior staffer, Peggy Hayes, has two children by Big Jim Korkoran? She and Big Jim have been lovers since his first campaign, and now the good senator is about to retire. The bill is a farewell gift to Peggy and the rest of his staff. S-107 is so complicated and arcane that implementation, let alone regulation, will be a nightmare. And who better to offer their services to keep the banks out of trouble than Korkoran's staff? Peggy Hayes and the rest of Korkoran's merry band can name their compensation—and be worth every penny to the banks when it comes to avoiding regulatory complications and fines. They'll be set for life."

Tom took a deep breath and sighed.

Her voice dropped. "Will you give us two months to correct

some of the structural problems and bad apples? After that, you can make up your own mind about whether you want to vote for Peggy Hayes' payoff or not."

"You can fix these issues in two months?" *Who is this woman?*

"I think so. The debt crisis and the too-big-to-fail problem? That, Senator, I can't fix. The current administration won't allow it. As currently implemented, regulatory contradictions make it impossible for banks and institutions to do business without violating some aspect of the law. That allows Attorney General Ramey and the Department of Justice to shake them down for ten or fifteen billion apiece whenever they need the funds."

"You make America sound like the third world."

Her smile held no humor. "Can you give me the two months?"

"What do you get out of it, Ms. Simond?"

"If we handle Penwick internally, we can avoid more pointless regulations and a scandal that could trigger an international panic. If we can squelch the growing abuse of derivatives, we defuse a destabilizing practice that will eventually lead to long-term losses and more government interference. Third, I prove that you can work with me to solve problems without cumbersome regulations."

He shifted uncomfortably in his chair. He had the feeling he was out of his league. No, worse. He wasn't even sure what the game was. But she intrigued him. "What the hell. It will take two months just to finish reading the damn bill."

"Thank you, Senator." She studied him thoughtfully. "You've impressed quite a few people here. Can I ask a personal question?"

"Shoot."

"If I could grant you any wish, outside of your daughter's health, what would it be?"

"That's easy. I want the bureaucracies reined in, a sane tax code, and a thriving American economy where people can start and grow businesses again. I came to Jackson to try to learn how to fix the country."

"The political class has a lot of vested interest in keeping their cash cows."

He locked eyes with her. "I'm sure that's true, but I don't want to see this country crash down in ruin or splinter in civil war. And I'll do whatever it takes to keep that from happening."

She studied him for a long moment, as though judging the quality of his soul, then she passed him a sheet of paper. "I had a close friend who suffered from osteoarthropathy. It's a nasty disease. Since then, we've been funding research into the causes and a potential cure. It's up to you, but you might call that number. They could probably see Jessie over the Thanksgiving break."

He stared at the clinic name, phone number, and address. "Turks and Caicos?"

Her gaze was green ice. "They don't like the regulatory environment in the United States. They're doing cutting-edge genetic research. And in sensitive cases for high-profile people, a trip to the islands can be passed off as a simple vacation instead of a major news story."

He felt a little numb. So, the payoff for putting a hold on S-107 was a trip to an elite off-shore medical clinic? Interesting. "I understand." To regain his composure, he added, "Now, if you could just do something about the Russians."

"One thing at a time. Good day, Senator," she said to dismiss him. Her eyes had returned to the papers on the desk.

As Tom rose, he felt like an insecure six-year-old on the playground of a new school.

He started for the door. Damn. The way she'd said it, she might have regarded Leon Platnikov as just another detail to be attended to.

On the way down the hall, he broke into a sweat. Fifteen minutes ago, he'd thought he understood the rules. It was just beginning to dawn on him that maybe he, a United States senator, didn't know anything.

CHAPTER SIX

***

TAYLOR HAD CHOSEN THE POSITION WITH GREAT CARE. SAGEBRUSH COVERED THE SLIGHT rise, and he and Bennie had been able to excavate a hollow from the gravelly soil. It conformed to his body, masked any heat signature, and the lip created a perfect rest for the rifle. Nothing had been left to chance. Burlap wrapped the rifle's barrel and long suppressor; his scope, similarly shrouded, included a hood to preclude even a glint from the sun.

Beside him, Benny barely moved as he kept an eye to the fifty-power spotting scope. Both men wore ghillie suits—fabric nets into which they had woven sprigs of sage and grass that blended seamlessly with the surrounding vegetation.

A thousand yards to the west, the Jackson Hole airport basked in the midmorning gleam, while behind it the rocky, gray splendor of the Tetons rose like some kind of perverted antediluvian teeth. Brilliant veins of snow filled the high crags and clefts, contrasting with the remarkable blue of the Wyoming sky.

The hollow echo of a rifle shot carried on the breeze. Hunting season was in full swing as men wearing blaze-orange pursued elk on the adjacent feeding grounds surrounding Teton National Park.

Sunlight enameled the cars in the distant airport parking lot, and tourist traffic whispered past on the highway.

"Ten thirty-five," Benny murmured as he shifted his arm and checked his watch.

"Flapjack will call when she leaves the hotel." Taylor snugged the rifle butt to his shoulder and settled on the cheek rest to stare through the Nightforce scope.

A Subaru pulled up before the departure doors, and a man and woman stepped from the vehicle. "See the woman in the red coat? Give me the dope."

Benny checked his Kestrel—a 4500NV that computed wind speed and direction, altitude, temperature, barometric pressure, and humidity. Touching the buttons, the little computer made its calculations."The range is eleven fifty-two meters." Benny double-checked the computer. "Adjust nine-point-four mils elevation, one-point-six mils left for windage."

Taylor adjusted the rifle until one of the tiny dots in the scope's Horus reticle centered on the woman in red as she lifted a suitcase from the Subaru's back hatch. "Got it."

Eye to the spotting scope, Bennie said, "Take the shot."

Taylor took a half breath, watched the tiny dot jiggle with his heartbeat. As the dot settled between heartbeats, he thought: *Now.*

"Bang, you're dead."

Through the scope, Taylor watched the target kiss her husband before the man picked up the suitcase and walked into the airport. The woman, still smiling, slid into the Subaru's driver's seat, closed the door and drove off, unaware.

Benny stiffened, pressing a finger to his earpiece. "Flapjack says she's about to leave. She's in a tan Chevy Suburban. Two-car detail. Blocking vehicle is a white Denali. The vehicles just pulled up in front of the hotel."

"Rock and roll," Taylor whispered.

The next time they ran the drill, it would be Chantal Simond in their sights.

CHAPTER SEVEN

***

WHEN SHE WAS HIRED IN NEW YORK TWO WEEKS EARLIER, BRENDA HAD BEEN GIVEN *CARTE blanche* to set up Chantel Simond's security for the Jackson Hole Economic Conference.

Brenda's first meeting with Chantel at the Jackson Hole airport had surprised her. She'd expected a mature woman to descend from the corporate jet. Instead, she got an elegant, flaming-haired beauty in her early thirties who could pass as a supermodel. Chantel dressed immaculately in tailored designer labels and, as the head of her hyper-efficient staff, left no doubt as to her intelligence or competence.

Brenda did not know what role Chantel Simond had played in the just-concluded conference, but the woman's clout was readily apparent. The yearly event was big, attended by the Fed Chairman and his minions, the high mucky-mucks in charge of the big banks, the Secretary of the Treasury, and a cadre of the financial world's magnates. Following in their wake trailed a small horde of journalists.

Throughout the week, Chantel had taken private meetings with a who's who of American finance, including the president's chief economic advisor. And more to the point, they'd come to her, climbing the steps of the Wort Hotel to her top-floor suite.

Finding a room in Jackson during the economic summit was tough enough, but Chantel Simond had rented the historic Wort Hotel's entire top floor for herself and her staff of six. From a security standpoint, the choice had been masterful and allowed complete control of access.

So far Brenda's job had been routine, though she'd taken every precaution. Often to the irritation of cabinet-level dignitaries, self-important politicians, and the privileged hyper-rich. Brenda had hired the best: veteran professionals in the field of executive protection. Her team functioned like a well-oiled machine. So far everything had gone by the book, without the least hint of a threat.

Alahiri must have thought the same thing before I ambushed him.

All that remained was to get Chantel to her corporate jet, where it waited at the Jackson Hole airport fifteen miles to the north. But ever since dreaming of Bill, worry had been chafing at Brenda's soul—that irritating sense that she'd missed something.

As Brenda waited on the carpet outside Chantel Simond's suite door, she checked the stairway one last time. Happy Gonzales glanced up from where he stood on the landing below. He gave her a thumb's up.

In Brenda's earpiece, Stud Meyer's voice said, *"We're ready. Looks clear, ma'am."*

Brenda nodded to herself, turned, knocked three times, waited for four seconds, and knocked twice.

The door opened and Brenda smiled at Kelly Patterson as she stepped out into the hall. She'd known Kelly for ten years, ever since Kelly had been a sergeant in the 1st Armored Division. Kelly had served three tours in Afghanistan, had a Bradley blown up around her, and picked up a Bronze Star.

She'd married Brenda's brother, Mark, a couple of years back—a classic love story.

Kelly was dressed in white slacks, a classy sweater, and wore a long black wool coat from Versace. The red wig proved a dashing contrast to her normal brunette, and the green contacts were unsettling. Up close she'd never pass for Chantel Simond, but it would do from across the room. Both women had the same fit physique.

"You ready?"

"Good to go, Brenda."

Brenda took a breath. Something was wrong. She could feel it like invisible tentacles reaching for her, but every possible security measure was in place. It was probably just the jitters. In the back of her mind, Bill whispered, *probably not*. She clamped her jaw, staying frosty as she led the way down the stairs; Happy stepped in behind Kelly to cover the rear.

On the first floor, Cap Smith and Brownie Phillips nodded and fell into a classic diamond formation as they crossed the lobby. Cap opened the main door, checked the street, and walked to the waiting vehicles. Bill Anderson and Pete Williams were ready in the idling white Denali, eyes on the buildings across from them.

Brenda opened the door on the tan Suburban as her team covered Kelly's route. The woman ducked in and slid across the seat to leave Brenda room. Cap slapped the roof as he closed the door, and they were off.

"We're rolling," Brenda said into her shoulder microphone.

"Roger," came the reply in her earpiece.

As they made the right around the hotel, a black-haired woman stepped out of the employees' exit. Dressed in a housekeeper's uniform, she accompanied a genial looking man wearing utility coveralls. A worn leather tool belt was thrown over the guy's shoulder. The two climbed into a battered Dodge Ram four-by-four pickup, fired it up, and backed out into the street.

Brenda called into her mic, "Anderson?"

Anderson's Denali braked.

The Dodge rumbled loudly and shot forward into the street, apparently in a hurry.

At the corner, a policeman examined the interloping Dodge, and waved them through.

Brenda caught a brief glimpse of the famous elk-antler arch on the square and turned her attention to the highway that would take them north. But for the pickup, it had all gone with perfect precision.

At the wheel, Adam Wilson tucked the Suburban's front bumper to within a couple of feet of the Denali's tailpipe eliminating any chance of a vehicle slipping between them.

Then they were out of town, passing the elk refuge.

"Airport? We're ten minutes out," Brenda said into her mic.

"Roger that. All clear here."

Brenda leaned back in the seat. "Stay frosty, everyone. We're not home free."

Kelly laughed. "No, but almost. What a great job! I always wanted to see Jackson. My God, the Tetons are beautiful. Maybe Mark and I need a vacation. Ski season's coming. I haven't been skiing in years. Just walking around town would be relaxing. You know, like a mini honeymoon."

"And to think," Brenda told her, "the best you could do when it came to a man was a grinning idiot like my brother."

Brenda had introduced Kelly to Mark in a forward operating base east of Kabul; she'd seen the stars shine in the woman's eyes. And wild man Mark had fallen like an anvil. Who said there was no such thing as love at first sight?

For an instant, the thought left her wistful. Even her impetuous brother had found someone and settled down. And with Kelly, Brenda's best friend in the whole world. Why couldn't Brenda find someone?

She mostly knew the answer to that. The demands of running a business like executive security entailed a certain catlike awareness that just precluded long-term relationships. But the fact was she scared the hell out of most men. Her last paramour had told her she had eyes of a corpse, "glazed with death". It had hit her hard because she knew what he meant. Two years ago, she'd watched a marine step out of a helicopter after a three-day firefight with no sleep. The rest of his company was gone. The man could barely put one foot in front of the other to get to his cot. What she remembered most was his expression: wide glistening eyes...alive with death.

Maybe there's too much adrenaline junky in my genes? Or maybe I'm too "frosty" for anyone with a heart.

If so, she'd inherited it from her father. During his career in the army, Hal Pepper had earned the nickname "Leather Guts" from his troops because emotion was a foreign word to him.

Brenda took a long look out the back, relieved to see no traffic behind them. So far, so good. The final choke point would be the airport as they made their way to the Wyoming Air hangar. The good news there was that it was wide open, and two of her men had been keeping an eye on it for most of the morning.

"Anything happening, Bill?" she asked into the mic.

"Just the pickup about a hundred yards ahead," Anderson replied.

Minutes later, the loud Dodge turned west at Airport Junction, a puff of diesel exhaust accompanying the truck's acceleration as it roared toward the airport.

"On deck, people," Brenda called as her detail made the turn. She could see her team's rising tension. If anyone was going to make a move, the airport would be their last chance.

Ahead of them, the Dodge Ram pulled into one of the parking places in the long-term lot. Brenda watched it as they passed, worried. The two people inside met her gaze and looked away. All perfectly normal.

They drove by the Jackson Hole terminal and proceeded to the Wyoming Air building. Behind the charter service hangar, Simond's gleaming Gulfstream waited. Set against a background of drifting Wyoming clouds, it looked regal.

As the vehicles pulled up before the terminal door, Randy Bascom loitered outside, smoking a cigarette, and holding a cell phone to his ear as if in earnest conversation with someone. He gave Brenda a slight nod as the vehicles stopped. Doors opened as if choreographed; her security detail stepped out into the morning, eyes scanning the surroundings.

"Last chance for fame," Brenda joked as she walked around to open Kelly's door.

Kelly took her hand and stepped out, flipping her red wig in a tease. "Yeah, well, if I'd only had the money to go with the wig, I..."

The supersonic crack and impact of the bullet merged into a single terrifying *pock-pow*!

Kelly hit the pavement like a rag doll, her head smacking hard enough that one green contact popped from her eye.

Brenda screamed, *"Threat!"* as she threw herself on Kelly's body, protecting her friend, and pulling her pistol.

Brenda's team scrambled to cover her, drawing weapons, and lunging into position. A cacophony erupted in her earpiece, everyone asking where the shot had come from.

Brenda only looked down when Kelly shuddered beneath her. "Kelly?"

As she watched, Kelly exhaled a final red froth from the hole in her throat.

Then, with a jolt, the Wyoming clouds morphed into a stark Afghan sky and the black pavement faded to tan soil. Bill Solace lay there, dying. And there was nothing she could do to save him.

CHAPTER EIGHT

***

THROUGH THE ENTIRE FLIGHT TO THE ISLAND, CHANTEL KEPT FINGERING THE BASE OF HER throat. Intact. Healthy and warm. But for Brenda Pepper and her absurd insistence that Kelly Patterson impersonate her, this same living tissue would be blown away: a ragged hole filled with splintered bone, torn tissue, and coagulated blood.

As the jet spooled down on the Simond Island airfield, she took a deep breath and collected her laptop. At the forward cabin door, she nodded to the flight attendant. Janeesh and Ricard—her two most trusted staff members—stepped out onto the stairs.

The tropical night breeze blowing in off the Caribbean carried the scent of saltwater and flowering palms. The hangar, tarmac, and waiting vehicles were bathed in bright white lights. The last of her staff was climbing into the waiting van. Luggage would be taken later.

At the bottom of the steps—dressed in loose-fitting white cotton—her father, Renaud Simond, stood with his arms crossed. His patrician face looked pinched. The breeze mussed his mane of white hair. Tall, tanned, and fit, he would have passed for fifty, right up to the moment he fixed those hard-green eyes on a person. Assuming eyes were a reflection of the soul's crucible, Renauld's had survived fires that would have melted tungsten.

As she descended each step, her heart beat harder, her palms began to sweat. She wanted to scream, *It's not your fault!*

But she wouldn't. Couldn't. History was reality.

And so, too, were the roles she and her father had chosen to play so long ago.

"Chantel?" He didn't quite hide the strain. The regret. "I mean, dear God, when we heard..."

"I'm fine. I'll deal." But even as she said it, the image haunted her: Kelly Patterson's body, bleeding through the throat, lay limp and broken on the pavement. Battle as she might, Chantel's normally disciplined brain hadn't been able to drive that image from her mind.

That would have been me.

Chantel stopped just short of her father, swallowed hard. She desperately longed to step forward and wrap her arms around him the way she had when she was a little girl. But that most fundamental of human needs—the urge to touch and hold—were no longer hers to enjoy.

The wounds had disfigured them both.

Since that day, he had never dared to touch her. Not even so much as the offer of a hand as she was leaving a vehicle. Guilt—like an ugly reef—lay beneath the turbulent waters that separated them. For Renaud, physical contact with his daughter was symbolic of a long-dead sin.

God, I'm fucking tired of being alone.

If there were someone, anyone, that she could just talk to. One human being to another. She'd tried with Val, only to discover that psychopaths might be great at sex, but they sucked when it came to intimacy.

As she watched, the corners of her father's mouth quivered; his night-hooded eyes tightened. With a short nod, he broke the impasse and turned. "It's bad enough that this is the third attempt, Chantel. But this time a woman died."

"Her name was Kelly Patterson."

He led the way to the waiting vehicle, an electric cart that he favored. "How did this even happen? Surely there must have been some warning. Why was this woman impersonating you? Was this your idea?"

"I thought Brenda was overreacting when she proposed it." Chantel climbed into the cart and set her computer case on the floor. "That she was trying to impress me. Dress as a maid? Go out the service entrance and get in a pickup truck? What kind of idiotic high theater was that?"

"So what made you agree?"

"The look in Brenda's eyes. The tone in her voice when she said, 'Because if it was me, that's how I'd do it.'"

"Chantel, was this some elaborate charade to gain your confidence? A set-up to ingratiate—"

"Kelly Patterson was Brenda Pepper's best friend. Married to her brother. I saw them. Those women loved each other. I walked by the body, saw what it did to Brenda."

She hesitated as the cart accelerated. "Dad, you've got to get your head around this: I'm alive because Kelly Patterson's throat was blown out *in place of mine.*"

"Chantel, these people are paid to take such risks. It's part of the job."

She shot him a sidelong glance. "Sure. When I was watching Kelly Patterson putting on that wig... Shit! I've done nothing but replay it over and over in my head. Abstract philosophical arguments are one thing. Living it—with a dead woman on the ground in front of you—hits you right down in the pit of your gut."

She changed the subject. "But what's passed is past. Who did this? The first name to spring to mind is Brian. Inga really wanted him to step into Fallon's position."

"We're still working on that." Her father's expression pinched. "If it turns out he's behind this, it will mean war within the family. It could tear us apart."

"Devon's people should have been able to comb it out of the databases within hours."

It was Renauld's turn to give her the sidelong glance. "The fact that Devon doesn't have a name yet? That tells me we are dealing with someone dangerous. Someone with intelligence and resources."

"This is the third attempt. The first two could have been random. A woman is dead. I can't live like this."

He pulled up at the mansion door and set the brake. Leaning on the steering wheel, he studied her in the glow of the house lights; the musical song of the tree frogs added tremolo in the background.

He said, "Inga really wanted to see Brian step into Fallon's position at Simond International. She's always resented the fact that your grandfather placed your uncle in charge of The Foundation's banking interests. While assassination isn't beyond them, my gut tells me it's not Inga and Brian. Something's happening, Chantel. Devon wouldn't come right out and say it, but I think he's worried sick."

"I won my appointment by one vote. That's got to leave Brian bitter right down to his toes. If anything happened to me...?"

Renaud gestured his frustration. "Enough of that for now. Tell me about the meetings. What was your take away?"

"Even without the threat from Russia, the United States will continue headlong down the path toward disaster. They've had two failed presidencies in a row. No substantial structural changes are even being considered, let alone implemented. The Fed created their monster and stepped into the saddle. Now they can't think of a way to rein it in, and it's running so fast they can't jump off before it goes over the cliff. Participation in the labor force continues to drop. The tax increases to cover the COVID relief debt have sucked the life out of productivity. With no incentives for businesses to invest, banks are increasingly forced to pursue ever-riskier short-term profit. The politicians are sucking what they can from the system before it finally breaks and comes crashing down. They figure they'll be insulated from the fall-out by their millions and clout."

Renauld nodded at something in his head. "Then it's just a matter of time. We'll have to move carefully to cover our positions. I trust you to take whatever steps you deem necessary."

"I saw Tom Ortega. Robert said he might be of help on that damned banking bill."

"What do you think?"

"He's a pragmatist with values. Said he'd put a hold on Korkoran's S-107. Didn't even ask me for anything in return. Which buys us some time. He's smart enough to know what he doesn't know, and willing to humble himself by learning it. I reviewed Devon's surveillance data on Ortega's meetings at the conference. Unlike the rest, he's actually desperately searching for solutions. And he knows that implementing them is going to hurt."

"What should we do with him?"

"I think he should be president."

"Seriously?"

"The frontrunners in both parties are professional politicians catering to their radical bases. They know two things: how to win elections, and how to appeal to their most rabid ideologues. After the last two presidencies, either will further divide the country—and if the US collapses into civil war, the world will disintegrate in the vacuum. Whoever is in the oval office after this next election is going to have to deal with some serious shit. I'd rather have someone who could make a tough decision."

"You think it would make any difference in the end?"

"Given the amount we have invested in the United States, I'd rather have them limping along instead of going into convulsions and ruin. Ortega might make that difference."

"I'll discuss it with Robert. Do we have any hold on Ortega?"

"I offered him a cure for his daughter. I've already sent Regal the particulars. If he takes the bait, she'll have her labs give it priority."

Renaud gave her a weary and relieved smile. "God, it's good to have you home. It's sobering to think we might not be having this conversation." An awkward pause. "Chantel, I just want you to know that if I could go back..."

To cut him off, she said, "I've instructed Poul Hammond to hire Brenda Pepper."

For long moments he just stared at her, pain sharp in his eyes. Then, in a clipped voice, he said, "I'll have Mitch vet her. But given what happened in Jackson, don't you think Sonny would have a better—"

"After Jackson I don't trust any recommendation from anyone inside The Foundation. Especially Sonny. Pepper's military. And, Dad, if whoever is behind these assassination attempts is in the family, we're going to war."

CHAPTER NINE

* * *

THE PHONE IN TAYLOR'S HAND BUZZED RIGHT ON TIME. HE SET HIS GLASS OF WINE ON THE table and, from his high vantage, stared across the harbor. Monte Carlo looked somber under the cloudy Mediterranean sky. A cruise ship was docked next to the breakwater. Like ants from a riddled log, a stream of masked tourists filed onto streets they could only admire. A lifestyle into which they were allowed to peer, but never participate.

And now, with twenty million in the bank, and savoring the knowledge that he'd made the score a lifetime, he could sit back and enjoy it.

Taylor lifted the device to his ear. "Diga."

"*We have a problem.*" The voice on the other end sounded tinny, modified to defeat voice-pattern recognition software, which wasn't supposed to be a concern given the phone's cutting-edge technology.

"What problem? Benny saw the impact. Center-punched, right through the base of the throat."

"*You killed the wrong woman. This last-minute change in security, Brenda Pepper, was better than we expected. You shot a decoy.*"

Taylor pursed his lips, eyes on the expensive yachts riding in their slips. A decoy? Bitch.

"What do you want to do?"

"*Consider yourself on call. Another opportunity will present itself. It always does.*"

Taylor took a deep breath. "I'll inform my partner. In the meantime, how do you want to adjust the fee?"

"*According to the non-fulfillment clause in the contract, you are allowed time and expenses. The terms of the contract, however, remain unfulfilled.*"

A cold rage began to build in Taylor's breast. His island, a dream

fulfilled but moments ago, faded like a desert mirage. "I understand."
He had signed the damned thing. "You should receive a transfer of
funds by the end of the day."

"*That will be satisfactory.*" A pause. "*And given your professionalism, we authorize you to retain an additional one million above the
time and expenses.*"

He struggled to keep his voice under control. "Thank you."

He heard the connection click and slowly lowered the phone. The
cold rage continued to brew. Benny would be livid.

Throwing a ten-Euro note on the table, he stood, shoved his hands
into his pockets, and turned his steps toward the bank. Heedless of the
misty drizzle that began to fall, he nursed his rage.

It had been a long time since Taylor had made a mistake—even
longer since anyone had played him for a fool. Taylor would remember
Brenda Pepper every time he thought of his island. Especially after he
wired nearly nine million out of his and Benny's account.

The cunt ruined my record.

That was fucking unacceptable!

FINANCE

***

THE ORIGINAL "MAN BEHIND THE CURTAIN" WAS JACK SIMOND. GERHARDT WIESSE WAS more oriented toward operations. Upon Jack's decline with advancing age, it appears that he handed more of the responsibility to his son, Fallon Prescot Simond. Fallon, with a doctorate from the family alma mater at Yale, took to the job with remarkable acumen. From the 1980s through the early 2000s, Simond International's assets grew exponentially, fueled by the consumer boom in the West, by the opening of Russian resources, by the energy boom in the Middle East, and the rise and growth of Chinese manufacturing and cheap labor.

Meanwhile, Fallon's younger brother, Renauld, took on the role of a sort of Chief Executive Officer, acting as the coordinator for The Foundation's diverse and often disparate interests. Little is known about the man or his biography. Like his brother, he did attend Yale, was initiated into the Order of Skull and Bones, and graduated with honors. Then he disappeared from the public venue.

—Paragraph 10, The Helen Rudy Report.

CHAPTER TEN

***

"SHE WAS DEAD BEFORE SHE HIT THE GROUND," BRENDA SAID.

She stood before the window looking down on Avenue of the Americas in New York. The sixtieth-floor office was palatial; legal volumes, economic reports, and references filled bookshelves on the walnut-paneled walls.

That gut-kicked feeling wouldn't let go.

I killed Kelly.

"We're sorry for your loss." Poul Hammond, seated behind a splendid teak desk, watched Brenda through speculative eyes.

Hammond had hired her for the Jackson job. The guy was pale, with fine golden hair, and immaculately dressed in a gray-blue silk suit. He came off almost too effeminate in a city full of effeminate men. Not that that meant anything. Hammond had to have had an acute business savvy and killer instincts to have risen to such heights in cutthroat Manhattan's financial world.

This was not a man to underestimate.

To Hammond's right, a solid bank of flat screens, the sound muted, followed stock markets, the business channels, and international news. One monitor showed Leon Platnikov haranguing the press, then pictures of the Estonian capital where protestors were waving "Down with Russia" signs. Then came images of Russian tanks rolling across winter-white fields.

Another, on CNN International, showed buildings in flames behind blasted cars in some North African city. The camera panned across blood-stained sidewalks where men in loose-fitting white clothes wept and gestured their dismay.

"If we could, we'd like to offer some solace to Kelly's husband."

Hammond held a gold Mont Blanc pen in his left hand; below it a notepad rested on the blotter. His silk suit appeared freshly pressed.

Solace. You had to use that word? An image of Bill's smile formed behind her eyes.

The phone call to Mark had been one of the toughest she'd ever made. How did you tell your brother you'd just gotten his wife killed? Let alone live with the memory of his broken expression as you stood by his side while her coffin was unloaded from the belly of the airplane?

She knew the risks. Brenda repeated the lie she'd been telling herself.

"The Teton County sheriff seems to buy the story that it was a spent hunter's bullet. That it was an accident."

Brenda turned to study Hammond's expression. "How's Ms. Simond taking it? She looked pretty shaken when she walked past Kelly's body."

"Bad as this is, she knows it would have been her lying there on the pavement. Sending Chantel out in a maid's uniform, accompanied by one of your guys dressed as a janitor? Putting her in a rusty pickup truck, of all things? You saved her life, Brenda." Hammond's expression remained professionally blank. "What can you tell me about the shooter?"

"He's good. That was a long shot. Way long. Sheriff's Office dug the bullet out of the building wall. A 6.5 mm Berger used for precision long-distance target work. The conditions that day were ideal: slight breeze, excellent visibility, cool and little mirage. With modern ballistic computers, a quality rifle, and excellent optics, a trained shooter could have put that round in from nearly a mile." She swallowed hard. "Going for a head or neck shot? The bastard was showing off. Proving he's the best."

"It was hunting season. It could have been just a chance—"

"Bullshit. I've planned enough assassinations to know one when I see one."

Hammond tapped his pen on the notepad. "Simond International Holdings has its share of competitors. Removing her from the game would serve any number of parties."

"Which competitors? Give me names. Who wants her dead?"

"At this stage of the game, a list of names would be premature." Hammond glanced at his pad. "Your last assignment before we hired you was to keep a Saudi Prince's spoiled and psychopathic son out of trouble. Before that it was to squire his wives and family around New York while the kids bought over ten-grand in toys, most of which you and your people had to cart around. Before that it was keeping a pampered movie starlet from being busted for cocaine and ensuring the New York Four Seasons Hotel was reimbursed for the damage the little bitch did to their suite."

Brenda arched a combative eyebrow. Here came the pitch.

Hammond leaned back in his plush leather chair. "Given your professionalism and training, how do you feel when you're putting up with prima donnas? Carting their purchases, attending to their vanities and foibles? I understand you call them 'cocoon babies'."

Brenda gave Hammond her I'm-about-to-tear-your-heart-out look, and he visibly flinched. "Why do you care?"

"Female intel personnel don't usually see combat. But you did. And you earned a wall full of citations and made captain."

"Cut to the chase, please."

"We hired you for the Jackson assignment because Chantel's previous personal security chief was caught using proprietary information to line his own pockets. Good as he was, had he been in charge in Jackson, Chantel Simond would be dead."

"You're offering me a job."

"No more struggling along carrying boxes from over-priced boutiques. No more long nights in nightclubs watching celebrities make drunken and drugged jackasses of themselves, and then cleaning up their messes."

"I'm only here to pick up my check."

"We'll triple what you're making now."

Brenda filled her lungs and stepped back to the window, muttering, "TANSTAAFL."

"Tanstaafl?"

"There Ain't No Such Thing As A Free Lunch. What's the catch?"

"You will be privy to conversations and information of the utmost sensitivity, so we will monitor every call you make, every note you write, every step you take. But you've dealt with high security environments before."

"Sounds ominous."

"You start at four-hundred thousand a year, with a one-hundred-grand increase in six months. You'll enjoy remarkable amenities when you're off duty. But most of all, you'll be working with professionals. Unlike your current situation, no ego-bloated celebrities and silly rich kids who treat you like the hired help."

"My current situation—as you put it—is running my own company. The ability to say no if I feel like it. The way I'm saying no to you right now. No thank you, Mr. Hammond."

"Then you like babysitting spoiled fools and carrying their luggage?"

"What if I decide I don't like working for you?"

"Then we'll make the appropriate adjustments." Hammond leaned forward, gesturing with his pen. "Your reputation is that you're a straight shooter. According to our research, that's why you cut short your military career. Someone who trusted you died as a result of a superior's political decision."

Brenda stiffened as if she'd just been slapped. "Those are sealed, 'eyes only' documents."

"Why don't you at least give Ms. Simond a chance?" Hammond ignored her. "Most people in your business would—"

"I'm not most people." Brenda watched the traffic far below. Since COVID, Manhattan traffic had never been the same. Drivers didn't even honk anymore. A whole different world. How could Hammond possibly get access to secret military files? Her curiosity went into overdrive.

"You know that whoever is after Ms. Simond is going to try again. We believe you are the person to make sure they don't succeed."

"Mr. Hammond, I need to deal with Kelly's death. See if I can patch things up with my brother. Then maybe I'll consider it."

"So, next month you read 'Chantel Simond dead from assassin's bullet'. How does that make you feel about Kelly's death? How does that 'patch things up' with your brother?" Hammond paused. "All we're asking is a couple of days of your time."

"Just a couple of days?"

"What could it hurt?"

CHAPTER ELEVEN

***

POUL HAMMOND WATCHED THE MONITOR DEDICATED TO BUILDING SECURITY AS CAMERAS followed Brenda Pepper out of the building. A side door snicked open, and a man entered on silent feet. Poul slapped his hands on the edge of the desk. Turning to the newcomer, he said, "Well, there she goes."

"Interesting woman. Kind of attractive, in a deadly snake sort of way. Jeez, what eyes. Scary."

The man, in his late twenties, smacked a fist into his palm with a hollow pop. His hair was long, wavy, and blond with reddish tints. "When you suggested we hire Pepper for the Jackson job, who would have guessed she'd be that good?"

Poul leaned back in his overstuffed leather chair. "Robert, I knew she was capable. Outstanding record in the military. She came to my attention when she kept Sheela Takanabi out of the slammer and out of the media spotlight as well. But Jackson? I mean, after the first two attempts on Chantel. We needed someone who oozed competency."

Robert gave the monitors an irritated grimace, and his expression tightened when he noticed that the DOW was down by sixty. "We've got a lot on the line here, Poul. Things are getting tense if you know what I mean. Devon's started the last run on that predictive model. I know for a fact that he's anticipating bad news. It may be Russia and this loony Platnikov that sets it off. Or maybe something in China that old man Liu doesn't see coming. God knows we were blindsided by COVID. But I'm betting Devon's report is going to be worse than anyone anticipates."

"Chantel's had two attempts on her life already. What if the assassin had killed her? It would have precipitated chaos. The impact on the markets alone—"

"My sister is the most powerful woman on the planet." Robert turned, his eyes hard. "You understand that don't you? If Devon's news is bad, The Foundation will turn to Dad. Dad will turn to her. She's the one with the brains and the money."

"Maybe, but they *fear* Sonny. He's the one who—"

Robert laughed. "Are you really so dim? They'll be *looking* for a leader. Brian Heston and old Inga made a fight of it, but in the end, Brian doesn't have Chantel's brilliance. That's why the board ultimately voted for Chantel to step into Fallon's shoes."

"Perhaps. Assuming anyone can really fill Fallon's shoes. Especially given the challenges in the coming months."

Robert turned back to the window and stared down at the street. "You don't know Chantel. How she thinks, what she's capable of. If you think Pepper is scary..." Robert paused. "Me, I know politics. My concern is who emerges as The Foundation's leader."

"And you're betting it will be Chantel? When there's Katya, Chicago Liu, David, and the rest?"

"It's a matter of vision. Chantel sees the world in its entirety. The others see their slice of it."

"But, Renaud—"

"My father is hobbled by his preoccupation with morals, forever seeking to balance The Foundation's goals against the morass of his damned ethics. If Devon's model predicts what I suspect it will, someone will have to step forward and take the tiller."

"Then...what do we do?"

"For the time being, whatever Chantel wants."

"What about this senator your sister is so enamored of? How does he play into this?"

"Ortega?" Robert made an airy gesture with his hand. "If I read his psychological profile correctly, he has a hero complex. The kind who will step into the breach for the good of the people."

"Think you can get him elected?"

"As long as he's not an idiot." Robert took a deep breath. "Chantel sees something in him. Something that plays into her long-term plans for America. Like I say, she sees the big picture."

Hammond cautiously said, "Three attempts on Chantel? Renaud is going to be furious. Worse, you know that Sonny's going to be sniffing with his nose to the wind. And there's no telling how Valentine Wiesse is going to take it. Just the thought of Val gives me nightmares."

Robert glanced at Poul. "Want to bet on who Sonny fixes on first? My money's on that idiot, Stephen. Not only is he Brian Heston's son, but he's obsessed with Chantel. The guy gets a hard-on just being in the same room with her."

"She's his cousin."

"What's that got to do with anything? Made it even worse when Chantel was screwing Val. He's a cousin, too. Thought Stephen was going to choke on his own tongue."

Poul leaned back in his chair. "Chantel believes Pepper can keep her alive."

"Pepper still has to make it past Father's examination. I mean, that's like surviving the inquisition."

"What if Pepper makes it? What if she's even better than we think?"

Robert stepped over, slapped Hammond on the shoulder, and said, "Nobody's that good. And besides, you'll tell me if anything crops up that I should know about, right?"

Poul nodded absently, eyes straying to the monitor where NATO troops were huddled on a snowy Latvian border. "This is a dangerous game we're playing. The problem with dancing with the Devil? If you miss a step, you're really fucked."

"Hey, trust me. I know what I'm doing." Then Robert squared his shoulders and headed for the door.

For long moments after he'd gone, Poul Hammond sat motionless, his eyes locked in a distant stare. "You think you know what you're doing, Robert? Good for you."

Then Hammond chuckled. "Shit, you don't even know how many devils you're dancing with?"

CHAPTER TWELVE

***

POUL HAMMOND HADN'T LIED ABOUT THE PERKS. FROM THE MOMENT BRENDA HAD STEPPED onto the plane, she'd wondered if she'd fallen through the looking glass. Over the last two years, in the capacity of her job, she'd ridden in corporate jets, but never one as sophisticated as the Simond International Holdings Gulfstream. As Hammond had so astutely noted, she did believe that privilege was a debility. It made people feel secure. 'Security', however, was an illusion.

Four men and a woman—dressed impeccably—sat in a stylishly designed office area in the cabin front. A young Jamaican flight attendant served sandwiches, lattes, and cappuccinos from the galley.

Brenda had chosen to seat herself in the rear, beyond hearing, but it was apparent that the folks up front were slaving over some project, their laptops open, a series of monitors built into the bulkhead streaming data.

The flight from Teterboro had lasted seven hours, most of it over water. Judging from the angle of the sun they'd been on a south-south-westerly heading. Factoring in flight time, and the occasional islands they'd flown over, their unknown destination was somewhere in the eastern Caribbean.

The Gulfstream touched down on a runway on the northwestern side of a lush and green island. From the size of the hangars and heliport, Brenda had, at first, mistaken it for a commercial field.

But now, as she retrieved her bag and followed the executives to the tarmac, it sank in that this was a private facility with no fences, no public terminal.

When Brenda trotted down the steps into the warm tropical air, four no-nonsense security guys politely indicated that she was to accompany them in an electric van, while the executives headed for a classy car.

She rode past agricultural fields and banana and fruit orchards to an opulent mansion built into the side of a forested mountain on the island's west side. Something about it bothered her. After passing the gate, it hit her: but for the stucco-white walls, lush gardens, and copper-clad roofs, it might have been a military installation. Buildings and walls were situated defensively, like those in a forward operating base.

When the van pulled up on a cobble-terraced drive, another security officer—a geeky-looking guy who introduced himself as "Mitch" Mitchell—took over.

"Ms. Pepper, follow me, please."

He escorted Brenda to a small room just inside a side entrance in the mansion. This consisted of a windowless white cubicle with doors at either end. Mitch provided her with an excellent cup of coffee and made her comfortable in a curiously designed chair in front of a stunning mahogany desk.

Mitch said, "You'll need to fill out some papers and answer a series of questions."

"Sure."

He left.

For hours, polite, well-dressed men and women filed through. Some asked her to fill out questionnaires; others asked her specific questions about her past, her political persuasions, her friends and family, her sexuality, and ambitions.

Brenda had been around long enough to recognize a psychological evaluation—and this one was both thorough and sophisticated.

Of all the questions, the ones that bothered her the most were posed by a young woman in a white lab coat: "You are standing at a railroad switch. A train is rapidly approaching. If you throw the switch one way, the train will be diverted onto a short siding behind which is a school full of children. On the station platform stands a young scientist who has just found a cure for a mutated hemorrhagic fever virus sweeping the country. Even as you watch, he slips and falls onto the mainline rails, breaking his leg. Do you throw the switch and save the scientist, or the children?"

Her mind filled with images of Maluf, she heard herself say, "I'll save the scientist."

"You are on the battlefield. Your position is being overrun. On your left flank are ten companies of newly deployed recruits, fresh from boot camp. On your right are three companies of battle-hardened veterans. You have time to make one evacuation before the enemy wipes them out. Who do you save?"

"I take my veterans."

The questions continued to come, rapid fire.

The grilling had opened doors she'd rather have left closed. Now, alone in the aftermath, she leaned back and massaged her forehead, trying to shut off memories of friends, comrades, and teammates. Images flickered of Iraq, Afghanistan, Pakistan, Africa, and so many places she longed to forget.

When the last of her interrogators left, Mitchell appeared.

"I'll escort you to the restroom and then bring you back, understood?"

"Perfectly. Thanks."

When she returned to the cubicle, she sat down and thought back over the interview.

Well, kiss this job goodbye. But it's been...interesting.

CHAPTER THIRTEEN

***

IN THE MANSION'S COMMAND CENTER, CHANTEL STUDIED THE MONITORS RECORDING Brenda Pepper's heart rate, blood pressure, galvanic skin response, pupil diameter, ear temperature, and facial muscular tension.

A separate monitor, via a satellite link, displayed the ongoing psychiatric evaluation at a Swiss clinic specializing in personality disorders and categorization. A psychiatric team was poring over Pepper's responses and physiological reactions to the specific questions she'd been asked.

Mitch entered after having seen to Brenda Pepper's needs in the interrogation room. He drew a fresh cup of coffee from the machine and shot periodic glances Chantel's way. His attention was mostly directed at the island security feeds and routine monitoring. With visitors on the island, his staff was being particularly vigilant.

Chantel turned her attention to the closeup of Brenda's face. She could almost read the woman's knowing expression.

She thinks she failed. That she was too heartless and mercenary.

The door opened, and Renaud strode in with Pepper's folder tucked under his right arm. He took a moment to scan the readouts from Switzerland, and then reviewed a couple of the interrogation transcripts.

"Not exactly what I expected." He glanced up, meeting Chantel's eyes. "Are you sure about this? Is that the kind of woman you want overseeing your security?"

Chantel nodded thoughtfully. "She was brutally honest, Dad."

"Brenda, the clinic's psychiatric evaluation suggests that she might be purposefully provoking us. That she really may not want the job. I mean, there should have been some attempt at accommodation whereby she at least tried to anticipate what we'd be looking for in an employee."

Chantel pointed at the folder. "That's her jacket, isn't it? You read her official record?"

He nodded, eyes on Brenda Pepper's image in the monitor. Her biometric stats indicated a woman engaged in uncomfortable reflection. "The captain's military record is exemplary. Think it's been edited for our benefit?"

"If some agency is running her, she's the best we've ever seen. Nor can StatNco turn up anything indicating she's compromised. I think she's really what she says she is."

"Chantel, if her personality profile is correct, she's suffering from post-traumatic event disorder. She's got more than her share of—"

"I know her weaknesses." Chantel fought a slight smile. "Call it a hunch. I think she's exactly who I've been looking for."

Renaud pursed his lips, gave her a slight shrug, and asked, "You're not doing this because of guilt, are you? Or some sense of obligation."

"Go talk to her, Dad. You're more familiar with guilt and obligation than I am."

She saw the slight flinch, the freezing of his green gaze. But it was too late. It had been too late for over a decade.

CHAPTER FOURTEEN

***

A MAN IN HIS SIXTIES STEPPED INTO THE SMALL INTERROGATION ROOM. HE WORE A LOOSE white cotton shirt, sail-cloth pants belted with black leather, and comfortable goat-hide shoes on his feet. But it was the way he carried himself, the hawkish green eyes and lean, tanned face that drew attention. Entering the room, he owned it. His demeanor, the way he moved, reminded Brenda of a combat-hardened general.

She rose, fighting the instinct to salute.

"Captain Pepper," the man greeted in a cultured voice. "I'm Renaud Simond."

"My pleasure, sir. But I'm retired. Just plain old Brenda Pepper these days."

"I'd like to address you as captain if you don't mind. I think you've earned it." At Brenda's nod, Simond asked, "How was your trip?"

"It beat the hell out of the middle row in economy."

Simond smiled, saying, "Have a seat." Then he lowered himself into the other chair, the desk between them. "Want something to drink? Me, I'll have a soursop margarita." With a casual gesture of his hand, he added, "Consider yourself off duty. You've had a long day."

"What's soursop?"

"A local fruit. Ugly looking green thing covered with spines. But when mixed with Triple Sec and quality tequila, it makes a remarkable margarita."

"Two of those."

Simond stared frankly at Brenda before saying, "No matter what the outcome here, I want to personally thank you for saving my daughter's life. I can only guess at the pain and loss you're feeling over Kelly Patterson's death."

The knot of grief hardened under Brenda's tongue. "She knew the risks."

"That doesn't lessen the pain, or the second-guessing after the fact. As an old friend of mine once said, 'Living is a dangerous business.'"

"Your old friend is a very wise man."

A middle-aged black woman entered with two drinks on a tray. Brenda took hers, and let her gaze scan the walls, ceiling, desk, floor. How had Simond communicated the drink order?

Brenda stared at the light green liquid with its salted rim. After the woman's departure, Simond indicated her glass as he lifted his own and sipped.

Brenda tried it, found the flavor unique and satisfying. She couldn't stifle a faint smile.

Simond missed nothing. "I'm glad you like it."

"So, how'd I do on the psych evaluations?"

"You have a remarkably quick mind, Captain."

"At a young age I was taught to parse things to their fundamentals. Whittle your way down to the basics, and most solutions become self-evident."

"Is that what you did in Jackson?"

Brenda took a deep breath, submerging the memory of a bullet blowing through Kelly's neck. "If you're good at killing people, it's just a matter of switching paradigms. If I can solve the adversary's problem about how to get to the target, I have a better chance of keeping him from succeeding."

Simond then asked, "If you would be so kind, I'd like to know why you switched from covert operations—assassinations and snatches, if you will—to protective details."

"An officer, a man I admired and respected, was killed because of someone else's negligent security."

"But, as I understand from your psych eval, you don't believe in security. You think it's an illusion."

"Knowing it's an illusion makes me better at my job."

"And when it comes to Chantel?"

"Whoever's behind this will try again. Which leads me to wonder: if I go to work for you, am I on the side of the angels? Or will I serve the demons?"

Simond ran supple fingers down his glass, as if lost in thought. "Where do you see the world in twenty years, Captain?"

"Ask me something easy, Mr. Simond."

"You've been all over the globe, living it, talking with the people. A quick and analytical mind like yours will have formed some opinions."

Brenda sipped her drink, enjoying the exotic taste. "We're running out of resources. We're scrambling just to keep the basics together. The Middle East is a bloodbath of revolution and civil war as the Iranians and Saudis use their proxies to duke it out. Russia's trying to dominate Europe through intimidation. This new guy, Platnikov, is worse than Putin was. On the other side of the world, if China doesn't go to war with Japan and Southeast Asia over control of land and sea, they're headed for a scrap with India. Central Africa can be defined as murderous chaos. When they're not butchering Christians, Muslims are murdering each other in the streets from Indonesia to Morocco. Global population continues to rise dramatically. Fueling this is climate change."

She paused before adding, "And then there's COVID and the staggering and destabilizing blow it's given to the world economy. Throw that into the mix, and I don't know what you get except ever more desperate."

"So, for the sake of argument, if you break it down to the civilized— call them the advanced states—and the barbarians, say for example ISIS, the Taliban, al Qaeda, Hezbollah, and the like, who's going to be ahead twenty years from now?"

"The barbarians."

"Really? Why?"

"Because when people run out of food, water, or security, they get desperate. Barbarians appeal to the emotions. They offer a way for those who are suffering to strike back, an opportunity to attain something, even if it means dying in the process. Throw God or political ideology into the brew and the hopeless feel like they've regained control. Strapping on a suicide belt beats remaining a helpless victim."

"But if we fed people, offered them security, a job...?"

"We're supposed to have nine billion people on this planet by 2040. We can barely feed the seven something billion we've got, and we're running out of water, arable land, and resources. Right now, there's some guy in Yemen who's on the edge. He can't read or write, and he's watching his children waste away from starvation and die of COVID. He's got nothing to lose. And he's not alone. Six billion hopeless people just like him are seething around the globe."

Simond stared thoughtfully at his glass. "I'm curious about some of the answers you gave in the interview. Take the question about the train. Why did you save the scientist?"

"His cure for an epidemic will save more people in the end."

"And choosing three companies of combat vets over ten companies of raw recruits?"

"In the end, my vets will keep more of my people alive and kill more of the enemy."

"That sounds callous, Captain. Certainly not in tune with popular enlightened sentiments."

"Mr. Renaud, I've had to make those choices for real, and I now live with the memory of human beings who died as a result."

He nodded, pensive. "I understand that you're well-read in history. So...it's the final battle. You're in charge of a division defending Washington D.C.. The barbarians are attacking in force. Given the assets that you control, and the time before relief can be sent by the rest of the country, you have a choice: You can defend the Smithsonian with its scientific and historical collections, the museums, the Library of Congress, the White House and Capitol, and the major monuments. Or you can retreat to the countryside and protect the people. You cannot do both. One way, you save the foundations of American culture, science, and heritage. The other, you save the lives of twenty million Americans. Which do you choose?"

It took her less than a second. "I'll save DC."

"Why?"

"Because the survivors will need that symbol and what it represents."

"So, Captain, are you on the side of the angels? Or the demons?"

Brenda gave him a grim smile.

SECURITY CONCERNS

* * *

THE QUESTION IS ASKED: WHAT ARE THE NATIONAL SECURITY IMPLICATIONS FOR THE UNITED States of America and our allies?

At this time, to the delight of conspiracy theorists, a full under-standing of The Foundation's role in world events cannot be calcu-lated. The suggestion, however, given The Foundation's implication in pivotal events during the second half of the twentieth century and first two decades of the twenty-first should be of major concern. The Foundation's fingerprints can be found actually directing the Cold War, apparently playing both sides against each other during The Foundation's rise to power. The key component appears to have been the use of ex-Nazis by both sides. In the west, politically useful Nazis had their records expunged by high-ranking government officials. The State Department was complicit from the beginning through the Office of Policy Coordination under the supervision of Frank Wisner, who created false papers and identities prior to bringing these individuals to the United States to work in intelligence, science and engineering, and finance.

A similar program was implemented by the Soviet Union in their aerospace and intelligence services.

CHAPTER FIFTEEN

***

THE VIEW COULDN'T BE CALLED ANYTHING LESS THAN SUBLIME. MOONLIGHT SHONE ON THE Caribbean like silver spilled over the sea. Far to the west, a layer of low clouds frosted the star-shot night sky. Around the mansion, a wealth of tree frogs and insects drowned the darkness in a tremolo of song.

Brenda leaned on a stucco balcony, letting her gaze search the distance where the faint lights of a ship marked the horizon.

Behind her, the door to her room stood open, revealing the plush interior. They called these guest quarters? A five-star hotel would be hard-pressed to compete—and she'd been in some of the best. On the flat-screen TV across from her couch, the sound muted, people picked through the ruined remains of a refugee camp in Jordan after a raid by armed gunmen. Coupled with food shortages in western China and the outbreak of civil war in Kyrgyzstan, nothing in the news was good.

Hard to believe that world was the same as the peaceful moonlit paradise she now gazed upon.

She'd been asked to limit her movements to the balcony and no further. Given the discreetly located cameras and roving security she'd observed, someone was keeping close tabs on her activities. Simond International continued to both intrigue and worry her.

A door opened at the far end of the balcony. A woman stepped out into the night. She wore a casual pantsuit, her hair back in a ponytail. Brenda recognized Chantel's athletic stride as she approached in the balmy air.

"Hello, Captain."

"Good evening. I used to be Brenda. What happened?"

"Dad likes to call you captain. If you stay, I'm afraid it will stick." She stopped beside Brenda, leaning to stare out at the sea. Brenda caught the faint scent of soap and a hint of lilac, which might have been the woman's only concession to vanity. Such a far cry from the high-maintenance divas Brenda had been pandering to for the last couple of years.

"Your father is a formidable man."

Chantel glanced thoughtfully at her; her green eyes masked by the night. "He doesn't always take time to meet new people. He made an exception for you." She paused. "What did you think of him?"

"He's one of the most impressive men I've ever met. I didn't expect to end up in a philosophical discussion."

"He missed an appointment, which is even more unusual. I haven't seen him so delighted in months." She paused. "You treated him as an equal, and that's a rare thing these days."

"He gave me a lot to think about."

"How so?"

"My relationship with morality and ethics is usually obscured by the pragmatic concerns of the moment. I'm rarely allowed the luxury of contemplating the higher implications."

"Do you ever wonder if you've become a monster?"

Brenda's hands unconsciously twitched. *A hollow-eyed monster. A cold weapon.* "Why do you ask?"

"Because I wonder that about myself."

"Does everyone in your family have a degree in philosophy?"

"Sort of. My grandfather, and then Dad, beat it into us from the very beginning. We..."

The door through which Chantel had arrived opened, and a young man hurried forward. He said, "Excuse me. You asked to be informed. The LIBOR is up twenty-five basis points."

"Thanks, Ricard."

The young man turned and left, closing the door behind him.

Chantel turned back to the sea, thoughtful in her consideration of Ricard's information.

Brenda let her think.

"That's a bigger jump than we anticipated," she said at last. "The Euro will be down in the morning."

"Is that good?"

"We shorted it last week. We'll buy tomorrow before the markets have time to think it through." After a pause, she added, "And to everyone's horror a certain Mr. Penwick's fingerprints will be all over this."

"I can see how your previous security got in trouble." What did they expect Brenda to do with such information? Chantel was talking about subverting international banking.

"Sometimes I talk without thinking. Forgetting anything I say would be integral to your job description."

"To set the record straight, I'm not into making a killing in the markets. But I take it, that's what Simond International Holdings does?"

"Investment, forex, currency, stocks and bonds, that's pretty much our business."

Brenda smiled at the simplification. She had seen the caliber of people who'd made their way, hat in hand, to Chantel's Jackson Hole suite.

"Captain," Chantel began, "I actually came to personally thank you for what you did that day. I've been trying to come to terms with the fact that Kelly Patterson died in my place. I keep seeing her, remembering her lying there in the blood..."

"Let's get down to it, shall we? Tell me about those other attempts."

Chantel straightened, and her red hair caught the light and shimmered. "You've read the reports."

"Yeah, but who do you think is behind it?"

"I make a lot of enemies, Captain. With strategic buys I can ruin a bank, devalue a currency, bankrupt a corporation. Even a nation. Just the act of killing me would inject turmoil into the markets."

"How?"

"People trust me to do the right thing, soften the blows if you will. God help them if my brother were to take my place. Robert doesn't think things through." She laughed. "Rather than wonder who'd want to kill me, ask who wouldn't?"

"Anyone who wants stable markets?"

She turned abruptly, asking, "What do you expect to gain from heading my security?"

"Not sure I'm going to head your security yet. Hammond asked me for a couple of days. But something about all this"—Brenda gestured to take in the exotic setting—"has my antennae twitching. It's too good to be true. As much as I liked your father, something tells me he has his dark side."

"You can be certain of that."

Brenda shot her a measuring glance. "And, you, too. A woman your age—no matter how smart—doesn't summon the president's chief of staff unless she's got a big stick behind her back."

After a long pause, Chantel said, "Money is power, and my battlefield is every bit as brutal as yours was in Afghanistan, Captain. And sometimes I make the same choices you did when it comes to combat."

"My goal was to keep my country secure and destroy her enemies before they could get to Main Street. What's yours?"

Again, Chantel took her time before answering, "To keep it *all* from collapsing. Do you know how close we came in 2008? And again, with COVID? Since then, it's been a delicately choreographed dance to save the Euro, stabilize the rupee, slowly deflate the dollar, prop up specific financial institutions—"

"And you're doing this out of the better angels of your nature?"

"We're doing it because if the world financial markets go under, national economies collapse. If they disintegrate, more than seven billion people go berserk because of something called deprivation theory."

"I think I just had this conversation with your father."

"You did. We're obsessed by it." Moonlight turned Chantel's face pale as she looked up. "Our world is as fragile as a house of cards, Captain. Something as simple as a labor dispute in Mumbai could cause a fuel shortage in India that disrupts food distribution. Bare shelves in the grocery store trigger a panic, people riot. And what happens next?"

"The government tries to maintain control, tightening the screws, which makes the people madder. If it goes too far, some event triggers anarchy just like what happened in Somalia, Syria, Central African Republic, Chad, or Yemen."

"You're talking about national impacts. What happens when it's a *global* economic collapse? Not just the big multinationals, but banks of all sizes down the little guy on the corner? Instant, massive, global deflation? Paper money worthless? Stocks cratered, markets crashing. Unredeemable bonds. Default everywhere. Assets vanishing by the second. Without a solvent bank, what's a check—no matter how much you write it for—worth? Your credit card is just a meaningless piece of plastic to the guy down the street siphoning gasoline out of his car and selling it."

Brenda took a deep breath. "Point made."

"We're self-sufficient here."Chantel made a grand gesture to include the mansion and island. "The island's volcanic. Our energy is geothermal. We can grow, fish, and process for all of our basic needs." Her delicate eyebrow raised. "But who wants to survive on a luxury island when it's surrounded by a desolate world? No stroll down Fifth Avenue. No Paris to enjoy coffee on the Champs Elyse. The 'Rocks' in Sydney are abandoned. Rome is nothing but ruins. No opera at la Scala in Milan. London is a no man's land of cannibalistic gangs."

"If it comes to that, I guess this island won't be such a happy refuge."

"It will be a prison." Chantel's eyes glittered. "I, for one, will do everything in my power to keep that from happening. Even if I have to sell myself to the demons to do it."

CHAPTER SIXTEEN

***

LIKE EVERYTHING IN LIFE, THE SENATE CAME WITH A PECKING ORDER. AS A FRESHMAN senator, Thomas Ortega had been assigned a cramped office deep in the guts of the Dirksen Senate Office Building. Better quarters with big windows, additional square footage, and the trappings of authority were reserved for powerful senior members with clout.

Ortega accepted this with aplomb. Nothing to date had left him with any illusions about the "new guy's" status no matter how spectacular his election victory might have been. Even in that greatest of political prizes, Ohio.

He'd spent his life working his way up from the bottom, first as a Latino kid in the Texas school system, graduating as valedictorian. Then through four years in college before he enlisted as a lieutenant in the Navy. His greatest trial came after he'd qualified for BUD/S training; they'd stripped him down to nothing but guts and determination. He'd earned his trident after two rollbacks and been posted to SEAL Team 3. Six years later, a shattered tibia and ankle forced him into civilian life. He had married Jennifer and followed her back to Ohio to start his first business in her hometown of Chillicothe. Endless conflicting regulations and ever-increasing taxes had hobbled his business until it turned him political. Three terms in the legislature had prompted him to run for the United States Senate as a dark horse. Given no chance by the pollsters, he'd won the primary, and then, to the amazement of even his own party, he'd handily won the election.

The hard knocks of life had also taught Tom Ortega that the universe came with a cosmic balance. And while he'd worked for everything he'd ever achieved, what God and luck gave with one hand, they took with the other. His daughter Jessie—over whom he and Jennifer fawned—was born with congenital osteoarthropathy, a painful condition of the joints that would leave her crippled, deformed, and in constant pain for the rest of her life.

He considered that as he reclined at his senate office desk and stared at his daughter's photo where it stood next to the computer monitor.

A knock at his door admitted Trevor Hughes, his hair combed, a red tie loosely knotted at his throat. "Boss? You asked for a heads up on this guy Penwick? Google just pinged us that he's been arrested in London."

Tom turned to his computer. Finding the story, he clicked the audio and watched it stream.

"Investigators from Scotland Yard, in cooperation with the FTSE, announced this evening that well-known financier Colin Penwick was arrested as he tried to leave the country. To the dismay of the financial community, Penwick has been charged with fraud and has been linked to alleged manipulations of the LIBOR, the rate at which international currency is loaned between banks. Penwick's ill-gotten earnings may have netted in the tens of millions. Based on an anonymous tip, authorities were able to arrest Penwick moments before he boarded a private charter for Cuba."

The video showed a ruddy-faced and handcuffed man in a suit being loaded into the back of a police car.

"So," Tom mused. "She did it. My God."

"Who?"

"Never mind."

He turned his attention back to his daughter's photo. From his wallet he removed the piece of paper Chantel Simond had given him. The clinic's phone number seemed to mock him with its promise. Dare he call? What would he owe Chantel Simond if he did?

Damn! How did a man quantify the ethical implications? So far, he owed Simond nothing.

"I'll see him *now!*" Korkoran's stentorian voice boomed from the reception area.

As Trevor protested, "Excuse me, but you can't just barge in here," in modulated tones, Tom stood and opened the door to the outer office.

Senator "Big Jim" Korkoran, as he liked to be called, towered over Trevor's desk. He clutched a sheaf of papers in his right hand, his face florid. The man's eyes glittered; his suit coat stretched as he hunched over the nervous Trevor.

"Can I help you, Senator?" Tom greeted cautiously.

Korkoran's hot black eyes sought Tom's as he said, "What's the meaning of this shit?" and waved the papers. "You put a fucking *hold* on my bill?"

"That's right."

"What the hell kind of game are you playing?"

A passerby in the hall slowed, gawking, entertained by the show.

"Trevor, if you'd see to the door, I'll discuss the situation with the good senator in my office." He gestured. "Come on in, Jim. Have a seat. Can I get you a coffee?"

Trevor sidled around the big man and clicked the outer door shut, then stood uncertainly, wary gaze darting back and forth.

"I'm not here for bullshit, Ortega. You put a fucking hold on my bill!"

"I'm not done reading it." Tom led the way into his office, picking up the remaining six hundred and forty-seven pages of S-107 from the sideboard. "This is what I've still got to wade through."

"*Reading it?* What the fuck do you need to read it for? I've told you what it says, what it does." His eyes narrowed. "Ah, I get it. Think you're gonna hold me hostage, huh? Well, you got another thing coming. You don't pull a chicken-shit stunt like this. You come to me first, tell me what you want. Then, maybe, we work out a compromise. Your pet for mine. Thought you'd already figured that out."

"I'm not looking to hold you hostage. I'm reading the bill, Jim. Just like I said. I know you want it out of committee, but I'm not voting until I know what Korkoran-Hardy really says." Tom smiled. "And how it's going to affect the banking industry when it's finally implemented."

Korkoran's eyes narrowed to slits. Trevor stood tensely to the side, his face growing paler by the instant.

"They got to you in Jackson." Korkoran crumpled the papers between his fingers. "The fucking bankers bought you off, didn't they? Let me guess, a couple hundred thousand in campaign contributions? Maybe played up this Ortega for President pap we've been hearing on the talk shows? Well, let me tell you something. If you kill my bill, use it as a publicity stunt, or a bone to throw a bunch of chicken-shit bankers, I'll see to it that you're crushed. Got that?"

Tom felt his hackles rising and crossed his arms. "Gee, wrong, wrong, and wrong! Good thing you're not on a game show. I told you what I'm doing, and why I'm doing it."

Korkoran pointed a knobby finger. "You may have been a hot-shot SEAL, but you're in a whole different game here, boy. Last chance, remove your hold."

"I will...after I finish reading it."

"Then I guess it's hardball between you and me from here on out."

Tom cocked his head, reading the rage in Korkoran's burning gaze. "It's your call, Big Jim. But before you commit yourself to a bloodbath, it's pretty easy to get DNA these days. Your wife doesn't know about Peggy's kids, does she?"

The corners of Big Jim's lips twitched. "How could you...?" With an oath, he tossed the crumpled hold onto the floor. "You son of a bitch!"

"And there's no reason she should hear it from me," Tom continued casually. "I meant what I said: I'm reading the bill. And so far, it looks like a nightmare of complexity and obfuscation. Now, get the hell out of my office, and I'll make up my own mind about whether or not I'm supporting S-107."

Korkoran turned, ripped the door open, and stalked out into the hall.

Trevor wiped his sweating face. "Jesus! What just happened here?"

"Reality reared its ugly head, Trev. Now, if you'll excuse me, I've got a long-distance call to make."

"To where, sir?"

"Turks and Caicos. I think after this week Jennifer and I could use a break from the usual for Thanksgiving. And who knows? Maybe some sunshine would do Jessie good, too."

CHAPTER SEVENTEEN

***

ON HER BALCONY THE NEXT MORNING, BRENDA ATE A BREAKFAST OF LOCAL EGGS WITH bright yellow yokes laid atop a slice of ham, cinnamon-fried plantain, and hominy grits topped with a tongue-jolting hot sauce. Below her, the Caribbean sparkled in turquoise majesty.

A prison? Those had been Chantel's words to describe the island. *So, you take this job? What if you want out? Does the prison snap shut around you?*

She speared the last of the plantain and was chasing it down with superb black coffee when Renaud Simond, wearing a tan suit and a white shirt open at the collar, emerged from the side door. He clutched a sheaf of paper in his right hand.

Brenda instinctively stood only to be waved back to her seat by Simond. "Sit, Captain. I appreciate the gesture but finish your breakfast."

As Brenda seated herself, Renaud's hard green eyes took her measure. "I would have preferred to have given you another couple of days to consider your future, and if our continued relationship would be a good fit. Something, however, has come up. Hence, my first question to you: What is your assessment of how to deal with the threat against my daughter?"

"Personal security is always defensive, Mr. Simond. Generally, that's the best that you can do. In Chantel's case, we know someone is out there with an agenda. If her enemies are wealthy enough and committed enough, eventually they will kill her."

Simond smoothed the papers he held. "You only speak of defensive action. The other course—for which you are uniquely prepared—is to hunt the son of a bitch down."

Brenda gave him a sober appraisal. A flutter tickled her gut, like volunteering for a hazardous-duty assignment: a turning point. If she agreed, she'd be working as an assassin, not a security chief.

Brenda set her coffee down. "You and I need to be clear on a couple of things. First, we're talking about a major investment of personnel and cash. Second—and I'll pull no punches here—this isn't the movies. Taking down people with these kinds of resources will be messy and difficult."

"She's my daughter."

"There will be serious legal ramifications, maybe involving a host of different countries."

"I do not give my word cavalierly, Captain. But should anything happen, I swear that I will exert every pressure to obtain your release."

"You sure you want to involve yourself?"

"I'm not a nice man, nor is Simond International a beneficent organization. We have an agenda based on an unforgiving and incontrovertible assessment of the global situation. In the past we've made choices that led to regrettable outcomes. We will no doubt do so again in the future. But we *will* have the courage to make those decisions, right or ultimately wrong. Is that a problem for you?"

Brenda turned her coffee cup in its saucer. "We're back to throwing the switch on the railroad track, aren't we?"

"Always."

"Mr. Renaud, my instincts are telling me to run like hell and get as far away from Simond Island and Simond International as I can."

"Good instincts." He smiled appreciatively. "Anything in particular bothering you?"

"Once I'm in, is there ever a way out?"

His smile faded. "There's always a way out. Some are just more palatable than others. Given the stakes for which we play, we both assume a certain amount of risk should you accept our offer of employment. The safest course for both of us would be if you packed your bag and took the next flight back to New York."

Damn it, he was daring her to get on that airplane. Telling her that if she didn't, the choice would be irrevocable.

Hell, she'd gotten out of worse places when it went to shit. Maluf, for one. She'd just have to play this very carefully, keep her wits about her. Recognize if she were getting in over her head.

"Kelly Patterson and I were friends long before she met and married my brother. I got her killed." She smiled bitterly. "Then again, maybe I'm just an adrenaline junky, and you're offering me a high."

He handed Brenda the papers he'd been holding. "Here's what we've been able to dig up so far. The Jackson shooter may be a man who calls himself Taylor. That's according to what we can mine out of the international cloud metadata." He paused. "We know he's high-dollar. He won't take a job for less than three million."

"That's insane!"

"Is it? What's a life worth when hundreds of millions, or a couple of billion dollars is at stake? Someone lost a fortune shorting stocks the day before the attempt was made on Chantel in Jackson. News of her death would have sent markets crashing. So if someone can make twenty or thirty million on the market by killing Chantel, just how much would they be willing to pay an assassin?"

"Jesus. Maybe I'm in the wrong business."

"Getting back to Taylor, my sources tell me his greatest vanity is his record. You spoiled it in Jackson. Rumor is that he's livid, had to return his rather substantial fee to whomever hired him, and will not rest until Chantel is dead. And maybe you, as well."

Brenda took the papers, scanning the sparse information. The following pages displayed a series of photographs taken at various airports in the Rocky Mountain region. Any of the individuals might have been the man calling himself Taylor.

Simond said, "And that brings us to the next problem. In two days, we have an emergency meeting with our colleagues. Chantel must attend. Pending your ultimate decision, we would still like to retain your services to keep her safe."

"Where is this meeting?"

"An island off Venezuela. It's a luxury retreat originally built by Hugo Chavez and rented for our purposes. Very secure. Some of the most important and influential business leaders in the world will be attending, so we're interfacing with numerous security details. You've met Mitch Mitchell, head of my personal security. Mitch and his team have been alerted and will be flying out in two hours to advance the location."

"You trust these folks you're meeting?"

Simond's eyes turned predatory. "To the contrary, Captain, there's a very good chance that one or more of them is the perpetrator behind the attacks on Chantel."

CHAPTER EIGHTEEN

***

THE PINK JEEP MIGHT HAVE BEEN STRAIGHT OUT OF A MOVIE WITH ITS RED-STRIPED AWNING. Five-year-old Jessie had loved it at first sight, her dark eyes lighting with wonder as she pointed, saying "That one, Daddy!"

Now, from her expression, it appeared she wasn't so sure of her pick as the hard-riding vehicle bounced its way down the potted asphalt on the Long Bay Highway. The term "highway" apparently had fundamentally different definitions in Provo—as the main island in Turks and Caicos was called.

Tom glanced at Jennifer as she pulled back a strand of long brown hair that had blown loose. Open-sided Jeeps, Jen was now discovering, were airy. But at least the eighty-degree ocean breeze was a welcome change from Chillicothe.

"You alright, sweetie?" he asked over his shoulder.

"Hurts, Daddy. But don't stop. I can take it." The way she said it brought a pang to his heart. A five-year-old girl shouldn't have to be gutting out a car trip like a prospective SEAL in BUD/S training.

"That's my girl."

The strain shone from Jennifer's brown eyes and reflected from the tightness at the corner of her mouth. She still blamed herself for Jessie's disorder, especially after finding the problem lay in her own genetics.

"It's gonna be alright, Jen." Tom turned his attention back to the road as they wound down the strip of asphalt. The pavement was edged with white sand that gave way to lush vegetation. Residences and businesses bathed in the midday glare; the older ones were sun-faded, while the newer had that anticipatory gleam of a hopeful future. Locals walked along bearing plastic bags, and wore colorful tee-shirts, shorts, and sometimes sandals.

"You don't even know these people, Tom. Why would they help us?"

He shrugged, one hand on the steering wheel. Spotting the clinic's sign, he took a left and drove down a sandy lane lined with palms and salt grass. "This is another chance, babe. That's all. And hell, if there's even a hope it will help Jessie, I'll try it."

She was giving him her worried look as they entered a paved parking lot. The spaces were mostly occupied by Mercedes, BMWs, and Jaguars. The three rather ratty looking and rusted Japanese sedans had rental logos.

Tom pulled up in front of the door and killed the engine.

"We're here?" Jessie asked from the back, staring thoughtfully at the clinic. "It doesn't look like a hospital, Daddy. There's only one floor."

Actually the place kind of looked like Tom thought it should: modern, new, chrome and glass mixed with stucco-clad concrete, and tastefully landscaped. Through a gap on one side of the building he could see the sparkling blue waters of the Turks Island Passage.

Jen climbed out, her long legs pale below her shorts. Walking around, she helped Tom lift Jessie out, and balanced the little girl on her leg braces. The stainless-steel contraption with its straps helped to reduce the weight and stress on Jessie's swollen and inflamed joints.

Tom's heart skipped as he watched Jessie's face tighten in the familiar expression of pain.

"I could give you a ride," Tom suggested.

"Gonna walk, Daddy."

"That's my little trooper."

Tom hopped back into the Jeep and pulled it into one of the spaces beside a waxed BMW. By the time he made it to the door, Jen and Jessie were already inside.

The reception area might have been in Cleveland: couches and chairs lined the wall to the left; potted plants stood in the corners; and low-end tables sported thumbed magazines. A couple of secretaries behind the desk were taking Jessie's name and inspecting Jen's passport.

Tom hadn't crossed the lobby before a door swung open. An attractive, fortyish, blonde woman in a white lab coat emerged calling, "So you're this magical Jessie we've been hearing about?" The woman dropped to one knee, sticking out a hand. "I'm Doctor Mead. Welcome to White Coral Clinic."

"Hi," Jessie managed shyly, unable to muster the courage to extend a hand.

Dr. Mead stood, hand offered to Jen this time, as she said, "I'm Catherine Mead. We're glad to have you come all this way, Ms. Ortega. And you, too, Senator, welcome."

They both shook her hand, Tom saying, "You came very well recommended."

"Simond International funds a great deal of our research." She bent down again, meeting Jessie's worried stare. "And we don't take just anyone. But you, Jessie, are most remarkable."

"I am?"

"You are. It's because of your joints. Do you know why?"

"It's called osteoarthropathy." The medical term sounded odd rolling off Jessie's little tongue.

"That's right. And what makes you special is that you shouldn't have it. It's a disease for much older people with damaged nerves. We've never seen a case like yours. That's why we're going to fix it."

"You *are?*" Jessie said excitedly.

"Doctor, please." Jen had that warning tone in her voice. "We do our best not to raise unreasonable expectations."

Catherine Mead winked at Jessie—who seemed completely taken by the woman. Then the doctor stood. "Ms. Ortega? We've thoroughly reviewed Jessie's records, read all the evaluations, and most of all, we've analyzed that blood sample you FedExed. Understand that Jessie has damage that has to be reversed, and it won't happen overnight. But assuming we don't run into a complication, my guess is that within three months, Jessie isn't going to need those braces."

Jen seemed to grapple with the woman's words. "Don't...Don't make promises you can't keep. We've talked to some of the finest—"

"Surgeons? Orthopedic specialists?" Mead smiled faintly. "Yes, we know. We're not going to treat the symptoms, Ms. Ortega. We're going to correct the problem at its source, a malfunctioning gene. And we're going to do that by triggering the right epigenetic DNA to grow new blood vessels and nerves that will allow Jessie's joints to function and develop normally."

Tom glanced down to see a glow of wonder on Jessie's face. "You can really do that?"

Catherine Mead's level gaze met his. "If we'd had any doubt, Senator, we wouldn't have wasted your time to come down here."

Jen struggled to control herself, the corners of her mouth quivering. "Dear God."

Tom Ortega struggled to hold back tears.

If this works Chantel Simond can have my very soul.

...And she probably knows it.

CHAPTER NINETEEN

***

CHANTEL WAS REVIEWING THE HANG SENG CLOSING FIGURES WHEN JANEESH LEANED INTO her office to say, "Your father wants you to know that Regal and Robert are on the patio. Can I get you anything to drink?"

Chantel massaged the back of her neck. "Maybe a Pelegrino with a twist of lime." She pushed back and stood, feeling every muscle knot. "How does Robert look?"

"Too handsome for his own good," Janeesh told her wryly. "He's got that smirky expression. The one he gets when he's in some kind of trouble. Must have left some woman panting in his absence."

"You've never liked him, have you?"

"He's your brother," Janeesh said laconically.

Chantel grabbed her notebook, gave Janeesh a thank-you smile, and strode out of her office, her mind on the data she needed.

The patio extended from the southern side of the villa, an elevated, four-sided protrusion that gave views in all directions. While it appeared architecturally exotic, the actual design dated back to the sixteenth century when European fortifications were undergoing rapid evolution in response to the introduction of the cannon. For the moment, she tried not to think why that would be necessary at the mansion.

Stepping out onto the flagstones, she made her way to the shaded table where her father, dressed in white cotton, leaned forward to stare at a computer screen. To his right sat Regal, Chantel's younger sister. Regal leaped to her feet, a grin cracking her generally serious expression. But for blue eyes and another two inches of height, she might have been Chantel's carbon copy. Regal had dressed in shorts that exposed athletically toned legs and wore a yellow cotton shirt tied at her narrow midriff.

"How's the queen of agriculture and biotech?" Chantel greeted.

"Still feeding the world a million mouths at a time," Regal told her. "Heard about Jackson. My God, Chantel, you saw this woman get shot?"

"I can't close my eyes without seeing it again and again. I met Kelly Patterson, talked to her. And she's dead in my place."

"Any idea as to who's behind it?"

"It's not like I have any shortage of enemies, but we know it's someone inside the family. At first, we thought maybe Inga and Brian, but now? Could be one of the Wiesses, one of the Takanabis. Not everyone was happy to see me pick up Uncle Fallon's reins."

"Must be weird," the second man at the table said, climbing to his feet. In his twenties with flowing red-gold hair, Robert stepped close, folding Chantel into a hug. "How ya doing, sis?"

"I'm keeping it together, Robert. Work will get me through. At least, that's what I make myself believe." She pushed back, inspecting her brother with a critical eye. "Looks like minding politicians has softened you up. That's not fat hanging over your belt, is it?"

With a narrowing of the eyes, his expression tightened. He quickly stuffed his loose shirt down into his pants to display a lean waist. "The day I get fat, you can take me out and shoot me, bitch."

"Love you, too, little brother," Chantel told him as she seated herself.

Renaud was watching them through half-lidded eyes. Sometimes she wondered what he really thought of his children. He'd never said, never hinted. Not after what had happened—what he'd been forced to do. She'd heard that all relations between siblings were complicated. Most brothers and sisters, however, were allowed to grow up like normal human beings. They didn't live with dark secrets and physical scars in the shadow of 'Big Data'.

Regal was giving Robert her skeptical look, as if she knew something about him that she didn't like. Nothing unusual in that—Robert made a habit of being unlikable.

"It's good to see us all together again," Renaud began, closing his computer. "I appreciate your willingness to meet prior to the announcement of Devon's research."

"It's not going to be good, is it, Dad?" Robert flopped back in his chair, the breeze off the Caribbean teasing his long hair.

"If Devon is calling The Foundation together, it's because he wants us in one place, face to face, to begin planning for the end."

Chantel nodded to herself, having come to the same conclusion. "We're in a pretty good position financially. I just need direction from the council to begin moving assets. We're going to have to make some hard decisions."

Renaud glanced at Regal. "Where are we with SimondAg?"

Regal tossed her hair back, pushing a bound report toward her father. "That's a précis. One of two copies in existence. I'll leave it up to you as to whether you want to present it to The Foundation or not."

"Give us the short version," Robert insisted.

"The short version is that we're continuing to purchase prime agricultural land, and through our corporate subsidiaries, we currently control twenty-nine percent of US agricultural production, twenty-two percent in Europe, and fourteen percent in Asia."

"How long until we control half in the US?" Robert asked.

"Five to ten years, depending on how much capital we commit." Regal shrugged. "That's for scattered parcels. For large tracts of contiguous land, it's going to take longer. Push too hard, and not only do prices skyrocket, but the locals get nervous."

"And the science?" Chantel asked.

Regal gave her a thumb's up. "Our microRNA work is a success. I've had our molecular geneticists working on *Triticum*. That's wheat to you, brother. We've modified the DNA to produce an additional twenty percent yield in hotter and dryer growing conditions. But the big payoff, very hush-hush, is the tailored microRNA gene we've included."

"The what?" Robert asked.

Regal glanced back and forth, lowering her voice. "The gene codes for the production of a short bit of RNA. Only twenty-two nucleotides long. When the wheat is eaten and digested, the microRNA is freed in a person's gut, and some of it is absorbed, eventually making its way to the cells."

"Whoopie," Robert threw his hands up. "Then what?"

Regal's expression cooled. "If those cells happen to belong to a woman, bro, it causes the genes that monitor progesterone production to methylate, to turn off."

"Mass birth control with no one the wiser," Renaud mused. "But we're ten years too late." He glanced at Robert. "What's the political situation in America?"

"Strained." Robert made a face. "From our monitoring of the NSA we can plot a four-way split in the country. The Northeast is going one way, the South another, the Rocky Mountain West is doing its thing, and the West Coast is headed in its own direction. The plan was originally to paralyze American influence in the world, and we may have been too effective in doing so. This guy Platnikov is pushing the US and Europe right to the edge."

"What about my guy, Senator Ortega?" Chantel asked.

Robert pointed a finger at her. "Really good call, sis. The guy's come through like a champ. He's got a hold on Korkoran-Hardy, and Big Jim is furious. Ortega's got his daughter in White Coral Clinic as we speak."

Chantel glanced at Regal. "What's the prognosis?"

Regal leaned forward. "Knowing the little girl was a priority, we immediately ran her genome. I've had several of our best geneticists and molecular people working on it round the clock. We've got a gene therapy protocol that should reverse the kid's symptoms. She'll never be one hundred percent, but your senator should really sit up and take notice."

Chantel granted herself a moment of satisfaction; then she turned back to Robert. "What's your opinion of his viability?"

"Chantel, he's kind of a boy scout. Plays too much by the rules for my taste."

"That's because you've never found a rule you could live with. God knows what fool shit you'd try if we didn't have Hammond keeping an eye on you."

Renaud had been watching his son through veiled eyes. "Depending on what we learn from Devon, it may be time to tamp down the partisan rhetoric in the United States."

"Inga will pitch a fit. She and Brian want a socialist reformation."

"Sure," Regal agreed. "So Inga can control the bureaucracies that control the people. She's not going to want to give that up. Not given our models for limited resource distribution."

"She may have to wait to become the wizard behind the American curtain," Renaud said. "If America descends into civil war, she'll end up with nothing but ruins to govern. Ortega might be the key to slowing the American decline. Robert, assuming we can control him, can you get him elected?"

Robert shrugged. "We're a little late for this election cycle, but the guy's positives are in the high seventies among the voters who recognize him. We'd have to pull our campaign team out from under Thad Calloway, but just doing that is going to make a huge statement, especially since Ortega's a Republican."

Chantel asked, "Will Ben Mackeson and his people be amenable to that?"

Renaud told her, "They'd better. We *own* them."

Robert continued, "The hard part is resetting the ground game, controlling the caucuses and primaries at the precinct level. After that, it's just a matter of ensuring the media cooperates. We have controlling interests in most of them. We'll be monitoring the NSA data to perpetuate positives and suppress the negatives. We've got ways of generating and proliferating social media in favor of Ortega and neutering anything against him. StatNco software controls eighty percent of election results. As long as Ortega is within five percent, we can put him over the top without anyone so much as suspecting manipulation."

"Yeah?" Regal asked, "How'd that work during the Trump election?"

Robert flipped her the finger in response.

"Chantel?" Renaud asked with a lifted brow.

"Yes, do it," she said.

Regal nodded her agreement.

Renaud told his son, "I guess you've got a president to make."

"Calloway's history, Ortega's in." Robert studied Chantel, then gave her a smile. "Too bad your sniper isn't as easy to deal with."

Chantel lifted her gaze to stare at him. He looked almost smug. "Don't be concerned, little brother. I have resources you don't know about."

CHAPTER TWENTY

***

AS THE ATR BOUNCED AND SHUDDERED ON TOUCHDOWN, BRENDA STARED OUT THE WINDOW. The pilot reversed the props before neatly wheeling the airplane to a stop before a white-painted hangar that housed a Gulfstream IV.

From the air, the island had looked like a big green kidney surrounded by a white line of fatty sand that contrasted with the crystalline Caribbean water. The airstrip lay on the western, or leeward, side of the island and was accessed by a paved road that led to the huge beachside mansion with its outlying villas and big central swimming pool. A marina, sporting expensive yachts, had been built on the northern end. What must have been workers' quarters had been chopped out of thick forest in the island's middle.

As the ATR throttled down, the flight attendant rose and went to the cabin door.

"We're here, people," Mitch Mitchell called to his team of ten. Bodies shifted, unbuckled, and began collecting gear from the overhead and under the seats.

Mitch remained an enigma. The guy was in his late forties, slight of build with stooped shoulders, and wore thick glasses. Faded green cargo pants were belted to his hips, the pockets loaded; scuffed running shoes clad his feet. A photographer's vest hung open over a short-sleeved cotton shirt. On first impression, the guy looked like a dork. And that might have been why he was so good at his job.

Brenda recognized a good team when she saw one. Mitch ran his detail with military efficiency. These guys, and the solitary woman, Dana Riccio, functioned like a well-oiled machine. Brenda saw it in the way they interacted: long-time associates who trusted one another.

So far, Brenda had been treated respectfully, but with an aloof caution. Not only was she new and an unknown, but Chantel's previous security had proven such a disappointment.

The last one out, Brenda grabbed her pack and followed Mitch as the detail leader descended to the hot, white-concrete tarmac. She took in the thick forest on one side where it crowded the tarmac. Lots of good cover there. On the other side, the Caribbean lapped at stone riprap just below the concrete. It was a security nightmare.

Cases of equipment were being unloaded from the ATR's cargo hold. A white-painted Blue Bird school bus rumbled past the hangars and pulled to a stop with rusty sounding brakes. The driver opened the door.

"Join me, will you?" Mitch asked Brenda as his team loaded their gear and climbed aboard.

Brenda stowed her pack and dropped into the seat beside Mitchell, who asked, "So, how's the job so far?"

"New."

"Mr. Simond said you're going to be hunting Chantel's attacker. What do you need from me?"

The bus jolted forward, gears grinding.

"For the moment, a briefing. I hear you've been with Simond for more than a decade. Some of your guys helped stop two previous attempts. Mr. Simond tells me that one of the people coming here might be behind the attempts on my principal. From your experience, which one would that be?"

Mitch's left eyebrow lifted. "That's a tough call. Playing for the stakes these guys are? Could be any of them, several of them in cahoots...or just as easily, someone from outside."

"I read the security briefing on the plane, studied the aerial photos and maps of this island, but you've been here before. What are we getting into?"

"The island security is better than most, but not perfect. Venezuela being what it is. While we're here a patrol boat will be circling the beaches, waving off anyone who gets too close. Armed patrols will be crisscrossing the forest and monitoring the shores. They've got cameras scattered around the island, most of which work most of the time. The motion detectors are hit and miss, but better than nothing." Mitch smiled thinly. "Me? I hate this place, but it's not my decision to make."

"How about in the mansion?"

"We've got the second floor, south wing. We'll put our own monitoring system on the balcony doors and windows. My people will control access to the hallway at all times. We're only here for two days so the villa staff won't need to access the rooms for any reason. We're using special security measures to ensure the food and drinks are safe with joint security for the receptions and banquet."

"Sounds like you've got it covered."

"Not from a sniper, or, God forbid, somebody out in the forest with an RPG."

Brenda pursed her lips. "I'll do reconnaissance, check out the ground to see what kind of opportunity it presents."

Mitchell's glasses made his brown eyes look geekish. "You have experience with that?"

"I ran SpecOps teams in Afghanistan. Deployed with them on special occasions." She smiled sadly. "My brother was a sniper with the Rangers. Runs in the family."

"Must have made for interesting meal-time conversations on holidays."

"We never talked about it." *Too private.* "What else do I need to know? Who should I pay special attention to? I assume Chantel has history with some of these people. Any hidden land mines I ought to be familiar with?"

Mitchell shoved his glasses up on his nose. "Yeah, a whole minefield full. There are family ties, business ties, policy spats, intrigue, and politics. The old generation is being replaced; turf wars are being fought. Not everyone thought that Chantel was the right person to take over Simond International when her uncle died last year. A lot of bad blood over that. Like any big corporation—especially one built on family—the camouflage of smiles and handshakes barely hides the scabs and scars."

"Family?"

Mitchell gazed at her through lens-enhanced eyes. "Most of these people go back to two families, the Simonds and the Wiesses. The Foundation—the board that's going to be meeting here in the next couple of days—was established by the two patriarchs, Jack Simond and Gerhardt Wiesse. They came out of the Second World War with enough money and assets to build this entire organization."

"Simond International Holdings?"

"That's just the financial arm. SimondAg owns a host of subsidiaries—"

"Whoa. The biotech GMO seed firm that everyone likes to hate?"

"That's them." Mitchell's shrewd eyes noted her reaction. "The Foundation also controls StatNco."

"Never heard of them."

"You wouldn't have. They're into 'Big Data', predictive models, writing the software that runs the computers. Then there is Wiesse Extractive Industries. They own every kind of mine you can think of and have controlling interests in most of the global energy giants. And if they don't, they've developed and licensed the technology that makes oil and gas happen. Then there's the manufacturing consortium. Old Felicia Wiesse-Takanabi still runs it as if she were thirty-five instead of in her seventies. David, her son, holds the title of CEO, but Felicia oversees the daily activities. You'll hear a lot about the Takanabis in the next couple of days."

"Takanabi? Related to Sheela Takanabi? The movie star?"

"She's Felicia's granddaughter. Has nothing to do with the business. Look, these people have to be the best of the best. Most of them have been groomed for positions within The Foundation from the time they were kids. It's an ultra-competitive environment that doesn't forgive failure. The ones who don't measure up, or have the smarts for business, are given allowances and cut loose. Sheela's one of the latter."

"I handled security for her in New York about a year ago."

"She as much trouble as the news and social media say?" Mitchell asked.

"I don't talk about clients."

"Yeah, I've heard that." He raised a finger as the bus pulled up before the mansion. "The guy you want to watch for is Charles Wiesse, he's called 'Sonny', Gerhardt's oldest son and Felicia's younger brother. I guess you'd say he's the black sheep. His business persona is in the international arms trade. He knows everybody in

armaments or knows someone who does. He's the guy they call on
to fix ugly little problems."

"So he knows how to hire an assassin."

Mitchell's eyes seemed to grow behind his glasses. "If he does,
you *didn't* hear it from me. Now, I need to get everyone situated, and
then we'd better be getting to work."

Brenda shouldered her bag, wondering, *What hell is this? The
Godfather on steroids?*

CHAPTER TWENTY-ONE

***

BIG JIM KORKORAN HAD REPRESENTED GEORGIA IN THE UNITED STATES SENATE FOR THREE terms. This was his last. The senate had been fun, ego-boosting, and worth every second he'd put into it. But Big Jim had plans, and given his age, they required that he make a change if he was going to revel in the rewards. A man could give up the senate with its perks when he would be compensated by a couple million a year in salary as a "political" consultant for Dynamil Industries. They'd get their money's worth since Big Jim had written most of the regulations governing their activities. Plus, he had plenty of clout in the Pentagon as well as on the Hill and with the bureaucracy. Additionally, he had already hired an agent to represent him to the networks and cable news channels as a "contributor". Two ghostwriters were at work on his tell-all biography. His literary agent had brokered a million-dollar advance for the book, and the publisher was salivating over the outline.

In short, life was good, and the future looked even brighter. With the passage of Korkoran-Hardy, Peggy and the rest of his staff would step from his senate office, right into prosperous careers with the big banks. So would several members of his immediate family. Peggy and the kids would be well cared for, and he'd get to see them every time he was in New York.

Assuming that cocky upstart asshole Ortega didn't manage to scuttle the bill.

Peggy knocked at his door, leaned in, and said, "William Petroski to see you, Jim."

"Send him in."

The overweight young man in an ill-fitting gray suit filled the doorway, his grin exposing yellow teeth. "How ya doing, Senator?"

"Fine, Bill. Just fine. Have a seat. Can I get you anything?"

"Yeah, one of them special lattes with whipped cream!"

"Peggy, could you be kind enough to run down a latte for Bill?"

She'd lingered in the doorway after Petroski had bulled his way through and gave Jim her familiar two-fingered salute indicating the affirmative before she disappeared.

"Have any trouble with the investigation?" Jim asked as he leaned back, placing as much distance between himself and Petroski as possible.

Petroski grinned—as if proud of his hideous teeth—and settled his bulk in the overstuffed chair on the other side of Korkoran's desk.

"No trouble. This one was a cakewalk. Ortega's people were blogging and tweeting the whole time, bragging about all the people the senator was meeting at the conference."

Petroski reached his sausage fingers into his suit coat, made a face as he fumbled about, and extracted a thumb drive. "Got the guy's whole schedule lined out: who he met with, and sometimes what they talked about. Pretty much everything was public. Luncheons, cocktails, usually with the senator dealing with a limited number of people. After COVID, these things are so much easier to keep track of. He did have breakfast with Secretary Johnson from Treasury, but Johnson's not a partisan when it comes to Korkoran-Hardy."

Peggy knocked, smiled, and stepped in to hand Petroski his latte. She efficiently closed the door behind her on the way out.

"So, no one at Jackson got to him?" Korkoran asked as Petroski slurped at the whipped cream atop his drink.

"Didn't say that," Petroski looked up, a mustache of white on his upper lip. The man's eyes narrowed. "I'm sure that a lot of the bankers expressed opposition to S-107, but never in a setting where they could have put pressure on Ortega. The guy took one very private meeting in Jackson."

"With whom?"

"You're gonna love this, Big Jim. It was with Chantel Simond." Petroski grinned, still unaware of the whipped cream on his lip. "In her hotel room."

"And who is Chantel Simond? She with one of the banks?"

"She's one of the big wheels at Simond International Holdings,

Jimmy. And a pretty hot number. Redhead, nice tits, long legs. I mean, she could lead me around by the dick any day of the week."

"You're saying she screwed him?"

"Naw. He wasn't there long enough. But if someone put the squeeze on Ortega in Jackson, that's the best bet."

"Simond International Holdings? I mean, yeah, I think I've heard of them. Foreign, right? But what kind of leverage would some obscure international investment corporation have on Ortega?"

Wariness hardened behind Petroski's normally gloating brown eyes. "Thought I'd anticipate exactly that question, so I tried a little snooping. Now, Jim boy, I'm pretty damn good when it comes to slipping past firewalls. I can get my fingers under their skirts and up into their panties right to the honey pot."

"And?"

"And Simond slapped me down like a two-year-old caught trying to hack Amazon." He sucked at his latte then smacked his lips. "Maybe five companies in the world have security that good."

"So, my question remains: Who the hell is Simond International Holdings?"

"You're the senator with the bohungus-sized club. I'd start asking around, Big Jim. Start with NSA. They've got the databases, and you're on the intelligence committee. Man, there's got to be a national security angle there someplace." Petroski shook a chubby finger in warning. "But you better think about it first. Call it a hunch. You might have the biggest balls in the room, Jimmy, but if you go lighting matches in places Simond International would rather keep dark, you might get your fingers burned."

CHAPTER TWENTY-TWO

***

AS BRENDA HAD EXPECTED, THE FORESTED TERRAIN SURROUNDING THE MANSION proved to be a sniper's wet dream. A trace-work of manicured paths wound along the tree-covered slope, allowing easy ingress and egress. In her preliminary survey of the grounds, Brenda plotted more than a dozen potential hides. Each provided concealment, an unrestricted field of fire, and facilitated exfiltration. Too many to counter with security—and a well-trained sniper like Taylor could easily find a couple dozen more.

The entire second floor of the south wing was exposed to the point that should Chantel so much as step onto a balcony, or peek out a window, the sniper had a clear shot.

Meanwhile, Mitch's team had gone to work on the mansion, nor did they do it alone. The building was a hive of security activity as eleven other teams went about securing their principals' living quarters, the kitchen, and the ornate hall with its huge wooden table and chairs. They started sealing windows, checking ductwork, and securing the small gymnasium. Half of Mitch's time was spent in meetings coordinating with the other teams.

Brenda thought she was up on the latest security technology, but some of the equipment she was seeing left her feeling like she'd just walked onto a science fiction movie set. She kept hearing terms like "entangled particle communications" and "molecular phase monitoring" along with "anti-mini-drone jamming frequencies". These seemed to be Jaime Sandoval's realm of expertise. The gizmos that kept appearing out of his equipment box were nothing short of the fantastic.

While the entire team showed proficiency with weapons, Sam

Gunnarson quickly established himself as the guru and go-to guy. Each member of Mitch's team demonstrated a specialty that left Brenda envious.

The problem was that everything they'd brought to the island was defensive. The trick equipment was all calibrated for surveillance and communications security. In Brenda's rush to make the flight, she hadn't had time to consider, let alone come up with, the equipment or personnel necessary for a counter-sniper operation.

"Quite the operation you've got," she told Mitch when she finally buttonholed him later that afternoon.

"And what did you discover, Captain?" He glanced disdainfully at her sweat-darkened clothing, streaked as it was with grass stains and vegetative matter.

"A sniper's paradise." She jerked her head in the direction of the slope behind the mansion. "We can keep the curtains closed so he can't make a visual. But if it were me, I'd have a laser mic trained on the windows, use it to pick out Chantel's voice, and take her out."

Mitch shrugged. "Assuming you could get a sniper in position."

"Given the local security guys I ran into out there, I could infiltrate teams with no problem."

Mitch winced. "Okay, I'll have Jaime Sandoval rig something on Chantel's window to muffle the vibrations."

"On all the windows," she countered. "If it's just one, you might as well put up a neon sign saying, 'This is it.' And what if he figures that one Simond is as good as another? He could take Renaud in Chantel's place."

Mitch ground his teeth in irritation. "Alright. All the windows, but that's a couple hours more work than we anticipated."

"Given the cover out there, I'll need a thermal imaging device. Something to spot his heat signature. Cooperation with whoever passes for a marksman among the local guys. Should be some ex-army—"

"Whoa!" Mitch threw up his arms. "Captain, stand down. We're not going to war here. First, I don't have a thermal imaging device. Not a lot of call for one here either. You're trying to make a good first impression. I get that but given the short notice before this meeting was called, not even your Mr. Taylor would have time to get here, let alone figure a way onto the island."

"You don't get it, Mitch. Taylor's one of the most—"

"Look, I've got a lot on my plate. I'm barely going to be ready as it is. I'll give you the curtains and window vibrators. But that's it. How you keep Chantel from exposing herself to a shot is your business. Make do, Captain."

CHAPTER TWENTY-THREE

***

THE FOLLOWING DAY AT THE AIRSTRIP, BRENDA WATCHED THE SIMOND INTERNATIONAL Holdings Gulfstream spool down. Worry, like a nasty little animal, gnawed angrily at her peace of mind. That sixth sense that had so often plagued her before things went to shit literally vibrated in her subconscious.

The bus was back, this time secured and driven by Kamal Rasheed—another of Mitch's team. At Brenda's insistence—and despite no little skepticism from Mitch—the vehicle's windows were curtained to prohibit Taylor from making an opportune shot during the short drive to the mansion.

As the Gulfstream's cabin door opened, a covered walkway was wheeled up. Designed to keep dignitaries dry in the event of rain, it now screened the passengers from observation. Rasheed carefully eased the bus next to the ramp, blocking any shot at the bottom of the stairs.

Brenda took a final look, satisfied that she'd precluded the majority of shot angles, and nodded to Mitch. At his signal, the first of Renaud Simond's staff made their way down the steps and hurried into the bus.

Fifth down came Chantel; a computer bag hung from her shoulder. She'd dressed in a charcoal-gray Rodriguez suit, the skirt and jacket tailored to her body. She met Brenda's eyes and gave a slight nod as Brenda stepped in beside her.

"Any trouble, Captain?"

"No." Brenda covered the woman as she stepped onto the bus, then indicated a seat midway down the aisle. It would be on the ocean side for most of the trip. Snipers didn't like bobbing around in open water at midday while waiting for a shot.

Seating herself beside Chantel, Brenda said, "Sorry about the curtains, but if you can't see out, they can't pick a target inside."

Chantel's green eyes reflected troubled thoughts. "That bad?"

"My motto is 'better safe than dead'. And once you get to the mansion, don't open a curtain, even to look out and check the weather. The glass is thick, but not enough to stop a high-velocity round. Mitch's team has secured the building itself, and I give his job a thumbs up. But I can't guarantee the grounds. Anytime you leave the room, I'd like to be with you. It will be tempting to take a walk, step out for a breath of fresh air, or just take a stroll in the halls, but any unnecessary exposure is the sort of opportunity Taylor could be waiting for."

Chantel's eyebrow lifted. "Do you really think they could sneak a shooter onto this secure island?"

"If I were trying to get to you, I'd already have six two-man teams on the ground and operating here."

Chantel sucked in a breath and looked away. "One of these days you're going to have to tell me about your military service."

"No, ma'am. I don't."

Chantel gave her a sidelong look.

Regal descended the stairs, immaculately dressed, her red hair pulled back professionally. Then came Robert, wearing a flamboyantly tailored cream-colored suit with oversized lapels, his flowing hair looking like Fabio's.

The last of the passengers was Renaud, a phone to his ear. The look on the tall man's face communicated worry as he listened to his caller.

Chantel carefully said, "There will be confidential meetings held on the side. Some of which deal with proprietary information. For those I will need privacy."

The bus lurched into motion, Rasheed no better at shifting the ancient transmission than the driver had been.

"On those occasions could I talk you into wearing one of Jaime Sandoval's communicators? I can be just outside the door, or wherever. All you need to do is thumb a transmit button and say the keyword, 'threat'. I'll hear it in my earpiece and be through the door in a flash."

"And if I find myself trapped in a conversation I'd like to escape, I can thumb the communicator, include the word 'rescue' in a sentence, and you can knock and tell me I'm needed somewhere else."

"Happy to. Are there any special people I should be keeping an eye on? Anyone with a vendetta?"

A churning lay behind Chantel's eyes, her posture instinctively shifting. Her voice lowered. "Val."

"You mean Valentine Wiesse, Charles Wiesse's son?"

Chantel chewed her lip for a second, eyes narrowing. "Mitch must have filled you in. Val's had a thing for me for years. Once upon a time, before I really knew him, we were... Well, he's not the type to gracefully fade into the sunset."

"Got it." Another macho asshole that considered women 'property'.

"Brenda, it's not likely that he'll make a scene, but if he does, let me handle it. You don't know the kind of man he is, what he's capable of."

"Okay, he's yours to deal with as you will. Up to a point."

"I mean it. His father Charles, everyone calls him Sonny, is probably the most dangerous man on earth, but Val? The term psychopath was probably coined just for him. You *do not* want to be cross-wise with either of them."

Brenda considered, then asked, "So, in your opinion, do I consider them the most likely employers of our mysterious Mr. Taylor?"

As the bus pulled up at the mansion, Chantel shook her head. "If either of them wanted me dead, they'd do it themselves. Especially Val. He enjoys personally attending to such things."

Chantel turned hard green eyes on Brenda. "And be aware, you're an attractive and competent woman. Just the sort Val finds irresistible." She paused. "If you involve yourself with him...? Well, I'd hate to lose you."

CHAPTER TWENTY-FOUR

***

FOLLOWING CHANTEL SIMOND'S ARRIVAL, BRENDA FOUND HERSELF ABSORBING INFORmation by the bucketful. Mindful of her status as a newcomer, no one came right out and told her, but from snippets of conversation, she was able to figure out that the meeting had been called by StatNco, the company that specialized in data collection and analysis. And they'd discovered something critically important to The Foundation.

Which left Brenda with the problem of just what exactly The Foundation was. Mitch had said it was a sort of family. And as the day passed, the roles various members played began to clarify. The Simonds were wheeler-dealers in finance and agriculture. Regal Simond—only in her late twenties—headed the huge agricultural conglomerate. The woman carried herself like a queen, whereas Chantel was always coolly in possession of herself, something fiery lay behind Regal's eyes.

Robert, like the model on a cheap Romance bookcover, came with a lady-killer smile, perfect physique, and devilish azure eyes. He was the younger brother Chantel had referred to dismissively. To think of him as a power player behind American politics stretched credulity, right up to the point that he started to talk intimately about the president, senators, and congressmen. At that moment, he dropped into his true element.

The Wiesse branch controlled extractive industries like mining and energy development along with heavy manufacturing industries, mostly in the United States and Europe.

The Takanabi tribe, it seemed, concentrated on Asia—and in particular the electronics and tech industries. Various members of the family were politically influential, sometimes through marriage.

Through bits and pieces, Brenda deduced The Foundation's influence covered most of the globe.

Of one thing, however, she was certain: Charles "Sonny" Wiesse was universally viewed with unease and suspicion. And his son Val gave people the jitters. Apparently, they served as enforcers, eliminators: the strong-arm tactical team.

So, what's the big surprise from StatNco? The question kept repeating in her head. The whole thing was like a conspiracy theorist's worst nightmare.

The mansion teemed with people. The security personnel, like Mitch's people, were dedicated professionals. The staff, assistants, or whatever one wanted to call them, scurried about with papers and cell phones and seemed oblivious to anything but the immediate tasks on their plates.

Each floor of the residential areas was off-limits to the others. The communal areas, including the lounge, the great hall, lobby, gymnasium, swimming pool, and dining room, seemed to be a no-man's land, though constantly monitored by all.

Brenda's attention focused on Chantel, who'd been given a plush suite with separate sleeping quarters, a marble bathroom, and living area with couch, wide-screen TV, fireplace, and wet bar.

There Chantel established her office; her assistants, Janeesh and Ricard, commandeered the desk, each with a computer and headset that tied to the satellite communications center. They might have been in a sweatshop for all the attention they paid to the luxurious surroundings.

The information they periodically reported to Chantel was mind-numbing: minute-by-minute updates on international markets and currencies, pending regulations, price fluctuations on precious metals, and various future markets among them. Most of it made no sense to Brenda.

What did was the escalating tensions between Russia and the NATO countries. Backed by the US, markets were falling, the dollar down by seven percent. The more ominous the threats by Platnikov, the higher the price of natural gas.

"Where does this end?" Ricard wondered aloud.

Brenda devoted herself to a position near the door, listening through her earpiece as Mitch communicated with his security detail. As a result, Brenda was aware when each of the conference parties arrived.

She turned to where Chantel bent over the desk and frowned at something on Janeesh's computer. "You asked to be informed when Felicia Wiesse-Takanabi arrived. Mitch just gave the word. She and Taki are in the lobby."

Chantel looked up, switching mental gears. Her eyes tightened. "Are David and Katya with her?"

Brenda touched her throat mic. "Mitch? Chantel wondered if David and Katya are with her."

"*That's an affirmative on Katya. No sign of David. Katya's accompanied by about thirty security and staff. No sign of Georgi.*"

When Brenda relayed the information, Chantel straightened, took a couple of paces as she thought, and said, "We figured Taki would come. He's no doubt delighted to get out of Tokyo. But if Katya's here, Felicia must have put her foot down. Katya hates these things as much as Georgi loves them."

Janeesh leaned back in her chair. "If Georgi's not here, it's because he just couldn't take a chance on leaving Russia right now. With Platnikov solidifying leadership, no one knows who's going to survive. Georgi was one of Putin's rising young stars. No telling how that might tar him."

Brenda listened, completely captivated. *Who are these people?*

Chantel braced hands on hips. "No matter what his previous alliances, never forget that Georgi is Katya's son, and Dimitri Sokolov's grandson. Georgi sucked Russian intrigue with his mother's milk. He's got enough allies on all sides to see that he ends up on his feet and well placed in the new government. Russia is still Russia—money, connections, and power are all that matter."

Ricard propped his chin on his hand. "Katya's being here means that whatever StatNco discovered, it's going to have a huge impact on Russia. She didn't get where she is by accident: for years she was the liaison between SVR, GRU, and FSB."

Mitch's voice in Brenda's earpiece announced, "*Brenda? You might let Chantel know that we see Chicago.*"

Brenda cleared her throat. "Repeat. You can see Chicago? Roger that." When Mitch didn't correct her, she turned, "Um, I assume this is code. Mitch says he can see Chicago."

"Not code, Captain."

"The plot thickens," Janeesh murmured as she refocused on her computer monitor and began taking notes.

Chantel massaged the back of her neck as she stepped over to the wet bar and poured a cup of coffee. "Chicago is one of Felicia's daughters. They named her after her birthplace. She married an old goat named Liu Xian." A pause. "You follow Chinese politics?"

"No."

"Liu's in the Chinese who's who. He was a kid during the Cultural Revolution. In the nineties a party boss took a fancy to Liu's wife, chucked Liu in prison, and took her. The experience reordered Liu's sense of priorities. Smart guy that he is, he's one of the economic architects of modern China. He's survived despite Xi Jinping's animosity. The two don't get along, but Xi is smart enough not to move against Liu. The man essentially designed and implemented the SEOs—"

"The what?"

"State-owned enterprises. China Petrochemical Corporation, China State Shipping Corporation, China Telecom. Each five-year plan has had his fingers all over it. Oh, and that party boss that took Liu's wife? Somehow he ended up breaking rocks in some forgotten prison on the Mongolian border."

Ricard absently added, "Which is one of the reasons even Xi won't move against him."

Chantel sipped her coffee. "Now I can't say that Felicia orchestrated it, but Chicago was eighteen when Liu first met her in the company of a Japanese trade delegation. One thing's sure, despite the age difference, he worships her, values Chicago's intellectual and technical input. In a real sense, the two of them built modern China."

Built modern China?

"Anyone else I need to know about?"

Chantel hesitated. "The Hestons. The matriarch is Inga Simond-Heston. She's knocking on 80 now. Won a Nobel Prize in mathematics a couple of decades back while she was head of the economics department at Harvard. She'll be here, as will her son, Brian Heston."

"Brian Heston? The one who headed the Department of Commerce? Was Secretary of the Treasury for a while?"

"That's him. He was my main competitor for control of Simond

International. Thinks the position should have been his. But if any of them cause me trouble, it will be Brian's son Stephen. Since I'm here, he'll definitely be in attendance. The guy's one of the most brilliant systems and games theorists alive." She winced. "And he's going to want to dominate every spare moment I have."

"He practically drools," Ricard added from where he leaned over his screen.

Brenda replied, "I know the type."

Chantel added, "He's a nice enough guy, but a little weird."

"Call that an understatement," Janeesh muttered under her breath. "Think obsessed. If you didn't live on an island, he'd be slipping through the gardens with binoculars just to get a peek and pine."

"I'll do my best to limit your exposure." Brenda cocked her head, studying Chantel. "Obsessed, weird, stalker types tend to go to extremes when the person of their dreams doesn't return their affections."

Chantel shot an irritated look at Janeesh, then shook her head. "He's a mathematician. Not the hire-a-killer kind of guy."

"Are you willing to bet your life on that?"

Chantel shrugged, but suddenly she didn't look nearly as confident.

CHAPTER TWENTY-FIVE

***

FOUR WINDOWS OVER. SECOND FLOOR. SOUTH WING. THAT WAS CHANTEL SIMOND'S ROOM. Taylor stared through his thermal-imaging scope where it fixed on the large glass window. Through the scope he could detect the heat signatures of four people. But which one was Chantel?

That was the twenty-million-dollar question.

And Brenda Pepper? Which of the ghostly figures represented her?

You cost me millions, bitch! She'd humiliated him. Spoiled his perfect record.

So, who do I want to kill more? Chantel Simond or Brenda Pepper?

Two individuals spent their time seated at what Taylor supposed was a desk. A third stood most of the time. The fourth figure moved back and forth. Occasionally one or another would retreat to the bathroom.

Camouflaged in their ghillie suits, he and Bennie had been in position for three hours now, looking like the rest of the forest floor. Taylor lay on his belly; the scope-topped Sako, chambered in .338 Lapua, rested on its bipod and butt-rest. The laser rangefinder verified that his hide lay an exact one hundred and seventy-five meters from Chantel's room. The shot would be a piece of cake.

If the woman ever presented herself at the window.

So far, the curtains had been drawn, and no one had so much as peered out.

He'd mulled the possibility of taking a shot anyway. His chances would be one in four. Assuming that Chantel was in the room.

Taylor studied mathematical probability. Living in Monte Carlo as he did, he occasionally idled away his time in the renowned casino. While he did not gamble himself, he often observed. The roulette table fascinated him. He could spend hours mentally wagering on red or black, odd or even, using the occasion to calculate his winnings or losses, adding and subtracting the figures in his head as a brain game to keep his faculties acute.

One night he would have made nearly a million, another he would have lost well over that figure. The exercise was sufficient to prove that probability wasn't only theoretical. Had he been gambling with real money, the casino would have been ahead by nearly two hundred thousand Euros.

No, he would wait. Though every passing hour increased his and Bennie's chances of discovery, they were far enough off the trail, and the guards lazy enough, to allay significant worry.

When he did get the shot, he and Bennie would trigger the beacon and have fifteen minutes to beat feet down the trail to the windward side of the island where they'd hidden their inflatable boat. Ten minutes after that, a waiting drug-runner's submersible would collect them. Eight hours later they would be in Caracas.

Again, he marveled at his client's organizational skills. Forty-eight hours ago, he'd received the call, and here he was, infiltrated onto the island. Every detail had been worked out, his travel a miracle of superbly executed and timed procedures.

"Someone just entered the room," Bennie whispered from where he peered through his own thermal scope. With the background chatter of insects, birds, and tree frogs for cover, an eavesdropper couldn't have heard them from five feet away.

Taylor watched one of the occupants walk to the door, listen, then open it. He picked up the new heat signature as the fifth figure entered. This one was tall, a wavering and indistinct human image. A second of the room's occupants walked over, obviously in conversation.

"The one who opened the door would have been Pepper." He fixed the crosshairs on the heat signature, his finger itching to take the shot. "But that second? Chantel?"

"Or one of her staff." Bennie slowly reached back to brush an insect off his hand. "If nothing else, we'll tag her when she finally goes to bed."

"She'll be the one sleeping in the master suite," Taylor murmured under his breath.

CHAPTER TWENTY-SIX

***

MITCH LED THE WAY DOWN THE HALL, FOLLOWED BY CHANTEL AND RENAUD. BRENDA brought up the rear as they passed Dana Riccio and John Cammack. The two agents guarded access to the second-floor hallway.

Descending the grand stairway, they crossed the lobby to the hall, now filled with people.

As all eyes turned their way, Chantel told Brenda, "Normally security stays along the wall. Tonight, I'd like you close in case I should need you, but not so close that I have to introduce you."

"Yes, ma'am."

Everyone in the room would understand why Brenda was standing closer to her principal than the rest of the security personnel—and if the assassin were here, he or she might be rightly worried that Chantel suspected his or her identity.

Mitch stepped discreetly to the side, taking his place in the thin line of men who stood with arms crossed, or talking, their eyes never leaving their principals.

"Renaud, Chantel, good to see you!" The greeter looked fiftyish with a slight belly. He was balding, wore casual clothes, but a thin black tie secured his collar.

"Devon," Renaud took the man's hand. "You're looking well. I'm assuming that whatever you've called us together for, it wasn't just to enjoy our company."

"We'll save that for the meeting tomorrow." He turned, lifting Chantel's proffered hand. "And you're looking lovely. Nice job fixing up that LIBOR trouble. You tied up Colin Penwick like a bow." His brown eyes narrowed. "And that business in Jackson Hole? Absolutely unimaginable. The shooter? He's good. Very good. Don't worry. We'll find the guy."

"Thank you, Devon."

Next came an elderly woman Brenda would have described as "stately and elegant". My God, what presence. She held the room in the palm of her hand. Tall, with erect posture and perfectly coiffed silver hair, she had a patrician face that—though marked by the years—reflected a seasoned beauty with its straight nose, firm cheeks, and strong mouth. Her intelligent eyes sparkled as she kissed Renaud's cheek and took Chantel's hands.

"Felicia," Renaud greeted. "You remain as remarkably beautiful as ever."

"And as cunning," she retorted, flicking an evaluative glance at Brenda who stood discreetly two paces back. Then Felicia turned her attention to Chantel. "I hear you've aroused someone's ire. Three attempts? Perhaps someone thinks you've become too good at your job, sweetheart. You've increased the bottom line by what, twenty percent since you took over? Perhaps old Renaud here, thinks he's being upstaged."

Chantel lifted a challenging eyebrow. "Twenty-eight percent actually. And if father was worried about my performance, he'd just have me strangled in my bed some night. Making a public spectacle of my death would be unseemly."

Renaud seemed to take it with aplomb, but Felicia Takanabi threw her head back and laughed. "Yes, indeed, that's my favorite cousin." Her blue gaze cooled. "You always were my favorite, you know. How's your sister?"

"Regal will be here in a couple of minutes." Renaud's voice remained calm; his face expressionless. "She's in the process of building two new facilities and had some last-minute calls to make."

"Of course. Given what I've heard, the young lady is going to own world agriculture by the time she's thirty-five. I've heard of her microRNA. Remarkable work. Even if my desiccated hips have spit out their last child, I'm still not eating what she's selling. Now, I've taken too much of your time."

Brenda noticed that the others had stood back respectfully. As Felicia inclined her head and stepped to the side, a striking platinum blonde wearing a phenomenal diamond necklace stepped forward to embrace Renaud. She brushed kisses over his cheeks. Her low-cut and form-fitting black dress revealed the kind of body a twenty-year-old would envy. Dark fishnet stockings accented the woman's toned calves, and high stilettos added to the effect.

"Renaud," she purred with the faintest trace of a Russian accent. "It has been too long." She pushed back, an expression of worry on her perfect face. "You are well?"

"Katya, my darling. Doing marvelously. Where's David?"

"Meetings in Beijing. Poor sweetie. Chicago, bless her heart, provided us with some information. One of Liu's, shall we say, competitors? He will no longer be a problem for several of our Chinese factories. But don't worry. I will give David a full report."

"Tell him I send my regards."

Katya gave Brenda an unpleasant glance, then turned thoughtful eyes on Chantel. "I am so sorry for your recent troubles. You know you can call on me at any time. If you come up with a name? Someone behind this? I have people who can remove problem."

The way the ex-Russian agent had said it, she might have been referring to a landscaping service.

"There he is!" An older man in a tuxedo gracefully shuttled Katya to the side, grabbing Renaud's hand. "Oh, go on, Katya, peddle your assassins elsewhere."

"We talk later," Katya promised with a cool sidelong glance at the newcomer. Like an elegant leopard, she sauntered over to a middle-aged Japanese man who was talking to a blond Adonis wearing a perfectly tailored suit.

"Sonny," Renaud greeted, shaking the man's hand. "Good to see you again."

Brenda went tense. Sonny? The one everyone seemed to fear? Looking at him, he might have just stepped out of a Fifth Avenue fundraiser. Though he had to be knocking on 70, Sonny looked like a dapper movie star—a Robert Duval face and presence topped by a shock of silver hair.

Then his eyes met Brenda's, and in that brief instant, her gaze locked with an ultimate predator's. Some deep-seated instinct caused her to tighten her grip on her purse with its concealed pistol.

He seemed to read her reaction, a glint of satisfaction in his eyes as he turned to Chantel. "Any leads on who is behind these attempts on your life?"

For once Chantel seemed reticent as she said, "Not so far." Then, as if she'd steadied herself, added, "If anyone had a lead, I would have thought it would be you. Father's sent the information your way, hasn't he?"

Sonny's expression sharpened. "This guy Taylor is a possibility. Slippery character. Trained by the French. One of the most talented snipers in the world. My solution would be to buy him off—double what the other side is paying. Much to my surprise, however, I've discovered that he's something of a curiosity. Doesn't drink to excess or gamble, has few vices that would give us a handle on him. The thing that seems to motivate our Mr. Taylor is maintaining his record of kills." Sonny's eyes took on a distant look. "Most admirable."

"You're not the one being shot at," Chantel retorted.

His smile turned cold. "No one would dare."

An awkward silence ensued until Renaud asked, "What will it take to employ a countermeasure?"

Sonny smiled wistfully. "Very difficult. He has protection from several governments that employ his services...an entire network of agencies and organizations. At first hint that we were sending counter-measures, they would tip him off. It may take time to find the right crack in his armor. And, as you know, Monte Carlo is a difficult place to run a counter operation."

"You are not adding to my peace of mind." Chantel crossed her arms.

"We'll get him." His lips thinned, eyes glittering. "Were he to succeed, it would imply weakness on our part. That would be bad for business."

Chantel began, "Then I—"

"I have another suggestion." Sonny raised a hand to stall her. "I'm sure that Valentine could be induced to ensure your security. It would mean a relocation, allowing us to place you somewhere safe until we can deal with the problem."

Sonny shot a dismissive glance Brenda's way. "I'm sure that Captain Pepper is most qualified; however, these are extenuating circumstances. Taylor isn't a run-of-the-mill thug."

At the slight, Brenda managed to keep her expression professional.

"Ah!" Sonny cried. "Here comes Valentine now. Join us, won't you, Val?"

The blond Adonis moved with an athletic grace that reminded Brenda of an alpha wolf. A dashing ivory silk suit with matching tie emphasized his broad shoulders and narrow waist. Beneath he wore a powder-blue shirt; diamond cufflinks glinted as he spread his arms wide. His smile flashed perfect white teeth. The contrast of his sparkling eyes, tanned features, and straight blond hair gave him a weathered look.

"Chantel," he cried, stepping close for a possessive hug. Chantel didn't reciprocate. "You're more beautiful than ever. How are you? Can't say how worried I've been over these last few months. More than once I've considered ditching everything and coming to see you."

"Good to see you, too, Val." Chantel deftly retreated from the hug.

Brenda may have been the only person in the room who saw the barest flicker of malice cross Renaud's face before his social mask fell back into place. Chantel's jaws were clenched, and she took a step back from Val, increasing the distance between them.

"Renaud," Valentine greeted, oblivious to Chantel's reaction. Tendons swelling, he took Simond's hand in what was no doubt a painful grip. "You're looking well."

"You, too, Val. It's been too long. Good work on that Indonesian problem." Renaud's smile had turned plastic.

"Child's play. They were clumsy." Val's smile widened, a sudden animation in his face. "Turns out that the provincial minister they were in collusion with was in poor health. An unexpected heart problem. And at his age? Who knew? His successor has no doubt decided to occupy himself with other concerns that have nothing to do with our operations."

Brenda filed that for future consideration. They had Indonesia in their pocket.

Valentine turned back to Chantel. "As my father no doubt mentioned, I've given thought to your recent circumstances. I have some ideas."

Chantel's smile remained coolly professional. "Thank you, Val. I'm quite safe for the moment."

For the first time, Valentine glanced in Brenda's direction in what was meant to be a casual appraisal. His eyes fixed on hers, the effect almost physical. Then he ran an evaluative gaze up and down her body. Brenda's muscles tensed, her throat going tight as his expression subtly changed. She was used to men stripping her bare in their imaginations, but Valentine Wiesse's self-assured appraisal hinted at a deeper appreciation than base lust.

"I must make your acquaintance." He stepped forward, offering his hand. His eyes never left hers as he asked, "Captain Brenda Pepper, isn't it? Remarkable work in Afghanistan. I doubt you know what a blow you gave the Haqqani in that Maluf operation. Not only did you eliminate Abu Alahiri, but your airstrike also took out the real brains behind Alahiri. A Saudi who called himself El Ankaboo."

"The Spider?" Brenda started. "He was there?"

"Along with the rest of Alahiri's inner cadre." Valentine's pupils darkened. "Colonel Solace recommended you for the Silver Star. It was in his paperwork when he was killed. But when General Alexander took over the operation, he saw to it that the paperwork was never submitted. Given the number of civilian casualties, he thought it politically inadvisable."

She blinked. She could see Bill lying in the dust as clearly as she had that day two years ago. *You recommended me for the Silver Star?*

Valentine's conspiratorial expression sent a shiver of adrenaline through her as he said, "Classified documents are the most fun to read." He paused. "Oh, and by the way, good job keeping our beloved Sheela out of jail in New York last year. Wasn't she a pain to deal with?"

Woodenly, she answered, "I don't discuss clients."

His smile seemed genuine, intimate. "Of course. No doubt the way you dealt with Sheela brought you to Poul Hammond's attention. Remarkably good call by that little weasel. It certainly paid off in Jackson."

Brenda didn't respond. She looked straight ahead, past him. Bodyguards weren't supposed to be the center of attention.

His warm laughter hinted of challenge. "You're on duty. It's boorish of me to distract you. But tell me, you almost made the Olympic team at Stanford. Do you still enjoy fencing?"

She gave him a curt nod. *How does he know?*

Aware that Sonny, Renaud, and Chantel were studying her, Brenda carefully repositioned herself so she could keep an eye on the room, but a tingle of adrenaline ran through her.

"Brenda?" Val called as she sought to recover. "Perhaps, when time allows, we could cross foils?"

"I doubt Ms. Simond will instruct me to use my time that way."

Val smiled. The sort of thing he'd no doubt practiced on a lot of women. It was perfect. The man had a cobra's kind of magnetic attraction: beautiful and deadly. He exuded the self-possessed virility that enticed a woman to see how close she could get without being bitten.

He'd been in her classified files? He was a foreign national, for God's sake.

Brenda kept her expression bland but noted that Val was watching her with a knowing anticipation on his handsome face, as though he could read her thoughts.

CHAPTER TWENTY-SEVEN

***

BRENDA PEPPER HAD ACHIEVED BOTH RANK AND SUCCESS BY FOCUSING SOLELY ON THE mission and dismissing distractions. Nevertheless, she remained acutely aware of Valentine Wiesse. She couldn't help but notice how gracefully he carried himself as he slipped from conversation to conversation, laughing, a model of poise and levity. Everyone's best friend.

Nor could she miss the reserve with which the others treated him. Chantel had insisted that if Valentine had wanted her dead, he'd have attended to it personally. Brenda wasn't so sure about that.

Worse, Val wasn't the only male interested in Chantel.

Stephen Heston might have been a cliché. The mathematician arrived an hour after Brenda's encounter with Val. He stepped through the entrance, escorting his Nobel Laureate grandmother, her raised hand in his. Inga Simond-Heston swept in wearing a stunning charcoal-gray suit coat and matching skirt. Her white hair, piled high, was held by a diamond-studded comb. She'd gracefully disengaged from her grandson's arm and joined Chicago Takanabi in a conversation.

Brenda was intrigued to note that none of the people over fifty in the room had yielded to dying his or her hair. Their egos, apparently, needed no such props.

"Chantel!" Stephen cried the second he was free and nearly broke into a run as he hurried over to hug Chantel. She'd been right: He was like a puppy, his face lighting, brown eyes worshipful.

Nor had Valentine missed it. The look on Val's face was one of pity—as if the skinny and awkward systems theorist in the oversized suit had any chance against the god-like Greco-Roman presence Val cast throughout the room.

After fifteen minutes of Stephen, Chantel shot a pleading look

Brenda's way. She didn't need the "rescue" code to step forward and interrupt Stephen's monologue about mathematical variables.

"Ma'am? Ricard has some new information from Zurich," Brenda said when Chantel turned to her.

"Steve, you've got to excuse me. I'll just be a minute."

"Sure thing," Stephen shot an irritated glance Brenda's way. "But... you're coming back, aren't you?"

"Of course."

"Good, because I can't wait to tell you about my new program. It has financial applications, too. No one has measured macro-trends in consumer behavior as a predictive means to evaluate equities with quite this level of sophistication. You see if you plot—"

"Hold that thought." Chantel raised a finger, her smile so strained even Stephen Heston should have seen through it.

The young man stood, oblivious, his mouth hanging open. Then, recovering, nodded too vigorously. "Okay. I'll be right here. See you soon. And if I'm talking to someone else, just come get me."

As they passed through the hall doors and into the lobby, Chantel asked, "Do you still think Stephen might be a potential threat?"

"He reminds me of the accountant that lived down the hall in the *Ghostbusters* movie. You know. The guy that kept locking himself out of his room?" Brenda's gaze swept the lobby, then double-checked the stairs. She took a position on Chantel's right, her hand in her open purse to grip her .40 HK compact. "Turned out he was the Key Master, remember?"

As they started up the stairs, Chantel added, "Val rolled you for a loop, didn't he?"

"He caught me by surprise. It won't happen again." Brenda stepped ahead, checked the landing, and nodded to Cammack and Riccio where they maintained their stations at the hallway entrance.

"He wanted to see what you were made of," Chantel said softly as they started down the hall. "That roguish charm just melts a woman. And, God, he knows how to use it. But underneath? He's all psychopath."

"Understood."

Chantel gave Brenda a worried glance. "I know that look, Captain. He intrigues you."

"I'm not paid to be intrigued." Brenda knocked twice when they reached Chantel's door, waited five seconds, and knocked four times.

Inside, someone knocked twice and then once in return. The all clear.

Brenda opened the door, her pistol ready, and let the portal swing wide to expose Ricard.

"All's well," Ricard told her, and Brenda led Chantel in, locking the door behind her.

Janeesh called through a stifled yawn, "We need you to look at some data on the rupee."

"In a bit," Chantel told her assistants. "I need some time with Brenda. Go get something to eat. Be back in fifteen minutes."

After Brenda let them out, she turned. "You're not planning on going back?"

Chantel ran fingers through her hair and shook her head. "I need to see what's going on in India. We're prepositioned against the Russians in most markets. If India panics, we'll take a loss. But first we need to talk. Drink?" She stopped at the bar, peering at the bottles.

"I'm on duty."

"How about soda with a lime?" Chantel was pouring Macallan into her own glass.

"Sure. Thanks."

Drinks in hand, Chantel stepped over to the desk, saying, "Sit."

Brenda settled into a chair as Chantel handed her the soda and dropped across from her. The woman's green eyes narrowed slightly as she studied the computer screen. Then with a shake of the head, she closed the laptop. For long seconds, Chantel gazed thoughtfully at Brenda.

Finally, she said, "You and I need to be honest with each other."

Brenda sipped her drink, the soda bubbling on her tongue. "Yes, ma'am."

"I'm sure you recall all the questions when you arrived on the island?"

"Of course."

"The chair we sat you in is a remarkably sophisticated biometric unit. Think of it as a very advanced lie detector. One of Taki Takanabi's companies makes them, and they cost a stinking fortune.

To put it simply, that grilling you went through was to determine if you were a spy."

Brenda turned her glass with casual fingers. "Evidently it passed me."

"Along with the psychological profiles, we throw in questions from every intelligence agency. We always get a hit, a reaction, when an agent reads a question he's had before. You only reacted to the ones from Army intel. Which is why you're here."

"I see."

Chantel vented a weary sigh. "After tonight, what is your impression of the family?"

"I'd say you make the Knights Templar and Illuminati look like Disney creations. The Foundation has controlling fingers in everyone's pies. International finance, mining and manufacturing, electronics, research, and wow, classified intel?" Brenda nodded to herself. "Katya is inside SVR and GRU. This guy Liu is a big wheel in the Chinese central committee. And Sonny?" She shook her head. "I'm having a hard time buying it. They're all too..." She made a face.

"Perfect and powerful?" Chantel smiled her amusement. "Not a dud among them? These are the survivors, Brenda. The few who lived through the hell that was our grandfathers' making. Those who don't measure up? Aren't bright enough? They get taken care of, given menial projects."

"It sounds so..."

"Draconian? Ruthless? Inhuman? Those are all words we use to describe ourselves." Her expression betrayed a deep wound. "From the time we're born, we're programmed. Mentally conditioned. Trained to compete. Our educations are what you would call extreme, unforgiving, and comprehensive." She paused, her lined brow hinted at dark and terrible things. "The ones who can't take it...fail... Sometimes it's not pleasant."

"Who determines?"

"We're given projects. Success is self-evident. Which leads to the next level, and so on. To date, I haven't failed. Nor has The Foundation. We've stopped three nuclear wars over the last seventy years."

"By pulling strings behind the scenes?"

"As an American, how does that make you feel?"

"Uneasy." Brenda met Chantel's eyes. "So, what's the end game?

World domination?"

"Sorry. You're not in a movie. There are limits to what we can and cannot accomplish. The world is too big, random, and messy for any single entity to control. And then there's what we call 'agency'. Look at the Trump election. Or the fact that Xi Jinping blindsided us with the COVID release. Devon has a statistical model that proves that political stability caps out at a couple billion people sharing a similar socio-cultural value system. As the numbers rise above that populations begin to fission and government breaks down. So, while we can't control governments—well, most of them, anyway—we can nudge them in certain directions."

"Nudge them?"

"Yes, which brings us back to Devon. Remember him?"

"Balding guy with the tie and brown loafers. He's supposedly the reason we're here."

"He and his sometimes-lover Rusty Patton are the brains behind StatNco. StatNco controls most of the companies that write computer code. Contractors for military, economics, agriculture, international trade and banking, you name it. And yes, NSA tracks everyone's email, social media, and credit card use, which is handy because we mine their metadata, analysis, and interpretation. And Russia's, and China's, and Germany's, and so on down the line, because, ultimately, they're using StatNco code."

Brenda's heart skipped. "But the amount of data..."

"Huge. For the last year or so, Devon and Rusty have had teams putting together a model. They ran it last week. Tomorrow they're going to tell us the results, and I already know it's not going to be pretty." Chantel hesitated. "Which brings us to End Game."

Brenda straightened in her chair.

Chantel flipped a strand of hair back. "The Foundation goes back to the end of the Second World War. My grandfather, Jack Simond, was best friends with a Nazi industrialist named Gerhardt Wiesse. They had gone to university together and married each other's sister if you can believe. And Gerhardt—which wasn't his real name by the way—survived the war with a fortune, but lost his entire family, his home, his country...all blasted to ruin. At the time, Jack and Gerhardt figured it was merely a matter of years before a third world war would destroy everything. Seventy years and billions of dollars later, The Foundation is the result." A beat. "And the world hasn't blown itself up."

Chantel sipped her scotch. "The cold war almost went hot several times. Thanks to The Foundation's influence with some of the key players, it didn't. It took time, but there was a reason Gorbachev finally succeeded. We bought another thirty years."

"*You* bought?"

Chantel absently smoothed her fingers over her glass. "If we focus on major players like Russia, Europe, China, and Japan, we miss hotheads in what seem to be insignificant countries like Pakistan, or Zambia, or Chechnya."

"Looks like you missed Russia's resumption of the cold war."

"We thought the West would call Putin's bluff over Crimea and eastern Ukraine. Our only recourse was to finally ruin Putin and devastate the Russian economy. If you ever need proof that we're not perfect, Platnikov came to power."

Brenda tapped her drink with her fingernails. "It's a hard sell if you want me to believe that you're a humanitarian organization dedicated to the best interests of mankind."

"We're much too pragmatic to be humanitarians. How much do you understand about terms like quantitative easing, liquidity, the devaluation of currency?"

"Essentially printing money and borrowing, writing each other IOUs. Like with the debt, right?"

"We made a killing, and not just in the US, but through the European Central Bank, and in China, not to mention the emerging markets like Brazil, India, and Russia. The tried-and-true idea was to borrow, spend, and stimulate the global economy as a short-term shot in the arm. To get elected, politicians enacted a slew of social welfare programs, most of which were a waste. Which meant they needed to raise taxes—what they call revenue—to at least make a dent in the deficits. The social programs, like the Affordable Care Act that you're familiar with, overran all of their budgets. Governments are playing sleight-of-hand games, just like kiting checks at the end of the month. You hope something comes in before the banks figure out the scheme. Governments have been trying to buy time for their economies to recover and begin creating wealth, which, with inflated and devalued currency, could be paid back without damaging economies. Then came COVID which just made things worse. That idiot Xi had no idea of the unintended consequences his little 'experiment' would have for the world economy. The debt incurred has to be paid back with printed money."

"I don't understand how printing money makes it easier to pay back."

Chantel spread her hands. "It's an old trick that goes back to the tyrant Dionysus of Syracuse. He had debts, so he collected all the one-drachma coins in the city, restamped them as two-drachma coins, then paid off his debt. Here's a grossly oversimplified example: a government has annual tax revenue of twenty dollars and a money supply of one hundred dollars out in public circulation. It wants to sell bonds worth ten bucks. Brenda Pepper, looking for an investment, shells out ten dollars for the bonds they offer. The deal is that in ten years, they will pay you back your ten dollars plus fifty cents interest. As the ten years go by, they print more bills, until they have a money supply of a thousand dollars in circulation. More money means that prices go up on everything by ten times. A gallon of gas that once cost fifty cents now costs five dollars. But the government is now bringing in two hundred dollars a year in tax revenue, so when you cash in your bond, they easily pay you the ten-fifty they owe you."

"But the buying power of the money I get back is worth ten times less."

Chantel swirled her scotch in her glass. "The hope is that a nation's GDP grows at a rate faster than the devaluation of the currency."

"I keep hearing that world GDP has been flat for a long time now." Brenda took another swallow of her soda. "Which brings us back to end game. What is it?"

Chantel studied her scotch, tilting the glass to watch the amber liquid shift. "Tomorrow, Devon will tell us how much time we have left. Because of something called social inertia—the fact that people like things as they are—I'm betting thirty years. Dad thinks twenty-five. And in answer to your question about end game, if the world is about to collapse, The Foundation is going to try and fulfill Jack Simond and Gerhardt Wiesse's original intent. We're going to try to cushion and direct the crash in order to save something of civilization."

"Do you think it will really be that bad?"

"Brenda, the world is feeding seven and a half billion people on just-in-time inventory and the climate is changing. Brush wars are flaring up all over the globe. What happens when the distribution system gets over-strained and breaks down? What do a billion starving people do? Just sit in their houses and die? No, they turn on each other like starving rats."

"Which means entire cities will be rioting, looting, murdering and stealing." The images forming behind her eyes were terrifying.

"You live in New York. You think the BLM and COVID riots were bad? What if you turned off the electricity and water? Stopped the trucks from delivering food? No elevators, lights, heat, or sewers? No gasoline? Credit cards are worthless? How long would it take before people were murdering each other in the streets just to obtain a loaf of bread or a bottle of water?"

Chantel Simond took a long drink of her scotch and said, "The Foundation will be making difficult choices. And we'll live with the consequences. As you did outside Maluf. Your airstrike saved your team and took out Alahiri, Ankaboo, and his staff. In doing so you killed eighty-six innocent men, women, and children."

Chantel paused, as if searching for words. "I'm known as a cold-hearted bitch, but you saved my life in Jackson. I wasn't sure that bringing you here was a good idea. And tonight, you got a feel for what The Foundation is. Before you get in any deeper, I'm offering you a way out."

Brenda took a deep breath, thinking, *For God's sake, Brenda. You silly bitch, go pack your bag and get the fuck out of here while you can!*

CHAPTER TWENTY-EIGHT

***

CHANTEL CONTINUED, "I CAN HAVE YOU OFF THE ISLAND TOMORROW MORNING WITH A
million-dollar severance package. There will be nondisclosure agreements that you will have to sign, and you will be monitored for a time to ensure compliance."

"And the alternative?"

"Tomorrow, the gloves come off. After that, leaving...well, it won't be so easy given the information you'll be privy to."

"In for a penny, in for a pound?"

Chantel held her gaze. "I think you'd be an incredible asset to my team, but it will come at a price."

"You're playing God with the End of the World, and you want me to help?" Stunned, Brenda sat back in her chair.

The knock at the door was in the proper sequence.

As Brenda rose and walked to the door, Chantel said, "Be honest with yourself, Brenda. I'll need your decision tonight."

Brenda, pistol easily accessible, stepped to the side and opened the door to admit Janeesh and Ricard.

"Are you ready for us?" Janeesh asked, yawning. The woman blinked haggard and bloodshot eyes.

"Brenda and I just finished." Chantel stood. "Janeesh, how long since you've slept? It's been more than twenty-four hours, hasn't it?"

Janeesh gave her a silly grin. "I'm fine." She indicated the laptop. "Let me show you the data, I think we need to short the rupee."

Chantel waved her off. "Go get some rest."

"You'll have questions."

"You're not going to be of use if you're narcoleptic. At least take a nap. You can flop on my bed for a couple of hours." Chantel's expression hardened. "That's an order."

"Yes, ma'am." With a nod to Brenda, Janeesh stepped through the bedroom door and closed it behind her.

Brenda stared vacantly at the floor, trying to come to grips. God, it was like some impending nightmare. Take her million and leave? Go home to West Virginia and lay in supplies at Mom and Dad's farm?

How did a person prepare for the collapse of the international monetary system and the end of civilization as she knew it?

Chantel seated herself before the laptop. "Alright, Ricard. What have we got?"

Ricard had no more than bent over Chantel's shoulder when a *pock-pow!* rang out. The second *pock-pow!* made Brenda lunge for Chantel, grab her by the shoulders, and hurl her to the floor. A *pock-crack!* split the air where Chantel had been. The laptop danced on the table, display dark where the bullet had center-punched the screen.

Brenda twisted her fingers in Chantel's coat as she pressed the stunned woman flat on the floor.

"Ricard, damn it, get down!" Brenda screamed.

Ricard dropped to the carpet, a confused look on his face.

"What's happening?" Chantel cried.

"Quiet." In the sudden silence, Brenda listened, her heart pounding. The only sound was the faint whirring of the laptop fan. And then, from behind the bedroom door, she heard a familiar wet gurgling followed by a rattling gasp.

Son of a bitch! Janeesh!

Accessing her throat mic, Brenda cried, "Mitch? Code one! Repeat, code one! Shots fired."

"Code one. Roger that. Stat?"

"Extracting Chantel."

"Roger that. On the way."

"Shooter is outside. Repeat, shooter is outside. High-power rifle."

"Shooter outside. High-Power rifle. Roger that."

Brenda tuned out the sudden chatter in her earpiece as Mitch called orders to his people. To Chantel, she said, "Belly crawl. No hands or knees. Get behind that wet bar. When you get there, stay down!"

Chantel trembled and nodded.

"Go!" Brenda hissed.

Chantel scuttled forward.

Brenda waved at the wide-eyed Ricard. "Go! Stay behind her!"

The man seemed frozen, then flopped his way after Chantel. Brenda crawled along behind, keeping herself between Ricard and the curtained glass.

Her flesh tingled, anticipating the impact of a bullet. Adrenaline's lipid rush lent her speed.

Only when they were behind the wet bar, did Brenda take a deep breath. "Everyone okay?"

"What the hell's going on?" Chantel demanded in a shaking voice, starting to sit up.

"Down!" Brenda jerked her down again. "Wait for the all clear."

"What about Janeesh?"

Brenda ground her teeth, remembering the death rattle. "You stay here. I'll check."

Brenda rose to a crouch, slipped around the end of the wet bar, and charged for the bedroom door. Flinging it open, she stopped, upright, shielded by the partitioning wall. She withdrew her flashlight, covered the lens with her fingers, and shone a sliver of light onto the bed.

Janeesh lay atop the bedspread, her head to one side, wide eyes staring emptily. The woman's bullet-shattered right arm lay at an impossible angle. Blood—still leaking from the wreckage of her chest—pooled on her right side, soaking into the covers.

CHAPTER TWENTY-NINE

***

I SHOULD BE DEAD.

In the chef's tiny office adjacent to the kitchen, Chantel sat at a paper-strewn desk, a cup of hot cocoa cradled in her hands. The terror of what she'd just experienced kept repeating in her mind: Brenda jerking her out of the chair. The *crack-pock* beside her ear. She'd felt Brenda's frantic heartbeat through her shirt as the woman pressed her to the floor. And then the desperate scrambling crawl to the safety of the wet bar.

Images haunted her: the glittering pain in Brenda's eyes when she returned from checking on Janeesh; how Mitch's team had burst into the room; the way Brenda ordered them to form a human shield around her; and the rapid evacuation from the room to this small and cramped office deep in the mansion's guts.

Brenda saved my life.

The woman now guarded the doorway, her pistol in hand, expression grim.

Janeesh? Dearest God, not Janeesh.

Janeesh had been with Chantel for ten years. Yes, she'd been an outstanding employee. Qualities like intelligence, tenacity, and a willingness to work thirty-six hours straight were rare enough, but Janeesh had had some intrinsic understanding of Chantel's personality. Never quite an intimate, she had been a confidante, a respectful pillar of support.

Murdered?

Grief, rage, and disbelief all sought to burn free.

Got to control myself. Be cool. Can't show weakness.

It was all she could do to keep from shivering, from breaking down and bursting into tears.

Brenda tensed as Renaud pushed the kitchen door open. Hal Parducci and Taco Carbajal stood just outside, MP5 submachine guns in hand, to control entry.

Renaud strode past counters, pans, and stoves, as if powered by an implacable force. His face was set, a fire behind his green eyes. Oh, Chantel knew that look. The few times she'd seen it before had always ended in tragedy.

"Are you alright?" His voice trembled as he stepped past Brenda and dropped to his knees before her.

Chantel took a deep breath, met his eyes, and barely nodded. Stumbling for words, she asked, "Who *are* these people?"

"We don't know. We've got security searching the entire island. Jaime Sandoval shined a laser through the bullet holes and onto the slope. Whoever the shooter was, he's running for his life." Renaud's fist clenched. "How the hell did they do it?"

"Thermal imaging scope." Brenda bit off the words. "With the blinds closed, all he had was heat signatures. The only way he could be sure of his target was when Chantel went to bed. He couldn't have known it was only Janeesh taking a nap."

Then to Chantel's surprise, Brenda knotted a fist in rage and snapped: "Damn it, Mitch! I told you!"

"Told Mitch what?" Renaud asked, rising, his piercing eyes burning into hers.

"I asked for a thermal scope to search for heat signatures on that slope. I could have coordinated with a counter-sniper to take the son of a bitch out."

Renaud stared at her, lips twitching from throttled emotion. "Counter-sniper? We're *supposed* to be on a *secure* island!"

"Dad," Chantel said softly. "You were the one who thought Brenda was a bit overboard on the window closures and the anti-eavesdropping glass vibrators. She was the one who said she could have had several teams working on this island in spite of the security."

Renaud's voice strained. "Janeesh is *dead*! It could have just as easily been you!"

Chantel stood, desperately relieved to take charge, to no longer be the helpless victim. Placing calming hands on her father's shoulders she looked into his eyes. Rage-tense muscles quivered under her touch. "But I'm alive. Wouldn't have been if Brenda hadn't thrown me to the floor."

"It shouldn't have happened in the first place."

"But it did."

In ominous tones, Brenda said, "There's more to this. Every window on the Simond floor was masked and blacked out. Even with advanced imaging gear, Taylor had to know exactly which room Chantel was occupying, which bedroom was hers."

"Dear God." Renaud swallowed hard, looking sick. "So, it *is* one of us?"

Taco Carbajal pushed the kitchen door open, calling, "Sir? Valentine Wiesse is asking—"

Val burst past the guard saying, "Sorry, Renaud. Ol' Taco here can shoot me if he wants, but I'm going to see Chantel."

Chantel bit off a curse. *Damn it, not Val. Not now.*

Renaud, still ashen, waved Taco back, and took a deep breath as Val strode purposefully up to Chantel. Eyes worried, he asked, "You alright, Fox?"

At the term, Brenda's eyebrow lifted slightly. As quickly, the woman professionally blanked her face.

Chantel's lips bent in a weary smile; she let him take her hands. "Yeah, I'm fine. But Janeesh is dead. The gunman mistook her for me."

Val's eyes tightened in that old and deadly way. "He can't get off the island. The second patrol boat is already out. Even at night, if he's on a boat, radar will ping him."

He paused for emphasis. "And then he and I are going to have a little session. There's a cement blockhouse back in the woods—admirably outfitted and soundproofed, I might add. A place Maduro's agents used to dissuade dissidents and political opponents. It even has an incinerator for the remains."

"You're not going to catch him," Brenda predicted.

Val's eyes, like blue ice, fixed on Brenda. "And how do you know this?"

"If he had a foolproof way onto the island, his exfiltration was just as carefully planned." Brenda held Val's measuring glance in a most dangerous way. "Your father said the French trained him. You don't seem to have too much trouble checking highly classified files. Get me the guy's address."

Valentine's eyes glittered—one predator to another—as he said, "If facial recognition software can be trusted, the man we think is Taylor will be found. As soon as we locate his shooting position, perhaps we can recover a strand of hair...something that will allow us to recover DNA, or even a fingerprint."

"What about the databases?" Renaud asked. "Surely StatNco can mine the metadata to get a line on the guy. He has to fly in and out of France, most likely Nice, since he lives in Monaco. Surely there's a financial trail. We have records from every bank on earth, for God's sake. Monaco is a small enclave. His image has to be on security cameras there."

Val smiled coldly. "As soon as I have a word with Devon and Rusty, I suspect Mr. Taylor's life is going to become very interesting. And short."

He shot Brenda a conspiratorial look. "Maybe you and I can take him down together?"

The cold anticipation in his voice sent a shiver down Chantel's spine.

"As long as we do it *my* way," Brenda insisted.

God, Brenda, you're playing with fire, challenging him like that.

She didn't need this. Not now. Not with the *crack-pow* of a killer's bullet impacting in Janeesh's body still echoing in her memory. Two women were now dead in her place. At any second, without warning, a bullet could blow her body to pieces.

The world was coming apart.

I can't stand this!

CHAPTER THIRTY

***

"ANYTHING GOES WRONG? YOU DO AS I SAY," BRENDA ORDERED.

Chantel jerked a nod. "Alright."

Brenda led the four-man detail that escorted Chantel to the hall and timed her arrival for the last minute, having ensured that Chantel had a seat in the rear, near the door. It was a position from which she could be evacuated quickly when the presentation finished. Having to withstand the gauntlet of pity and concern from the Wiesse and Takanabi factions would have been added torture now that the impact of Janeesh's death was sinking in.

That Chantel looked as composed as she did after the heartbreak and stress of the night spoke volumes about her character. Somehow, she'd partitioned off the grief, made herself function.

While Janeesh's death hadn't torn an emotional hole in Brenda the way Kelly's had, a burning rage and frustration remained. She'd hunted her share of bad men, including Pashtu drug lords who sold children to the sex trade, but what was brewing inside was qualitatively different.

As Brenda had predicted, Taylor—if that's really who the trigger-puller had been—was long gone. While his sniper hide had been located, not a trace of the man or his spotter had been found.

Brenda stood in the back of the great hall and watched The Foundation's movers and shakers seat themselves around the stunning central banquet table in preparation for Devon Czykowski's PowerPoint. *So, which one did it?*

Damn it, she just had to know.

Is that why I'm still here?

Looking around, the sobering reality dawned that she was in the midst of some of the most coldly powerful people on the planet. Chantel had offered her a flight out. A chance to leave—and a million-dollar incentive to do so. But a security professional didn't just walk up to a woman who'd barely avoided assassination and say, "So, I quit. Can I have my million?"

Besides, Brenda wanted Taylor almost as much as she'd wanted Alahiri.

She cataloged the faces. They were powerful people indeed, used to having their way. Any one of them might have ordered the assassination.

Could it have been crafty old Felicia? The woman had a bitter expression on her thin face. Or perhaps her missing son, David? Katya was another possibility. Today she looked like a blonde ice-goddess the way her hair was piled high, and she sat straight-backed. She'd have access to some of the finest snipers in the world given her ties with Russian clandestine operations.

And then there was the Takanabi crowd. Taki, the electronics magnate, had controlling interests in east Asian electronics industries from Korea to Singapore, and throughout Silicon Valley. His sister, Chicago Takanabi-Liu, needed only to ask her aged Central Committee husband for assistance. Old Liu could have orchestrated the entire operation, utilizing the best within China's sprawling military.

And there sat Sonny, arms propped on the table, his narrow mouth pursed. When he glanced Chantel's way, the man's eyes narrowed as though in promise of violence. If the scuttlebutt about the extent of his arms trade was correct, the guy knew more mercenaries than the pope knew cardinals. He, Devon, and Taki Takanabi formed a sort of triumvirate when it came to electronic intel and data gathering. Maybe dad didn't like the fact that Chantel had thrown his son over?

Valentine, of course, couldn't be dismissed, but somehow Brenda couldn't see him using a surrogate. Chantel was right about that. The guy had been too excited about the chance to rendition the assassin off to that secluded blockhouse back in the forest. Word, too, was that his preferred method of assassination was through exotic technology like dart guns, drones, poisons, and electrocution.

And you dated him? Let him call you Fox? Brenda glanced sidelong at Chantel, wondering how that had worked.

On the other side of the table, Inga Simond-Heston had a notebook out, her face thoughtful as she wrote on a fresh page. She looked like a way-too-rich college professor, her hair immaculate, gaze distant. Despite her appearance she sat at the table with the perfect composure of an equal.

Beside her, Stephen kept shooting worried glances at Chantel, as if itching to leave his chair and rush over. Or was that just a cover, a role? Given the choice of overtly dangerous hyenas and piranhas in the room, dismissing him as a suspect was almost a given. Assuming that is, that Brenda could convince herself that unrequited love wasn't a motive for murder.

Yeah, sure.

And dork though he might be, the guy was smart. His specialty was game theory? Whoever was using Taylor as a playing piece was doing a masterful job of staying a step ahead.

Finally, there was Chacon Gutierez Wiesse. He sat in the back opposite Chantel, with his two attendants behind his wheelchair. The guy was eighty-seven, an Argentine industrialist who'd married Valerie Mathilda Simond. He'd been a crony of Peron, Allende, and a host of other South American dictators. Brilliant at acquisitions—and with Renaud Simond's financial support and counsel—Chacon had ridden the wave, always bailing just before an economic or political collapse left investors in ruin.

Like a dying vulture, Chacon watched the proceedings, thin arms propped on his wheelchair's armrests, brown fingers laced like a priest's in prayer. Tubes ran from an oxygen bottle to his aquiline nose. The man's keen black eyes, however, missed nothing.

He's an unknown.

"Let's get started," Devon called from the front. He fixed on Chantel. "As you all know, an attempt was made on Chantel last night. Thank God, it failed."

The room filled with applause, all eyes going to Chantel, who inclined her head in recognition.

"You also know that the assassin appears to have escaped." Devon spread his arms. "Valentine, Sonny, Taki and I have already discussed this untenable situation, and I assure you, we'll deal with this swiftly and surely."

"God have mercy on the guy," Sonny growled loud enough for the room to hear. Grunts of approval seconded his comment.

"Now, given the sudden uncertainties we've just experienced"—Devon clasped his hands—"we need to make this short and to the point."

Katya called, "Cut to the chase, Devon. We're sure that your conclusions are accurate, data superb, and statistics impeccable. What is bottom line?"

Devon cocked his head, meeting Katya's eyes. "The bottom line is five years at the outside."

"*What?*" Renaud cried, his voice lost among the others.

"Are you sure you don't want to see the data?" Devon asked.

"Five years?" Taki Takanabi asked.

"It's a mathematically derived probability," Devon replied. "You understand probability, don't you? We're talking about the most likely outcome of chance events. Not an absolute. For example, all nations are now in a race for critical resources. The earth is running out of rare-earth elements, palatable drinking water, arable land, and dependable energy. The scrambling between Russia and the West over Poland and the Baltic states is symptomatic. Xi released COVID as a test run to determine the best way to implement a world pandemic to eliminate rival states. In the last few days, it's become obvious that with a simple miscalculation, the entire world could explode.

"The current territorial squabbles between China, Japan, Vietnam, and the Philippines in the South China Sea are over oil on the continental shelf. Pakistan remains a soggy sugar cube—one that could disintegrate at any moment. India is already bursting because of its rising population, and climate change threatens their agricultural production.

"The Middle East is in flames."

Chicago Takanabi called out, "We're doing our best to keep tensions from escalating beyond the point they already have. Unfortunately, with social media, we do not control the press with the precision we once did. But getting back to the point, which variables are the most problematic?"

Devon pointed. "Katya, could you address the Russian situation?"

Katya's polar-cold gaze swept the table. "We have intelligence that Platnikov is going to solidify his power by moving on Baltic states. He expects to do this by June at the latest."

Brenda's gut went sour. NATO couldn't let him.

Devon said, "Platnikov is the most immediate threat we face. But political instability driven by social deprivation, disruption of food production and distribution, climatic effects on weather and agriculture, and after the success of COVID, newly adapted pathogens anywhere around the world could be a precipitating event. Nor do the regional conflicts show any sign of abating."

Devon paused. "We monitor most of the governments and can anticipate and blunt their more egregious actions. But as you've seen from social unrest across the globe, entire populations can rise up over what seems to be an insignificant event. And they can do it virtually overnight. As deprivation increases, this will become an even more random variable which we cannot control."

"But you can anticipate social unrest through the metadata, can't you?" Chicago Liu asked. "We know from social media when the people are agitated. You have descriptive statistics for that."

"We do," Devon agreed, pulling absently at his tie. "Our problem is that there are so many populations in ferment, the triggering event could come from anywhere. The sub-Saharan belt, Iran, Pakistan, Eastern Europe and Muslim Russia, most of South America, Indo-China, even the ever-increasing political polarization in the United States. Americans are already killing each other in the streets. All that's necessary is the spark that sends the masses over the top. Nor can we predict what that spark will be."

"We're taking steps to defuse American political tensions," Robert Simond said from one side of the room. "We have a potential candidate for the next election. His election should buy us some stability, provided the rest of the world doesn't go up in flames."

Brenda stared in disbelief. *They have a candidate?*

"But, Devon, you must have some predictive ability," Felicia snapped.

Devon gave her an apologetic shrug. "Generally, yes. But we can't account for the random effect of agency. Sometimes an opposition leader can be assassinated, and nothing happens. Look at what happened when we got rid of Putin. A week later, a grocer, who seemed inconsequential, is shot to death by mistake, and the country erupts in flames. Why one event triggers chaos, and another doesn't? That, we can't tell you. Think back. We missed the revolt in Tunisia, but correctly called Syria. In the social sciences this is called agency, the effect that a random individual can have on popular perception. The function of agency can almost be random. The higher the stresses within a population, the more susceptible they are to agency."

"Do not lecture us on social science," Katya's voice dipped. "Our concern is what to do if you are correct, and we only have five years."

"Or less," Devon replied testily. "Remember, I said that five years was the highest probability for when the world global system would reach critical mass. Factor in weather, for example. A sudden reversal of atmospheric circulation around the Tibetan Plateau would reduce precipitation along the Himalayas and in Southeast Asia. Regal, do you have data on the impact?"

A pale Regal Simond glanced around the room. "Two billion people would starve within three months. We would have the same result from an outbreak of a recently identified strain of rice-specific fungus that we're currently studying and trying to suppress. If it spreads before we can modify or kill it, it could reduce harvests by sixty percent or more. We're also concerned about a potential corn blight in the American Midwest."

"So, Devon," Renaud said, "you're saying that the fragility we see in international banking extends to the physical and social spheres."

"Very much so," Devon answered. "I was going to get to international finance, but precarious as things are, socio-cultural or environmental factors are just as likely to disrupt either commodity production, or worse, distribution. Both systems are vulnerable. Or a political act could be the precipitating event. If a messianic leader comes to power in Pakistan and launches a nuclear attack on India, the global system will cascade."

"Go back to this precipitating event." Inga Simond-Heston spoke in a remarkably cultured voice. "Part of our success over the last couple of decades has been predicated on the integrated global economy, what that reporter, Thomas Friedman, called the Flat Earth. Even subtle perturbations can have effects way beyond their expected proportions. A typhoon destroying an engine-control chip factory in Taiwan can cause the shutdown of a German automotive assembly line. That shut down, in turn, can cause an overstock of tires in Brazil that leads to layoffs. Those in turn can trigger a riot that initiates the collapse of the government. The complexity of the system cannot be understated."

Devon rubbed the back of his neck. "Those are exactly the variables we've figured into the model, Inga. You reviewed the categories, and we relied on so much of your own research. What you just said makes my point: the global economy is so specialized, complex, and inter-dependent, it's become a precarious edifice spun of delicate crystal. If a strand cracks, even if it seems to be unimportant, the entire system begins to shatter."

Inga took a deep breath, adding, "And once that begins, nothing we can do will stop it."

"That's why we're here," Devon told her, his voice weary. "This is your notification. We are past the point of no return. Assuming we can contain Platnikov, we may have five years before everything comes crashing down. Or, though improbable, it might happen tomorrow. Every day that passes increases the probability of a precipitating event. If we make it past the five-year mark, consider it a gift from God. But when that critical event happens, it's going to get very nasty, very quickly."

"How nasty?" Sonny Wiesse asked.

Given his expression, Devon might have been contemplating his own grave. "It depends on the variables, but it will be fast. Under optimal circumstances, if we can direct the crash, we might have ten years to drop world population to a sustainable two billion people. But that's if everything works out our way."

Brenda gritted her teeth. *They're talking about five billion dead, and not one of them flinched.*

"But the current world population is seven and a half billion." Chicago Takanabi noted. "Most of them in Eastern Asia."

"And so is most of the world's manufacturing capability," Taki Takanabi said. "Our industries will be unsustainable."

Devon raised his hands for silence. "Here's the alternative: If the wrong variables play out, ninety-nine percent of the world's population could be dead within a year of the precipitating event. The majority of the survivors will be isolated to pockets in the Southern Hemisphere. Places like South Africa, Australia, the tip of South America. The rest will lie under a radioactive haze and nuclear winter."

CHAPTER THIRTY-ONE

***

A STUNNED BRENDA ACCOMPANIED CHANTEL AS THEY LEFT THE ROOM TWO HOURS LATER. Trying to absorb everything she'd heard, she shook her head at the impossibility of it.

The thing was these people believed it!

Chantel gave her a sidelong glance. "How does it feel, Captain? Me, I've got a runny sensation in my guts. Like all of a sudden, being targeted for assassination isn't such a big deal."

"It's just a statistical model. Devon himself said it was a mathematical probability. It's just a wild guess."

"It's also a mathematical possibility that you could make one hundred consecutive rolls at the roulette table and have the ball always land on red fifteen. The laws of probability don't prohibit it, but would you bet your life on it? You heard Devon. Something's going to give, and when it does, the world is going to fall apart."

"Surely we can do something."

Chantel's eyebrow arched. "We? Who is *we*? Governments—even if presented with Devon's data and assuming they could understand it—are run by narcissists and sycophants. The notion of working in unison to stem an inevitable collapse is simply beyond their ability, let alone comprehension. All they know is Us versus Them."

"Catastrophe can be one hell of a motivator."

"Captain, the first priority of government is to perpetuate more government. If the politicians have to do it at the expense of their own people, so be it."

Brenda bit her lip. Nothing she'd seen—even in the US with its Democrats against Republicans and their inflexible party loyalty—argued against Chantel's assertion.

As they walked down the hall, Chantel sighed. "Seriously, can you really see Americans, Iranians, Russians, Saudis, Chinese, and Argentines sitting at the same table, making decisions that would hobble their self-interest?"

"No."

Chantel waved back toward the meeting room. "We knew it was coming. The Foundation was *built* on that premise. All cultures, economies, and systems ultimately fail. But did you see their faces? If The Foundation council was stunned by Devon's announcement, how do you expect a mere president, prime minister, or dictator to get his limited mind around the end of the world? And the common people? They'll retreat to some religious insanity to save themselves."

"But if Devon's data are real...I mean, someone needs to be told."

"Who?" Chantel smiled in sad amusement. "Even if you could communicate Devon's data to the world, make everyone understand, do you think people would *do* anything? Or would they choose to *believe* that something, faith in God, or luck, or a miracle, is going to save them?"

"Yeah, you're right. When the shit comes down, they'll pin their hopes on a miracle. They always do."

"It's a herd mentality. Despite the sciences of geology, genetics, biology, physics, anthropology, and archaeology, four-out-of-ten of your Americans still insist on believing that the earth was created a mere six thousand years ago. Almost thirty percent of them think the sun revolves around the earth. That's the power of faith, Brenda. I explain it as a deep-seated psychological *need* to self-delude. Ignorance is always easier."

Brenda took a deep breath as they stopped before Chantel's new room. "Last night you offered me a way out."

Chantel's cool green gaze fixed on Brenda. "That was before... God, what am I saying? Of course. You can still leave. I'll make arrangements—"

"If Devon's right, how bad is this really going to be?"

"We've studied archaeology and history. With each collapse vast amounts of knowledge are lost, often irrevocably. Think about the science, literature, and engineering that vanished when Rome fell, or when the lowland Maya self-destructed. This time it's going to be global. As deprivation increases, the electricity will go off, and poof, the information superhighway, all the knowledge stored on computers and in the cloud is gone. Vanished."

"Electricity is everywhere."

"Not after a string of EMPs are laid across the sky."

"There will still be books."

"Yeah. Right." Chantel's voice had a desperate ring to it. "Rome was full of them. Most fed fires when the barbarians pounded their way in and the night got a little chilly. Which is why today we can still appreciate the art and talent displayed in the collected works of Nicander of Colophon."

"Who?"

"The guy was a contemporary of Theocritus—of whom you've also never heard. You see, Nicander's literary works kept Mog the Bloody and his pals warm the night after they'd sacked the biggest villa on the Palatine Hill and wore themselves out gang-raping all the patrician women. Or haven't you heard about things like ISIS destroying the Iraqi museums and burning the Mosul libraries?"

"I heard." *I saw.*

"What about our technical knowledge, Captain? It's not in print these days. Things like the human genome? It's too vast to be printed on paper. Most scientific journals are now electronic. All it will take is a string of atmospheric nuclear detonations. In an instant, the compendium of medical, geological, biological, genetic, engineering, physics, computer and materials technology, weather, and a host of other sciences will be gone. Along with Facebook and Twitter, Nook and Kindle, and grandma's family photos on the PC."

Chantel continued to hold Brenda's gaze. "You asked how bad it could be? There's your answer, Captain."

Everything...gone.

"And you think The Foundation can stop it?"

"Assume we're lucky. We might save enough to start over, cushion the collapse. In the midst of the chaos, we may even have time to ask ourselves questions about the morality of our choices. But what's moral? A Somali pirate will tell you one thing. An upper-middle-class housewife from Marin County will give you a whole different answer."

When Chantel reached for the knob to open the door to her room, Brenda blocked her hand. "So, you're saying it's The Foundation or a new Dark Age?"

"Listen to me." Chantel took Brenda's hand in a warm companionable grip. "Get on that airplane tomorrow and fly home. Spend some time with your family. Make your peace. Forewarned, maybe you can hide your family in some remote corner of the world."

The hall turned suddenly colder. Brenda shivered. "But if I can keep you safe, maybe America will survive."

"Trying to protect your country again, Captain Pepper? Honestly, I'm not sure I have the time to make a differen—"

"Somebody is sure. They're trying to kill you to stop you."

"Captain, I don't have a way out. You do. Think about that."

CHAPTER THIRTY-TWO

***

ANNOUNCING HIMSELF BY A LIGHT KNOCK ON ORTEGA'S OFFICE DOOR, TREVOR HUGHES leaned in, his tie swinging. "Senator? Your three o'clock appointment is here. It's a Mr. Poul Hammond."

Ortega pushed the report he'd been reading to the side and looked up as Trevor led an immaculately dressed man into the room. From his styled white-blond hair all the way down to expertly shined custom Italian shoes, the guy smacked of being too perfect. Sparkling blue eyes and a smile full of dazzling teeth filled the guy's face as he stuck out a manicured hand and said, "Senator, thank you for taking the time to see me."

"I'm delighted to be of service. I understand that you're with Simond International?" He indicated Trevor. "Could Trevor get you something? Perhaps coffee? Tea? A soda?"

Hammond inclined his head slightly, a clever smile bending his lips. "Rumor has it that you keep a bottle of Texas whiskey hidden under your desk. A special small distiller."

"Trevor? Two glasses please," Ortega waved Hammond to a chair as Trevor left. Reaching down, he pulled the bottle of Garrison Brothers from the bottom shelf of his bookcase. "I wasn't aware that my bottle was common knowledge."

"It's not," Hammond told him as Trevor entered, placed two tumblers on the corner of the desk, and closed the door on the way out.

Ortega splashed a finger for himself and raised a questioning eyebrow as he poured for Hammond. Something about the guy...well, he was just too much of a dandy to take seriously. Hammond stopped Ortega at two fingers, took his glass, and sipped. He grunted satisfaction and leaned back, the glass resting easily in his pale hand.

"Talk like this," Hammond began, "should be initiated over a good hard drink."

"And what talk is that?"

"In a moment, Senator. I understand that Jessie is making progress at the White Coral Clinic?"

Ortega felt his stomach tighten. Payback time? But if so, what handle could Hammond try to use? He and Jennifer had paid all expenses out of pocket to avoid even the slightest hint of impropriety.

"She's doing remarkably well," Ortega replied. "Jen, my wife, is still down there with her. Jessie's like a whole new girl. She's in pain, but her joints are healing, growing new nerves and muscle. I'm going to fly down just as soon as the Christmas recess allows."

"I'm so glad to hear that." Hammond might have been commenting on rice futures given the concern in his voice. "We wish her the best. But I suspect you'll want to cancel that trip."

"For what reason?" Here it came.

"Something has come up. Do you know Ben Mackeson?"

"Not personally. He runs presidential campaigns. Smart guy."

"He'd like to take a meeting with you on the fifteenth. If you don't mind, he'd like to include Julie Zapruder, Tamarland Bizhenov, and Patrick Nelson. Depending on your schedule, they'll be adaptable."

Ortega frowned, took a sip from his whiskey and ran it over his tongue. "Um, why me? They bat for the other team. I'm certainly not blocking the president's legislation. Nor would my influence sway my colleagues. I'm the new guy on the block."

"Good point. But imagine the impact if they were interested in forming an exploratory committee to determine your feasibility as a presidential candidate."

Ortega straightened in his chair. "You haven't been taking that Ortega for President thing seriously, have you?"

"To put it bluntly, you're the best candidate on the horizon. Your story resonates with conservatives, independents, and even some liberals. You're not just a war hero, but a SEAL. You've run a business, and you have a grasp of the actual trouble the country is facing. We've had a string of failed presidencies. People have lost faith in the administration because of failure after failure with health care, foreign policy, and what they perceive as general ineptness. People are exhausted and hopeless after years of Republicans and Democrats fighting each other."

"What about Governor Falco? He's already got his organization. He's been all over Iowa and New Hampshire. Not to mention that as a governor, he's had the experience of running a government. Then there's Ed Brown and his Texas organization. He's been preparing for four years for this run."

Hammond's expression tightened. "They're not the right men for the times. Falco, in the final analysis, will be unelectable. Irregularities in his campaign finances, coupled with kickbacks on highway projects, not to mention the ten-year affair he had with Sally Swing, will come out once the press really fixes on him. Ed Brown will be vulnerable over his brother-in-law and first cousins. Too much of a honey deal on the stadiums in Dallas and Houston, not to mention preference on a state canal project."

"What about Senator Calloway?" Ortega asked. "He's already got a toe in the water. His wife's family has plenty of money."

"Zack is a possibility. His wife's family would enable a run. Turns out, however, that they've dealt profitably with organized crime through the years. And it'll be red meat for the liberals because they've got an adversarial relationship with their employees."

Ortega took a moment to organize his reeling thoughts. "The first question is always: 'How much money do you have?' I'm hardly in the position necessary to swing the billion-dollar campaign necessary to run effectively."

"Julie Zapruder is the brightest bulb in the inventory when it comes to campaign finances. She wouldn't have considered working for your campaign if she didn't think she could find the donors. The same with Tamarland Bizhenov. Tam's genius is in organizing the ground game at the precinct level, social media, and voter turnout. He lit up at the idea of selling Thomas Ortega, SEAL, and loving father. He's already got a package that crosses Latino values with white conservatism, and you've never been a social right winger, but more of a Libertarian when it comes to individual rights."

This time, Ortega took a full swallow, letting the whiskey warm his belly. "Which brings me back to asking, why me? I'm a junior senator from Ohio. What gives you the foggiest idea that I'd be a good president?"

Hammond reached for the bottle, pouring another finger into Ortega's glass. "As I told you, something's happened. You're painfully cognizant of the national debt and the deficits left behind by COVID relief, not to mention the gaping political divide that's tearing this country apart. My superiors have come to believe that in the near future the country is in for a real financial shock. And then there's Russia."

"You're telling me? We could be in the middle of World War III by spring."

Hammond's curiously blue eyes met Ortega's. "This isn't a favor. Just the opposite. We've looked at the field, and given a choice of who has the best chance of handling an economic and social collapse, we've come to you."

"I understand that, but I still don't get it, Mr. Hammond."

"I told you this was the sort of conversation that should begin over a hard drink. Here it is in a nutshell: If you run, and are elected, your presidency will be the last chance to save this country. On that, I give you my word."

CHAPTER THIRTY-THREE

***

WITH A SATISFYING *PING* BIG JIM KORKORAN'S DRIVER LAUNCHED HIS BALL STRAIGHT AND true. More by luck than skill, his ball arced through a gap in the trees and landed at the angle of the fairway, setting him up for par.

The Florida sun beamed down; white fluffy clouds marched across the pale blue sky. Far up I-95, Washington was hunkered down for a blizzard, most of the government shut down. Being here, enjoying the day, reminded Big Jim of all the good things in life.

"Nice shot," Vince Pacheki admitted as he dropped his number three wood into his bag. "I may regret betting you a hundred bucks a hole."

"You may at that." Korkoran slipped his own driver into his bag as they climbed into the cart, Pacheki driving.

"Alright, we're far enough out." Pacheki shot him a sidelong glance. "What's so important you had to drag me out here? And don't give me that appropriations crap."

"I need a favor."

"We're friends, Jim. Don't even suggest compromising my ethics. We're under a fucking magnifying glass after the latest security breach. I mean, like balancing on a tightrope. If you want anything on anyone, I may or may not be able to help. Especially if it's an American citizen, and more so if they've got juice."

"Nothing so nefarious, although I know you guys slip around the rules anytime you want. I even heard of a guy checking up on a cute girl he met in a bar. Copped her phone records, social media, credit cards. Knew so much about her he had her in the sack by the next Saturday night. Poor gal thought she'd met Prince fucking Charming the way he flipped her switches."

"Prove it."

"I'm not interested in proving it." Big Jim smiled. "Yet."

"Look, we know that a low-level—"

"Simond International Holdings," Korkoran interrupted. "Who are they? Really? I want to know all about them, especially Chantel Simond."

Pacheki let the cart roll to a stop, his flat brown eyes on Korkoran's. "You don't want to go there."

"Why not? She's not an American. Simond International's got offices in New York, Chicago, and L.A., sure, but they're Swiss, with an office in the Caymans. So what's the deal?"

"Remember when I mentioned the part about juice? Simond and the rest of their clan? When it comes to juice, they're Florida citrus. You don't mess with them, Jim."

He'd never seen Pacheki look so serious. "What clan?"

"The Foundation."

"Huh? What the hell are they, some sort of charity? Gimme a break. You're the deputy director of the NSA. If you've got something on these guys, spill it. That or I'll have you sitting in a hearing by the end of January where the whole country can listen in."

Pacheki closed his eyes in defeat. "Alright, but you swear on your honor that this is not only off the record, but if you want a long and happy retirement with Dynamil, you'll never breathe a word. Not to anyone. Not your wife, not Peggy, and for sure not to a reporter or colleague."

"So, are you trying to tell me that this Foundation is a secret American asset? Something clandestine?"

Pacheki looked out at the manicured golf course. "If I'd known you were going to ask about The Foundation, I'd have scheduled a root canal instead."

"Cute. I asked you a question."

"And I don't know the answer, Jim. What I do know is that they're big and spooky. International finance is only part of The Foundation. There's arms dealing, industry, electronics and software, energy production, mining, and agriculture. They've got their fingers in all kinds of pies."

"So, it's a sort of cartel?"

"You might call it that." Pacheki slapped the steering wheel. "Hell, I

don't know! I've just heard things. Rumors. Like you really don't want to go poking around in their business, and if you try, they'll know. Bad things happen to people when they fuck around with The Foundation."

"Now you're really scaring me," Korkoran chuckled.

"Then I'm finally getting through that thick skull of yours."

"Come on. You're the NSA. They're foreign nationals. I think this Foundation of theirs might be a threat to national security, maybe tied up with terrorism. You guys are the best eavesdroppers in the world. Do a little listening in for me, will you? You don't even need FISA approval."

"You don't want to do this, Jim. I'll tiptoe around the edges, but that's it. I'll get you what we've got, but then you've got to back off. Promise me that."

"Or what?"

"Or I'll decide if I want to be seen attending your funeral."

CHAPTER THIRTY-FOUR

***

THE WRONG FUCKING WOMAN? TWICE IN A ROW!

Taylor laid the satellite phone on the table as if he were in a trance. A feeling he'd never experienced before, a cold lump, as if someone had stuck block ice in his belly, left him stunned.

That miserable fucking bitch!

"Trouble?" Across the table from Taylor, Bennie's brown eyes missed nothing. His facial muscles tensed as he took another swig from the bottle of Sol.

Around them, the cantina crowd chattered on, unaware as they picked at spicy roasted chicken, sipped iced beer or rum drinks. Most were Oaxacan locals with a couple of tourists tossed in. Taylor had chosen the place because they wouldn't stand out.

"The woman on the bed? It wasn't Chantel Simond, but her assistant. Someone named Janeesh."

Bennie lowered his beer and muttered, "Fuck."

"Yeah, fuck, alright."

"What did the client say?"

"He's unhappy." Taylor reached for the bottle of Jarrita soda. "I told him no charge."

"It was the highest probability, man. It was Chantel's bed, for Christ's sake! It was the only shot you had. Hell, I told you to take it. It was that, or you weren't going to get a shot. Period. Call the client back, tell him—"

"No. We do it for free."

Bennie's lips twitched, his jaw hardening.

"Don't say it," Taylor whispered, raising a hand in warning. "All we've got is our reputation. We lose that, we got nothing."

"So, what are we gonna do?"

"We go to war. Before we kill her, we make Brenda Pepper pay. She's the real problem. Then we blow a hole in Chantel Simond that a truck could drive through. After that, the record remains intact."

CHAPTER THIRTY-FIVE

***

THE SMALL CONFERENCE ROOM—BURIED IN THE DEPTHS OF THE SIMOND VILLA—WAS A remarkably comfortable room with flat screens on the walls, a projection system, and voice-interactive computer interface.

Brenda Pepper, who'd called the meeting, was already seated at the conference table across from Mitch and Sam Gunnarson when Chantel entered. Renaud appeared in the doorway behind her as Chantel took a chair at the far end where she could see all the participants. She was still stunned, overwhelmed by events. Wondering how the hell she was supposed to keep herself together.

Her father took the seat at the head of the table, his somber attention on Brenda Pepper, his expression a curious mix of hope and worry.

Chantel had flown in from The Foundation conference two days before—the Simond contingent having left in advance of the others. Her stunned staff had spent the time since trying to cover for the deficit left in the wake of Janeesh's murder. The load felt doubly heavy on Chantel's shoulders as she fought the instinctive need to seek Janeesh's input. The loss was finally hitting home like a kick in the gut.

The Foundation's entire financial empire had to be reorganized. It was a herculean task; nevertheless, Chantel had agreed to Pepper's request for a war council.

"Let's get to this," Renaud said, voice crisp.

Brenda took a last sip from her coffee, placed the cup on the table beside her notepad, and glanced around. "I realize I'm the FNG—the new gal—and in many ways, an unknown quantity. I also understand that although I've expressed my commitment to work with you people, I'm going to be under suspicion and some sort of probation. Which is as it should be."

Renaud's response was measured by a slight nod. Mitch's placid demeanor was a front; he and his entire team were smarting, sleep-deprived, having just flown in after dismantling their security.

Brenda laced her fingers together. "Here's our problem: After Devon's revelations, Chantel isn't going to be able to do her job if she's worried about a bullet coming out of nowhere."

As if I didn't have enough demons grinning at me from my nightmares. Chantel rubbed her tired face.

Renaud nodded again.

Brenda continued, "This guy Taylor killed my best friend in Jackson. Then he killed Janeesh at The Foundation meeting. That's twice that he's murdered someone important to us, and twice that he's come close to killing Chantel. And that's twice he's done it right under my nose. That, people, is unacceptable."

She let the statement hang as she glanced from face to face, finishing with a special intensity as she met Chantel's eyes.

Renaud asked, "I assume you have a strategy?"

Brenda laced her fingers together. "I've trained snipers, fielded them, and lived with them. My brother is a sniper. This is personal for me. But it's also personal for Taylor. Twice now, he's failed to complete his mission. Sonny said that this guy's greatest vanity is his kill record. At this very moment, he's obsessing over Chantel. He's not going to rest until his record is one hundred percent."

"So, what do we do?" Renaud asked.

"I'm only beginning to assess the capabilities The Foundation has through StatNco, the Wiesses, and individuals like Katya. If I knew the full extent, I'd probably be stunned."

Yes, you would.

Pepper ended by saying, "I want to use those resources to hunt this son of a bitch down and kill him."

"At the same time, he's hunting Chantel," Mitch noted.

"That's the game," Brenda agreed. "His cunning and resources pitted against mine."

***

Throughout, Mitch kept his gaze on the table, avoiding Brenda's glare. Renaud had reamed him pretty hard after he'd learned Mitch turned her down for thermal gear. Now he said, "With Chantel's life in the balance?"

"No other choice." Brenda glanced Chantel's way. "He's left us with only two options: either I take him out, or Chantel has to be locked away in a secure room inside the villa here."

"Impossible," Chantel told her. "Given Devon's assessment, I have to attend to things personally. And then there's The World Economic Forum on Davos in January. Too much is at stake."

Even her father was clueless about the extent of what she was going to attempt.

"We can't just keep her safe through tighter security?" Renaud asked.

Mitch, eyes still downcast, said, "A sniper of Taylor's talent increases the security envelope. Anywhere Chantel goes, we would have to control a mile radius in all directions. That's way too much terrain in the wild, and absolutely impossible in an urban environment." Mitch thoughtfully stroked his chin. "And if we place too much emphasis on countering a sniper, we might miss someone impersonating a maid or doorman who steps close and pulls a trigger."

"Mitch is right," Brenda agreed. "But we've got an even bigger problem: someone inside The Foundation hired Taylor. Alerted him to where Chantel would be, told him which room. Then facilitated his infiltration and exfiltration from the island." She paused to make her point. "Who?"

"I'm working on that." Renaud's gaze was distant. "What bothers me is why now? Is it because Devon has a date for the collapse? If so, how does Chantel's death provide any advantage to the other families? Given what's coming, Chantel is indispensable."

Am I, father? Maybe someone knows exactly what they're doing.

"How so?" Brenda asked.

Renaud glanced at Chantel—who nodded her approval—then said, "When the collapse comes, currencies will be worthless. We need to convert our holdings into physical assets, but it's a delicate juggling act. Right up to the end Chantel must balance liquidity—the ability to shift large amounts of cash—against a developing disaster. Do we buy a refinery in Indonesia, or Montana? Depending on how the collapse unfolds, that decision might have to be made at the last second."

Brenda nodded. "I get it. Not only do you need to come up with a lot of eggs, but you need be able to shift them into different baskets as the situation evolves."

"To do that, we need last-minute cash," Chantel told her. "But if I hold it for too long, it's suddenly worthless paper."

"How does that affect the other players in The Foundation? Say Katya, or Liu?"

Renaud shrugged. "They depend on Chantel's ability as much as anyone. Simond International is the bank. And Chantel has a remarkable talent for doing the right thing at the right time."

"Maybe someone got to one of your members? You've got to be on US, Chinese, Russian, and just about everyone else's radar. Surely the NSA, State Department, CIA, and who knows whom else is keeping an eye on you. Maybe they decided you were too much of a threat and decided to take you down?"

To Brenda, Chantel said, "NSA, CIA, SVR, FSB, MI6...they can't send an email across an office without us knowing."

The woman stared at her in disbelief.

Welcome to our world, Captain.

"Governments are the biggest threat we face," Chantel told her softly. "We spend a great deal of time keeping our fingers on the political pulse, supporting the right politicians, and making sure we don't get cross-wise of their supposed 'national interests'."

Renaud told her, "If a government department or bureau were behind any blackmail or extortion, we'd know. They've tried it often enough. At first hint, we would deal with it."

Brenda whispered, "Unfuckingbelievable." Then in a louder voice: "I'll leave uncovering a traitor inside The Foundation to you folks. For now, I want Taylor."

"What's this strategy of yours?" Mitch asked.

"Hunting snipers is a tricky business. It's done carefully, with planning, resources, and no little risk. I need complete information on where Chantel has to travel, whom she has to see, and control over all the details. This will be a battle of wits. It will be fought in the shadows, and when it's over either he's dead, or I am."

Renaud turned his attention to Chantel. "It's your call."

How far could she trust Pepper?

A deadly fire lay behind the woman's eyes.

Brenda, if you're not the woman I think you are... She heard herself
saying, "Do it."

Mitch sighed, saying, "Whatever you need, Captain. And if we
don't have it, get me a list."

A wounded love filled her father's eyes as he said, "Very well,
Captain, hunt that piece of shit down and kill him."

So, it's you and me, Brenda.

Killing Brenda Pepper would be one of the more distasteful things
she'd ever have to do if she were wrong.

CHAPTER THIRTY-SIX

***

THE CAR DOOR SHUT WITH A THUMP OF FINALITY, AS IF SEVERING ANY CHANCE OF RETREAT.

So, I'm committed.

Tom Ortega took Jen's hand. Uncertainty lay behind her eyes as the black Lincoln pulled away from the Washington Hotel curb. The doorman was already walking toward them, a welcoming smile on his face. Tom took a deep breath, and told Jen, "It's just a meeting."

"God," she whispered, "Suddenly it's too real. I mean, how can this be happening?"

"Tempest in a teapot. We'll talk about it, and someone will say, 'We'll get back to you,' or, 'We'll see what the money looks like,' and two months from now, everyone will have forgotten."

Tom started forward, almost dragging Jen into motion as he smiled at the doorman. Stepping in from the cold, he found the Washington Hotel to be every bit as ornate as he remembered, the lobby all polished and shining.

"Senator?" A young man in a gray suit stepped forward. "I'm Tino Reyes. If you'd follow me?"

Reyes led the way to the elevators, used a key to access the executive level, and pressed the button.

"I can't believe Jessie let you get away," Tom said off-handedly, trying to alleviate both his and Jen's stress.

She shot him a quivering smile. "She's doing so much better. She dotes on Dr. Mead, and she's healing, Tom. It's a miracle."

The elevator chimed moments before the door opened.

"This way, Senator, Ms. Ortega." Reyes led them down the richly carpeted hall to one of the corner suites, used his key card, and ushered them into a lavishly appointed corner room. Billowing curtains were gathered at the windows where slanting sunlight cast beams on two couches that faced each other across a coffee table. A silver cart, room service at its best, stood to one side. It sported plates of fruits, cheeses, berries, melon slices, and cold cuts with a variety of breads.

From the wet bar came the sounds of an espresso machine at work.

"Could I get you something to drink?" Reyes asked. "I can make your favorite Americano, Senator. Ma'am, we have rooibos tea just for you."

"Fine," Tom and Jen answered in unison, smiling nervously at each other.

As Reyes turned away, an older man stepped out of the bathroom, drying his hands on a towel. "Ah, Senator, here you are. Right on time. I'm Ben Mackeson, and it's a pleasure to meet you. Mrs. Ortega, Jennifer, we're so glad you could make it."

Mackeson was a tall man, his facial features having the gravity of carved stone. Black hair faded into white at his temples, and piercing black eyes took Ortega's measure. Mackeson shook each of their hands and gestured toward the couches, saying, "Have a seat. The others are on the way. Julie had a few last-minute figures to go over. Patrick was reviewing some files."

Tom led Jen to the closest couch and seated himself. "I have to tell you, this all comes as something of a surprise."

Mackeson lowered himself across from them, hunched forward, hands on his knees. He stared hard into Ortega's eyes. "Then let me ask the first question. Do you have the guts to go all the way?"

Tom chuckled dryly. "If I had any quit in me, they'd have beaten it out of me before they pinned that trident on my chest. My question for you is why are you switching sides?"

Mackeson's hard lips bent in a smile. "What makes you think I've got a side? I'm here for one reason, Senator: The country is in trouble. You might be able to fix it. If we do this, I want to win. Period. You offer me the best chance to do that."

The door opened, and Julie Zapruder, followed by Patrick Nelson and Tamarland Bizhenov, stepped through. Zapruder was in her late forties, had started as a volunteer for Gore in the late '90s and soon became a fixture in Democratic campaigns. She wore a peach-colored dress with a single strand of pearls at her throat. Her severe face barely cracked a smile as she shifted the thick files she carried, introduced herself, and shook hands.

Patrick Nelson was closing on forty, a dark-haired Harvard-trained lawyer who reveled in his reputation as a hard-core partisan, dirty-tricks master, and legal genius when it came to campaign law. He was the go-to guy when it came to ground game at the local precinct and state level.

Ortega turned his attention to Tam Bizhenov, the social media and statistical guru. A thirty-year-old, first-generation American, his father had made his reputation and fortune as a Ukrainian computer hacker and had come to the US at the behest of a Seattle computer tech company to take charge of their cybersecurity. His son, Tamarland, had taken to the new world like a predatory fish in the pond of social media.

Drinks were handed round, and the others took seats on the opposite couch. Zapruder slapped down the files. "Okay, I think we're ready."

Tom took the initiative. "When it comes to campaigns, you're the dream team. Why me?"

It was Nelson who spoke. "It's time for a change. The planet's on the verge of world war. We've lost the Middle East to Russia and Iran, and half the world's about to come unglued. China's whipped us with COVID, taken Hong Kong and Taiwan. Now they're sewing up the South China Sea.

"The country is staggered after two failed presidencies. Economically and politically, the economy's stagnant and declining under crushing debt, secession movements are gaining traction, and the radical right and hard left are in a virtual state of war. There's a chance that you can heal some of the political wounds. Otherwise, we're about to come apart at the seams. The word that's circulating is 'dry rot'. That's what people are saying about America."

"Not to be indelicate, but part of that's your own doing through the Biden years." Tom sipped at his coffee and found it too hot. "You all made your names demonizing your opponents, convincing people that my side would destroy the country."

"At the time that's what it took to compensate for the Trump years. That's changed," Mackeson said uncomfortably. "Senator, you picked up Independents and a reasonable number of Democrats with your Libertarian bent. Tailor that message a little more, and you've got a winning ticket."

Tamarland rubbed his hands together, as if in anticipation, as he said, "From my research, eighty-two percent of the American people believe we're going to become involved in a war for the Baltics that we can't win. The trend is that America is in decline. Respect for government is the lowest ever measured, and even the socialists consider it to be antagonistic to their best interests. Unless something changes, our data suggests that the Northeast, South, Rocky Mountain West, and West Coast are going to seek their own remedies. For many, secession is no longer a lunatic abstract. The people are looking for a leader, Senator. Someone who will just be honest with them."

Tom leaned back and considered. "If we're going to turn this thing around, we're going to have to gut a lot of sacred cows. Entitlements—especially Social Security and Medicare—being the biggest of them."

Mackeson sighed. "No one said it would be easy. But from Tam's data, for the first time, people are scared enough that they'll be willing to make sacrifices." A beat. "But it will take a real leader."

"Provided they see a light at the end of the tunnel," Tamarland added. "By the end of your first term, they've got to see progress."

"Employment and health care are the biggest concerns." Zapruder cocked her head. "Any ideas?"

"Employment's easy," Ortega replied. "Get the government out of small businesses and provide them operating capital. That worked in the Trump years until COVID. Health care? That's a tougher nut to crack. The expansion of the Affordable Care Act has cratered American medicine. Too much graft and free money in the system. It has to be decentralized—and the fat cats will unleash unholy hell when the government spigot is turned off and their billions go away."

Tam pressed the tips of his fingers together. "That battle will have to be waged. But we'd have an ally in the people. They're fed up. It's just a matter of channeling that disgust in the right direction."

Mackeson said, "In our opinion, we're on the verge of the greatest national disaster since the Civil War. We need a Lincoln. Are you willing to give it a try?"

Ortega glanced at Jen, who looked pale and stunned. She met his eyes and gave a slight nod.

"Since this is just exploratory, let's take the next step."

Mackeson chuckled. "Consider it more than exploratory. I think you'll be the next President of the United States."

"Provided there are no skeletons in the closet." Nelson leaned back, laying an arm on the couch back. His dark and predatory eyes fixed on Tom's. "All I've been able to turn up are some traffic tickets when you were a kid, a couple of times you fiddled with grass, tried cocaine once, and there's a DUI that a chief petty officer managed to quash because you were about to be deployed."

He paused. "Anything else you want to tell me now? Because, believe me, if you so much as had a case of the clap, it's going to come out. A woman? Some campaign irregularities? Kickbacks to constituents? Irregular accounting in your business? A child out of wedlock?"

Tom grinned. "How on earth did you find that DUI? I mean, my God, I'd forgotten!"

"That's what we're here to discover, Senator. Your deepest, darkest secrets. Stuff that other SEALS might say. Guys you pissed off. Anything that might give the other side a handle to twist."

Tom sighed. "Look, I know how the game is played. I can guarantee you that someone, somewhere in my past, is carrying a grudge. And I did all the things young soldiers on the front lines do. Some of it wasn't pretty. But no, there's no hidden dynamite, affairs, crimes, or dirty dealings."

Nelson glanced at Jen.

She stiffened and shot a panicked glance at Tom. "I had an...an abortion. Years ago. Before I met Tom."

"You never told me."

"It wasn't your business." She shot a look like knives at Nelson. "But I guess it is now."

Zapruder said, "We can spin that right off the bat. It'll buy us sympathy with upper-income educated women."

Nelson paused, lifting an eyebrow. "Anything else that wasn't Tom's business that we should—"

"No," Tom told them. "My wife and my daughter..."

Jen put her hand on his arm, her pained eyes searching his. "Tom? Do you want to win this thing? If you do, let these people do their jobs. Maybe it's my turn to be as tough as you've always been." She turned back to Nelson. "I did some wild partying as a kid. There might be photos on social media. Got kind of crazy. Enough to finally scare myself into cleaning up my act. After that I worked on being a professional woman until I met Tom."

For the first time, Patrick Nelson smiled. "Now we're talking. I'll need the names of your old party friends. You never know what they might have. Maybe old videos, photos. We'll have our people check them out first, make sure we've got something on them *before* they decide they can make a name for themselves on television and Snap Chat."

Nelson turned back to Tom. "How about you, Senator? Anything coming to mind now that we're heading down this road?"

"What about Simond International?" Tom asked. "Chantel Simond recommended a clinic for Jessie. Poul Hammond set up this meeting. I've done absolutely nothing that would cross an ethical line, but they are players."

Ben Mackeson smiled as if he were the cat who'd caught the canary. "Nor will Simond do anything to compromise your ethics, Senator. Trust me on this; they know better than you how the game is played."

Tom shrugged in acceptance. "Then perhaps we should discuss money."

Julie Zapruder's normally sour lips bent into a smile. "That, Senator, will be the least of your worries. We have enough big donors. Given what they see coming, they're ready to back you. Nevertheless, expect long hours on the phone. Fundraising is always the most distasteful and grueling part of any campaign."

"What about organization? Nominations are won at the local and state level. It's people at the precinct level that really make the difference. Without that ground game—"

"It's covered. By this time next week, your name will be registered in every state. We'll have people at the precinct level ensuring you have the right delegates in caucus states and be laying the groundwork for the primaries."

"And we've got a lot of ground to make up," Mackeson stated. "No one since Bush has won with such a late start. But by this time next month, your name's going to be on everyone's lips."

"This is only an exploratory..." Tom began.

Mackeson made a cutting gesture with his hand. "Are you in or out, Senator? Tell me now, because by this time next year, I expect you to be the President-elect of the United States."

CHAPTER THIRTY-SEVEN

***

CHANTEL NODDED TO THE GUARD AT THE SECURITY DOOR. SHE BENT HER EYE TO THE RETINAL scanner and exhaled onto the breathalizer. An eyeball could be plucked from a person's head. Their breath, however, carried distinct traits that couldn't be faked. As the light glowed green and the lock clicked, she pushed the door open.

Valentine Wiesse sat on one of the couches in the "reception" foyer. His long legs were thrust out, his microcomputer in his hands. A frown lined his face as he studied the holo projection.

The waiting room, with its ocean views, tropical plants, comfortable chairs and refreshments, was actually a security screening facility. Sensitive scanners had already determined the contents of Val's billfold through RFID. Other sensors determined that he carried a loaded .380 Kahr pistol under his left armpit, and a garrotte wire ran through his belt. His body temperature was a placid 32 degrees Celcius, and his respiration, galvanic skin response, and heart rate betrayed no anxiety.

He rose, pocketed his small computer, and grinned. "Hey, Fox. I was expecting Mitch and a machine-gun-toting tactical team to escort me into your presence."

She stepped aside as he sauntered into the hallway, the faintest hint of cologne mixed with his normal animal scent.

"If you wanted me dead, it wouldn't be here, locked away in the dim vastness of Simond Island. It would involve abduction, removing me to someplace where you could take your time. Really make me scream, plead, bleed, and grovel."

His lazy smile didn't change; only the tightening at the corner of his eyes betrayed the truth behind her allegation. "You do know the strings to my heart, my love. But how about we go someplace private? Confidential?"

She read the intensity in his blue eyes, nodded, and led him up two flights of stairs, past the opulent dining room to a small salon with a humidor, ornate-and-well-stocked bar, and high glass windows. These she opened to the air with the press of a button. Then she tapped a code into the console set into the polished teak wall.

Turning, she asked, "Drink? I shut down the monitoring. Even Dad needs a place to retreat to where he's not under glass."

"Lime and soursop," he said, taking a turn around the room to inspect the fainting couch, the leather recliners, and inlaid tables.

She poured his fruit juice and splashed a finger of tequila añejo into a tumbler. Handing him his, she seated herself in one of the Captain's chairs that lined the bar and raised a suggestive eyebrow.

Val walked to the balcony, stared out at the Caribbean, and sighed. Returning, he seated himself in the recliner opposite her and sipped the drink. "Platnikov is going to start a war with the West in June. Katya has proof. Devon agrees. Sonny knows. I know. Now you know."

"Why come to me?"

He let his gaze trail down her body, as if caressing each of her curves in memory as he had once done in the flesh. "As well as you know me, I know you. You're plotting. You may actually be able to accomplish what I think you're going to attempt. It's a long shot. But if you were to take out Platnikov? By yourself? Your odds for ultimate success go up to at least fifty-fifty."

She took a sip of her tequila to cover the sudden shiver of anxiety. *He couldn't know!* "And what do you think I'm going to try and do?"

"A coup." He cocked his head, studying her. "My father hasn't a clue. Neither do the others. Me, I'm here to declare myself. Given what's coming, I think you're our only hope. I'm here to tell you I'm on your side, Chantel."

"Why choose me?"

"Because it's the last call. The gravy train is going off the tracks. The Foundation is about to rip itself apart. I may be a psychopath, but I'm a smart one. You're going to need allies. In the coming scramble, I stand to gain the most if you come out on top."

"Nothing comes for free, Val. What do you want in return?" She hesitated. "Me?"

He sipped his drink. "That didn't work so well last time."

"Damaged goods I think you said."

He waved it away, eyes calculating. "We all have words we'd like to take back. You're going to need an enforcer. A number two."

"Why only number two?"

"Because I don't have your talents when it comes to juggling the bits and pieces of the grand scheme. You comprehend the whole, and how all the parts work together to create harmony." He pointed a finger at her. "And someone has to help you keep it together, Chantel. Because I know how close you are to the edge. To shattering like a dropped glass."

"Maybe I'm tougher than you think." Damn it, he'd always known how to play her.

"Platnikov is the key. He wants to start a war. Georgi and Katya are too weak to stop him. If he attacks the Baltics, Devon says our world dies next spring. To have any shot at controlling The Foundation, you need a symbolic act. Like single-handedly taking Platnikov down. To do it you're going to have to get close. In his lair. He's going to want you in his bed. Can you keep the demons from breaking loose while he's screwing you? Going to bet everything on Captain Pepper? She's new, shiny, and exciting, but you don't know if you can trust her. Let alone if she'll stick."

She took a deep breath—the flashback like a snap of the fingers—spun images of the black phantom slashing at her naked body. Her legs were forced wide. The blood. The pain...

"It's okay, Fox," Val said softly as she forced the nightmare away. "I think I know how to do this. And maybe we can learn something about your new best buddy Pepper at the same time."

CHAPTER THIRTY-EIGHT

***

THE BEST WAY TO THWART A SNIPER IS TO DENY HIM A SHOT. TO DO THAT THE TARGET HAS to be anywhere except where the shooter expects him or her to be. That's the golden rule.

As long as Chantel stayed on Simond Island, she was fairly well protected. The island security was state of the art, and thermal imaging would pick up anyone who stepped off the beach and shagged his or her way up into the forest wearing a ghillie suit. Security was at a fever pitch; Mitch's people were fuming over Janeesh's murder.

Brenda wasn't sure that she, herself, could have inserted a team onto Simond Island given the thermal scanning and scrutiny every nook and cranny was finally being given.

That meant if another attempt were to be made it would be off-island, somewhere out in the world where Simond security couldn't control every avenue of approach, monitor each potential shooting position or field of fire.

Chantel, however, couldn't go to ground. She had places to go and business to conduct. A world to save. The entire Foundation was stepping into high gear. Three generations of plans were being put in motion.

God, did I make the right decision by involving myself with these people?

Backing out at this stage wouldn't be an option.

Brenda stared down at the world map she'd pulled from the Simond library. Dots indicated the places on Chantel's itinerary for the next three months. Seven cities, starting with Zurich in three days.

Taylor was out there, somewhere, planning, biding his time.

Whoever his client in The Foundation was, he or she would know Chantel's schedule. Taylor could advance the locations, pick and choose his time and place.

But where?

Announcing herself with a light knock, Chantel leaned in at the library door. "Val Wiesse is here. War meeting in the conference room in a half hour. Thought you might want to sit in."

"What's it about?"

"That trip to Zurich? I think we're going by way of Russia."

CHAPTER THIRTY-NINE

***

WHEN BRENDA ENTERED THE CONFERENCE ROOM THIRTY MINUTES LATER, HER NOTEBOOK in hand, Renaud, Chantel, Mitch, and Regal were already seated.

Val, wearing a white muslin shirt and tan cotton pants, rose, smiling. "Captain Pepper! You've been on my mind since the conference."

An almost physical jolt went through her when he took her hand. His blue eyes sharpened, pupils expanding as if he, too, felt it.

"Good to see you, Mr. Wiesse."

Val's charming laugh was accompanied by a roguish smile. "Mr. Wiesse? Oh, come. I'm Valentine to my colleagues...and Val to my friends. You're among the latter, Captain."

Brenda tactfully disengaged and stepped around the table to a chair Chantel indicated.

Val—amusement still lingering on his lips—dropped into his seat opposite her. Renaud had watched with veiled eyes. Regal, however, had a predatory look, as if witnessing a calf being led to slaughter.

"Very well," Renaud began. "What have you got, Val?"

Valentine Wiesse's demeanor changed like a switch had been thrown. He glanced around the table, meeting their eyes one by one. "As you know, Georgi wasn't present at the meeting. That same weekend, on Leon Platnikov's orders, he was up to his curly eyebrows planning the takeover of the Baltic States and a destabilization of the eastern NATO countries."

Renaud straightened, asking, "Surely Platnikov isn't thinking about actually going ahead with it? The Crimean and Ukrainian conflict almost collapsed the entire Russian economy, investors fled like rats from a sinking ship, and Ukraine is like a cancerous boil in Russia's flesh. The aftereffects cost Putin his job. Europe and the US will go crazy."

Val leaned back like a lounging tiger. "Oh, he's serious, alright. He thinks that in the long run the territorial gain will offset short-term economic sanctions and drive the price of oil even higher. Using Crimea as a model, his agents are already implementing phase one, which is to create the impression of a threat to ethnic Russians in the Baltics. Next comes the propaganda campaign, followed by directed civil unrest. If you remember, there've been cyber attacks on Baltic governments and media. The disruption of the electricity grids, water, and basic services has been taking place for a couple of years now. Those were dry runs to discover weaknesses before the big strike. This will all be capped by a covertly orchestrated massacre of ethnic Russians just prior to the invasion date. Which, Katya informs us, is to be June 22nd, this year."

He paused. "The same date Hitler initiated Operation Barbarossa against Russia in 1941. Platnikov loves his ironies."

Chantel gave him a sharp look. "That's only six months away."

"Platnikov wants to move fast. Since Putin dropped dead from unknown causes"—he smiled—"the West has relaxed and occupied themselves with their own squabbles. Good old Leon wants to have his people in Vilnius, Riga, and Tallinn before anyone has time to organize.

"Possession being nine tenths of the law, depending on the West's reaction, he can offer to negotiate over Estonia first. Then he'll dicker over Latvia if forced. But he's going to keep Lithuania and the link to Kaliningrad. He's gambling the West won't think it's worth nuclear annihilation."

Renaud was taking notes. "What about Poland and the rest of eastern Europe? You mentioned that Platnikov wanted to destabilize them."

"Platnikov's goals are two-pronged. A constant stream of weapons, aid, and supplies are being shipped from Eastern Europe to the Ukrainian resistance. SVR and GRU agents are going to orchestrate a series of coordinated assassinations, terrorist bombings, cyber attacks on government and banking, and industrial sabotage to disrupt Poland, Hungary, Romania, and the Czech and Slovak republics. Leon's plan is to throw them into confused disarray, thereby cutting off support to Ukraine and adding to his 'reasonable' intervention in the Baltic States. But who knows? If he sees an opportunity—especially to get rid of the missile defense network and drive a wedge between Eastern

Europe and NATO—he's going to use it."

Chantel asked, "And Katya confirms all of this?"

"She does. It's called the Gorky Plan, and the extent of it is only known to a handful of Leon's closest allies in the army and intelligence services."

"Why come to us?" Regal asked.

"Because after discussing it among the Wiesses and Takanabis, we think it's too dangerous to allow good old Leon to proceed. Devon concurs. We're already teetering on the brink. Such a destabilizing event will precipitate disaster."

"And if we agree, how do you expect to stop Platnikov?" Chantel asked.

"That's where *you* come in." Val pointed at Chantel. "You can get close to Leon Platnikov. Katya and Georgi have ruled out mundane assassination. To Russia, that would be like a slap across the face. We need something more refined and...shall we say, non-incendiary."

"You mean, Putin's sudden death hurt us."

He fixed Regal with his twinkling blue eyes. "What about some previously diagnosed genetic disease? A sudden catastrophic immune response? Perhaps a metabolic disorder? Something slow."

Regal nodded thoughtfully as she tapped on her tablet. "We ran his genome last year when Georgi forwarded the sample. Just a minute. Yes, here's his file."

Her fingers played across the screen as she opened menus and input commands. "Searching for deleterious genes, and...yes. Okay, got it."

"Got what?" Chantel asked.

"Platnikov has a pair of methylated homozygous deleterious alleles on his sixth chromosome. Using an adeno-associated virus, or AAV9, I can deliver tailored microRNAs that will demethylate, or turn on those genes."

"Which will do what?" Val asked mildly.

Regal fixed him with a cold blue stare. "Activating those genes will signal cells in the immune system to begin producing exosomes. Uh, call them message molecules that will shut down Platnikov's oligodendrocytes. Oligodendrocytes are the cells that create myelin, the protein which essentially insulates nerve sheaths in the brain."

Val rolled his eyes. "What?"

"Think dementia."

Val chuckled, as if at his own ignorance. "How long?"

"From ingestion?" Regal shrugged. "Two weeks until he's visibly impaired. Maybe a month before the effects become debilitating. Figure him for dead in six to eight weeks."

"Traceability?" Renaud asked.

"There's no chemical signature, Dad. No residual toxins in the tissues. Even if some lab isolated and made note of the adeno-associated virus, most of us have been infected at one time or another. In short, it's everywhere."

Chantel was nodding thoughtfully. "Mental incapacitation? What better way to cast doubt on his plans and policies?"

Brenda blinked. *My God, they can actually do this?*

Val slapped the table. "I love this plan. Two questions: how long to make the virus, and when can Chantel leave?"

"Three days on my end." Regal was staring at something on her tablet. "The bottle can be delivered to you *en route*. I'd say change the plans. Stop in Zurich on the way to Moscow and my people can make the delivery there."

"Three days," Chantel agreed. "I'm good to go."

Brenda stared around the table in stunned disbelief. *We're going to assassinate the Russian president?*

CHAPTER FORTY

***

"DON'T YOU THINK IT'S A HARD SELL?" ALEXIS SHERMAN ASKED FROM BEHIND THE BULWARK of her plexiglass desk. Studio lights blazed down, and the cameras zooming in might have been predatory Jurassic beasts. Her oversized "The Alexis Sherman Show" coffee cup rested at her elbow. Guests always received a coffee cup as a souvenir.

To Tom Ortega's amusement, he'd only been offered tap water in a paper cup. Anyone who'd been through SEAL training and survived SERE understood psychological warfare. The intentional slight and additional brusque treatment in the green room had been meant to provoke.

For Tom, the challenge was not to be distracted by the fact that he hated Alexis Sherman—right down to her trademark spiked blue hair and glossy red lipstick. The studio lights almost turned the latter iridescent. He hadn't wanted to do the show. Downright refused at first. Unless a guest agreed 100% with Alexis and her super progressive agenda, they never escaped with their dignity intact. And the woman was a master when it came to insulting an opponent's intelligence and questioning his integrity. Her rabid fans loved it, and that made this MSNBC's hot new venue.

"Of course it's a hard sell," Tom told her, leaning forward. "Alexis, no one wants to hear bad news. I don't want to be the one to give it to them. But someone has to. How long do we have to keep stumbling our way down a rotting pier before we figure out that with just another couple of steps, we're going to be floundering in the water?"

"So it's back to the failed policies of the past?" She rolled her eyes dramatically. "Back to making the rich richer. You're not just throwing the poor under the bus; you're using their blood and bones for traction! When is enough *enough* for you people? Once your campaign donors squeeze the last penny from the people, what are they going to want next?"

"How about we don't throw the poor under the bus?" Tom forced himself to reply calmly. In his imagination he had his hands around her thin neck, choking her down. "How about we *don't* go back to making the rich richer. How about we try a different way? One that creates opportunity for all?"

"Yeah, yeah, cut the taxes and remove all holds on the robber barons of big business. Toss out regulations that protect little people from Capitalist vultures like you. Let the privileged lords of industry pollute our waters, rape the earth, and pour whatever crap they want into our food!"

"How about a sane third way?" Tom lifted a challenging eyebrow, refusing to go for the bait. "How about unleashing *small* businesses? How about telling our over-bloated regulatory agencies that they have to chop out seventy-five percent of the rules and regulations on their books?" He waved her down before she could explode. "And how about telling government agencies that if they fail in their mandates, they will be legally liable?"

"Are you joking? Let the people sue the government?"

"Yeah, is that such a leap? What happens if we allow business to sue federal agencies for incompetence? Since the government can sue businesses for incompetency, why not the other way around? Come on, Alexis! Don't you think that within weeks of passing such a bill that the deadwood would be shaking out of the bureaucracies like fleas out of a mongrel dog?"

"That will lead to a billion frivolous lawsuits! It will paralyze the government!"

"It could, but don't we all agree that the bureaucracy *is* incompetent? Business *can't* function because there are so many contradictory rules, and even within a single agency, a business complying with one rule, is automatically in noncompliance with another."

"You're saying that government *workers* are *incompetent?*"

"Not all of them. There's a small core of people who are really there to serve the public, but for most, it's a free ride to a paycheck and benefits. Wouldn't it be different if The People had a legal right to demand competence from *their* government?"

Her eyes gleaming as she prepared for the kill, she took a breath, only to hesitate when her producer said something in her earpiece. Looking quizzical, she swallowed, as if off-balance, and awkwardly nodded. In wooden tones, she said, "Yes, it would."

Tom, ready for the flaying, stared in disbelief as Alexis bitterly added, "I think I could get behind that."

Off to the side, behind the cameras, Ben Mackeson, arms crossed, was nodding to himself in satisfaction.

"I'm so glad to hear that, Alexis,"—he wondered how far he could push it—"given that you called me 'just another intellectual cretin' when I was elected to the senate. It goes to show that we can all come together behind a good idea."

Her jaw muscles bulged like bowline knots, her brown eyes smoldering. "Yes," she strained, "we can."

She said to the camera, "And after the break we have more news about the EPA taking another hideous, polluting coal-fired plant to court. Don't go away."

As the red light went out on the camera, she shot a hot look at the control booth, demanding, "What the *hell* is going on here?"

As Tom was unplugging his clip-on mic, Ben Mackeson strode forward, calling, "Nothing that your sponsors and management don't approve of, Alexis. Great show. Absolutely fantastic!"

Alexis Sherman, lips pinched in anger, grabbed her coffee cup from her desk. Heedless of its contents, she violently hurled it in the direction of the production booth.

As Tom walked off the set, he asked, "Wow, after this, I can't wait for Bill Mulloy at Fox News. He's the guy who called me a RINO sellout."

Mackeson's cat-and-canary grin grew wider. "Oh, don't worry about good old Bill. He knows which side his bread is buttered on. Like Alexis here, he, too, has to answer to superiors. The only thing these people care about more than skewering a guest is staying on the air."

CHAPTER FORTY-ONE

***

BIG JIM KORKORAN GLANCED DISTASTEFULLY AT HIS ESCORT. THE KID'S NAME WAS TAD Ellis. The young man looked to be barely out of his teens, wearing a cheap suit, a white shirt he'd probably picked up from an online sale, and a rayon tie. He even still had pimples.

Through what malevolent turn of events had a mere kid risen high enough in the NSA's ranks to merit such a high-level security position? Diapers notwithstanding, Ellis had been handed the job of escorting a high-ranking senator down into the NSA's deepest guts. This was the sanctum sanctorum, the "eyes only" records division.

The corridor they walked down could be called utilitarian at best. Fluorescent light bathed featureless concrete walls and closed security doors in a slightly green light. Their shoes made a clicking sound on the tiled floor.

"Here, Senator," Ellis told him, and swiped a key card over the security panel before tapping in his code. He opened the door, nodded, and held it while Korkoran entered. Ellis remained outside as he closed the door with a click of finality.

"Where the hell are we?" Korkoran asked as he took in rows of heavy canvas bags, many of them piled under what looked like an oversized laundry chute. The entire far wall was covered by an industrial-grade furnace. The monstrosity was giving off a muted roar. Complicated sheet-metal ductwork, fans, and hanging lights cluttered the ceiling. The place had a slightly acrid odor.

Vincent Pacheki had half of his ass perched on a heavy metal table that backed against the left wall. He was swinging his right leg, the left bracing him. He clutched a blue binder.

"This is the burn room," Vince told him, using the binder to indicate the piled bags. "Everything classified that doesn't go into the permanent record—and probably some stuff that should—comes here for incineration. You should feel honored. You're the first person from outside to set foot in here since the contractors built it. And, if anyone found out you were here, we'd both get twenty years in Leavenworth."

"What about Ellis outside the door there?"

"You never saw him. This meeting never happened. If anyone asks, you were upstairs in my office, going over budget."

"Wow, just like James Bond, huh?"

Pacheki handed him the blue binder. "You wanted The Foundation? Here they are."

"Thanks." Korkoran took the binder, flipping the cover open. He squinted in the light, skimming the first paragraph. "You know, you could have just messengered it over to my office."

"Not a chance. You read it right here." Pacheki checked his watch. "No one's going to check the burn room for another two hours. Plenty of time for you to read from cover to cover."

"What?"

Pacheki pointed at the furnace. "Soon as you're done, that report gets tossed in there."

"You're going to *burn* it?"

"Damned straight. And if you read that thing, instead of wasting your time talking about it, you'll know why."

Korkoran made a face and used a toe to pull an old metal chair under the brightest of the overhead lights. He dropped into the seat and began to read. By the time he reached page two, he muttered, "Holy shit!"

At page seven, he blurted, "No fucking way!"

By page twenty, he'd been stunned into silence.

Finally, he looked up, closing the binder. "This is someone's idea of fantasy! Like a bad novel. Assassinations? *Electing* presidents? Controlling the economy? International espionage? Who *are* these people?"

"They call themselves The Foundation."

"Impossible! This is the modern world. There are leaks, rumors, investigative reporting. The fucking internet, you know? No one can hide something like this."

"Sure they can. If they have enough money. If they control the right industries. Think about it. They're right there, out in the open.

Simond International, SimondAg, the various Wiesse and Takanabi corporations, the Hestons. It's perfect camouflage. They're just so central, they seem completely innocuous."

"Who in hell is the Bilderberg Group? Run by an ex-Nazi of all things? Union Banking Corporation? A pipeline for Nazi wealth? I mean, these people *started* the Trilateral Commission. The Council on Foreign Relations?"

"That's a recruiting ground," Pacheki told him. "A collection of powerful individuals from whom The Foundation can draw for like-minded talent."

"They had ties to the Nazi party, for God's sake! The fact that they have people sprinkled throughout the Fed? They make the Skull and Bones boys look like pikers. And my God, what they've done with Exxon and Chevron?"

"They *established* the European Central Bank. Played the West and the Soviet Union against each other for their own gain—that's the part that shocked me."

"How? The report doesn't say?"

"At the end of the war both sides were snapping up prominent Nazis for their technical skills. Think no further than Werner von Braun and NASA for an example. But the deeper recruitment was in the intelligence community. It didn't matter what kind of crimes they'd committed; SS officers were quietly integrated into the American clandestine services. After all, they'd been fighting the Soviets for years. The Foundation provided our ex-Nazis and the Russian ex-Nazis with channels of communication. You read the report. The founders, Jack Simond and Gerhardt Wiesse, were shipping millions back and forth between their enterprises through UBC, I. G. Farben's front companies, and through banks in Switzerland, and even Paris. Paul Warburg, head of the Fed, and Max Warburg, head of Deutsche Bank were brothers, for God's sake! The network had been established for decades."

"You're telling me that all Simond and Wiesse did was take it over, eliminate their rivals, groom their kids, and perfect the organization? And they succeeded?"

"On the American side, Jack Simond was tied in at the highest levels. His banks financed a lot of the American war industry in the early months of the Second World War. He was the architect of building 'the arsenal of democracy'. Roosevelt, the Dulles brothers, the Rockefellers, the Harrimans, General Marshall... I mean, the man was connected."

"And Gerhardt Wiesse?"

"Some have speculated that he was Heinrich Messer, known as 'the knife'. He was Speer's go-to guy, a financier for the Third Reich. But he worked in the shadows, let Warburg and Borman bask in the limelight. Messer and Simond graduated from Harvard together, married each other's sisters, had kids. Then Messer vanishes at the end of the war. Gone. And Gerhardt Wiesse appears magically in Italy in the spring of 46."

"That's ancient history." Korkoran tapped the report. "This is today. I mean, how do these people keep this shit secret?"

"They don't. There's lots of books and articles," Pacheki countered. "Remember the John Birch society? *None Dare Call it Conspiracy* by Gary Allen? Jim Marrs' *Rule by Secrecy* and *Rise of the Fourth Reich?*"

"Vaguely. Why didn't they squash them?"

"Why didn't the Clinton campaign sue Sweitzer over *Clinton Cash?* Because, leaving it out there—not making a big deal out of it—makes it look like the work of kooks. The majority of the people pay it no mind."

"I'm not a kook." Korkoran slapped his knuckles on the report. "We've got to take this to every committee on the hill, the Department of Homeland Security, the banking committee, the Justice Department. This is going to blow the lid off the—"

"You've read it. Now you're going to watch me pull out that drawer. Where I'll lay it inside and shove it into the fire."

"Damn it, Vince! Don't you get it? These fuckers have been playing this country like a puppet. Pulling the strings, subverting our elections in a way the Russians could only dream of. That son of a bitch Ortega met with Chantel Simond! She's got to be the one who told him to put a hold on my bill. He's in her fucking pocket!"

"Hand it to me. Right now, Jim."

Korkoran clutched the binder tight to his chest. "You read this, right? This is bigger than Watergate, bigger than Russia hacking the 2016 election, or the impeachment, or Trump's..." He blinked, dismayed at the implacable look in Vince Pacheki's eyes.

"Jim, I owed you one. We're not only even—you owe me from

here on out. Hand me the fucking report, or this is going to get very, very ugly."

Big Jim Korkoran reluctantly extended the report—an almost physical pain in his soul as Pacheki took it. "Just tell me why, Vince. What have they got on you?"

"Right now? They've got nothing on me." Pacheki looked down at the report in his hands. "You've never lived in a mob town. A place like Newark, or Chicago, with a corrupt political machine, have you? The Foundation is like that. You don't care that they're throwing elections, skimming a percentage off the local economy...as long as the trash gets picked up, the lights stay on, and the roads get fixed. The unspoken deal is that they won't mess with the common folk, and you don't mess with them."

"That's sick."

"Is it, Jim? I, Vince Pacheki, don't want to be noticed by The Foundation. After what you've read, neither do you. And should it ever come down to it, I'll swear on a stack of Bibles that this report never existed, and you were never down here."

And with that, he pulled the drawer out, dropped in the report, and slammed it shut.

"Yeah, yeah, I understand. I was never here." *In a fucking pig's ass, Pacheki! 'Cause this is anything but over.*

CHAPTER FORTY-TWO

***

MERRY CHRISTMAS! AND IT WAS. BRENDA HAD BOTH MITCH AND SAM GUNNARSON SUPPLY her with enough deadly new toys and communications equipment to almost distract her from what she'd gotten herself into. Last year she'd been spending the day with Mark and Kelly in their upstate New York cabin. Mom and Dad had driven up from West Virginia. A day of laughter, and the only family she'd ever had.

Gone. All gone.

Brenda leaned over Mitch's shoulder as he demonstrated the device. The thing was built inside a hefty Mont Blanc pen. By turning the top past its stop, it retracted the ink filler, opening a tube. Depressing the clip fired it. A combination of spring and compressed air shot a small dart at five hundred meters per second.

"That's all it takes," Mitchell told her. "The dart contains a micro charge that bursts a fraction of a second after impact. The neurotoxin is dispersed in the bloodstream. The moment it reaches the heart, it paralyzes the nerves."

"And it's completely undetectable?"

"Looks like a pen when it goes through airport screening."

"What else have you got down here?" She glanced around the armory. "I've trained on most of the firearms, but what are those?"

"Ah!" Mitch grinned as he turned to the rack. "Aerosols, perfume bottles, chapstick tubes, all containing various inhalants and contact poisons, nerve agents, or anesthetics. Wherever you go, no matter how innocent you look, you can keep Chantel as safe as if you were packing an MP5."

"I'll give it some thought before we leave."

"You'll need training."

"I'll take it." She glanced at her watch. "Chantel wanted to see me. I'd better go."

Mitch's eyes remained placid behind his glasses. "Captain? One last thing. I owe you an apology. Glad to have you on board."

She gave him a nod, stepped out of the armory door, and climbed the stairs. She'd only been given access to specific areas of the villa and made no effort to stray.

Locked in thought, she arrived at her quarters to find Chantel seated in Brenda's easy chair, a report open in her lap.

"I was on my way to your office," Brenda greeted, setting her bag of new toys to the side.

"Thought we'd talk here," Chantel told her, closing the report and standing. "You seemed a little taken aback when Val announced we'd be eliminating Platnikov. If you have reservations, I need to know now."

Brenda crossed her arms. "It's not every day that I'm sitting at the same table when someone decides to kill the Russian president." She paused. "Why you?"

"Because Platnikov was there when I met with Putin, offered Vladimir a way out before we lowered crude oil prices, crashed his stock market, and triggered the catastrophic devaluation of the ruble that led to Putin's removal and Platnikov's rise to power."

Chantel's lips pressed into a tight line. "As a result of that meeting, Leon's developed a certain fascination with me. Makes sense given his psychological profile. A beautiful, powerful woman would make the sort of conquest he can't resist. He'll let me get up close and personal."

"How personal?"

"Very, I'm afraid."

Brenda fought a wince, hesitated only a second. "So, what's the plan?"

"I confront him on the Gorky Plan, which is supposed to be top secret. I tell him he can ditch it or pay the consequences. It's only fair, right? Offer him an out."

"Think he'll take it?"

Chantel absently shook her head. "That's not his profile. He bought into Putin's dream of reestablishing the old Russia with all of its grandeur and prestige. He thinks Putin was too much of a glamour boy, taken with celebrity and cultism."

"So, what does he think he is?"

"Part mystical descendant of the Czars mixed with the courage and self-sacrifice of the Great Patriotic War, and heir to the technology and discipline of the Soviet Union." She made a face. "I really hate messianic leaders. They gain too many followers too quickly."

"Then...is it wise to enter his lair when he's got this perverted interest in you?"

Hard green eyes flashed Brenda's way. "Captain, perhaps you haven't been paying attention. In less than six months, Platnikov is planning to precipitate a disaster that will end with NATO and Russian troops in combat. Give me another option."

"I don't have one, but I don't like my principal walking into a situation where I don't have control." Brenda stepped over to stare out at the ocean. "Assuming there is a Gorky Plan."

"If Katya says there's a Gorky Plan, there's a Gorky Plan. She wouldn't be going to this length, handing me this opportunity if she wasn't worried."

"Why not deal with it herself?"

"Because I can get close to him without raising suspicion. He and I will drink from the same gift bottle of Hennessy Timeless, and he'll never know."

Brenda froze. "Wait a minute. The bottle with the virus?"

"Sure. I don't have the what's-it-called gene that he does. We're sacrificing a bottle of the finest cognac on the planet in the name of world security, and I'm going to get at least a snifter."

"Are you absolutely sure—"

"It's a tailored virus, Brenda. But now, here, look me in the eyes. Are you alright with taking Platnikov down?"

Brenda met her hard stare. "You said the alternative is nuclear holocaust. If for some reason it doesn't work the way you plan, and I get the chance, I'll take him out myself."

The flicker in Chantel's eyes might have been relief. "Thank you, Captain."

Chantel's mask fell back into place. "Now Val's got a surprise for you. He's down in the tennis courts. I said I'd send you down when we were finished."

"You think that's a good idea? Me and Val?"

"No, but he's a guest. And you're going to have to learn to deal with him eventually."

She studied Chantel's expression, seeing the worry deep behind her green eyes. "There's something you're not telling me."

Chantel took a deep breath. As she turned away, Brenda barely heard her murmur, "I'm too high profile to mess with. Surely he knows that."

CHAPTER FORTY-THREE

***

THE BLUE WATERS OF THE GULF OF MEXICO HAD SHADED INTO MUDDY BROWN AS THE shrimp boat rolled north with the swells. The name *Blue Belle,* **Gautier, Mississippi,** was barely visible on the stern. Beneath it a frothy wake boiled out as the boat plowed between the buoys that marked the main channel between the outer islands.

Blue Belle had seen better days. Taylor glanced at the scarred gunwale, paint missing in patches that exposed salt-weathered wood. In the wheelhouse, the silent captain stood like a post; a grease-stained John Deere cap perched sideways on his wiry gray hair. The two deckhands sorted and folded heavy yards of green-brown net, having finally tired of casting furtive gazes at Taylor and Bennie.

"Nice touch, that yacht," Bennie replied, bracing himself as the *Blue Belle* rolled over a series of larger swells. "I'm starting to miss it."

"You're only missing that brown-tanned girl in the bikini."

"Yeah. I'm gonna be missing her for the rest of my life. The stuff dreams are made of. Still, making the run from Belize in luxury like that, only to transfer to a stinking bucket like this? Man, that's what I call a step down in the world."

"The client knows what he's doing." Taylor reached into his pocket for a toothpick before chomping down on it. "The way we're coming in? There's no customs, no cameras. Just a rental car waiting for us when we step off the dock."

"Wonder who the target is?"

"Doesn't matter. He's pissed the client off. But I do know he's a big wheel in Washington D.C.. The client lists him as 'high value'. The guy lives in Virginia, and he's got a daily routine. Never varies. Piece of cake."

Bennie twitched his lips in irritation. "I'm just glad the client's giving us another chance. After two misses?"

Taylor felt the heat under his collar. "The client understands where that particular problem lies. And, Bennie, after we attend to this first thing? You and I are going to be doing a little hunting of our own. I've had the client do a little research for us. I've been getting to know all about Brenda Pepper. The bitch has cost us twenty million. Ruined our reputation. I want to punch her where it will hurt the most."

Ahead of them the Mississippi Gulf Shore was broken by the cluttered white buildings and ramshackle docks of Gautier. No wonder it was still standing, it wasn't worth a hurricane's time to wash it away.

Taylor looked down where his water-proof weapons locker was secured to the deck.

Just wait, bitch. Yours is coming.

CHAPTER FORTY-FOUR

***

BRENDA TROTTED DOWN THE STAIRS TO THE TENNIS COURT TO FIND VALENTINE WIESSE, looking fit and trim, his golden hair glinting in the sunlight.

"Ah, here you are!" He stood, right hand lifting a fencing mask and jacket, a foil in his left. "I recall that you prefer the Italian foil. Myself, I enjoy the French. Three bouts, five points each. If I take the match, you have a romantic supper with me."

Brenda stopped short. "Not a chance."

Val gave her a deadly smile. "One way or another, you and I will cross blades, my dear."

Half an hour later, panting for breath, Brenda lunged; she beat Val's blade to initiate a compound attack. With a circle parry, he deflected her foil. Only by maintaining contact with a fast glide and twist *in quartata* did she avoid a touch.

Disengaging, she leaped back, instinctively dropping into *en garde*. Even as she did, Val attacked, his lightning *raddopio* accompanied by a thrust at her inside low. She parried *septime*, holding his blade on the *forte*—or stronger lower third of her foil. She let his blade bow past her side as his momentum bent her tip in for the touch.

She was fencing the match of her life, her heart hammering, adrenaline firing her veins.

Her first hint of trouble had come when she donned her mask and asked, "Where's the *piste*, the strip?" referring to the fourteen-by-two-meter strip on which a match was held.

"No *piste*," he'd told her. "That's for games. If you ever have to do this for real, no one's going to pay attention to the rules."

She'd given him a salute, and said, "Very well, *en garde. Prêt. Allez!*"

At her first attack, he'd feinted, touched her with a stop-thrust, and followed up slashing her across the mask with a vicious cut before hitting her outside high line twice more in succession.

"Black card! Damn you! That's illegal!"

He'd fallen back into *en garde,* his foil tip dancing evilly. "I said no rules. Only hitting the target counts. Come on, *Captain* Pepper. *Prise de fer,* take the steel. Fight this out as if your life depends on it, because, Brenda, my love, I would have just killed you if this were for real."

And then he'd attacked in earnest. For the first few minutes, she'd survived by falling back on the fundamentals while her brain reactivated partially fossilized neural pathways. Then something clicked, the years falling away as muscle memory returned, and old instincts flickered to life.

She had him now, keeping him at bay with technique, weaving a defense of parries, countering his superior reach with skill. Valentine Wiesse was good, but she was better. And damn it, fencing like this, not for points, but for blood? Each time she countered one of his dirty tricks, her grin went wider.

For blood!

She vaulted back and to the side, reveling in the freedom of movement. She recovered the right of way, beat his blade to the side, and lunged as if for a simple attack on his low outside. She knew him now. He'd attempt to parry *octave.*

As he fell for the feint, she flicked her tip to catch him full in the low inside. The perfect *trompement.*

"Touche," he admitted, gasping for air and stepping back. "That's fifteen. You win, damn it."

She brought her foil up in salute, whipped it down, and pulled her mask off.

On rubbery legs, hair clinging to her sweat-streaked face, she hobbled over to one of the benches. "Dear God, that was great." She made a face at the burning in her thigh muscles. "And, son of a bitch, I'm going to pay for it tomorrow."

He was grinning, face beet red, when he pulled off his mask and tossed it to the side. He dragged a sleeve over his drenched face. "Nothing like living dangerously, is there?"

"I'm eating alone tonight."

"My offer still stands."

"No." She tugged the jacket over her head, grateful for the cooling breeze, and leaned back on the bench to gulp air. That his gaze had fixed on her breasts—now rendered in 3D by her perspiration-soaked tee-shirt—should have pissed her off.

Instead, she noted, "You do know that staring like that is rude."

"Consider it reverential admiration. How did you ever get by in the American army?"

"By beating the hell out of any jackass who stared at me like that and focusing on my job."

He pulled his jacket off and dropped onto the bench beside her. "I do appreciate your candor."

Brenda fought the urge to squirm as she caught his scent— something deep in her core warming under his very masculine interest.

"There are many ways to live dangerously," he said softly, as if reading her traitorous body.

"Something tells me that sex with you would be like pulling the pin on a hand grenade."

"The only thing better than a beautiful woman is a smart one." He shifted his gaze and looked out beyond the tennis court to the tree-covered slope. "But perhaps you do not understand my intentions."

"Wanna bet? You play for points. To win. And you don't give a damn what you have to do to get it."

"That's rather bitter."

"After the three bouts we just fought, I know you down to your soul, Valentine." At his mocking smile, she added, "I got where I am today by making sure my brain had veto power over sexual arousal."

"I'll keep that in mind." His eyes had a devilish twinkle. And as quickly, his mood changed. "Am I really to believe that you've joined us heart and soul?"

"Given what we're facing I'm not sure I have a choice."

"Who are you, Brenda Pepper?" His gaze now reflected blue ice. "Four months ago, you ran an executive protection firm. Today you stand behind one of the most influential women in the world, apparently ready to ride off and help assassinate one of the most powerful men alive."

His eyes, the color of a dark-and-deadly sky, fixed on hers. "Tell me why we should believe you...trust you?"

Brenda swallowed hard, her heart beginning to pound. God, she felt like Clarice Starling trying to stare down Hannibal Lecter.

She tried to see past his black pupils to his soul. "I don't give a damn if you trust me."

"Oh, I think you do. I also think you're just starting to get a handle on the load Chantel is carrying. You're wondering if you're up to the job."

Brenda took a deep breath, stilling her rising unease. *This guy is a jackal.* "First, it can't be easy wandering around with the weight of the world on your shoulders. Second, she's about to leave for Russia to assassinate Platnikov. Third, she's dodging a world-class sniper's bullet sent by someone in The Foundation. Can I protect her? The only thing I know for certain is that I will die trying."

Thoughts raced behind his eyes. "Chantel plays her own game. By her own rules. Do you know that?"

"Are you trying to share a secret with me?"

Valentine's cold eyes barely changed. "One of these days... Well, my beautiful and enchanting woman, I hope I don't have to kill you."

Like a falcon, he bent forward and kissed her. It lasted barely a second. Nevertheless, the gentle, yet urgent, way his lips worked on hers triggered a warm cascade inside her. One of his hands cupped her shoulder, while the other conformed to the back of her head.

Heart racing, she tore herself away and shot to her feet. "Do that again, and I'll break your jaw."

As she wheeled and stalked away, Valentine Wiesse threw his head back and laughed in delight.

CHAPTER FORTY-FIVE

***

FROM HIS MANSION'S EXPANSIVE FRONT WINDOW, BIG JIM KORKORAN COULD SEE THE SURF rolling in. Curling breakers pounded the sand, only to fall back in a foamy rush that robbed each successive wave of any chance for glory.

Years ago, the Korkoran clan had made a tradition of retreating to Jekyll Island for Christmas. They had a real tree—a twelve-foot Georgian pine—in the great room and a roaring fire in the big hearth. His kids, and now grandkids, reveled in the gaudy splendor of too many expensive presents.

He cradled a cup of hot chocolate accented with peppermint schnapps—a long-time favorite that dated back to his youth. Mostly his drink was sour mash. The only time he succumbed to the hot chocolate was here, in this place. Anywhere else and he would most likely have hated it.

Teeny, one of the grandkids, squealed with delight as she scored on her new hand-held video game. The great house smelled of turkey and trimmings. Leftovers from Christmas dinner. Glancing at his watch, he had almost a half hour before supper. Taking one last look at the gray day outside, he padded into his study: an Edwardian extravaganza. Stained walnut walls sported expensive artwork; floor-to-ceiling bookcases were filled with volumes he'd never touch even if he had the time. The back wall was dominated by a gigantic and ornately carved mahogany desk.

Flopping into the high-back leather chair, he used the remote to activate the giant flat screen on the opposite wall. The news was shit. Had been for days as the good anchors and producers took the week off. Still, it didn't hurt to...

"CNN reporting. Again, we confirm that the deputy director of the

NSA, Vincent Pacheki, has been found dead of a single gunshot wound. Deputy Director Pacheki, age fifty-two, was found face-down on a jogging path he was known to frequent outside his home in rural Virginia."

The image showed a draped gurney being rolled out of the woods and loaded into the back of an ambulance.

"Pacheki, best known for his testimony before Congress on the NSA eavesdropping scandal, is a close confidante of the president, and was considered one of the most powerful men in Washington. His death has ignited a firestorm of speculation."

Attorney General Ramey's face filled the screen. *"We're very early into the investigation. I will not speculate on who, how, or why, but make no mistake, we will uncover the facts behind this cowardly act, and the guilty party will pay to the fullest extent of the law."*

Big Jim Korkoran stared vacantly, his mind spinning, as he remembered the fear in Pacheki's eyes.

The words came back to haunt him: *"I, Vince Pacheki, don't want to be noticed by The Foundation, and after what you've read, neither do you."*

CHAPTER FORTY-SIX

***

CHANTEL WAS PACKING THE LAST OF HER BAGS AFTER PICKING THE SUIT SHE'D WEAR for her confrontation with Platnikov. At the knock, she opened her door to Renaud.

"Mind if I come in?"

She stepped back as he walked into her private quarters. The rooms were in the mansion's upper northwest corner with a balcony and views of the Caribbean, beach, and forest. Her bedroom, office, and bath lay off the main room with its couches, table, and floor-to-ceiling bookshelves.

Her father stopped in the main room, taking in the mostly utilitarian furnishings. He walked over to the one opulent piece: a desk commissioned by Winston Churchill. As he ran his fingers down the smooth teak, he said, "You don't have to do this, you know. There are other ways."

"This is it, Dad. We've known it was coming. Planned for this day. I've already set it in motion with sell orders. By the time I return, we'll either have won or lost."

His expression pinched with concern. "Platnikov wasn't part of the plan. That's what I meant by you don't have to do this. I mean, what you might have to do to—"

"If it comes to sex, I'll deal with it. Val's got a plan. And afterward, I'll settle with the Lius and Takanabis."

He studied her with his serious eyes. "Anything that you need from me? You ask, do you understand?"

"Sure."

"Don't trust Katya. I've looked at this from every angle and can't see how she'd gain by double-crossing you. Maybe, in a couple of weeks, after David realizes how far we've gone, it might be different. But she always plays her own game."

"I know."

"Devon is an asset you can depend on. He knows what we're doing and why. He's integral to any success we're going to have."

"I know, Dad."

"And Val? I just—"

"I'll deal with Val. You deal with Sonny." She pointed a finger at him in emphasis. "Poul knows you're dealing with Sonny. He's reallocating assets to purchase the defense upgrades for the island. The important thing is that you either bring Sonny on board, or at least keep him neutral."

"Yes, ma'am. I'm just..." He shrugged, face reflecting the conflicting emotions he couldn't form the words to convey.

"Like I said, we've known the collapse was coming for a long time."

"I wish there were another way."

"We all do. But there isn't." She gave him a fleeting smile. "Now, if you'll excuse me, there's a world to try and save."

He nodded, a glimmer of futility behind his eyes. "When you get back. I want an evening. Just for the two of us. There are things to say. About your brother...your mother..."

"Can't change the past, Dad."

He shook his head stubbornly, wetting his lips.

Before he could say anything, Brenda's knock came at the door.

"Gotta go," Chantel snapped irritably.

"Good luck." He straightened, face tense. "And, Chantel, I want you to know that I'm incredibly proud of—"

"Sure, Dad. See you when I get back."

Desperate to escape, she fled for the door.

CHAPTER FORTY-SEVEN

***

TAYLOR, TRAVELING AS VERNON SNOWE AND WEARING CHEEK INSERTS, LIP ENHANCERS, and glasses to distort his intraocular diameter, stepped off the United flight and into the terminal at Chicago O'Hare. He missed the pre-COVID crowds. Made it easier to disguise himself among the masses. Following the desultory line of passengers, he made his way to the nearest bar and found Bennie. His spotter perched on a stool in the back, a drink before him.

Taylor pointed at Bennie's computer case where it sat on the only unoccupied chair. "You saving that for someone?"

Bennie checked his watch. "I was, but she's overdue. Go ahead. Sit. But if my wife comes, I'm going to ask for it back."

"No problem."

Bennie never made eye contact as he removed his computer case and said, "Hope she's not just checking her email." Then he went back to his drink.

It was an old code.

Taylor pulled his phone from his pocket, scrolling to his email. Opening the one marked "dog food". He found the sixth word, seventh sentence.

Zurich.

"What'll you have?" the bartender asked.

"Nothing. Gotta go."

Taylor slipped off the chair, throwing his coat over his shoulder. To Bennie, he said, "Hope your wife catches the next flight."

And then he was on the way to ticketing.

CHAPTER FORTY-EIGHT

***

CHANTEL BUCKLED HERSELF IN NEXT TO BRENDA. THE SIMOND 737, CALLED "BIG BIRD", was on the descent and final approach to Zurich. "Almost there. Our people on the ground are ready."

Brenda nodded. "Thanks for letting me do this my way."

Chantel considered the best way to handle the situation with Brenda. In addition to the woman's skills, and the debt Chantel owed the woman, she intuitively liked Brenda Pepper. She wanted Pepper on her side. With Janeesh gone, the longing was almost desperate. A fact that scared Chantel down to her bones.

I don't exactly have a track record of great interpersonal relationships.

She needed only to look forward a few rows to see Val's head for that truth to hit home.

Brenda had brooded for most of the flight, alternately staring into space, or reading the weapons manuals Sam Gunnarson had provided. James Bond would have salivated over some of the deadly little gizmos now residing in the captain's purse. But the brooding was something deeper, more troubling.

If she can't back me up? If I can't go through with this at the last moment?

"Want to talk about what's bothering you?"

The 737 jolted and swayed as Brenda said, "It's nothing."

"Val?" Chantel asked quietly, her heart hammering.

Brenda shot her a hostile sidelong glance.

Chantel made a dismissive gesture. "Brenda, I don't meddle in other people's private lives unless something infringes on their ability to do their jobs. Val has lured stronger women than you into his bed. Generally, they end up as wreckage. I liken it to committing suicide with ecstasy."

"You survived."

She looked in Val's direction, remembering tears and pain. "After a fashion."

And now I have to let Platnikov touch me?

A cold fear stirred. Panic lay a hair-trigger away.

Brenda was watching her like a cat. "This thing with Platnikov. Is that why you've been so pensive on this trip?"

Chantel tried to swallow her fear. "We can't make a single mistake. You must do whatever I tell you to." Her gaze shifted. "Platnikov has a history..."

Images flashed through her brain; things she'd read in the report Val had given her after takeoff.

With that, Chantel unbuckled, rose, and slipped across to her seat. After securing herself for landing, she bowed her head, letting her hair obscure her face.

He's going to touch me.

And I'm going to scream. Or burst into tears. And then he's going to rape me, and rape me...

CHAPTER FORTY-NINE

***

BRENDA LOOKED OUT THE WINDOW AS THE SIMOND INTERNATIONAL 737 TOUCHED DOWN on the runway. Big Bird was a statement of The Foundation's wealth and clout. The thing was a sybaritic flying office.

She took a deep breath as the airplane taxied toward the cargo hangars, and the two cabin attendants announced their arrival at Zurich.

Looking out the window, Brenda could see the main terminal—a sprawling gray monstrosity of steel and glass. A certain amount of hubris had gone into naming Unique Zurich Airport. It looked like something gone wrong in the merging between mutant Transformers and a psychotic erector set.

As the Big Bird rolled to a stop, Brenda caught Chantel's eye. The woman opened her computer case. "If the cars are on schedule, they should be on the tarmac."

Brenda repositioned her HK pistol in its inside-the-waist holster and made her way forward as Chantel joined Ricard at the office desk and opened her computer. Any semblance of worry had been replaced by a focused concentration. One of the cabin stewards was swiveling the cleverly designed chairs into place for the conference attendees.

Brenda began pulling down the window shades. Val watched, hand concealing his mouth, a curious speculation in his expression. She gave him her deadliest glare as she passed his seat.

The second steward was disarming the door. Brenda inserted her earpiece and keyed the mic, asking, "Simond security? This is Big Bird. Report, please."

"All clear. Can we pass the first vehicle?"

"Roger that."

Brenda bent to the nearest window, watching the stairs being wheeled up even as the engines spooled down. Beyond the hangars, snow-capped mountains were shrouded in cloud. The day had a gray overcast.

Three long black limousines crept out in a line escorted by airport security.

As the stairs rolled up, the steward undogged the heavy forward cabin door. Cold air, damp with the smell of burned jet fuel, washed over Brenda as she took a position at the door.

The first car pulled up; an older man with white hair and a heavy black wool coat emerged. *Herr Scheinich,* Brenda thought, placing the face from the photo she'd studied on the long flight.

She kept a wary eye out as the man climbed the stairs and his car pulled forward, allowing the next in line to take its place.

"*Bitte?*" Brenda asked, indicating she was about to frisk Scheinich. The man's florid face reflected his irritation, but he grudgingly spread his arms. Using one of Jaime Sandoval's body scanners, Brenda could see right through his clothing down to the pacemaker in his chest.

One by one, she admitted the three men and one woman who emerged from the cars, and as the cabin door was closed, escorted them back to where Chantel greeted each, speaking what sounded like perfect German to Brenda's ears.

Holding the meetings on the airplane had been Brenda's idea. A last-minute schedule change calculated to throw an assassin off-balance. She glanced through the window. *Are you out there, Taylor? Even now, is your rifle trained on the door, just waiting for Chantel to frame herself for the shot?*

If they'd gone into Zurich itself, there would have been hundreds of places along the roads, in the tunnel, or at the hotel, where Taylor could have found a shot. Nor could Brenda have safely delivered Chantel to the banks whose entrances faced the pedestrian-only Bahnhofstrasse.

"It will be an inconvenience for them," Chantel had mused, "but I suspect they'll deal with it."

When the bankers seated themselves in the plush chairs around Chantel's desk and began opening their cases, Brenda took a position in the front of the cabin.

As the day wore on, she would periodically peer out the small window port in the forward door. Misty rain continued to fall, and she studied the surrounding buildings, cataloging the windows, the distant rooftops, and high-rises.

Stilling her thoughts, she tried extending her senses as she had on missions. Sometimes—like the day Bill Solace was killed—she could feel the enemy, as if there was some psychic awareness of the hatred and danger.

But not today, not here, inside an airplane with its fuselage and insulation like a wall between her and the world. Nor could she find that quiet place where hints of subconscious awareness tickled her with insect-like feet.

Instead, the drone of voices—often rising in passion as Chantel delivered an ultimatum—or the hum of fans and the click of computer keys where Chantel's staff worked with the bankers interfered like a fuzzy static.

It was hard to believe that Chantel was preparing for the end of the world.

Val's words returned to haunt her: *Chantel plays her own game.*

Brenda glanced back at the woman as she was insisting that certain Malaysian assets be reallocated. With the stroke of a pen, an entire nation's finances were being rewritten.

The whole thing was like a lunatic's dream come true.

Brenda turned her gaze back to the rain-streaked window, staring through the plastic. She could see Taylor in her imagination as he hunched over his scope. The crosshairs fixed on her window, on her blurry face. His finger poised over the trigger. He was thinking: *Should I take the shot?*

CHAPTER FIFTY

***

THE BUSINESS OF REORGANIZING SIMOND INTERNATIONAL'S FINANCIAL EMPIRE WAS immense. StatNco's predictions about which countries and industries were likely to fail had led to the creation of a complicated strategy for disengagement and divestiture of assets.

Chantel and Ricard had been seated at the office desk, heads together, as they alternately tapped on their keyboards and studied monitors. Most of what they were discussing was over Brenda's head as they brought up data on Southeast Asia.

Big Bird had real-time communications and virtual office capabilities. Devon's face periodically appeared on a monitor as Chantel asked for information on population, demographics, infrastructure, and politicians. What, for example, could rare-earth-element mining have to do with electronics manufacturing in the US and factories in Singapore, Vietnam, and Taiwan? And why would population density in Indonesia have any bearing on the stocks Chantel was ordering Ricard to sell?

How did Chantel keep it all in her head?

The team had been focused like lasers on their computers in the aftermath of the Zurich meetings. They were choreographing a dangerous dance, seeking to rearrange assets and holdings without precipitating a crisis as they pulled money out of specific regions, countries, and industries.

All of this was being coordinated as Big Bird winged eastward over Russia. Brenda leaned against what she suspected was a teak bulkhead and watched an almost manic Chantel as she huddled over a communications console, interfacing with her team back in the Caribbean.

The ominous bottle, delivered to the 737 by courier on the last day, rested in its ornate box. More than once, Brenda had noticed Chantel's expression turn glassy when she fixed on the box.

"Who'd have thought it was that complicated, eh?" Val asked, causing Brenda to jump as he appeared at her shoulder.

Brenda shot him a sour look. "Clear your throat or something when you're sneaking up on me."

"My apologies." He looked anything but sorry.

Brenda crossed her arms defensively, an action that seemed to amuse him. "I wouldn't want to be in Chantel's shoes. The wrong move could set off a panic that triggers the end of everything. How would you live with that, knowing you brought the world down?"

"She has nerves of steel." He glanced at her. "You've seen the scars?"

"What scars?"

"Ah, you're not as close to her as I thought."

"Meaning?"

He shrugged. "Are you ready for Russia?"

"As ready as I can be. We're met at the airport by several limousines. They transport us to some dacha out in the country where Chantel meets Platnikov. We have dinner, they drink"—she gestured toward the brown-paper-wrapped bottle—"we spend the night. Next morning the limousines take us back to the airfield. We fly away." *If we're still alive.*

"We spend the night?" Val's lips quirked. "She didn't tell you?"

"Tell me what?"

"Leon Platnikov was one of Putin's hand-licking lackeys. He was there the last time Chantel met to discuss Russian aggression and world finances. Chantel threatened Putin with economic disruption unless he backed down on Eastern Europe. When Putin dismissed her and proceeded to take all of Ukraine, Chantel pulled her magical strings, depressed oil prices, destroyed most of Putin's wealth, and threw the already teetering Russian economy into crisis.

"Now Platnikov's the big boss. But Chantel fascinated him. What sort of woman could do this? He was entranced not only by her beauty, but her power. She's become an obsession of his. He's only serviced by redheaded women. He's even had some of his girls surgically altered to look like Chantel."

"Jesus."

"Why do you think the meeting is to be held at his private dacha?"

"Is she out of her mind?"

"What is a little risk when you know Platnikov is going to throw a dying world into turmoil? Knowing that millions would be drawn up in a maelstrom if Platnikov launches his takeover of the Baltic States? That if he has misread the Americans, or the Chinese, it could precipitate global war? How then could The Foundation soften the blow? Direct the coming collapse?"

Brenda took a deep breath. "Chantel said Platnikov has a history. She didn't elaborate, but it seemed to throw her into a funk. I asked for a file that I still haven't been given."

"Russia has had years to refine the arts of torture, abuse, and degradation. Platnikov once had a mistress he suspected of working for German intelligence. The story is that they pulled her teeth and screwed metal straps into her mandible and face to brace her jaws at just the right angle. Then they stapled her nostrils shut. Strapped her to the floor...and after Platnikov took the first turn, a line of his men drowned her by ejaculating and urinating into her mouth. That's Platnikov."

"That's fucking sick and...and knowing that, she's still going?"

"The Gorky Plan is not theory. Platnikov *will* act. NATO and the US? It *will* be the trigger to global conflict. As it escalates, there will be a nuclear exchange." In a carefully modulated voice he added, "Chantel understands. To get him to drink that bottle, she will do anything she has to."

Brenda bit her lip, wondering, *Dear God, how does she do it?*

Val seemed to be peering into her soul. "Any future for humankind depends on what Chantel does in the next thirty-six hours. My concern is you."

"Me?"

"A wrong word from you, a negative look or expression, could tip off Platnikov. Worse, you might take it upon yourself to play the hero. Use one of Gunnarson's clever little toys to try to save Chantel. That would doom us all. If you get her killed..." The look she gave him would have frozen fire.

"I've got her back. No matter what it takes."

"See that you do, Brenda." He glanced back at Chantel, a somber expression on his face. "I wouldn't like to lose her that way...or you, either."

CHAPTER FIFTY-ONE

***

THE LIMOUSINES WERE WAITING ON THE SNOW-CAKED TARMAC AT THE FOOT OF THE JETWAY
stairs. Exhaust rose in white puffs from the tailpipes, and a security
agent dressed in a black greatcoat, head topped by a fur hat, stood
expectantly by the rear passenger door.

Chantel took one last look through the window as she waited by
the front cabin door. Brenda had already seen to delivering their two
overnight bags.

Brenda approached down the aisle, the bottle of cognac resting in
the crook of her right arm, her purse slung over her shoulder. Stress
filled every line in the woman's face.

Chantel tried to smile, only to feel it crumble. The tickle in her gut
came from a barely throttled fear. She took a deep breath to still it.

*This isn't anything women haven't been doing for millennia. If they
could bear it, so can you.*

The black phantom slashed out of her nightmares, sending a prickle
through her body. She barely stopped herself from fingering the outline
of the scars beneath her dress.

"Captain?" she greeted.

"Ready."

Chantel hesitated and glanced around the safety of Big Bird's warm
cabin. In the rear, Ricard and her people were bent at their computers,
frown lines incising their foreheads as they changed the future of a planet.

But Val had already left. The plan was in motion.

*God, I just want to fly away! What's the line from Luke? 'Take this
cup away from me?'*

"Captain, from the moment we leave this airplane, there can be
no mistakes. You must do anything and everything I say. No argu-

ments. Every movement and word will be observed. The stakes..." Chantel fought down a sudden surge of anxiety that felt as if it would burst her chest.

"Chantel"—a deadly earnest filled Brenda's eyes—"I'm with you. We'll do whatever we have to do."

"It might mean that I..."

"*Whatever* it takes, Chantel."

I'm not alone.

A sweeping sense of relief mixed with the building horror.

She could do this.

"Alright, Captain. Let's go."

CHAPTER FIFTY-TWO

***

BRENDA GLANCED AT HER REFLECTION IN THE ORNATE MIRROR IN PLATNIKOV'S DACHA.
The thing was an antique, the frame sporting raised images of satyrs, wood nymphs, and leaping stags; the whole clad in golden leaf. The woman in the reflection stared back, eyes filled with fear.

The mirror fit the room: splendid, with a vaulted ceiling painted with angels; a huge canopy bed; fantastically carved and upholstered furniture; and a marble fireplace. The place looked like it was part of a museum.

Taking one last glance, Brenda wondered how many prominent Russians—how many party bosses and powerful nobles—had stared into this same glass? And how many had died horribly before their time? Disappeared, never to be heard of again, their names struck from all record?

This was, after all, Russia.

Val's story of Platnikov's "execution" of his mistress kept replaying, nightmare-like, in her imagination.

Come on, Captain. Where are the guts that let you walk through a Taliban-held town?

She'd been in Pakistan, wearing a burqa, wandering a market in Wana, a town in Waziristan, in an attempt to locate a known weapons smuggler. She'd had the guts then.

Visions of dark cells, beatings, torture, and an endless line of men taking their places as her naked body was gang-raped... The feeling of her teeth being pulled, screws cutting through her cheeks and jaws... She shook her head to forestall the thought of being strapped to the floor, the first man lowering himself...

No one lives forever. You will deal with it. Use one of Sam Gunnar-

son's innocent deadly toys and check out.

Knotting her muscles, she burned some of the nervous energy, forcing herself to concentrate on the mission.

"I really don't like this," Brenda repeated, then glanced down at the ornate cognac box that stood on the inlaid nightstand. A fortune in liquid wealth that would kill a man and change history if everything worked according to plan.

"Your opinion is noted," Chantel remarked from where she sat at a desk reputed to have belonged to one of Czar Nicholas II's advisors. She was in the process of fixing an ornate hair clip—a glass or crystal cylinder with golden rings fixed on either end—into her red hair.

Chantel might have been carved of ice. Incredible, knowing, as she must, that Platnikov insisted that his sex toys look like her?

Shake off the nerves. It's just another mission.

Brenda let her gaze roam the room again. It was a given that their every word and action was being monitored.

At the desk, Chantel checked her watch, rose, and smoothed her form-fitting dress: white with black trim, tailored with pockets. Brenda had forgotten the designer's name. Something Italian. Though smacking of the professional, the silk fabric left nothing to the imagination as it emphasized Chantel's breasts, slim stomach, and curved hips.

Platnikov would be drooling.

"Time," Chantel said an instant before a knock came at the door. She picked up the cognac and arched an eyebrow, as if at an internal thought.

Brenda slipped her purse over her shoulder, reassured by the deadly pen in its front pocket. Nerving herself, she took the lead, stepping to the side as she opened the door and let it swing wide.

All she had to do was stay alive and free until the car came to pick them up at six the next morning.

The man outside had a military crew cut. Despite being dressed in a suit that barely hid packed muscle, he still came across as a thug. The scar on his chin marred a face that seemed carved from blocks. Then he turned on a heel and started down the hall in what Brenda imagined was a SPETZNAZ swagger.

Was he one of the beasts who'd contributed to the German agent's death?

Keeping track of the doors they passed—all closed—Brenda memorized their route. She and Chantel were led into a monumental hall with art-covered walls, elaborate woodwork, and a roaring fire in the hearth at the opposite end. Statues, splendidly rendered knock-offs, of Greek and Roman classics lined the walls; the difference was that she'd never seen classical statues with such anatomically impossible genitalia.

A masterpiece of carved and inlaid wood, the central table dominated the room. Like soldiers at attention, tall-backed chairs flanked each side.

Two gold-filigreed plates sat across from each other at the far end before the fire. Silverware gleamed in the light from the overhead chandelier burning real candles.

The guide extended a meaty hand toward a wooden-wheeled drink service to one side, asking in strained English, "I get you something?"

"Vodka," Chantel replied. "Your best. Straight."

A slight glint of appreciation broke their guide's stony features. Taking a cut-crystal glass in his oversized fingers, he removed the stopper from a bottle, poured, and extended it to Chantel.

She handed the bottle of Timeless to Brenda, took the proffered glass, and toasted, "*Nostrovia*" before tossing it down.

"Ah, you drink like Russian!" a voice called cheerily from behind.

Brenda turned to see Leon Platnikov, his burly form clad in a strikingly antique-looking tuxedo complete with red sash. He walked with a slight limp, a smile on his thin face.

Her first thought was that he looked smaller than on TV, but his dark eyes held that almost maniacal glint. Blond hair had prematurely turned to silver, though he was only in his early fifties. He approached Chantel and kissed the back of her hand.

"You look lovely as always," he said through a thick accent.

Chantel replied in Russian.

"Ah, and what is this?" Platnikov turned and indicated the bottle Brenda held.

Chantel nodded graciously. "I've heard you have a fondness for the best cognacs."

"Could it be Hennessey Timeless? You will share with me later? Yes?"

"With pleasure," Chantel replied with a gesture that cued Brenda to step forward and hand the bottle to Platnikov.

The Russian president took the exquisite cognac, admiring it in the light. Then he handed the bottle to the goon, who placed it on the drink cart.

Brenda discreetly stepped back, her attention fixed on her stoic opposite as he resumed his position beside the drink cart. He missed nothing as she adopted an at-ease stance. The purse's weight on her shoulder felt oddly reassuring. One of the security personnel had pawed through it on their arrival, closely examining the hairspray, lipsticks, and personal effects.

"Felix!" Platnikov cried. "Vodka." Then he asked Chantel something in Russian. She shook her head and replied.

Felix filled a second glass before handing it to Platnikov.

Platnikov lifted his glass and uttered what sounded like a toast. He swallowed it in a gulp, eyes never leaving Chantel's.

"You know why I'm here," Chantel told him.

Platnikov made a dismissive gesture. "Good to see you, too."

"The last time, we severely disrupted Putin's economy. And that was over nothing as ambitious as the Gorky Plan."

Platnikov went still. His mouth hardened. As quickly, he chuckled, holding the empty vodka glass up to watch the dancing flames through the cut crystal. "Oh, my. Gorky Plan? You are here over hypothetical military exercise? Something drawn up by generals, for generals, as exercise in planning?"

Chantel raised an eyebrow. "Another time, perhaps, if we had been consulted, we might have agreed. Right now, however, we would prefer that June 22nd remain a notable date only in the history books."

Brenda watched Platnikov's expression darken.

"What *you* prefer...?" He chuckled bitterly. "But what is this? Business before food? Come, let us eat. Then, on full stomachs, I will tell you how Gorky Plan has been...yes, miscommunicated to your colleagues. Allow me."

With a single fluid motion, he tossed his glass into the fire, took a step, and held Chantel's chair as she seated herself at the table.

In a sidelong glance, Brenda caught Felix's barely suppressed smile. The cat-that-ate-the-canary kind of smile. And periodically he'd look her way, his eyes filled with promise, as if he were anticipating something to come.

What if the traitor in The Foundation is Katya? What if this is her way to be rid of Chantel? Handed over to a man capable of making her disappear without a trace?

Alone as they were, it would be so easy. Katya could skate, Platnikov taking all the blame.

Can I take Felix?

With a hard swallow she told herself: *Not fucking likely.*

CHAPTER FIFTY-THREE

* * *

"LET'S JUST BE HONEST," TOM ORTEGA SAID TO THE REPORTER, HIS VOICE RAISED OVER the rally behind him. Despite his fatigue, he kept his smile warm for the cameraman who stood behind the young woman. "We can't possibly service a debt of *five trillion* dollars. Not with the current economy."

"And your solution?" She gave him a charming smile, cocking her head coquettishly.

"Unleash small businesses. If I were in the White House, in my first one hundred days, I'd order the bureaucracies to cut regulations by two-thirds. For example, New Hampshire is filled with small farms raising chickens, pigs, and grass-fed beef. But it all has to be shipped to a USDA plant in Virginia for processing. I talked to a young man today who wanted to open a meat packing plant to serve his local market. He was told it would cost over three hundred thousand and take two years just to get the permitting pushed through. And then the USDA regs conflict with the FDA regs, which conflict with the state regs. That's insane.

"Another business, a small foundry, isn't going to expand beyond the father and son who work there. They told me flat out, 'We could triple our business making household items for custom homes, but we can't afford the employees.' I mean, what's happened in this country when taxes are so high businesses can't *afford* to hire more help?"

"Your critics say you want to remove regulation from big businesses, give them free rein."

"Yeah, makes a good tag line, doesn't it? I think we've had too much of big business. After all, their lobbyists have ensured the regulations are written to give them the advantage."

"Well..." She paused pensively "They're not going to give that up easily, are they?"

Ortega shrugged. "I didn't shy away from a hard fight in Afghanistan. Why would taking on big businesses be any different? Besides, people hired by small businesses who are creating wealth become customers for those same big corporations who are lamenting their bottom lines in the current economy."

"Thank you, Senator." She turned toward the camera, adding, "And, as you can hear in the background, Senator Ortega's message really resounds with the people of Manchester."

Tom disengaged himself, seeing Ben Mackeson where he beckoned by the door.

Shaking hands as he made his way to Mackeson, he turned, gave a final wave, and let Ben escort him into a quiet hallway behind the banquet room.

"That went over well," Tom told him.

"Julie has her people working the crowd." Mackeson's brow lined. "I was keeping score. Even some of the skeptics were nodding at the end."

Tom loosened his tie, sweating from the lights. "I overheard one guy. He kept saying, 'Yeah, it sounds good now. But wait until he's in office.' I mean, how do we make people understand we really mean it?"

"Figure that out, my friend, and you'll have the country eating out of your hand." Mackeson's tone changed. "In the meantime, something's come up. Mark Dagget's here. He showed up a half hour ago, listened to part of your stump speech, and gave Tam the high sign. Tam took him up to your room."

"I wondered when the RNC was going to make an appearance."

"Then I guess you no longer need to wonder."

"I suppose he's here to put pressure on me." Tom stepped into the elevator and stared up at the ceiling panels as Mackeson pushed the button for their floor. "The last time I dealt with the party at this stage in a campaign, they were a little less than enthusiastic."

"Gee? I wonder why?"

Tom led the way to his suite. Stepping in, Marcus Dagget rose from the small couch where one of the volunteer staff had given him a cup of coffee. Across from him the TV was on MSNBC.

Dagget had spent years in the party, having built his reputation running a polling company that had actually predicted the Trump election before hiring his expertise to various candidates. Turned out that he liked directing voter trends more than measuring them; he had sold his business the first time the party had dangled a paycheck in front of his nose.

"Hello, Marcus." Tom shook his hand and indicated the TV. "MSN-BC? Is that just a bad habit or an addiction you'd rather not admit to?"

Now in his early fifties, Dagget had the polished look of a professional. His smile might have been molded of plastic. "Just keeping up with the opposition. You got a full fifteen minutes on Chris Hayes. The question that preoccupied them was 'What does Tom Ortega think he's trying to prove?' Which made me wonder exactly the same thing."

Mackeson headed for the small counter where a bottle of Macallan resided. "Oh, come on, Mark. I'd have thought you learned that lesson in Ohio."

"What we learned in Ohio was that Tom, here, was a fresh face. But the problem is that a novice candidate can get lucky when his opponent self-destructs in front of the cameras. Presidential politics? That's a whole different animal with a lot of teeth."

"Get to the point, Marcus."

The man inspected his coffee for a couple of seconds, as if picking his words. "The point is that Gene Falco is our preferred candidate. He's earned it. Paid his dues. And right behind him in line is Ed Brown. We learned our lesson with Trump. The last thing the party needs right now is a wildcard splitting the vote."

He looked up to meet Ortega's eyes. "You're good, Tom. We understand that. And down the road, you've got real potential. But take your time. Build your base. And when the time comes—"

"The time is now, Marcus."

"Don't waste your momentum before you're ready. That's all I'm saying. You shoot the works now, you'll be labeled a loser."

Mackeson stepped forward. "I don't take chances on losers, Marcus. Bitter experience should have taught you that."

"That's just it," Marcus shot Ben a hard look. "I've got a lot of people asking what the hell you're doing here. You're the enemy. And we're supposed to suddenly think you've come over to our tent? There's a lot of suspicion about what's really behind your move."

"It's simple. We think the country needs Tom Ortega. Oh...don't give me that look. You've been watching the same news reports. The world's teetering on the edge of the abyss. The radical right and Antifa are killing each other in the streets. Platnikov is about to move on the Baltics. Do you really think that Gene Falco can sit across the table from Leon Platnikov and negotiate anything? Tom's a SEAL. Been in the shit. He's got a credibility you should be salivating over."

For long moments Dagget stared, as though trying to see through Mackeson's bland expression. "Drop the bullshit. It's a nice publicity move. But after what you've done to Republicans over the years, you just change? Like putting on a new shirt? I'm supposed to buy that?"

"It's a free-market economy. Buy whatever you want."

Dagget made a face. "Tom, whatever he's after, you know he's playing you. Maybe they really are afraid of you in the long term. What better way to cut your nuts off than to dangle the possibility of being president, let it get down to the wire, and just when it starts looking good, stab you in the back with some sort of malicious accusation? Dear God, they can ruin your career overnight, you innocent sap."

"Marcus..." Mackeson warned.

"Fuck you, Ben. I didn't think even *you* were capable of something so shitty."

"Fuck yourself, Marcus," Mackeson snapped. "I'm in this to elect a president. And once you get off your fucking high horse and think this thing through, it's going to hit you like a thrown rock that if I was going to pull a stunt like that, I sure as hell wouldn't do it myself. Now, get the hell out of here! And come election night, you can lick my shorts before you're setting foot on that stage to shake Tom Ortega's hand. And on that day, when people wonder where you are, I'm going to make damn certain they know all about it."

"Whoa!" Tom stepped between them, arms out. "That's more than enough. Both of you."

"You haven't heard the last of this." Marcus tossed his coffee into the trash. He started for the door, wheeling, finger pointed. "Tom, this isn't Ohio. You're going to need money, organizational support, and endorsements. And as long as you're involved with that son of a bitch"—he jabbed a finger at Mackeson—"you're getting jack shit."

Then he was out the door, slamming it behind him.

Tom reached over, taking the scotch from Mackeson's hand and downing a belt. "Well, we just played hell."

Mackeson grabbed the glass back, chugging the rest. "I think you better get your shit wired tight, my friend. Because if I had any doubts before, they're gone now. I'm going to elect you president if I have to buy every vote in the country just to bury that prick."

"Can we do it without the party?"

"Tam Bizhenov has people in every state in the Union collecting signatures and filing the paperwork to put you on the ballot as a Republican. The biggest challenge right now is to whisk the ground game away from the party at the precinct level. It'll be a little tricky, but I can't wait to spin this. By the end of business tomorrow, every news outlet in the country is going to be talking about why the RNC wants to cut your throat."

CHAPTER FIFTY-FOUR

***

ANXIETY BUILDING, BRENDA WATCHED NO LESS THAN SIXTEEN COURSES SERVED AS WAIT staff entered and left through a remarkably concealed door between two statues.

Chantel sampled everything, limiting her consumption.

Only after dessert did Platnikov push back his chair. "You like?"

"One of the finest meals I've ever eaten," Chantel told him with a smile.

To battle the jitters, Brenda mentally rehearsed ways to kill Felix. The man had stood through the entire meal without as much as a flicker crossing his hard expression.

"Now, what is this silliness about Gorky Plan?" Platnikov leaned back, an arm on the table. "I know you have sources. Perhaps they do not understand."

Chantel laid her napkin to one side. "We not only have more sources than you do, but better ones. If you move on the Baltics now, the West will not back down. After Ukraine, NATO has drawn the line. They will *not* remove their troops. A Russian incursion will lead to combat. The situation will escalate. Iran will attack the Persian Gulf and Saudi Arabia. Tensions in the three-way triangle between Pakistan, India and China will escalate to a nuclear exchange. North Korea might be down for the moment, but it will strike South Korea."

"Which is good time to move, no?" He shook a chastening finger. "Cut to chase, yes? The world is about to explode. America and Europe are mired in debt and political strife. They cannot afford conflict. They will deal over Baltic States rather than hold this line you claim. China looks longingly at Southeast Asia and at Africa for salvation. India is about to collapse of own weight. Is new world order. Russia is self-contained, resilient, with resources we have barely tapped. We only need to give rest of world a push. After Europe and America fall apart, we pick up pieces we need. You and your people have same goal. Want to come out on top? Work with us. Can share in resources. Not such bad deal, eh?"

Chantel seemed to think on that. With a ghostly smile, she shook her head. "The only problem with your scenario is that the West *isn't* going to negotiate or back down. If it comes to confrontation, it *will* go nuclear. Come on, Leon, you've read the GRU and SVR reports just like we have. You *know* NATO's contingency plans. Unlike the Cold War, this won't be about just ideology, it will be about grasping at straws. Too many people won't have anything left to lose."

"Why you care? Forewarned, you make billions on war industry."

"We *lose* billions when the global markets collapse. Then we lose *everything* when it goes nuclear."

"West will not fight. They are broke after COVID, *da?* Will is gone." His mouth quirked bitterly. "When we take Baltics, West is distracted. Iran takes Middle East; China takes Southeast Asia and Japan. NATO and EU splinters into separate interests, unable to react to anything, *da?* Is ultimate weakness of Europe. French, Germans, Italians, British. For two thousand years little countries in Europe squabble like children. America is weak. On verge of civil war and secession. Whole country breaking up. Republicans would rather fight Democrats. Is cheaper, less risky, to just let Baltics go. Sniveling Americas will say, 'Their war. Not ours.'"

"That's your final word?"

Platnikov said something in Russian, no give in his expression. Then in English. "Or perhaps we come to other arrangement?"

"Meaning?"

"I have soft spot for good friends. Special friends. Friends who can have place in new Russia."

"I wouldn't make a good mistress, Leon."

"Who said anything about mistress?" Platnikov's expression turned keen. "I am thinking of, um, partner. Someone to share ideas, enjoy same passions."

"Passions?" She laughed. "People say I'm more robot than woman."

"This I do not believe."

Chantel toyed with her napkin. "I would come at a very high price."

"To me, you are Helen of Troy. For Helen, Greeks went to war. For you? What is Russia's destiny in comparison?"

She held his eyes for a long moment. "Brenda? Could you bring that bottle over?"

Brenda fought the urge to give Felix a measuring glance as she retrieved the bottle and two snifters. She tried to appear relaxed as she walked over to the table, setting the bottle before Chantel.

Platnikov turned his attention to her. He fixed first on her face, then his gaze traced down her body with growing interest.

He said something in Russian, but at Brenda's incomprehension, asked, "You are security?"

"Yes, sir."

"Nice security." Then he shot a crafty glance at Chantel. "She go everywhere with you?"

"She does."

Platnikov's gaze followed Brenda as she retreated to her place, her skin crawling at the lust in his eyes. Then his attention returned to Chantel, as if seeing her anew. "How important is stopping Gorky Plan? Really?"

"I wouldn't have come all this way, Leon."

"Perhaps there is way to...sweeten deal." Then he spoke in Russian and inclined his head in Brenda's direction.

Brenda noticed that Felix couldn't stifle the slight grin as he glanced at her in open appraisal. Her back stiffened instinctively.

What the hell was going on?

Chantel tapped her fingernails on the cognac bottle. "A...delay? For an indefinite period?"

Platnikov's smile widened. "I am not robot either. Let us say Gorky Plan delayed pending additional study. Time to truly determine that West will not precipitate military clash with Russian troops sent to stabilize chaotic conditions in faltering Baltic states? I do this for *special* friends, *da?* Act of good faith with new partner who brings valuable expertise to new Russia."

"You would give your word, knowing we could make your life miserable if you didn't follow through?"

"For my Helen?" He seemed to think on it, then shot another lascivious glance Brenda's way. "*Da.* I do this for you."

"That being the case, maybe we can come to some accommodation."

Platnikov seemed to swell, a victorious smile bending his lips.

"To the three of us," Chantel said challengingly.

Brenda's mouth had gone dry, her nerves knotted like swollen rope. *Three?*

"I think we open this bottle in my personal quarters." Platnikov lifted the cognac and rose to his feet.

Chantel rose from her chair, her face drained of color. "Brenda, it seems that Leon has invited you to share his cognac." She paused, her green eyes trying to read Brenda's soul. "Just the three of us. Alone."

CHAPTER FIFTY-FIVE

***

LEON PLATNIKOV'S PERSONAL QUARTERS WERE EVEN MORE OPULENT THAN THE REST OF the dacha, and the walls were hung with erotic art rendered in a classical fashion. Men and women with muscular naked bodies, their skin flushed and sweat-streaked, were locked in improbable copulation. Thick fur rugs carpeted the floor, and Brenda's eyes were drawn to the great four-poster bed surrounded by giant mirrors.

Platnikov led the way with his eyes gleaming.

Felix stopped at the door and shot a last look at Brenda. With a nod, he closed the door behind her, evidently to stand guard outside.

"What you think?" Platnikov asked, raising his arms, the cognac bottle held high. "Is good place to transact special friendship, *da?*"

His method of transaction couldn't be misinterpreted as Chantel stopped short, fixing on a painting of a muscular man whipping a naked woman. She was on her knees as she performed fellatio on a second man, his back arched, muscles tense. His expression reflected an agony of bliss.

"What?" Platnikov cried. "You not like?"

Chantel seemed frozen, eyes glazing with panic.

Shit, she's losing it!

Brenda stepped forward. "The art looks Renaissance in style." She pointed to keep Platnikov distracted. "That one, with the four interlocked men and women. Caravaggio used that technique, didn't he?"

As Platnikov turned, Brenda bumped against Chantel, whispering, "Guts, girl," and giving her a nod of reassurance. She'd seen more explicit stuff. Usually in cheap magazines passed surreptitiously among male soldiers on forward operating bases. But not as fine art.

Chantel recovered in an instant, shot Brenda a look that said "I'm okay", and stepped forward. "So, Mr. President, now that the foreplay's over"—she checked her watch—"we've got ten hours until our car picks us up. How do we want to negotiate our special friendship? Perhaps with a glass of cognac?"

Platnikov turned to a carved marble bar, retrieving glasses. With a flourish he broke the seal and poured.

Chantel strode across the fur-covered floor with her old grace to take one of the glasses Platnikov had filled.

Clinking it in a toast, she stared into the Russian president's eyes as she drank. Then she turned, saying, "Brenda, consider yourself off duty. Come join us. Leon, pour her a glass and let's see if we can get the captain to let her hair down a little."

Brenda took the glass he offered, her stomach crawling. *Good God, I'm drinking a deadly virus. Do I have the gene? No one said.*

Platnikov gulped his cognac, his entire attention on Chantel. She lifted an eyebrow in return, meeting challenge for challenge. But Brenda could see the little quiver at the corner of Chantel's mouth.

At that moment, the lights flickered, then continued to burn brightly.

A faint smile curved Chantel's lips, as she said, "How about a game, Leon?" Taking the bottle, she refilled his glass. "We'll take turns. You drink, and I'll take something off. I drink, you'll take something off. Same with Brenda."

Me?

Chantel held Platnikov's eyes as he lifted his glass, taking a sip. At the same time, she slipped off her suitcoat and rested it carefully on the marble bar. She lifted her glass to sip.

Platnivkov removed his red sash, a delighted smile lighting his face.

When they both turned to Brenda, her mouth went dry.

She removed her suit coat as he lifted the glass and gulped.

A flicker of what might have been relief crossed Chantel's face, then she returned her attention to Platnikov. "How do you see this working? You and me together? Given the right authority, I could turn Russia into the banking capital of the world." She sipped as Platnikov removed his coat.

"How does this help me?" he asked before taking a drink.

"In two years, I could give you the Baltic states without a shot being fired." Chantel unbuttoned her blouse and sensuously let it fall to the floor.

Brenda started.

Platnikov eyes went glassy as he stared at the scars that marred Chantel's pale skin. Two angular slashes ran from the upper left shoulder to disappear into her bra and emerge below her right breast. Another ran diagonally from the right ribs, then down under her skirt.

"Is true," Platnikov whispered.

"Brenda's turn," Chantel's voice wavered as she changed the subject. "Take a drink, Leon."

As he sipped, Brenda laid her blouse atop her coat. Platnikov didn't seem to notice. His gaze remained fixed on Chantel's scars as though he were imagining the sexual game that must have caused them. One he would have very much enjoyed to play.

"The banks, Leon?" Chantel asked softly. "Are they mine?"

"*Da,*" he whispered breathlessly. Gulping cognac, he stared as Chantel unsnapped her bra and let it fall. The scars had missed her left nipple but followed the curves of her round breasts.

She sipped cognac before adding, "Your stock exchange is a laughing stock. Simonov and Vashenko have to go first. Then we'll deal with the others. I know you get a percentage, but by having Simonov and Vashenko—powerful as they are—eliminated, the others will toe the line. Those who don't, can be arrested."

"Why I do this?" he asked, mesmerized by Chantel's breasts.

"Now you get a paltry ten percent of Simonov and Vashenko's profits from their rigged market, and I can attract billions in investment if the players know the market's fair. FSB has more than enough evidence to put them away for a couple of centuries."

Platnikov nearly ripped the shirt from his body, then his fumbling fingers reached for his belt.

"Take your time, Leon. Don't spoil the game," Chantel teased. "It's Brenda's turn."

For the first time, Platnikov fixed on Brenda as she undid her bra and let it fall. He took a deep breath as he fixed on her breasts, wetting his lips with his tongue.

He might be one of the most powerful men in the world, but he's only a man.

Platnikov was already drinking, gulping it down as Chantel let her skirt slide down her legs.

"This game is too slow," he growled, kicking off his shoes, and dropping his pants. His silk boxers stood out like a tent.

He inclined his glass toward Brenda and sucked down the last swallow as she undid her skirt and let it drop.

Chantel only paused to refill his cognac, brushing against him in the process. Her mere contact caused him to suck a quick breath. As he drank, she slipped her panties over her hips, adding, "And I want control of your aerospace industries. To do that, Kalinov and his cronies have to go."

"Consider him gone," he said too quickly, yanking his silk shorts down to expose himself.

He turned anxious eyes to Brenda and drained his glass to emphasize his hurry. She slid her panties over her hips and let them fall. Filling her lungs, she locked eyes with the monster and smiled her most deadly smile.

Yes, look at me, you piece of shit. We've already killed you, and you don't have a fucking clue.

Brenda kept an eye on Chantel. Platnikov had chugged down plenty of cognac. How far did they have to take this?

Brenda glanced at her purse; it would take one shot from the aerosol spray to put Platnikov out.

But then what? When he awakened, he'd know he'd been had.

Chantel's orders had been to follow her lead.

So, can I actually go through with this? Let him touch me?

"And now for a special prize, Leon," Chantel told him coyly, reaching for her coat where it lay on the bar. From one of the tailored pockets, she removed a plastic-backed foil pack, the kind pills were packed in.

Pressing a capsule out, she'd raised it to her mouth when he asked, "What is pill?"

Chantel stepped close, reaching down with her other hand to grasp his erection and squeeze. "How long does an orgasm last? Five seconds, maybe six?"

She indicated the pill. "This is one of Regal's creations. Works on the centers of the brain. Make's an orgasm last for twenty to thirty seconds. Brenda and I can entertain each other long after you're spent, but since I'm here, I'm going to enjoy every second."

She tightened her grip again, making him shudder as he asked, "Works on men?"

"Same chemistry." She brushed her lips across his left cheek. "Want to try?"

He cried something in Russian and she popped it into his mouth. Letting him go, she pressed a second pill from the foil and swallowed it. The third she tossed to Brenda.

Then, reaching down again, she took Platnikov by his "handle" and started for the great bed. Over her shoulder, she called, "Come on, Brenda. Let's make this a night to remember."

CHAPTER FIFTY-SIX

***

AT THE SLIGHT TOUCH, TAYLOR CAME AWAKE. HE BLINKED, TRYING TO CLEAR HIS muzzy thoughts of fragmenting dreams. He lay on a blanket atop a table. The walls in the room were plastered, a ceiling fan turning slowly overhead.

"What's happening?"

Bennie stepped back to the chair where he sat behind tripod-mounted fifty-power binoculars and raised his eyes to them. "Activity. Some of the staff are setting the veranda table."

Taylor sat up, rubbing his face. "What the hell does the client think we are? Ping pong balls? What time is it?"

Bennie checked his watch. "A little before one in the afternoon here. Screw the jet lag. We can sleep on the boat when the job's done."

"We damn well better get this one right." He flicked open his tablet and pulled up the photo. Taking his time, he studied the target's facial features. They damned well couldn't afford another mistake.

Rolling over, he repositioned the padding to cushion his body and fitted himself to the rifle where it rested in its brace. He'd always liked the 300 Winchester Magnum. This one was a Remington 700 action in a bedded Macmillan stock with a twenty-six-inch barrel. The suppressor was a custom-built job that added another two feet to the overall length. At his request, the weapon had been topped with a twenty-power Nightforce scope with a Horus reticle.

Before infiltrating to the hide, he and Benny had zeroed the rifle and confirmed the ballistics on a remote stretch of beach. Now he lifted the bolt, reached for the cartridge box and, one by one, inserted three rounds.

Closing the bolt, he snugged up against the adjustable stock and settled against the cheekpiece. Through the scope, he had a clear view of the distant table where two white-coated women laid plates on a spotless tablecloth.

Do the job. Then you can get back to the real problem.

CHAPTER FIFTY-SEVEN

***

THE BARTENDER SET A GLASS OF BOOKERS ON THE SCARRED BAR AND GAVE BIG JIM KOR-koran a nod before retreating to serve two bikers who'd taken seats at the far end. In the background Lady Gaga belted out rebellious notes. Above the mirrored backbar with its various bottles, the Lakers battled the Celtics in what was undoubtedly an epic game.

Behind Korkoran, balls clacked, as two construction workers played straight eight beneath a cheap tiffany-style lamp.

The place was called Chris's, a local joint on the outskirts of Alexandria. A perfect place for an assignation.

Korkoran sipped his whiskey and glanced at his watch. He wore a plaid shirt, jeans, and a St. Louis Cardinals cap. The glasses he'd donned completely changed his appearance.

Veronica Wolf arrived ten minutes late, breezing through the door, wearing a dark blue parka, her raven-black hair in a ponytail topped by a woolen watch cap. Korkoran glanced appreciatively at her slim, jean-clad legs as she took a second look and walked his way. Hanging her purse on the chair back, she seated herself beside him.

"Sorry I'm late," she told him. "Took a couple of tries to find the place. And the snow's a bitch."

"Glad you could make it. What are you drinking?"

She glanced around in obvious distaste. "Something tells me I'm not finding a McNab Ridge chardonnay here." But as the bartender walked up, she called, "Just a Bud."

"Going incognito, huh?"

She gave him another speculative look, taking in his glasses and cap. "Guess that makes two of us. Why are we in a dive like this?"

"Because there are no security cameras. Chris, the guy who owns this place, has clients that don't like to have their activities recorded. And Chris relies on a semi-automatic riot shotgun for security."

"I'm assuming you've got a good reason for all the cloak and dagger?"

Korkoran waited until the bartender delivered her beer and walked off. "I've got a source in the FBI. They've got nothing on Vince Pacheki's murder. Forget the daily press conferences claiming progress."

Veronica had straightened, her expression wary. "So...what have you got, Senator?"

He glanced around, then softly said, "I know for a fact that Vince was looking into an organization called The Foundation."

"Never heard of them."

"That's the point. How about SimondAg? Simond Investments? Inga Simond-Heston?"

He had her full attention now, her dark eyes intense. "You mean, like the big ag company? The Nobel laureate? And her son Brian was the secretary of the Treasury?"

"Not to mention the Takanabi clan that's big in Asia. And then there's the Wiesses. Think global. And all tied together in one big family. It's like Spectre in James Bond, but for real. Vince was scared. Afraid his NSA investigation had been discovered."

For a moment she stared thoughtfully at him. "How do you know?"

"Vince and I had some mutual interests. I was looking into Thomas Ortega. Something about the guy isn't right. He's got ties to Simond International. Had a special meeting with Chantel Simond in Jackson. And now he's catapulted into the limelight."

"That's a lot to take in."

"Is it? It's all over the news that Marcus Dagget and Ortega are going to war. The Republican National Committee wants nothing to do with the guy. And, wonder of wonders, Ben Mackeson and his team of cutthroats switched sides at the last minute to support Ortega? What kind of clout does it take to swing that?"

Her face had lined, her mouth set. "And Pacheki was investigating Ortega? Something he learned at NSA?"

"I'd say tripped over. And it got him killed when he started asking questions."

"Jesus, if this is true?" Her voice went husky. "My God."

Korkoran sipped his whiskey. "Sounds like the story of a lifetime, doesn't it? Especially for an ambitious young political reporter with aspirations to the anchor's desk."

"Have you got any kind of proof?"

"Nope. But I saw the document Vince had put together."

"And where is this document now?"

"Burned. Right in front of my eyes. He said it was the only copy, and that putting it together had scared the shit out of him. His last words to me were that he didn't want The Foundation to know he'd been poking around. A couple of weeks later, he's mysteriously shot out on his favorite jogging path."

She leaned forward, excitement in her eyes. "What about this Foundation? I mean, how high does their influence go?"

"Right up to the tippity top. They elect presidents, buy votes, and corrupt governments. You ever heard of StatNco? Think in terms of global software. Their subsidiaries write the code that runs military, government, economic, global communications, agricultural, aviation, social media, and every other software. Their people designed the megadata systems that monitor data in the NSA, CIA, FBI, IRS, Health and Human Services, VA, as well as for the Russians, Chinese, Europe, you name it. I saw the organizational chart. Every major software firm in the world is linked through dummy companies to StatNco. Most of their personnel are in Bangalore, India. They even run most of the electronic tax returns for American tax consultants."

"If this is true..."

"You keep saying that. And I know your next question. How come no one's stumbled over this before? My answer to that is that The Foundation hides out in the open. A group of the richest people on earth, carefully pulling the strings from behind the curtain."

"Someone would have ratted them out."

"There are lots of conspiracy stories about them. All written by people you've never heard of. They're considered kooks. Conspiracy theorists. People no one would ever believe." Korkoran pulled a folded piece of paper from his pocket, sliding it across the bar to her. "I downloaded that from the SimondAg website. We all know the controversy over their genetically altered crops and livestock. But look at the amount they put into genetic research. And then there's their work on pathogens. Guess who netted nearly a trillion with their

COVID vaccine. Check the who's who on patents. SimondAg and their subsidiaries own most of them. My guess is that anyone important who threatens them mysteriously croaks in the most convenient ways. Heart attack, stroke, rare blood disease, COVID, or some other innocent appearing natural cause." He shrugged. "Or they just buy them off."

She shook her head. "I mean, we've heard this before. The Tri-Lateralists, the Illuminati, they've been the basis for novels for years. Conspiracy theories hide under every whacko's tin-foil hat."

"The difference is, I'm not a conspiracy nut, and I've never had a thing for tin foil. I called you because you're the brightest bulb in the pack. You figured out about me and Peggy, and when you came to me with it, you did me a favor by not publishing. Now I'm returning the favor. I think."

"You think?"

He stared earnestly into her dark eyes. "Veronica, if you make a single mistake, tip your hand, you could end up just as dead as Vince Pacheki."

After a pause, he added, "I mean that. Don't take this to your producer and start blabbing with your colleagues. My guess is that The Foundation owns most of the big media."

"That's nuts." But suddenly she didn't look so sure.

"You like research. Check it out. Ortega's an upstart, too late out of the gate. Compare how much positive press he gets compared to negative. Even at MSNBC. Even that incendiary blue-haired bitch gave him a pass."

For long moments she stared at the précis on SimondAg, data meant for potential investors, and then she slowly folded the paper.

"One thing I don't get," she told him. "If they have all these ways of putting pressure on people, why take Pacheki out like they did? Why not a heart attack?"

"Because what they're saying is 'Back off or you're next'. And my best guess is that they weren't sure who Pacheki had talked to, but that this was a good way to ensure that no one else would follow in his footsteps."

"And you say Ortega is involved in this?"

"Right up to his eyebrows."

CHAPTER FIFTY-EIGHT

*** ★★★

CHANTEL PLAYFULLY PUSHED PLATNIKOV ONTO THE GREAT BED, CRAWLING UP BESIDE HIM.

It's alright, she told herself. *I can do this.*

The quivering threshold of panic had passed. She was in control now. Platnikov was pulling her onto him as she said, "Wait, Leon. We've got all night. You just lay there. Brenda and I are going to make you happier than you've ever dreamed."

Brenda leaned close, whispering, "I've got knockout spray in my purse."

Chantel just gave her the slightest shake of the head. "Climb in bed beside Leon, Brenda. Let's start with his feet."

Chantel fought her revulsion as she took Platnikov's foot and pulled off his silk stocking. Wanting nothing more than to twist his toes off, she began massaging his soles, stroking, working up to his ankles. Only the tension around Brenda's mouth indicated the woman's disgust.

Platnikov had turned his head. Brenda followed his glance, stunned to see herself and Chantel in the mirrors. The woman's eyes widened as she realized how the cameras must be seeing them. Chantel could almost hear the woman thinking, *Don't fucking stare at yourself, fool,* which brought a smile to her lips.

Chantel fixed on Platnikov's erection. It brought memories bubbling up. *That* erection, the one that had ripped into her, painful, driven by his...

She stifled a whimper.

The black phantom giggled hysterically in her subconscious. Memories of pain and violation screamed out the ultimate betrayal. A sob started at the base of her throat. The knife slashed out of the darkness, and Chantel flinched.

"Chantel?" Brenda's whisper caused her to gasp, blink, and stare incomprehensibly at Platnikov's engorged penis.

God, don't go there.

Chantel made herself coo, forced little gasps as her fingers ran over Platnikov's hairy thigh.

Brenda ground her teeth and shot Chantel a 'I'm only doing this for you' look as she flipped her hair out of the way. Then she lowered her head toward the man's penis.

"Don't have to." Chantel sat back on her haunches, hands braced on her thighs. "He's out."

"Out?"

"The orgasm pill. It interacts with alcohol."

"Then, why aren't we out, too?"

"We took placebos."

"The cameras! His security is going to be here any moment." Brenda leaped from the bed, headed for her clothes.

"Stand down, Captain. We're fine." Chantel swept a lock of hair back, sucking a deep breath. "That flicker in the lights was Val's signal. He's working with Devon. The room has ten cameras, all under Val's control."

"Oh, wonderful. Val and Devon are watching?"

Chantel shrugged again. "Just Val."

Brenda considered, her lips twitched, and she faced the mirror and flipped it the bird.

It was all Chantel could do to keep from breaking into peals of hysterical laughter. That or tears. Anything to relieve the half panic and terror she'd just barely avoided.

Brenda asked, "What happens when Leon, here, goes to watch his video tomorrow?"

"Through the miracle of CGI and Devon's team, Leon's going to see some of the most awesome sex he's ever had. Even as he watches, a clever little virus begins to destroy the pixels. It will only add to his panic as dementia begins to set in."

"What about tonight? When he wakes up, the blackout is going to make him suspicious."

At that moment Platnikov gasped and began to ejaculate.

Chantel looked at the man with disgust. "I wasn't exactly lying when I told him Regal's team had created an orgasm drug. When he comes to in the morning, he's going to remember the most erotic night of his life."

Brenda grabbed up her clothes and began to dress. "Hope Regal's virus works. He sure drank enough of it. How do we get out of here?"

"We don't. And don't bother getting dressed. If someone comes to check, we're going to be right here, naked as bunnies, in bed with Leon. So come, make yourself comfortable."

CHAPTER FIFTY-NINE

***

MITCH OFFERED HIS HAND WHEN RENAUD STEPPED OUT OF THE HELICOPTER; HE WINCED at the piercing whine as it spooled down. His security detail—already in position—had their eyes on the lush vegetation lining Sonny's private heliport. Two of Sonny's security agents stood to either side.

With Mitch leading the way toward the white-stuccoed mansion, Renaud followed them to the huge double doors. As if on command, the right portal opened; Sonny stepped out with a smile on his face. He wore casual clothing, his shock of white hair catching the afternoon sun.

"Renaud, old friend. So good to see you." Sonny offered his hand. "Have any trouble?"

"None. Havana cleared us for landing without incident, and we even had a military honor guard. They saluted as we walked to the helicopter."

Sonny, looking pleased with himself, added, "Since I *own* the man in charge of Cuba's state security, I would have expected nothing less. Come, I have a meal prepared for you. I remember that you prefer local cuisine."

With Mitch following a step behind, Renaud walked at Sonny's side as they entered the cool recesses of the mansion. The building had been built as a fortress by a Spanish nobleman in the early eighteen hundreds. At a time of ferment and slave revolts, the edifice had been known as the *refugio*, the refuge. Sonny jokingly referred to it as *El Presidio*, the prison.

While the thing looked foreboding from the exterior, upon setting foot inside, it was to enter another world of opulence crafted from intricately inlaid hardwoods, polished marble floors, exotic mosaics, and gleaming brass fixtures worthy of Spain's greatest wealth.

In keeping with Sonny's passion, the rooms were decorated with historical weapons, each room having its own theme, from polished antique armor, swords, and shields to the harquebus, crossbows, and the occasional bronze cannon.

Sonny led the way to a side door and out onto a shaded patio. The *presidio* had been built on a rocky height above the Caribbean, giving the high veranda stunning views of the ocean and forested slopes to the sides.

A balmy breeze barely ruffled Renaud's hair as Sonny's staff held his chair and he seated himself at the table. Sonny dropped into the opposite chair, unfolding his napkin. Mitch and his team took up positions at the edge of the terrace.

"What can I get you from the cellar?" Then Sonny smiled. "I doubt that suggesting a Hennessey Timeless would be appropriate."

Renaud laughed. "Ice water to start, perhaps followed by a good red wine when we eat. You choose. Whatever you want to impress me with."

Sonny barely glanced at one of the uniformed women, and as she left, he leaned forward. "So, Devon has given us the news we've always dreaded. We are in the end days. I expected that you would come knocking on my door."

Renaud shifted to allow a glass of water to be placed beside his plate. "The first order of business is eliminating Platnikov. Given that you know about the bottle of Timeless, Val has no doubt kept you informed."

Sonny's thin lips bent into a smile. "Chantel will be doing us a great favor if she succeeds, though it will cut into my expected profits." He lifted a finger, forestalling any comment. "I should amend that to say my short-term profits."

"You have enough wars to go around for the moment," Renaud said drily. "Ukraine, the Middle East, South America, Southeast Asia—eventually something will explode beyond its borders and suck us all down."

"That, my old friend, is the way of things. Ask Archduke Ferdinand how these things happen. But you are not here to ask about the arms trade."

"I'm here to talk about The Foundation"—Renaud sipped his

water—"and where we're headed. Despite conflicting goals, we've always operated as a consortium. Now that the gloves are off, the ground rules are changed. We're in a very fragile position."

"A point accentuated by the attempts on Chantel's life. Someone already understands your changed ground rules and seeks the advantage." Sonny laced his fingers together, the fabric of his white shirt ruffling in the breeze. "Each faction will be looking to their own interests. Our tradition of compromise and consensus has been built on the premise that if you lose today, The Foundation will compensate you sometime in the future. With no future? You're right to be concerned."

Renaud leaned back as plates of fruit were placed before them. "If we go to war with each other, we're going to lose it all. You know that don't you?"

Sonny stabbed a slice of mango with his fork. "Devon's data and the reports he writes read the same for me as they do for you." He chewed the mango. "Odd, isn't it? In the beginning, Gerhardt, the reformed Nazi, was The Foundation's ethical pillar. Jack was the situational ethicist, willing to sacrifice all to see his goals realized."

"I worshipped Gerhardt," Renaud said. "Your father always made me think."

Sonny studied him through slitted eyes. "Odd that you should decide to be The Foundation's conscience. But let's get to the meat of the matter. Why should I throw my support behind you?"

"It's good that you brought our fathers into the conversation. They knew this was coming. Everything we've accomplished in their names...we could throw it all away if we turn on each other. Felicia *is* Asia. She dedicated her life and sold her body and soul to make Asia what it is today. Through marriage, money, and talent, she has managed to guide and ride the wave of Asian prosperity. She beat that into her children until she's got a finger on Russia, China, Japan, and Korea's beating pulse. Her offspring are true believers, and they've made their own sacrifices to get where they are today."

"Ancient history. What's your point?"

"My point is that we're going to have to sacrifice their region. Like you said, you've seen Devon's models. Eastern China, Japan, India and Pakistan, Southeast Asia, Europe, most of North America can't be saved. Too many people depending on complex technology and sophisticated and delicate distribution systems. When some critical part of the system fails—and deprivation rears its ugly head—millions of human beings are going to turn on each other like rats trapped in a bucket."

"So where do you see any glimmer of hope?"

Renaud speared a kiwi. "Assuming the collapse can be managed, parts of central South America, Central America and rural Mexico. Some of the American and Canadian west. Central Asia. Sections of Australia. Places closer to subsistence economy and away from major urban areas. Africa, ironically, looks pretty good."

Renaud gestured with his fork. "Not that there won't be huge dislocations everywhere. None of this is going to be easy, let alone doable. And if we can't control the use of nuclear weapons, we'll lose it all to EMP or nuclear winter. In that scenario, the few survivors will be like neolithic farmers when it's all over."

"The rest of us know this."

"Damn it, Sonny, knowing is one thing. Accepting it? Allowing it to happen? That's something else."

"What specifically do you want me to do?"

"If there is anyone they'll all listen to, it's you. They fear and respect you. If we're going to save anything, I need your backing in the coming months. We've got to make a lot of hard and unpalatable decisions. Afterward, we're going to have to live with them. Watch them unfold as billions of human beings starve, murder each other, and die horribly. But if we can survive that, our children will have to be able to work together and have enough resources to rebuild from the wreckage."

Sonny studied him as the plates were cleared and wood-grilled fish placed on the table. "You and I, we've never really liked each other. You don't approve of me, of my methods or what I do. Yet here you are."

"Your father made a fortune building the tools of Hitler's war machine. In the end, he lost everything he cherished. But he had the chance to rebuild afterward. I want to give the same chance to my children, and Felicia's, and Inga's, and Katya's."

Sonny took a bite of the fish. Washing it down with a sip of wine, he said, "We're also faced with a generational change. The young people are taking over. They don't have the same global view that you and I do."

"Chantel does."

"You expect her to follow in your footsteps? She doesn't have your charisma, Renaud. You've always been the voice of reason. She's cold and calculating."

"I accept my responsibility in that regard. Her brother... Well, a father doesn't always see his children objectively. I should have acted earlier."

Sonny sighed wearily. "Outside of the noble sacrifice for the good of humanity...which I'm not sure I believe in given the men I've known, what's in it for me?"

"If the world's population is decimated to a handful of neolithic farmers, to whom do you sell bombs and missiles?"

Sonny chuckled and wiped his lips with a napkin. "Now, there, Renaud, is a good point. Assuming I do this for you, and only for you. How do you see this working?"

"You, me, and Devon. A triumvirate. Like in Rome."

"That didn't always work out so well. Ask Lepidus."

"We don't have an empire for the taking to incite our ambitions. There is no imperial chair to fill. Just the opposite. If we fail, Chantel and Val inherit irradiated ruins."

"So you will be the voice of reason, Devon the man with the hard facts, and I make sure the rest fall into line. And if they refuse?"

"We have to make it so they won't." Renaud finished his fish. "Devon, Chantel, and I have the beginnings of a plan. The Takanabi and Liu faction won't like it but..."

The bullet blasted through Renaud's chest, blowing bits of bone, blood, and lung tissue across the table and spattering Sonny's white shirt.

CHAPTER SIXTY

***

AT A QUARTER TO SIX, BRENDA INSPECTED LEON PLATNIKOV'S ROOM. HER STOMACH WAS growling, having not eaten the night before. Leon snored where he lay twisted in the rumpled covers. The pornographic artwork made a mockery of his naked body with its arm flung out.

Here lies the noblest of Russians, Brenda's internal voice mocked.

She and Chantel had rearranged the furniture, emptied a couple of wine bottles they'd found behind the bar, and left them on their sides on the floor. To her eyes, the place looked like it had hosted an orgy.

Chantel—dressed in her immaculate suit—checked herself in the mirror.

The bottle of Hennessy Timeless stood beside the bed, one of the three glasses still holding a finger of the world's most expensive cognac.

"Time," Chantel said as she ran fingers over her skirt.

Brenda reached into her purse, removing the aerosol hair spray.

"Think you'll need that?" Chantel asked.

"Felix is still outside the door. Or his replacement. If he tries to stop us, a whiff of this, and he'll be out like a light. Might have to drag him in and strip him. Leave him propped in a chair like he'd fallen asleep."

Brenda walked to the door, opening it to find not only Felix but a second man. He, too, had the appearance of an over-muscled thug.

Chantel said something in Russian, pointing at her watch.

Felix replied, holding a hand up for them to wait as he entered Platnikov's quarters. Brenda watched him survey the disheveled room, a grin spreading on his blocky face. Then he walked over to the bed, bent over Platnikov, and assured himself the man was breathing.

Only then did he return, give them a curt nod, and lead the way down the hallway. Several turns later, Brenda was relieved to find the front door before her. Their two overnight bags sat mockingly to the side. A servant bowed and opened the door to the winter darkness beyond.

Passing the threshold, Brenda almost sighed with relief. Three black limousines idled in the snowy drive, white streamers of exhaust rising from their tailpipes.

The doors opened on the extended Mercedes in the middle, two suited men stepping out.

At the last minute, Felix leaned forward, a lascivious grin on his face. In Brenda's ear, he whispered, "I watch tape later, *da?* Imagine what next time will be."

Brenda gave him a cold stare—slipped the aerosol into her pocket—then led Chantel through the bitter cold to the waiting limousine. She nodded at the man holding the door and followed Chantel as she slid onto the seat in the dark interior.

As the door slammed shut, someone thumped the roof, and the car began to move.

Only then did Brenda make out the two men on the rear-facing seat opposite her. Both wore FSB uniforms, high-peaked caps on their heads. Each held a curious looking pistol.

"Captain Pepper?" the elder asked derisively. "You will kindly remove your purse. Carefully set it on floor and use toe to push it over to me. If you make me shoot, the tranquilizer's effects will not kill you, but they are most unpleasant to endure."

"Who are you?" Chantel asked as Brenda complied.

"What you call FSB. You are both under arrest for attempting assassination of President Platnikov." He grinned in the dim light. "And maybe for prostitution as well."

Brenda tensed.

Chantel, however, calmly said, "I think, Colonel, that you are in for a very interesting time when my special friend, Leon, hears of this."

"Perhaps." The man shrugged. "Anything you would like to confess before is too late? For instance, who you really are? Who you work for?"

"Confess?" Chantel said coldly. "Just my coming pleasure when I'm informed that you've been transferred to some mining camp in Siberia to serve out your years as a private."

"Your remark is noted for evidence," he returned. "Oh, and Captain

Pepper, or whatever your name is. You might as well remove your hand from door handle. Is securely locked."

The rest of the ride was in silence. The blacked-out windows allowed no view of the outside world.

When the car finally slowed for the last time and came to a stop, the doors were opened from the outside.

Brenda stepped out into a lighted garage; no less than ten FSB officers were covering them with the odd-looking dart pistols.

Chantel emerged beside her, followed by the two officers.

With her heels clicking on the concrete, Katya Takanabi, her pale blonde hair gleaming under the light, walked up and crossed her arms. She wore a fitted gray wool suit, her expression severe.

"Katya," Chantel greeted. "To what do I owe the pleasure?"

Katya's icy blue eyes didn't reflect her gracious smile. "Colonel Antonov, here, has stumbled onto interesting information concerning your visit. Attempting to corrupt the president? I always knew you had morals like alley cat. But Leon? Seriously? You allow repulsive old man like him to crawl on top of you?"

Brenda's hand slipped into her pocket, fingers wrapping around the aerosol she'd tucked there.

Katya would be easy, but what about the rest of them?

"Colonel." Katya turned her eyes to the FSB officer saying something in Russian.

The colonel jerked to attention and saluted. His lieutenant handed over Brenda's purse, then snapped a salute.

As he and his lieutenant were climbing back into the limo, Katya walked up to Chantel and carefully removed the gold-and-crystal hair clip. Holding it before Chantel's eyes, she said, "See? I even know about device. I fear your stay in Russia will be much longer than you anticipated, my dear. And nowhere near as pleasant as you may have expected."

The car door slammed shut on the limo, as if to accent the finality of Katya's words.

"So, she's the traitor," Brenda growled under her breath. She fought the odd urge to laugh as she struggled with her outrage at the betrayal.

Katya turned hard eyes on Brenda. "Oh, we are so much more clever than that, Captain. Or whoever you are." She flashed a cruel smile. "You will see."

Chantel fixed deadly green eyes on Katya. "If you do this, it will be a declaration of internal war. You do understand the consequences, don't you?"

Katya only pointed at a dingy looking delivery truck in the back of the garage. Two men were opening the creaking doors in the van's rear. "To vehicle, please. And enjoy stroll. It may be last walk you ever take."

CHAPTER SIXTY-ONE

***

AS THE VAN ROCKED, JOLTED, AND BUMPED, BRENDA FOUGHT FOR BALANCE IN THE CARGO box. The "seat" consisted of a large crate strapped to the bed at the head of the box. If Katya had made a mistake, it was that they weren't bound up like cocoons with restraints.

"How are you doing, Chantel?"

"Numb." The woman shook her head. "Emotionally...empty. Like there's nothing left after last night. I just want to cry."

"Nothing wrong with crying." Brenda braced herself in the rocking truck, feeling along the featureless doors for a latch. The steel was so cold it numbed her fingers.

"After that night I swore I'd never cry again. I've kept that promise. Well, but for once...leave it to Val to ruin a good thing." Chantel shook her head as if to rid it of devils. "At least we've destroyed Leon."

"I don't suppose you have some trick homing device, and that even now Renaud is swooping down from the sky to rescue us?" Brenda shouted over the gear whine and poorly muffled exhaust.

"That was the hair clip I was wearing. Recorder, RFID transmitter. How'd she know?" Chantel looked shocked and dismayed, her arms braced, feet sliding on the steel deck. "My God. Katya, of all people? She's always been a vindictive bitch. Has a cruel streak and piss-poor sense of humor, but this? I mean, what does she have to gain?"

"Free rein? Platnikov's going to be out of the picture in a month or two. The entire Russian government is going to be in play. How's Georgi positioned? Maybe she's got him groomed as the next president?"

"Now that, Captain, is a distinct possibility. She won't waste Platnikov's demise. And if it isn't Georgi, it will be someone she has her talons sunk into."

"So...what's going to happen?" Brenda made her way back to the box and seated herself. Pulling the little aerosol hair spray from her pocket she studied the can in the faint light from the dim bulb overhead.

Chantel closed her eyes as if in defeat. "My best guess? We'll disappear without a trace. Katya will have already laid the groundwork so that Platnikov takes the blame. And maybe a couple of others she's been laying for. He's going to be losing his grip on reality in the next month anyway. Delusions, false memories, erratic behavior. It will appear to anyone asking questions like he was behind our disappearance."

"Wish I had my purse. I'd use that pen. The bitch killed Kelly and Janeesh."

Chantel gave her a knowing look. "I doubt you'll get the chance. She'll be far away if I know Katya. She's got plenty of willing thugs to do her work for her." Chantel seemed to nerve herself. "At the end of this ride expect gang rape, a beating, and if Katya's feeling merciful, a final shot to the head before we're thrown in a hole in the forest and covered up."

Brenda nodded, her jaw set. "When the truck stops, you be ready. I'll go first." She lifted the aerosol. "Sam said I had five discharges in this thing. I'll rush them, try to take out as many as I can. When I launch into them, I want you to make a break. Run like hell for the nearest cover. As soon as you're out of sight, pick a direction and go. No stopping. If there's a road, trail, anything with packed snow that won't leave tracks, take it."

"What about you?"

"I'll buy you as much time as I can."

"They'll kill you, Captain."

"They're going to kill us anyway. If I'm lucky, I'll piss them off enough that it will be quick."

"God, you mean that don't you?"

Brenda held Chantel's eyes as the truck lurched. "You just promise me. You live, damn it. If anyone's going to save a piece of this world when the shit hits the fan, it's you."

"I won't forget."

"See that you don't." Brenda shivered. "At least they could have some heat in this thing. It's the middle of the fucking Russian winter, for God's sake."

The brakes squealed as the truck slowed, the driver grinding gears. "You got the plan?"

Chantel nodded. "Not that I'll get far in this cold, and dressed like I am." She stared down at her feet. "These shoes aren't made for running."

"Just don't give up."

Brenda winced as the wheels slammed through a pothole and tossed them against the wall.

The truck slowed, voices calling in Russian.

"What did they say?"

Chantel said, "Sounded like guards challenging the truck."

An answer was called back.

"That was the driver. Said he was expected for a delivery."

"Some delivery."

The truck lurched ahead.

Tell me we're not in a fenced compound.

The truck proceeded at a slower pace, barely crawling in second gear. Then it made a quick turn, swaying to a stop.

"You ready?" Brenda asked as she stood and walked to the steel doors at the back.

Chantel nodded, her expression shadowed as she faced the door. "Brenda. Whatever happens...you have my gratitude."

"We all die sometime."

She fought the butterflies in her gut as the padlock was unlocked. Balancing on her toes, she flexed to loosen her muscles.

So, this is it.

God, she was running on pure adrenaline, every sense heightened to the stage that each flash of light and sound hurt.

The door banged and began to swing out...

CHAPTER SIXTY-TWO

* * *

ED'S DONUT SHOP IN DES MOINES HAD PEOPLE PACKED WALL-TO-WALL, MANY OF THEM elbowing the local camera crews and reporters as Tom Ortega propped his butt against a table and gestured with the chocolate donut in his right hand.

"It's not an easy sell," he told the crowd. "We've got some tough choices ahead of us. And I guess I'm not a very good candidate because I can't promise you the moon. Currently, the government eats up a quarter of this country's GDP. That means that your tax dollars go into some bureaucrat's pocket and retirement plan when it could go to Ed here to open two more donut shops and hire another twenty of your friends and neighbors."

"What about Social Security?" someone called from the back.

"It's broken. Bankrupt." Tom called back. "Yeah, my opponents can quote you studies and statistics, but you can manipulate data any way you want to if you've got enough clever guys running the calculators. I mean, we've all watched the news, right? CNN, FOX, NBC, they have a conservative quoting one set of facts, and a liberal on the other side of the table quoting another. Both of them 'the Truth with a capital T'. But you dig into the real data behind the shenanigans, and Social Security's running out of money. The government 'borrowed' against the principal, and now they can't pay it back. Unless, of course, they print more money and devalue the dollar, which in the end means you'll get the money promised you, but it will be worth half as much."

"What would you do to fix it?"

"You want the truth, or a fantastic lie?"

"Truth!" someone shouted.

"Here are the hard facts: We're going to have to make some adjustments in payout." He held up his hand. "Now, wait! Hear me out. If we do this smartly, free up folks like Ed so they can hire more people, build better businesses, we can *generate* more jobs. But that means cutting the Federal budget and rolling back two-thirds of the regulations that you all have to pay for. We don't need five paper shufflers for every health inspector out in the field."

"What about minimum wage?" another called.

"What about it?" Tom gestured with his donut. "People, think this through. It's not rocket science. Let's say that we raise the minimum wage to twenty dollars an hour. That raises Ed's payroll cost by fifty percent, so he raises the price of his donuts by fifty percent to cover it. The same with every business. Instead of ten bucks for donuts and coffee, you pay fifteen, right?"

"Right," a woman up front answered.

"And the Federal government raises the poverty level from forty-five thousand to fifty-three thousand. So, what's changed?"

"But the light bill, water, internet service...?"

Tom shrugged. "They have to pay for labor, too. It's a shell game. Now, on the other hand, if Ed can put his time into making better donuts, and build two more restaurants, he's going to need another twenty people to work for him. And if the hardware store is expanding, and the dress shop will pay more for employees, he's going to have to compete for labor. He can only do that by offering better wages to keep his employees."

"But that's inflation!" someone in the back called.

"Tom?" Ben Mackeson called, "We're out of time."

"I've got to go. But I want to thank you all for coming out today. Now, I want to leave you with something to think about: Fixing this country won't be easy. You're going to hear a lot of screaming about how fixing things is going to ruin everything. And yes, it's going to upset a bunch of apple carts full of government free-riders. But ask yourselves this: What could Des Moines do with a couple of billion extra dollars in its pocket to spend on building Des Moines, instead of paying thousands of Washington bureaucrats to fill out forms for other bureaucrats to read?"

On his way to the door, he ended with, "God Bless you all!"

Whistles and applause followed; the people spilled out behind him as he made his way to the bus.

Tam Bizhenov's people were already working the crowd, taking signatures, signing up volunteers, passing out bumper stickers and signs. Tom had met every caucus captain in the state. The rapidity and competence with which Mackeson's team had organized the entire campaign seemed like magic after Tom's Ohio senatorial run.

Tom made his way to his seat and dropped onto the cushions where he stared at his chocolate donut. Ben Mackeson settled into the seat opposite him, a curious smile on his face.

"What?" Tom took a bite from the donut.

"You, you're magical. They love you."

"Then why do I feel so tired?"

"Because you're telling it like it is. Social media is on fire. They're calling you 'Honest Tom'." Mackeson paused. "You know it's not going to be that easy when you're elected. You're going to hit a wall of special interests that will fight you every step of the way."

Tom took another bite of his donut, gesturing to the crowd as the bus pulled away. "It won't be me, Ben. It will be them. They don't know it yet, but I'll take the first step, and they'll be the ones insisting that it be carried through."

"And if you're wrong? If the masses revolt when the cuts come?"

"Then the country is lost, and any kind of future with it."

CHAPTER SIXTY-THREE

* * *

AS THE VAN DOOR SWUNG OPEN, BRENDA DIDN'T HESITATE. SHE LAUNCHED HERSELF.
Rammed a shoulder into the panel. Knocked it wide. Then she was
on the ground, catching her balance. Hitting the door felt like she had
knocked one man to the pavement. Two others stood before her.

She barely had time to register the fact that she was at an airfield,
fuel-tank trucks to either side, cloudy sky overhead. On the snow-
packed tarmac, she planted a foot, charging the closest man. Clad in
coveralls, he threw his hands up, as if to stop her. She feinted, jabbing
the aerosol forward in a fencer's thrust. When she thumbed the button,
the can hissed, discharging its contents as Jaime had advertised.

Not waiting to see the effect, she ducked and twisted, yelling,
"Chantel! Run!"

As her first target screamed and clamped hands to his face, she
slipped on the snow, staggered, and turned her attention to the last
man standing. She'd barely leaped at him when her feet went out
from under her.

Tucking as she hit the frozen ground, she rolled, coming up on
one knee. Even as she propelled herself to her feet and leaped, she
recognized Val, his face wide with shock.

The man's reflexes were quick. He managed to catch her arm, his
grasp closing like iron.

At the last instant, Brenda hesitated, her thumb on the spray button.
Panting, she said, "This better be good."

Val's eyes were crossed, staring at the spray a hand's length from
his nose. Then a slow smile crossed his lips.

"Stand down, Captain."

"Why?"

"You're safe. You're free. And I'd appreciate it if you'd point that thing somewhere else and let me explain."

Brenda tilted her head, eyes narrowed. "How about I put you out now, and we do explanations later?"

"You could, but someone might come looking for you before we get you and Chantel quietly aboard Big Bird and get the hell out of here."

Reluctantly, Brenda withdrew her hand, heart still pounding. The adrenaline of combat surged in her veins.

Glancing to the side, she noticed the man she'd sprayed was on the ground moaning. The one she'd knocked over was huddled into a ball, grabbing his nuts and drawing fast breaths. Chantel stood at the corner of the truck, half crouched for a fast dash, eyes wide as she glanced from Val's face to the man on the ground.

"What did you do to him?" Val asked.

Voice shakey, Chantel said, "For all I knew, Katya might have really double-crossed us. He was down so I hit the ground and kicked him in the balls with everything I had."

Val shook his head as he took in the mayhem. From where they were folded atop a crate, he handed them both coveralls and caps. "Put these on. It's a short walk to Big Bird. Stuff your hair up under your hats so you're not *too* obvious. Though Katya's going to be in a ring-tailed snit over what you've done to some of her best agents."

"The bitch had us arrested." Brenda followed Chantel's lead, un-zipping the coveralls and tugging them up over her legs, heedless of what it did to her skirt.

"Layers within layers," Val told her. "Katya always plays a deep game."

Chantel zipped up her oversized outer gear, shivering from the cold. Brenda had never seen her in anything but the chicest of wear. The exotic Italian shoes poking out the bottom of the pants, however, were a dead giveaway.

"It's Russia," Brenda murmured as she stuffed her hair under a workman's cap. "Maybe nobody will notice."

"What?" Chantel asked.

"Thought you were supposed to be running?"

"I wasn't leaving you behind."

"Kind of defeats the purpose of self-sacrifice, don't you think?"

But Chantel was smiling, as if secretly pleased with herself.

"Let's go," Val called, shifting in his coat. "We're out of sight of the surveillance cameras here. And Devon's people will alter the other feeds."

"What about these guys?" Brenda indicated the two men in the snow.

"They'll deal." Val's lips thinned. "Call it penance for stupidity."

Once clear of the truck, Brenda could see Big Bird no more than two hundred yards away. Thin patches of snow remained where the plows had skimmed the surface.

It was all she could do to keep from glancing around; she forced herself into a steady and unconcerned walk as she followed Val.

The cold felt brutal, even through the coveralls. Thinking about it, Chantel would never have made it, not in cold like this, dressed as she was. She might have lasted fifteen minutes without some sort of shelter.

At the stairs, Val motioned them ahead. Chantel went first, arriving as the cabin door swung open. Brenda followed her in, to find two women dressed similarly. They said nothing, but as soon as Brenda passed inside, both women stepped out the door, heading down the steps. Each carried a plastic sack of something that might have been garbage.

"Two in, two out," Chantel nodded. "Someone's thinking."

Moments later, Val popped through the cabin door, swinging it shut behind him. His blue eyes were twinkling in contrast to his cold-ruddy skin. "Glad that's finished."

Chantel was already peeling out of her overalls, shaking her red hair free from the cap. "You want to explain why we were arrested and taken to Katya? If you were going to deviate from the plan, I should have been briefed. I've had the shit scared out of me."

Val took the coveralls as Brenda shucked out of them, hardly caring that his attention was on her bare legs where her skirt had been bunched up.

Val handed the coveralls to one of the flight attendants. "How about something warm to drink?"

"And eat," Brenda amended, her empty stomach gurgling loud enough to cause Val's eyebrow to arch.

"And eat," he amended.

Sprawled in the over-cushioned seats in the rear, Brenda could see the fire behind Chantel's eyes. Val settled across from them, handing Chantel a flash drive.

"This is it?" She studied the small rectangle.

"The only copy of your activities last night." Val leaned back. "Yours to do with as you wish."

"The only copy?" Brenda asked suspiciously.

Val met her hard glare and gestured innocence. "If there were another, say in my personal possession, and Chantel found out? I couldn't take the chance that my bank accounts wouldn't suddenly vanish. One doesn't cross Chantel."

"Or me, if you value the sanctity of your balls."

"Perhaps, Brenda. Though one of Katya's agents out there might argue with you." He leaned forward. "You were both magnificent. Platnikov doesn't suspect a thing."

"Then why the phony arrest?" Chantel snapped.

"Katya thought it prudent. The two FSB officers who picked you up? They've been problems in the past. Very suspicious of Platnikov and his motives. Let's call it an old score to be settled. There will be questions when Platnikov begins to fail. Certain individuals and factions will begin jockeying for power. Steps have been taken to cast doubt on the identities of the women who visited Platnikov. Hints given that they might not have been Chantel Simond and her bodyguard."

"But they know Big Bird landed here, that we were picked up and taken to the dacha," Chantel countered.

"They know that a 737 landed," Val agreed. "But not whose. The flight records are being adjusted accordingly. And who is going to believe that Chantel Simond, the aloof manager of the world's highest finance, would stoop to screwing Leon Platnikov in a wild orgy, especially when she's reportedly taking a meeting in the Cayman Islands at the same time?"

"And meanwhile, Katya has witnesses that the two prostitutes were arrested by FSB." Brenda nodded. "Officers who will swear the women were delivered to Katya."

"Who in turn interrogated them, determined they were prostitutes picked for their resemblance to Chantel Simond and her bodyguard, and then disposed of." Val laced his fingers together as a tray of steaming chicken and vegetables was placed before Brenda.

Brenda took a fork and pitched in.

Chantel added, "Let me guess. Katya's going to use this to remove several enemies in the same fell swoop?"

"Waste not, want not. By next week, she's going to have several of her biggest opponents on the mat. Two of the most troublesome oligarchs in Russian investments—"

"Simonov and Vashenko," Brenda guessed.

"Good for you, Captain."

"And the same for Platnikov's cronies in the banking and aerospace industries?" Chantel mused.

"Exactly," Val agreed. "Katya has Chantel's recorder. It will come as a bombshell that Platnikov would sell his old comrades out over a sexy woman." He paused. "You know, of course, that Platnikov had no intention of keeping his word."

"Another reason for having us arrested?"

"Katya knew that given the right bait the FSB would deliver you straight to her." Val shrugged. "Had you relied on Platnikov for transportation, you might have been delivered to someplace less salubrious. One of Platnikov's secret rooms in the Kremlin where he could call upon you when the moment seized him, to use as he would. He actually discussed it in several conversations we recorded."

Chantel's disgust was plain. "I would have liked to have known that in advance."

"Better for your performance that you didn't, Fox."

Brenda sighed, leaning back wearily. "God, you people run the damndest operations."

Ricard, who'd been remaining discreetly busy in the office, now shot to his feet. His eyes on the screen before him, he cried, "Dear God, no!"

Chantel turned. "What's happened?"

Ricard's expression seemed to fracture. "It's your father, Chantel. He's been shot!"

CHAPTER SIXTY-FOUR

***

RICARD AND THE REST OF CHANTEL'S STAFF WORKED IN SOMBER SILENCE, OCCASIONALLY glancing forward where Chantel sat in one of the plush seats, her head bowed. Her sightless eyes were fixed on the drawn window shade, images floating in her memory.

Her father's last words repeated in her head: *"Save me an evening when you get back. We need to talk."*

There would be no evening.

Her father was dead. Shot. Killed by a sniper's bullet.

And I know whose.

She swallowed against the painful knot under her tongue. The swelling grief in her chest was suffocating. She kept seeing his green eyes, filled with love and pride. How his rarely seen smile was usually for her. The tones of his voice echoed in her soul.

I loved you, Dad.

But she'd never told him. There were so many things unsaid. If only she could go back, explain how she felt, how she had loved and admired him. How important he had been.

I built that barrier.

"I'm so sorry."

Memories of that terrible night swam up from her nightmares. His face had twisted with revulsion and horror, as if he had borne the full responsibility.

Not your fault, Dad.

She watched his face change from incredulous disbelief to pain as she shoved her pants down to show him the blood staining the inside of her thighs, pulled up her shirt to expose the bruises and bite marks.

How her father had stormed off, leaving her. Alone. Hurting. Vulnerable.

She'd been crying when her raging brother had found her.

"You told! You fucking told!"

Her stomach convulsed at the memory. The slashing horror... morphing into the black phantom...

She remembered how the next day, Renauld's eyes had glittered, wounded and desperate as he'd stood over her hospital bed. Tears had streaked his eyes as he'd confessed, *"He's dead, Chantel. I killed him myself. I'm so very sorry."*

"Some things are just beyond us, Dad," she whispered to herself, struggling to keep the tears from welling behind her eyes.

And then Robert had found Mom's body.

"Not your fault either, Dad. She did what she did. Made her choice."

Deep down inside, the lonely little girl that she'd never outgrown threw her head back and shrieked in anguish and grief.

The tears came, hot and unbidden, to trickle down her cheeks. She had to find herself, take control. Dad would have wanted that.

Come on, Chantel. Think! What does this mean?

CHAPTER SIXTY-FIVE

***

BRENDA SAT ACROSS FROM WHERE VAL HAD ENSCONCED HIMSELF IN THE OFFICE CHAIR; A headset allowed him to address the monitor as he communicated with his father in Cuba.

She only caught snippets of the conversation, having taken a seat just far enough from Chantel to allow the woman her privacy. Each deeply muffled sniff, the furtive movements to wipe away tears, was like a stab to the heart.

No one was going to get close enough to witness Chantel's pain or see her vulnerable. Not while Brenda stood guard.

It had happened in Cuba, at Sonny's estate. A sniper's bullet out of nowhere. Renaud had been eating lunch with Sonny. Mitch had had no warning until he heard the supersonic crack of the bullet and its popping impact as it blew Renaud's body apart. The mushroomed slug had grazed Sonny's arm.

Reconstructing the shot angle, Sonny's security personnel had finally located an abandoned shack nearly a mile away. One of Sonny's men tripped a wire as they were trailing the assassins. The trailside mine killed two men.

By the time subsequent teams had cleared the trail of two other such devices, they descended to the shore and found nothing.

Taylor?

Had to be.

Brenda studied what she could see of Chantel's desolate profile.

The cold rage built. Renaud Simond had been one of the most impressive men she'd ever met. She recalled every conversation she'd had with him. Despite his position and power, he'd been thoughtful and poised. His preoccupation with questions of morality? Talking the talk was one thing; Renaud had struggled to live it.

The Foundation had just lost its ablest leader at the opening of its greatest trial. Surely that wasn't coincidental.

Val appeared at the side of her seat and knelt down. He shot a worried gaze at Chantel. "I just talked to Dad. Regal's taken possession of the body. The entire Foundation is up in arms. The usual cries of outrage and demands that the assassin pay."

"Does your father have any idea who sanctioned the hit?"

"Not yet. But he will." Val's eyes had turned glacial. "I've never seen him this livid. He and Renaud have had a tense relationship. But Dad always respected him. Really respected him. Worse, the man was his guest, on his turf. Sitting at his table, eating his food. He's outraged. And then there's the matter about being nicked by the bullet."

"Taylor?"

"Unknown. But I can promise you this: whoever it was, we're going to turn earth and sky upside down until we find him."

"Taylor's just the tool, and like a good shovel or rake, can easily be discarded and another procured. Your real objective is the person who hired him...and what it means for The Foundation."

"Precisely," Chantel said. She kept her face partially averted so they couldn't see her puffy eyes. "Brenda? Could you tell Ricard that there's no change of plans. Have him contact Taki's people. We're not canceling the meeting. And I definitely want Chicago there."

Brenda glanced uncertainly at Val. "Yes, ma'am."

Val asked, "What about Regal and Robert? They're headed to the island to meet your father's casket."

"Tell them I'll be there when I'm able. If they protest, remind them that I'm my father's daughter. I'll grieve when I can fit it into my schedule."

"Okay, Fox, but I don't think—"

"Val, when we land at Narita, outside Tokyo, I need you to carry a message to your father. Can you do that for me?"

Brenda could see indecision in Val's face as he said, "You sure you don't want me there to back you up with Taki and Chicago?"

"If I can't deal with them on my own, it's better to learn that now. No, I need you to deliver a message to Sonny. It's important,

Val. I'll have Ricard arrange a charter. You'll be on it the moment we land."

"Anything you need, Fox."

As Brenda walked back to where Ricard's team sat at their computers in the rear, she wondered, *The woman's father was just murdered. And we're still going to Japan?*

CHAPTER SIXTY-SIX

***

WHAT THE HELL IS CHANTEL DOING? THE QUESTION HAUNTED POUL HAMMOND AS INDEX AFTER index displayed global stock markets. The data, fresh from Rusty Patton at StatNco, detailed Chantel's latest trades. The Foundation's investment in Indonesia and Malaysia had dropped by fifteen percent in the last week.

In the wake of Renaud's death, he'd expected her to be distracted. Instead, the divestiture had accelerated.

When he turned to Southeast Asia, the statistics indicated a similar pattern. Chantel was moving money out of high-tech electronics, many of them profitable firms. He noticed the same trend in mining and heavy manufacturing, most of them Liu and Takanabi holdings.

Leaning back in his chair, he contemplated at the monitors lining his New York office wall. The major stock indexes in those regions showed that tech and industry had only dropped by three percent. Market analysts had labeled the movement as a "hiccup" and listed the stocks as "buys". For the short term, no one was panicking, but how long could Chantel taper their holdings without inciting a crash?

And more to the point, how was David Takanabi taking this? Asian high-tech and electronics were his bailiwick, and he wasn't known for his placid demeanor when someone was undercutting his babies. Nor was Liu going to react favorably at the decline in his industrials.

Hammond leaned back, thoughtful eyes on the New York skyline beyond his windows. His concentration was broken when his secretary's voice on the intercom announced Robert Simond's arrival.

"Send him in."

Moments later, Robert stepped through the door, his red-blond locks flowing over the collar of his gray silk suit. "She's done it."

"I know. I've just been looking at the stats. Southeast Asia is her first victim. That's going to set off the Takanabis and the Lius. It's going to be nasty. Each family is going to be fighting to keep its share of the pie."

Robert stopped short, left palm cradling his right fist. "Clever of her. She moved on Asia first. Her timing is impeccable."

"You really don't look the part of a grieving son. Are you even going home?"

"No one lives forever, Poul." He smiled humorlessly. "And Dad had to go sometime, so I've planned accordingly." He cocked his head. "I really thought they'd take him out with more subtlety, like poison or some nerve agent."

"He was your father."

"He was, wasn't he?" He paused for effect, then shrugged. "Here's the other big news: Chantel got to Platnikov. She's infected him with one of Regal's viruses. The guy's going to be a babbling idiot within a couple of months and dead by the end of February. Scratch Russian aggression in the Baltics from your late-night list of things to worry about."

Poul reached for his gold pen, twiddling it between his fingers. "That means Katya and Georgi—"

"Are cleaning house. Chantel just took out their biggest opposition. My dear sister has single-handedly stopped the Gorky Plan dead in its tracks. As soon as Platnikov's impairment is obvious, there's going to be a scramble to find a successor. Katya and Georgi are already laying the groundwork to come out on top."

"Chantel *infected* him? How?"

"With her bottle of virus-laced cognac in hand, the ice queen led him straight to his bedroom. From there...well, use your imagination."

"I'm trying, believe me. A Siberian winter has more charm than your sister. That must have been some kind of seduction."

"Platnikov wasn't interested in her personality. What matters is that Russia's neutralized for the moment. Turn your whiz kids loose. I want my portfolio adjusted accordingly and assets moved before the market catches up."

"I'll have them on it immediately." Hammond made a note on his pad. "With your father out of the picture, what happens with The

Foundation? Who picks up the mantle of leadership?"

Robert sighed as he walked over to stand in front of Hammond's desk. "Big sister's done what we feared she'd do. She's repositioned herself. We were afraid of a leader rising. Chantel is giving it her best shot."

"I see what you mean. She's handed Russia to Katya, and for whatever reason, Val seems to have taken the Simond side. Does that mean that Sonny's backing Chantel, too?"

"Sonny is on Sonny's side and no one else's. Nor do I know where the Hestons stand in this. But I can tell you that Chantel's thought it all through, and she's got a plan. As we speak, she's on the way to Tokyo. I just heard. Chicago's flying in from Beijing, and Taki's going to meet them both on his private island. Chantel knows that whatever she's going to do, it's going to be at the Takanabis and the Lius' expense. So, in a couple of hours, hot off her Russian triumph and weeping tears over Dad's foul murder, she's going to be sitting across the table from the two of them. My bet is that they're not going to like what they're going to hear."

"What if she sways them?"

"Then my darling sister clamps a headlock on The Foundation. It's always been a consortium that sought consensus. From here on out, she'll be calling the shots."

"How does Val fit into all this?"

"Now that, my friend, is always an unknown. Nor do we count the Takanabis out. David and Katya's marriage is in name only. While she may be able to influence David—Georgi is his son after all—he's going to take the brunt of this."

"Chantel didn't give you as much as a hint? Your father didn't let something slip last time you saw him?"

"My sister hasn't shared a secret with me since she was six. And Dad and I had a cooling of our relationship years ago. Hence my grief-filled wailing and gnashing of the teeth. But if Chantel's going to have trouble, it will be with David and old man Liu."

"Which might be why Chantel's meeting with Taki? He's the creative one with an instinct for developing technology and turning it into products. David's forte is manufacturing the stuff. If she's going to sell anyone, starting with Taki makes sense. He understands long-term ramifications. The same with Chicago. If Chantel can convince her, she can probably bring old man Liu along."

Robert nodded and walked to the window, eyes on the city beyond. "If Chantel can convince Taki and Chicago, she's got a chance, because whatever Chantel's planning it will have an impact on China. More than half of David's manufacturing is based there. His companies employ millions, building everything from automobiles to refrigerators, not to mention electronics."

"And if they don't buy it?"

Robert shoved his hands into his pockets. "We might see a whole slew of assassins lining up to take Chantel out."

CHAPTER SIXTY-SEVEN

***

CHANTEL—WITH BRENDA CLOSE AT HER HEEL—LED THE WAY INTO A SPACIOUS CONFERENCE room. Polished hardwood covered the floors. Huge windows on one side gave a breathtaking view of the surf crashing on the island's black volcanic rocks. A stylish conference table, surrounded by sixteen plush chairs, occupied the middle of the room. Instead of a boardroom it looked more like a futuristic set on a James Bond movie.

Their escort consisted of a serious-faced Japanese man of about fifty; he bowed and left on silent feet, closing the door behind him. Chantel stopped in the center, amused as Brenda took in the room with its wooden walls and white panels. A huge painting of a tree with improbable red birds dominated the wall beyond the foot of the table.

Moments later, the door in the rear slid aside to admit a dark-suited Taki Takanabi and Chicago Liu, who sported a form-fitting red silk dress.

Let the games begin. Chantel forced a steely smile onto her hard lips.

"Chantel!" Taki cried, walking over to take her hand. "I know you have received my messages, but let me say in person how shocked and dismayed I am. I share your sorrow. Whatever you need, you know that you need only ask."

Chantel searched his dark eyes, looking for any trace of gloating success, and found none. She'd considered marrying him once upon a time. Before that night. Now she recognized only a suppressed rage beneath his smooth face.

Chicago walked up, placing her arms around Chantel. "I am so sorry. We grieve with you. When the people behind this are found..."

Chantel pushed back, a granite-like hardness around her heart. "Thank you both. You have heard about Platnikov?"

Chicago, still off-balance, said, "To tackle Platnikov in his own dacha? And at such personal cost? An animal like him? I would not have had such courage."

Taki seemed to choose his words. "If reports from Russia are true, you have just done us a great service. Everyone is impressed. My people have been reviewing Devon's analysis of the ramifications. Within a month, tensions should ease in Europe and America. We should see a ten percent increase in sales where we expected a twenty-five percent drop." He shook his head. "But given your father's—"

"My father's death isn't at issue." Chantel gave them a cool smile. "I've been working with Devon, and circumstances have forced me to reallocate Foundation assets which will affect your operations. Given the gravity of my actions, I thought I should bring you up to date in person."

The cold rage intensified behind Taki Takanabi's eyes. Chicago, however, kept her expression neutral.

"Come," Taki gestured. "Take a seat. Chicago and I have already reviewed the data. To say that we were discouraged? That would be an understatement. Out of respect for your loss, we have agreed to temper our reaction."

Chantel slipped into a seat, lacing her fingers as she placed her arms on the table. Brenda took a position to her right. Her instructions were to look stoic and dangerous. Brenda fell into an "at ease" stance, jaw clamped, eye hard.

After Chicago had seated herself at Taki's elbow, she glanced suggestively at Brenda, and then said, "Perhaps, given the sensitive nature of the topic, we should speak in private."

"Captain Pepper has my full confidence." Chantel fixed on Taki. "Fallon taught me that you've always had a sixth sense about what some crazy engineer was designing in a lab somewhere, and how it could be adapted to the commercial market. In spite of occasional reservations, Simond International has unstintingly supported your projects from smartphones to tablets, and now teenagers are wearing headsets that interface with the human brain. Together, we've changed the world."

Taki traced a finger along the table. "Which leads me to wonder why you're shorting some of my most productive companies. My father is more than a little concerned."

"As am I," Chicago agreed. "What you're doing—"

"Is preparing for the inevitable," Chantel interrupted. She gestured at the painting of the tree with its long-beaked and improbably
feathered birds. "If you'd oblige, I'd like to bring Devon in on this."

"Screen one, please," Taki said, and turned his attention to the
painting.

The image faded into swirling colors that reformed into Devon
Czykowski's face. The man's thinning hair looked mussed, and he
stared at them through tired brown eyes.

"Devon," Chantel greeted, "I'm about to explain our actions in
Southeast Asia. Would you like to begin?"

Devon summoned a thin-lipped smile. "Very well, I'll give it
to you cold: Eastern and Southern Asia are unsustainable. There is
no other way to say this: There are too many people, and too few
resources. Renaud, Chantel, and I have been working on various
models, trying to anticipate what we can save and what we must
abandon. No matter how we run the permutations, when you figure
in population density, infrastructure, food production and carrying
capacity, energy, and most of all, redistribution of resources, we
can't see a way to soften the blow."

"I don't understand," Chicago snapped.

Devon repeated, "Too many people. The first concern is the electrical grid, and the second is the transportation and distribution of
commodities. Even if rural areas could grow enough food, without
sufficient fuel, there is no way to transport it. As basic requirements
like water, food, and energy grow short, deprivation increases. If the
system is disrupted in any way, distribution stops completely. The
moment people start turning on their neighbors, it's going to be like
nuclear fission. It will begin in the urban areas with rioting, looting,
and mass violence. Since we're talking about billions, once unleashed,
the turmoil will progress exponentially."

"But what does that have to do with electronics?" Taki asked.

Devon gave him a sympathetic look. "When the electricity goes
off, electronics become useless. People will be killing their neighbors
for food, not buying the latest smartphone or 6K interactive tv." He
paused. "Taki, it is inevitable. The social reaction to shortages will

end up disrupting the electrical grid."

Chicago demanded, "How?"

"Buildings will be looted and burned, which will damage the electrical infrastructure. Even if electrical workers aren't involved in the riots, who would risk his neck on the streets trying to repair severed power lines and transformers? Large portions of the population will attempt to flee the cities. The attendant demographic dislocations will further destabilize the situation as refugees seek food and shelter. The disruption will reach the electricity-generating facilities. Those closest to urban areas will be affected first. Workers will not be able to leave their homes, needing instead to protect their families and possessions. Roads will be blockaded as hungry masses seek to procure transportation and to seize anything valuable being transported by trucks. Even if the electricity-generating plants are protected by some miracle, eventually the spare parts to maintain them will be unavailable."

He paused. "Nor have we mentioned atmospheric detonation of a nuclear device which will destroy the power grid and its dependent electronic components immediately through an electromagnetic pulse."

Chantel added, "The combined damage to the water infrastructure during rioting, coupled with the loss of power, means the water system will fail. When that happens, people will be drinking from any source they can find, most of which will be polluted. Dysentery, cholera, and other diseases will sweep the survivors, adding to the fear and discord. You both know this. You've read the studies and seen the same models we have."

Beside her, Brenda took a deep breath. She was no doubt trying to visualize a city like Shanghai, its teeming millions rioting in the streets, autos burning and blocking thoroughfares, buildings looted and on fire.

Chicago said, "To know is one thing. To be faced with reality? That is another. But, Devon, why start with Asia?"

"It has two-thirds of the world's population in the densest concentrations. Currently fifty-six percent of the regional biomass goes to human consumption."

Devon fixed his weary eyes on the room's occupants. "China and India are at the top of our list, but after that, any country with a highly urbanized population that depends on extensive distribution networks will follow the same pattern. The more developed the country, the higher the population density, the greater the impact. We see the same for most of Europe, the United States...anywhere in the vicinity of a large urban center."

Brenda tensed, and Chantel heard the faint grinding of her teeth.

Yes, Captain. That's what's coming.

Chantel said, "Our immediate concern is to put together an operational plan. Taki, you're the innovative brain when it comes to electronics. Could you motivate your people to develop a secure data storage system someplace remote, perhaps a defensible island with an EMP-shielded storage facility? It should be designed to download as much scientific, technical, and medical information as possible. I'm willing to provide as much capital as needed to begin the project."

Taki's face reflected suspicion. "I would hope that you're not just throwing us a bone to defuse our anger. You acted without our consent. Father is furious."

"It was not your decision to make, Chantel," Chicago added. "The Foundation should have been briefed. A course of action agreed upon. We have started to implement our own plans, and you just cut the legs out from beneath us."

"I didn't have time," Chantel replied frostily. "My concern now is the development of an electronic data repository. We may have five years, or four, or even three. Had Platnikov not been eliminated, it might have only been six months. I dealt with Platnikov, and I'll attempt to deal with any other threats that develop."

"*You* are *not* The Foundation!" Chicago snapped.

"No, I'm not." Time to throw down the gauntlet. "Essentially, your perspective is Chinese. Devon and I have to deal with *global* realities. And Devon and I concurred that immediate action had to be taken. I came to you to explain our actions. To find out if Taki can design, and you can manufacture, the first of the repositories."

"The first?" Taki asked. "There will be others?"

From the monitor, Devon asked, "Do you want to put all of our eggs in one basket?"

Chicago turned her cold stare on Devon. "I take it that you agree with Chantel's actions?"

Devon nodded, his expression weary. "By taking down Platnikov, Chantel has bought us time. I ran the models for her. I trust her instincts. If you can build such a facility, it will be of immeasurable value after the collapse."

Taki grudgingly said, "If it's technologically possible, I know the people to design it."

Devon added, "It will need to be both self-sustainable—capable of producing its own food and power—and defensible from air and sea. Sonny can provide the necessary armaments if you have trouble with your militaries."

Taki—with a hard glare in Chantel's direction—said, "We've produced a prototype quantum qubit computer that, if perfected, could store that kind of information. With financing, I can obtain the talent needed to design the project."

Chicago added, "With the proper incentives and bribes, I can allocate the manufacturing facilities and most of the resources necessary." She narrowed her stare. "Though it will displease some in our military. Not to mention my husband."

"Or my father," Taki chimed in. "He has his own ideas about how to deal with the future. And that being the case, Chantel, we will *consider* your request. Do not think that we are on board. In addition, our response to your divestiture of our assets is still to be determined."

In as calm a voice as she could manage, she almost whispered, "I'm not here for a fight. I *need* your cooperation."

Devon told them. "I can forward the hard data if that would help convince you and your people."

"*I* need the data, Devon." Chicago's gaze never wavered from Chantel's. "Because if Chantel's playing some game of her own, there *will* be consequences. Even if it means tearing The Foundation apart and going to war."

CHAPTER SIXTY-EIGHT

***

BRENDA STARED OUT AT THE DARK PACIFIC AS BIG BIRD WINGED ITS WAY EASTWARD. SHE'D slept, eaten, and now tried to still ten thousand conflicting thoughts.

Rising, she stretched, and walked forward in the dark airplane past where Ricard and two of Chantel's staff slept in their reclined seats. At the desk in the office section Chantel sat over a computer, her face illuminated by the glow.

Brenda took a seat opposite and studied the woman. Chantel looked haggard, and there were dark circles under her eyes. Her normally composed features now pinched with worry as she tapped the desktop with a long fingernail; her other hand kept pulling at her hair.

"Can I get you something?" Brenda asked. "Coffee?"

Chantel dropped her head into her hands and sighed. "I'm tired. Not thinking straight." After a pause she raised her head, bloodshot eyes on Brenda's. "How did you read Taki and Chicago's reactions?"

"Pissed and dangerous. Is there a reason you didn't give them a heads up before you moved?"

"One either deals from a position of strength, or one doesn't deal. Not with either the Lius or the Takanabis. And coming in the wake of Dad's murder, I can capitalize on some sympathy. If I'd consulted with them first, they would have turned me down flat. Told me to start somewhere else. Probably Europe or the US, which they consider weak and expendable. But the fat is now crackling in the fire, as you Americans say, and the course set. They'll resent it, and I expect a few stinging rebukes along the way to remind me that they're still in the game, but my expectation is that they'll accept the inevitable."

"Sounds like a dangerous gamble."

"Risks have to be taken." Chantel studied Brenda. "Something else on your mind, Captain?"

"Why did you want me in that room?"

"Knowing what you now do, do you want out, Brenda?"

"There is no way out." She met the woman's cold stare.

"How does that make you feel? Angry? Scared?"

"Both."

Chantel smiled thinly. "I haven't forgotten that were it not for you, I wouldn't be sitting here. So, I'll be honest: I wanted you in that room hearing what you heard, because we're going to write off both American coasts."

"Is there anything you could save?"

"Depending on how the collapse unfolds—and if we get the time— parts of the Midwest and Rocky Mountain region will be self-sustainable. The coasts will not. We need places with energy, agriculture, and low population. Land we can control. The joker in the deck is if someone uses atmospheric nukes and EMP takes out the electrical grids. Then all bets are off. Devon's people will be monitoring for that as long as they can to give us a preemptive ability."

"Just how are you planning to do this?"

"That depends on if we can get Tom Ortega elected president. My take so far is that he's got enough sense that when the inevitable is laid out, he'll do his best to save as much of America as he can."

"He's *your* man?"

"I think that he's a lot like you, Captain. He'll be willing to save something if the alternative is losing everything."

"That's the dirty truth underlying this whole mess, isn't it?"

Chantel nodded; the depth of her fatigue again visible. "Something is always better than nothing. I just hope... Well, I've always had Dad. Like this great pillar of strength to lean on."

"Devon's on your side."

"For the moment. He only runs the data. Someone has to take the helm."

"You?"

Brenda watched Chantel's shoulders sag under the weight. "In the end, it's always me. No one else will make the hard choices."

Brenda thought back to Maluf, to the dead children. "I know what it is like to deal with the dead when they rise up in your dreams at night. I could stand it as long as I had Bill Solace to take some of the burden."

Chantel looked as if she were trying to peer down into Brenda's soul. "It won't be innocent villages and a couple dozen kids, Brenda. We're talking about the lives of billions. When the system breaks, it's going to be with inconceivable brutality and bestial violence."

"Maybe it was hundreds instead of billions, but it's still staring into the eyes of the dead."

"Would you sell your soul to the devil to stop it?"

Brenda took a deep breath. "I don't walk away from the dirty work."

"Then we are both cursed, Captain."

Brenda gathered herself to leave, but Chantel said, "About the scars. I appreciate that you haven't asked. I had another brother, Heinrich. Older. He was as brilliant as he was dark and tormented. A pathological narcissist with a sadistic twist. He'd read about the Egyptian pharaohs and how they married their sisters. If my father ever had a blind eye, it was for Heinrich."

"What happened?"

"I'd just turned seventeen. Heinrich was drunk. Locked me in a room. When I fought it just made him more brutal. When he finally passed out, I got the key. Even when I showed Dad the proof, he told me it wasn't Heinrich. Heinrich, of course, denied it. Dad took his word, locked me in my room until I'd confess who the rapist really was."

Chantel's gaze went dull. "Heinrich was in the process of cutting me to pieces, yelling, 'You told! You told!' when Dad burst in. I didn't see how it ended. I passed out from blood loss...woke up in hospital. I could have had the scars fixed. But I keep them as a reminder."

Brenda felt a shiver run down her spine. "What happened to Heinrich?"

"Father killed him. He considered it a lesson in taking personal responsibility."

For a long time, they just stared at one another.

"I don't know how you keep it together."

For the first time a flicker of desperation crossed Chantel's eyes. "Because, I don't have the luxury of failure. But Brenda, know this: I couldn't have come this far... Back in the dacha. When I saw that painting, knew that Platnikov... That bump and nudge saved my life.

And again, on the bed when I really fixed on his penis. The flash-backs..." She seemed to realize what she was saying, and snapped, "Well, never mind."

"Get some rest, Chantel. You're no good to anyone if your brain's full of cobwebs."

Brenda stood and walked back to her seat with a feeling of inevitability. No doubt Chantel had played her masterfully, but then, from the moment she'd boarded that plane to Simond Island there'd been no way out.

CHAPTER SIXTY-NINE

★★★

HAROLD "LEATHER GUTS" PEPPER MADE A FACE AS HE ROSE FROM HIS RECLINER. HE LOVED that chair. It had been a gift from Brenda and Mark when he had retired and moved back to the farm. The joke had been that he'd finally have someplace to take it easy.

On the TV across the living room, the morning news seemed anything but reassuring. NATO was mobilizing forces to repel a suspected Russian advance on the Baltics and Poland. Bloody war continued to rage between Sunnis and Shias in what was left of the Middle East. The mess in the Persian Gulf seemed endless, and gasoline prices were expected to be seven dollars a gallon by summer. A new and extremely lethal mutation of COVID had just been discovered. China, Japan, the Philippines, and Vietnam maintained a fragile truce after a Japanese F-35 was shot down, and a party of Democrats had stormed out of a session in the House, threatening vile retribution.

Ten were dead as Boogaloo, Proud Boys, and Antifa clashed in the streets of Baltimore on one coast and in Berkley on the other.

The only sane voice in the news seemed to come from Tom Ortega, who was ten points up in the polls in Iowa.

Walking into the kitchen, he muttered, "Damn politicians. I tell you, Julia, the country's headed to hell in a handbasket."

"Well, you could go down to the VFW and organize a military coup. Half the world's doing it, so you shouldn't be left behind." His wife glanced up at him where she sat at the kitchen table "socializing" with her Facebook friends.

He smiled as he stuck his coffee cup in the machine and pressed the button. As the cup filled, he glanced through the kitchen window at the frosty field behind the house. His John Deere was crusted with white hoar where it sat at the edge of the cornfield. The stubble of yellow stalks had been invaded by three turkeys that pecked at the cut stems. Beyond the fence and the county road, a gray-fuzz of trees covered the ridge that blocked the southern horizon. Snow still blanketed the slope.

"Gonna be a clear one today. What's the temperature outside?"

"About twenty," Julia told him. "Supposed to be up to the thirties today. Then another storm's coming in."

"Guess we'll have a fire tonight."

"Not without wood." Julia glanced at him over the top of her computer. "Funny how that works."

"That a hint, mother?"

"Never even crossed my mind. Anything from Mark?"

He shook his head. "Kelly was the world to him. With all the shit coming down, I was so happy when he didn't re-up. She sure made him settle down. A hardware store, of all things? Wish he'd come down here. Worry about him up in New York, drinking, brooding."

"You can't live his life for him, Hal." She paused. "I don't know what Brenda was thinking, dragging Kelly into that. But then, I never quite know what to think of that girl. What's this Simond company she's working for? I mean, what's gotten into her? She had a nice job in New York. Her own company. Good money."

"She's gonna get herself killed saving the rest of the world. That's what."

"She wasn't happy, Hal." Julia smiled wistfully. "Most of the time I think she's trying to be the woman you always wanted her to be. She worships you, you know."

They'd had that conversation often enough to have worn holes in it. He tested his coffee, burned his tongue, and set it down.

"Tell you what. How about I go split some wood and carry it in. In return, you cook a couple of hen fruits and some potatoes for breakfast."

"And you call that watching your cholesterol?"

"Maybe I'll go for a run later. I've been letting that slide. Getting fat."

She clicked a couple of keys and stood, arching her back. "Breakfast for wood? I'd call that a deal. But you be back here in twenty minutes. Don't want the food getting cold. And I know you. Once you start something, it's hell to get you to quit."

He walked to the door and grabbed his coat off the hook, then

270   W. MICHAEL GEAR AND KATHLEEN O'NEAL GEAR

pulled a Scotch cap onto his close-cropped gray hair. "Maybe I'll call Mark when I get back. Too many of my guys dropped themselves in a black hole and never got out."

"Might not hurt," she admitted as she walked to the refrigerator.

He stepped out into the cold air and watched his breath rise in white streamers. Morning sunlight was spilling into the valley in the east, sparking diamonds from the frost.

Rounding the house, he walked to the woodpile where six cords of bucked wood waited. Pulling gloves from his pocket, he plucked a sixteen-inch round of maple and set it on the splitting stump. The maul handle was thick with frost, and he wiped it off as best he could. Taking a stance, he swung the heavy splitting maul over his shoulder to put his weight behind it.

He never heard the bullet that killed him.

CHAPTER SEVENTY

***

BRENDA FOLLOWED CHANTEL DOWN THE LADDER AND ONTO THE TARMAC AT THE LANDING strip on Simond Island. With perfect timing, Regal drove up in one of the electric carts.

Chantel's smile died as she said, "If you're going to give me a lecture, forget it."

Brenda, following behind, saw the concern on Regal's face. "You deal with Dad's murder your way, Chantel. I'll deal with it in mine. We've got trouble."

"Taki and Chicago?"

"Not sure yet, though those waters are currently boiling." Regal hooked a thumb at Brenda. "She in?"

"She's in."

To Brenda, Regal said, "Then since you were there, maybe you ought to see it, too."

"See what?" Brenda tossed her bag into the small electric cart and climbed into the back as Chantel joined her sister up front. Regal never bothered to answer.

"Where's Dad's body?" Chantel asked.

"In a casket downstairs. I brought in a couple of guys from a funeral home in Vieux Fort to care for the body. He wanted a cremation. We can deal with that later." She bit back tears. "Mitch quit. He's taking it pretty hard."

"He doesn't have my sympathy at the moment," Chantel said through clenched teeth. "Who have you replaced—"

"I *refused* his resignation. No one knows more about the upgrades Dad ordered for the island's defenses. We're not wasting that kind of expertise." Regal pointed a finger. "And don't you fucking *dare* try and countermand my decision."

Chantel sighed, slapping her hands on her thighs. "Then what's the trouble?"

As they accelerated along the paved road up to the mansion, Regal, one hand on the wheel, told them, "Katya just sent us a video from a secure camera in the Kremlin. And, well, you'll just have to see for yourself."

When they arrived in the conference room, one wall monitor projected Devon's dour expression while Katya and Val watched from others.

Regal took a seat at the head of the conference table as Chantel, motioning Brenda to sit beside her, took another to her right.

"Very well," Chantel began, "What seems to be the problem?"

"This," Katya told them from her monitor, "was recorded last night."

Yet another of the monitors flashed to life across from Brenda. On it a conference room could be seen. The room might have been transported from the eighteenth century: ornate, with giant classical paintings framed in gold, thick carpets, and billowing drapes on the antique-looking windows. An intricately carved table dominated the center, and at its head sat Leon Platnikov. In the high-backed leather chairs to either side were seated generals in uniform and a collection of older men in suits.

In the audio, Platnikov grandiosely spoke in Russian. A voiceover translated into English. "And you ask for power? I give you power. Ha! I should call myself czar! For who can doubt me, yes? I want. I take! Even now I have Chantel Simond locked away. Yes, she is mine. An angel fallen from God to do with as I please! That is Leon Platnikov! He with whom no one shall fool."

"But Leon," one of the men protested, "who is this woman, and why should we care? We're here to discuss your ridiculous decisions." He waved a paper. "This directive you made to turn half of our economic production to lemons. Lemons? We do not understand what you're—"

"Lemons!" Platnikov cried. "All the world is using lemons, yes? And who dominates the lemon trade? Arabs! Filthy Muslim terrorists!"

His face lit, the muscles in the left side of his face twitching. "I control Chantel. She controls the lemons! Such things, you know, can be mixed with cognac! And the fucking? Yes, fantastic! Ask Chantel Simond! I could barely pry myself from her arms—"

"What are you talking about?" one of the generals cried as he threw his arms wide. "Lemons? Chantel Simond? Who is she?"

"A banker," one of the suited men growled. "I have checked. She is not even in Russia. Hasn't been."

Chantel leaned toward Brenda. "That's Uri Simonov. Katya's boss."

"Head of the SVR." Brenda placed him.

"Bah," Platnikov waved it away. "Your KGB spies can't find their penises with two hands...or even a furry squirrel. I have just come from Chantel." He cocked his head. "There! Hear her? Even now she cries out in pleasure."

"KGB? What's he talking about?" Chantel asked as the men in the recording listened and glanced back and forth in confusion.

But Platnikov, his grin oddly lopsided, seemed to be having trouble with his hands. The fingers kept twitching.

"There she is again," Platnikov told them, his eyes wandering as if seeking something illusive. "It's the pills, you see. Makes her crazy for me."

"Are you drunk?" one of the generals demanded.

"Only in..." Platnikov's face went blank. He blinked. "Cognac."

"Vassily," Simonov ordered as he stood, "get the president to bed. When he sleeps it off, we can discuss what this nonsense about lemons really means. Perhaps this is some code?"

"No! I have her!" Platnikov insisted. "In my room. Now."

But the others were rising while a suited man rushed in from the side, trying to help Platnikov to his feet.

The monitor went blank.

Regal emitted an audible sigh. "I don't understand. It's too soon."

"What is?" Devon asked.

"Dementia. He believes Chantel is in Russia. And what's this business about lemons?" Regal glanced around.

"An economic directive issued yesterday afternoon," Katya told them, her expression thoughtful. "Everyone thought it was some code word. Something perhaps posted by mistake."

"So, it's working?" Devon asked. "We've been seeing some odd things in the metadata."

Regal raised her voice. "You don't understand. Platnikov shouldn't be showing signs of dementia and motor control for another two weeks!"

"Which means...?" Chantel looked around the room, waiting for an answer.

Regal appeared tense and thoughtful. "I don't know what it means. We should have had months before Platnikov's decline. I've got to check with my team. Something's gone wrong."

"How wrong?"

"Wait a minute. Are you saying..." Devon didn't seem able to finish the sentence.

Brenda's heartbeat started to pound a dull rhythm in her chest. She could see it on their faces. Each of them knew, but none of them wanted to say it outloud. "Regal thinks this may be the precipitating event. Is that it?"

"Don't put words in my mouth!" Regal shouted. "I'm saying I don't know what it means. That's all!"

CHAPTER SEVENTY-ONE

***

THE LEATHER FELT SOFT UNDER HER FINGERTIPS AS CHANTEL RAN THEM OVER THE SPINES of her father's books. One entire wall of his office was composed of bookshelves. It was here, behind the polished hardwood desk, that Renaud came to relax at night. Here he would sit back in the great leather chair, a drink on the desk, and read from one of his volumes before going to bed.

This had been his retreat, his final redoubt.

Her father's presence filled the room, as if the man's soul, personality, and power resonated from the wood, the flooring, and the fixtures. If only she could spread her arms, gather his essence in and hold it to her as she hadn't been able to do in life.

Gone.

She found it hard to breathe, as if the air had become rarified. The knot of grief tightened under her tongue. Tears warmed behind her eyes.

"Damn it, no!"

A pause.

"Can't show weakness."

She sniffed. "You taught me well, Dad."

Stepping around behind the desk, she lowered herself into his opulent chair and laid her hands on the polished leather arms.

"Please, Daddy? I can't do this alone."

The tears came unbidden.

She had fifteen minutes. That long to cry and grieve.

And then she had to be the cold hard pillar the others needed. Demanded.

What if I'm not strong enough?

CHAPTER SEVENTY-TWO

***

BRENDA WAS SURPRISED WHEN CHANTEL HERSELF WALKED INTO THE SECURITY BRIEFING and took the chair that had always been reserved for Renaud.

Mitch, looking cowed, sat opposite Dana Riccio, while Sam Gunnarson, Jaime Sandoval, and Taco Carbajal filled the rest of the chairs in the command center conference room. The monitors behind them were dark with the exception of one projecting Devon's real-time image. The mood was somber.

"First, tell me what happened to my father," Chantel began, her gaze on the opposite wall where the island defense upgrades were marked on the big map. Then she fixed on Mitch.

He avoided her eyes as, point by point, he laid out their arrival at Sonny's *presidio.* "We took positions along the terrace. The usual protocol. Renaud and Sonny were eating, talking. Nothing looked out of the ordinary. It was the second-floor terrace. You've been there. We were told that Sonny's security had the perimeter. That they'd been warned about the possibility of a shooter in their briefing and had taken measures."

"But obviously, they didn't." Chantel took a deep breath. "Who knew Dad was going to Cuba?"

Mitch seemed to squirm. "Me and my team, Devon, the immediate family. Since the attempts on you, we've been pretty close-mouthed."

"How long before the trip was this planned?" Brenda asked.

"A couple of days," Mitch told her. "Just after Chantel, Devon, and Renaud agreed to divest in Asia. Renaud wanted to elicit Sonny's support."

Chantel asked, "Could Sonny have been behind it?"

Mitch's mouth pinched. "Doesn't feel right. I mean, if he was, his shooter would have had ample opportunity when Sonny wasn't in the line of fire. Given the shot angle, it's a wonder Sonny wasn't taken out with the same bullet. Almost was."

Chantel asked, "Do you have a graphic?"

Mitch opened a section of the table to expose a touch screen. Tapping it, he bought up a menu, accessed a file, and one of the monitors filled with an overhead of Sonny's estate in Cuba.

"Here's the second-floor terrace." Mitch tapped, and a blue dot formed. The shooter was here, about a half mile away. You can see the hut where he was hidden." Another dot of blue marked the location.

"Sonny was in the direct line of fire," he finished. Then he flicked his fingers to enlarge the scene. On the satellite photo, the table could be seen.

"Renaud was here, his back to the shooter. Sonny sat here."

"Brenda?" Chantel asked.

Brenda got her feet, studying the scene. "Is there any reason Sonny had to be sitting where he was? The setting couldn't have been arranged any other way?"

"Sure. He could have had his back to either the house or the sea, allowing a clean raking shot with no risk to Sonny."

Brenda shook her head. "If Sonny knew Renaud was going to be killed, he wouldn't have seated himself in the direct line of fire." She paused. "Any idea on the caliber?"

"Thirty."

Brenda considered. "Either a .308 or .300 Win Mag. Sonny definitely wouldn't have taken a chance." She turned. "That doesn't discount the leak coming from one of his people. Maybe the idea was to take out two birds with one stone."

"God damn it!" Regal cried, knotting her fist. "What the hell is happening to us?"

Chantel lowered her head into her hands, elbows braced on the table. "The fools are playing with fire."

"Who?" Regal demanded. "One of the Lius? The Takanabis? You're the one who decided to cut them off at the knees."

"Dad and Devon and I," she corrected softly.

"And they killed Dad for it!" Regal snapped. "But you didn't plan on that, did you? You're so engrossed in your little games, moving pieces around the board—"

"And you didn't plan on Platnikov losing his mind in a few days!" Chantel slapped the table, turning to glare at Regal. "Don't you get it? We've a chance. One small fucking chance to save something out of the coming apocalypse. It's a damn house of cards, Regal. Pull the wrong one, and there's nothing left. You get it? All your proprietary seeds? The ones good for only one planting? After they've grown, and you're not there to sell more, there's *nothing* to grow! You've outsmarted yourself and condemned millions to starvation in the process!"

"My labs—"

"Are *worthless*, Regal! You've got to have water, people, and energy to produce your seeds. And then you've got to get them to farmers. That means roads, ships, fuel, and security. A distribution *system* that's going to collapse. Once that happens, how are you going to get your precious seeds from Iowa to Missouri, let alone to India?"

Regal's brow lined, her face reflecting confusion. "But the trucks—"

"Can't run without diesel," Chantel told her listlessly. "Nor can wells pump water without electricity. And the grids *will* fail. Maybe not at once, but soon. And even if they don't, pumps need parts. Parts are made in Taiwan or China. They're made of alloys mined in South Africa or Chile. The ores are smelted in Malaysia or Brazil."

Regal looked stunned.

In a conciliatory voice, Chantel added, "That's why we need a plan, Regal. Some way to bring order when the chaos breaks loose. Dad understood. Dad had the authority and character to sell it to the others. For us, it means they killed our father. For everyone else, they may have killed any chance for the future."

Brenda swallowed past a knot in her throat. Chantel looked like a tortured saint. Damn it, the woman's father was lying dead on a slab in the basement. How did she find the strength and courage?

Regal raised a hand in defeat. "So, what's the plan?"

Chantel rubbed her eyes, looking for the first time as if she were on the verge of tears. "Devon and I are trying to make it work. That's why I had to go see Taki and Chicago. I had to try and make them see what's right before our noses. If I can convince them..." She shook her head. "It's hearts against heads. If they follow their hearts and pool their resources into a futile attempt to save eastern Asia, they'll take the rest of the world down with them. Annihilation."

Brenda realized her heart was pounding. Around the table, every face was pale, some barely breathing.

Regal had her eyes focused on an infinity only she could see.

"That still leaves Taylor," Brenda said, trying to calm herself. "And whoever's behind him."

Chantel sniffed as if in sour amusement. "We've got to take out him and the person who hired him. And if we don't do it soon, it will be a sign to the others that we're incompetent. Any influence we have is going to evaporate."

"So," Mitch said gingerly, "how do we find him?"

On the monitor, Devon's expression changed, and he placed a finger to his earpiece. "Excuse me. Something's come up. We just picked up a news report."

He seemed to hesitate as he fixed on Brenda. "I have some upsetting news, Captain. West Virginia, it's a local story. Your mother and father have been found dead in the snow outside their house."

Brenda—in stunned disbelief—said, "What? How?"

"One of the neighbors stopped by after your father missed his lunch at the local café. Apparently, Colonel Pepper was chopping wood when he was shot. Your mother was killed when she bent over his body. I'm so sorry, Captain."

CHAPTER SEVENTY-THREE

***

TREVOR HUGHES, WEARY TO THE BONE, CLOSED TOM ORTEGA'S SENATE OFFICE DOOR BEHIND him and checked to make sure it was locked. The hall was quiet, lonely at this hour of the night.

"Excuse me?" The voice was female, cultured.

Trevor turned, startled by the attractive young woman with large dark eyes and luxurious black hair. In a city full of beautiful women, she stood out, looking oddly vulnerable. A press badge hung on her immaculate jacket.

"Yes?" He tried not to stare at her perfect legs clad in black nylons.

"You're Mr. Hughes? Senator Ortega's chief of staff?"

"I am."

"Veronica Wolf. Total News Network. Um, I know it's late. It's just been a bitch of a day, but could you tell me when the senator's going to be back in town?"

"It's on his schedule. Just pull up the senator's website and—"

"I know. But, um, would he consider a one-on-one sometime when his schedule is a little less rushed?"

"I'm sure. You can contact the campaign—"

"Sorry." As if in weary defeat her expression seemed to collapse. "I thought maybe you could fit me in as special... Screw it. Just another thing gone wrong today. Sorry to bother you."

She turned away, shoulders sagging, looking on the verge of tears.

"Hey, wait. You okay?"

She turned back to him, a brittle smile on her face. "Sorry, I'm not thinking well. Got some bad news today. Friend of mine. It's just that... The way we work, you know? It just hit me like a brick. You're on the way up? You're always alone. I mean, there's no one you can just talk to. Have a drink with, that isn't looking for an angle, trying to use you as another step on the ladder."

He chuckled. "Yeah, know what you mean. I'm headed off for a quick meal and then an empty apartment."

"Same here. If you wouldn't mind..." Then she shook her head. "Sorry. Like I said, I'm not thinking well. Goodnight."

"Do you like pizza? I mean, awesome pizza? The place is nothing snazzy, and kind of out of way, but they make everything from scratch."

Damn. I sound too desperate.

He felt a flush warm his ears. Why did he always have to be an idiot when it came to attractive women?

"Hey, I didn't come here looking for a date. Just...dinner?"

"Beats eating alone."

She gave him a tenuous smile, her large dark eyes reflecting relief. "Been ages since I did something this crazy. Sure."

Oh, my God! She said yes. "Awesome."

CHAPTER SEVENTY-FOUR

***

EACH MEMORY OF BRENDA'S MOTHER AND FATHER WAS LIKE DRIVING A THORN INTO HER soul. She kept fixing on Christmas when she was six, suffering from the flu, and her father's warm arms held her so she could see the Christmas tree and the presents underneath.

Images of her mother, forever loving, maintaining the family during the long absences when Dad was deployed. Of how mom's brown eyes would soften on those rare occasions when she could provide some special treat for Brenda or Mark.

Something seemed to rip apart inside.

Across the lavishly appointed office, Chantel watched her with cool green eyes. The woman sat behind a desk, with reports piled on either side of the computer console.

Brenda knotted a fist and thumped it against her forehead. "He shot them down in cold blood. Because of me."

Then it hit her. "I have to warn Mark."

Chantel said, "I've already taken steps. Your brother's at his home just outside of New York. Whenever you're ready, we've got a scrambled line. You should talk to him."

Brenda rubbed her face, trying to sort through the crazy mixture of emotions. Grief and worry, guilt and hate, all mixed together with a growing anger that threatened to burn free in a killing rage.

Sucking in a lungful of air, she forced memories of her mother and father from her reeling brain, ordered her thoughts, and walked over to the desk.

"Okay, Chantel, I'm ready."

Chantel picked up the phone and pressed a button. She listened for a second, then handed the receiver to Brenda.

When Brenda placed it to her ear it was to hear the ring tone, and then Mark's voice. *"Hello?"*

"Mark? It's Brenda."

"Dear God, Brenda. Have you heard? First Kelly, and then Mom and Dad?"

"Look, this is going to be hard to explain."

She heard the silence, and then a pained gasp. *"What have you done, Brenda? What the fuck is going on?"*

"The guy's name is Taylor. He's been trying to kill the woman I'm protecting. Now he's coming after me and the people I love. I need you someplace safe where he can't get you."

Chantel said, "If he can get to Teterboro we can have him on a charter flight to somewhere safe. It's the least I can do."

Before Mark could digest what Brenda had said, she added, "Can you get to Teterboro Airport?"

"In New Jersey?"

"That's right."

"Yeah. I mean, sure. When?"

"Soonest. Right now! I'll call with more information within the hour."

"Damn it, sis! What's going on?"

"Tell you when I see you. I'm in the Caribbean. Now, soldier, beat feet."

"Taylor, you said?" He swallowed hard. *"I want the mother fucker, Brenda."*

"Stand in line, brother. Call you soon."

"I'll be on the road in fifteen. Figure it three hours to Teterboro."

"Watch your six. Don't forget you're being hunted."

"Roger that." The line went dead.

Brenda—feeling as if she were in a daze—handed the phone back. "He's going to want a piece of Taylor."

"Be honest with me, Brenda. Take your time and think it through. Is he a good fit for The Foundation?"

If they have my brother, there's no way I can ever escape. They can control me completely just by threatening Mark.

"My call for the present is to hold him somewhere safe until I figure out what to do next."

"Sure you're thinking straight? Your brother, as I understand it, is a trained sniper. You could use him."

"Maybe later. But not now. He needs to go to ground somewhere and lay low."

Chantel nodded, then thought for a moment before saying, "There's something else I want to talk to you about. What we did in Russia? I took a risk when Platnikov wanted you for a threesome. That wasn't the plan going in."

Brenda hesitated, trying to refocus on the new discussion.

"Not just any woman could have played the part you did. While we didn't have to, it's a relief to know that you'd have done whatever was required."

"I understand, ma'am."

"I just..."

"Yes?"

Chantel's brow pinched. She started to say something. Hesitated. Then in a more formal tone said, "Never mind. Moving on. Finding Taylor, doing it right, is going to take time. Meanwhile, I have—"

"We won't have to wait," Brenda said thoughtfully. "He's made it personal so he can bring it to a head. Right now, he's picking the place, laying his trap."

CHAPTER SEVENTY-FIVE

***

THE SPEECH WAS THE RAGE IN WASHINGTON, AND EVERY MAJOR NEWS ORGANIZATION WAS
replaying sound bites.

Tom Ortega leaned back on the couch in Ben Mackeson's campaign
headquarters, a cup of coffee in his hand. Around him, the campaign
staff watched the big-screen TV with rapt attention, computers forgotten, phones on their cradles.

On the screen, Leon Platnikov stood at a podium before the Russian
Duma. Several of his generals flanked him, along with Platnikov's
foreign minister.

"People ask about the Russian destiny," came the translator's voice.
*"Why should they worry? For millennia, Russia has remained resolute!
When Napoleon thought to thrash us and break us, we sent his clowns
staggering back in the snow! So, too, have we crushed the barbarians.
Our glorious ancestors won the revolution, pulling down the clownish
Czars! What simpletons they were!"*

"Who does he mean?" Mackeson wondered.

"Wait, here it comes," Ortega said.

*"And then came the Great Patriotic War. And what did the Americans
find as they sent their Panzers and storm troopers looting and burning
into Russia's heart? Death by the millions! We watched them weeping
in the bitter cold outside Moscow! We starved them in the snow at
Stalingrad!"* Platnikov pulled himself up. *"But the Americans haven't
learned. They are coming again! Massing their millions in Berlin and
Prague! I see them, preparing to betray us in our pact of peace."*

On the screen, the minister and generals were staring oddly at
Platnikov.

"Once again the snows of Russia await their delusional goals!

Luring them into our arms will be as easy as luring Chantel Simond into our beds! We will show them Russia's true love! Ah, yes, my countrymen, let us pull them into our embrace and open their soft white thighs to our caress!"

At Chantel Simond's name, Ortega straightened, even more bewildered than he'd been at Platnikov's confusing Nazis with Americans.

The screen flashed to a Fox anchor, a condescending smile on his face. *"Well, there you have it. Russian President Platnikov seems to have rewritten history. After all, in the Second World War, America was Russia's ally. And Fox News has discovered that Chantel Simond is an investment banker with Simond International. A spokesman for her office informs us that Ms. Simond hasn't been to Russia at any time in the recent past, making the Russian president's odd statements even more of a mystery."*

"He's lost his mind!" Mackeson cried.

The Fox anchor then added, *"Our Moscow bureau informs us that President Platnikov hasn't been seen since the broadcast this morning. A spokesman for his office informs us the president isn't well. And now, turning to our panel..."*

Mackeson muted the sound, looking around. "Alright, people. Let's get to work. We're going to have to revise the stump speech. Whatever's happened to Platnikov, it totally changes the dynamic in the Baltic States."

"Yes, but for better or worse? Who will replace Platnikov?" Tom asked with narrowed eyes.

"Anybody would be better. The guy's a lunatic."

"So was Rasputin. Luckily he wasn't in the number one position."

Tom shook his head. "Do you know how this is going to play in Russia? The people are proud of beating the Nazis. Then, to turn them into Americans?"

"And that bit about Chantel? Lured to Platnikov's bed?" Mackeson wondered.

Ortega said with a chuckle. "The Chantel Simond I know..." Then he remembered her saying, *"One thing at a time, Senator."*

He stiffened. *No, she couldn't have!*

CHAPTER SEVENTY-SIX

***

TAYLOR, HIS CARRY-ON BAG OVER HIS SHOULDER, EXITED THE TIRED-LOOKING AIRBUS 330 and flashed his COVID-FREE card at the gate agent. Then he followed the other weary travelers down the jetway and into the sterile corridor that led to passport control and customs. Leonardo da Vinci International Airport was one of Taylor's favorites. It processed thousands of international travelers, but despite its high profile, security—never an Italian strong point—tended to be lax.

To add to his advantage, he'd inserted cheek pads and darkened his skin. Mutton-chop sideburns augmented the effect, and special glasses created the optical illusion that his eyes were closer together than they were to fool the intraocular statistical program on facial recognition software.

At least for the moment.

Everything would have to be orchestrated. But then, Taylor excelled at the small details. Or he had until Brenda Pepper began mucking up his works.

From here on out, this would have to be played flawlessly. He'd thrown down the gauntlet. If Pepper were even half the woman her file indicated, she'd have to take the bait. And if he'd set the hook deep enough, she'd probably be bringing her enraged brother along with her.

He cleared passport control, his Tunisian identity sliding through the reader without issue.

Customs, likewise, was a breeze.

In the men's room, he removed the cheek patches, allowing his face to assume its normal shape. He checked his watch. Bennie should already be in the city and dealing with the usual contacts for a weapon and tactical gear.

Time to bait the trap.

Making his way out to the taxi queue, he shivered in the cold wind, hating the fact that he'd picked a garishly colored short-sleeve shirt and light cotton pants for his disguise.

When his turn came for a cab, he told the driver his destination, pitched his bag into the Alpha's trunk, and managed to clumsily knock his glasses off as he climbed into the back seat. In that moment, he flashed a quick glance at the security cameras.

Then the door was closed, and the silver-gray taxi was heading off on the long drive into Rome.

CHAPTER SEVENTY-SEVEN

***

THROUGH THE CAR WINDOW, MARK PEPPER WATCHED THE SOMBER WINTER FORESTS OF the West Virginia pass. Small plots of farmland, the soil winter-fallow, had been cut out of the thicket of trees. White frame houses, many with porches, passed by anonymously. The road wound down into the holler where older-model cars and trucks, marred by dents and dings, nosed into gravel driveways. Yards contained rusting bicycles, occasional swing sets, and cracked blue-plastic swimming pools that hearkened back to a vanished summer.

The little town of Slanesville showed signs of life, its café parking lot attended by a variety of pickups and sedans. The craft shops and antique dealers, however, had closed for the season. Just beyond the convenience store, Mark's driver took a left off the pavement, climbing up to the little Masonic cemetery.

Tires popped on gravel as the black Town Car rolled up and stopped beside a beige Yukon with Maryland plates.

"We're here, sir."

"Thank you." For all his vaunted courage, all he wanted to do was sit in that seat. Maybe forever.

In a matter of months, his life had unraveled like yarn stripped from a torn sweater.

Kelly's death had hit him like a sledgehammer's blow. One moment, she's flying off to Wyoming; the next, he's standing—as if in a nightmarish dream—watching her casket being unloaded from an airplane.

Even as the impossibility of Kelly's death was finally setting in, a neighbor finds Mom and Dad murdered, their bloody bodies frozen in the snow.

And then came the police, piecing together disparate facts. Kelly is shot in Wyoming. Mom and Dad in West Virginia. Where was he on those days? Were he and Kelly having problems? Was he or she having an affair? Who inherited? Did he have any reason to wish any of them dead? The grilling had gone on for what seemed an eternity.

He'd downed no more than four fast shots of bourbon after the last cop left before Brenda's curious phone call had sent him on the drunken drive to Teterboro. Mysterious men had placed him on a charter jet flight to Las Vegas. This morning they'd flown him back to Maryland. And through it all, strangers had been polite, but told him nothing.

"Mark, I need you to trust me. We're in the shit, brother. Please, do what these people say, and I'll get the son of a bitch who killed the people we love."

It had been her tone of voice, more than anything, that made him obey.

God, sis, just tell me you know what the hell is going on!

He took a deep breath, opened the car door, and stepped out into the damp air. Slinging his coat around his shoulders, he walked toward the Yukon, nodding to the driver who sat behind the vehicle's wheel.

As he did, the rear door opened, and a woman stepped out. Tall, redheaded, she regarded him with alert green eyes. Mark stopped short, having expected Brenda and not some immaculately dressed stranger. She seemed to exude an aura of power and competence, as though she were somehow more than a mere mortal.

"You're Mark Pepper?" she asked, offering a hand. "I'm Chantel Simond, a friend of Brenda's."

He took her hand uncertainly, feeling a firm shake. "You want to tell me what the hell is going on? Where's Brenda?"

The woman's green gaze didn't waver but studied him as if trying to read his soul. "She's hunting the man who killed your wife and parents. I'm here to see if including you in the hunt is a good idea."

"She sent you? To judge me?" He bristled.

"Only two people in the world know I'm here, and if she were one of them, she'd be very unhappy." A humorless smile bent the woman's lips. "Let's just say it's the price of old-fashioned honor, and my willingness to take a risk."

He shoved his hands into his pockets. Glanced uneasily at the gate just beyond the parking lot. "Look, I'm tired of being jacked around. So, whoever you are, Chantel Simond, maybe it's time to drop the cryptic shit and tell me why the hell I should give you so much as the time of day."

The woman's face tensed at his tone, only to soften into a knowing smile. "Taylor was trying to kill me when he shot Kelly. On the second attempt, he killed one of my few trusted friends. A little over a week ago, he murdered my father. To punish Brenda for thwarting him, he shot your parents. You may very well be next on his list."

She started for the gate, leaving him to follow.

Awash in confusion, anger, and grief, Mark followed her through the ornate wrought-iron arch and into the cemetery. Ancient oaks, their branches knotted, reached tiredly toward the cloud-thick sky, as though pleading for warmer weather.

"Which way?" she asked.

"Down here." He made his way past the weathered headstones and monuments, the grass beneath his boots spongy and dead.

There, in the southwest corner, the plot lay, just down the slope from the faded marble monument that marked his great great grandfather, Jonathan Pepper. He'd been killed by Phillip Sheridan's troops just over the mountain in the last battle for Winchester, Virginia. To its right stood the red granite slab that marked the grave of his mother's great grandfather, Eli Cory, who'd fought under Hancock on the Union side and lost a leg at the Wilderness.

His people had a long history of service, and here, too, had been laid to rest Harold and Julia Pepper. Come to this place before their time.

She walked up beside him as he stood over the new graves, his head bowed, shoulders sagging. For long moments he looked down at the strips of replaced sod. Each beat of his heart was like a blow to his bones. Grief tightened into a hard ache under his tongue, his vision swimming.

Memories of his youth, of Mom smiling, working in the kitchen, taking him to school, played in his head. He remembered the time Dad had come home unexpectedly and found him in the barn, drinking beer. How Dad had bought him his first rifle, a magical Marlin .22. Dad had taken him hunting that summer, and Mark had shot his first squirrel. How proud Mom and Dad had been, traveling to see him at the ceremony when he finally was dismissed from formation the day he finished boot.

Now they were down there, just under that cold sod and dirt, and he'd never be able to hug them, tell them how much he loved them.

Gone.

Dead.

Forever.

"You want to tell me what's really going on? Why this is happening to us?"

"The world is about to change, Mark. A lot of money can be made when nations and economies collapse. I'm in the way of those who would profit most by bringing it all down."

"When I got the call about Mom and Dad? I was drunk. I was still drunk when I got to Teterboro. I just didn't give a fuck anymore. Because I didn't, I just did what your guys said. I only asked that they pony up a bottle of whiskey when they stuck me in that motel room in Las Vegas."

"We didn't think it was our place to tell Brenda about the whiskey. She's had enough on her plate recently."

"If you know sis, you already know I'll do whatever it takes to hunt this shit bag Taylor down. So, a woman like you? Why come all the way here?"

"Your sister is one of the few women on earth I actually respect and admire. I was wondering if you were cut from the same cloth. After Taylor is taken care of, I might have a place for you. A chance to make a difference."

Bits and pieces of his soul, like a torn montage, formed inside. "I got nothing left to give anyone."

"You've got a good job in that hardware store. You don't have to go back to—"

"I did that for Kelly. And I loved it for Kelly's sake." He stuffed his hands deeper into his pockets. "Taylor? Thinks he's a sniper? I killed thirty-eight, confirmed, over there. What's this guy's count?"

"His reputation, Mr. Pepper, is that he's the best in the world."

"And Brenda's hunting him?"

"She is." Her cool eyes were taking his measure. What was it about the woman? She just had a presence, part energy and power, part danger.

"If this guy really is the best in the world, I'm the one who should be out there hunting him, not Brenda."

"If you decide to join us, you'll take orders from your sister. And, of course, me. Can you do that, Mr. Pepper?"

Can I?

She watched him bend down, slip his fingers under the re-laid sod, and scoop up a handful of damp soil. Clutching ground hallowed by his ancestors, he stood, thoughtful, and then dropped it back to the earth.

"Ms. Simond, all you have to do is find Taylor, and I'll take him out for you. And you can leave Brenda out of it."

"We've learned he's in Rome."

"Then let's go kill the son of a bitch."

Her smile struck him as a foregone conclusion, as if she'd known exactly what he was going say long before it passed his lips.

CHAPTER SEVENTY-EIGHT

***

CHANTEL WALKED ALONG THE ANGLED WALL SURROUNDING THE EXTENDED PATIO, THE breeze teasing her red hair. She stopped and stared out over the Caribbean. The distant glow in the clouds marked Vieux Fort's location some sixty miles to the north and over the horizon.

She recognized the soft pad of her brother's feet. Without turning, she asked, "You saw Father's body?"

Robert came to lean beside her, arms propped on the angled cornice. "I did." He craned his neck and expectorated, watching his spittle fall to the trees below. He knew she thought the habit vulgar, which, of course, was why he did it.

"How's the Tom Ortega campaign?"

"He's smart. The guy doesn't rattle easily. He's remarkably cool under pressure. Electing him is going to be a piece of cake unless he lied about skeletons in the closet, or does something stupid that we can't contain. Once he's in office, we've got him by the balls."

"Be careful, brother."

"With Ortega? I've trolled a couple of sex-bomb babes in front of him, late at night, with a hotel room close at hand. These were quality, mind you. Five grand a night, with PhDs. Nada. The guy's faithful to his wife."

"And you don't have any film for leverage? Poor little brother. But that's not what I meant."

"We've still got his little girl. Jessie. He'll do anything for her. Maybe a recurrence of the disease that—"

"God, you're dense sometimes! You threaten that man's daughter? He'll come after you like a berserk lion." She calmed herself, adding, "I've studied the guy. We'll get him in the end. But, Robert, it will be through shared interests, not by threats, coercion, or blackmail. Don't get cute, or it will blow up in your face."

"Yeah, yeah, warning noted." He glanced around. "Where's Pepper? Heard you made her permanent. People are starting to wonder about the two of you."

"Meaning?"

Robert gave her a sidelong glance. "Hey, I fully understand how tough it is to fill a person's needs with our schedules and how oppressive the security is. And it's been what, five years since you've had anyone in your life?"

"Actually, I suspect she's a solid heterosexual."

"You don't have a life, that's all."

"None of us do. Look at Regal."

"Her latest boy toy?" Robert said with a shrug. "Dumb as rock but hung like a horse. Comes and goes on her orders, doesn't have an aspiration in his head beyond living the good life."

He gave her a mocking, sidelong glance. "There's always Steve Heston."

"I'd rather shoot myself."

"The way I hear it, Taylor might do the job for you." He waved at the forest to their left. "I'm surprised Captain Pepper lets you stand out here."

"She's worked with Mitch. The island has been sniper-proofed while you've been away in America making presidents." She smiled wearily. "Pepper's on her way to Rome."

"Someone said that you went to see her parent's grave. Thought that was a bit extravagant. But Rome? Tossing in a bit of perk for good service?"

"Taylor's there. He left a crumb on his back trail."

"Sounds like she's walking right into his lair. You send any backup?"

"Her brother."

"Some backup. My people rounded the guy up for you, remember? Sloppy drunk. Said it was a miracle he made it to Teterboro without wrecking or getting pulled over for DUI."

"Brenda will keep him in line."

He flipped his long hair back, studying her through narrowed lids.

"So you met him at the graves? Cunning of you. Caught the poor sod at his lowest and extended the merciful hand. But...ah, I see. Now that you've got your claws sunk into the brother, you've got another handle on Pepper in case she doesn't share your ultimately pragmatic ethics."

"All tools have their place."

"You truly are one cold bitch."

"So they say. But you've never understood complexity, Robert. That's your fatal weakness. I can tell you that Brenda Pepper is going to be my salvation, and you haven't a clue as to what I'm talking about."

"Hope she's up to your lofty expectations. Me, I'll put my money on Valentine. My bet is that after Taylor takes out Pepper, it's only a matter of time before good old Val runs him to earth."

"Where did you get such a high opinion of women?"

"Must have been the sisters I grew up with, huh?"

CHAPTER SEVENTY-NINE

***

IF ANYTHING, CHRIS'S BAR WAS LOUDER THIS TIME, WHICH WAS ALL TO THE GOOD. BIG JIM Korkoran had just taken his second sip of whiskey when Veronica Wolf breezed through the door dressed like a harried housewife. She parked herself on the stool beside him and shrugged out of a worn-looking North Slope coat.

"You look beat," he muttered.

"Long night." She grinned. "That boy never had a chance. Two lonely young professionals. Pizza. Then a couple of drinks, and next thing, we're at his apartment."

"Whose apartment?"

"Trevor Hughes'. Did you know he used to race motorcycles? The guy still works out." She focused absently on the bottles on the mirrored backbar, a silly smile on her face.

"Must have been good."

"He was too quick on the trigger the first time. Out of practice, but when he caught his second wind? I mean, damn!"

Korkoran glanced sidelong at her perfect body, the jealous part of his male brain irritated. She still had the glow.

"Outside of getting your chimes rung, did the young man share anything of interest?"

"Chantel Simond gave Ortega the number of a clinic. You know how you were talking about SimondAg? How they're doing advanced genetics work? The good senator's daughter has that bone disease. The place is called the White Coral Clinic. Got an address in Turks and Caicos. Apparently, they've got a cure."

"SimondAg, huh? That's run by Chantel's sister, Regal." He took another sip of whiskey. "Ortega dotes on that little girl. He'd do just about anything for her."

"Like sell his soul to Chantel for the cure?"

"That's a hell of a lever." He paused. "Did Hughes seem suspicious?"

She shot him a saucy smile. "Do you think I just fell off the turnip truck yesterday? The guy's lonely, working twelve-hour days. And he worships Ortega. Loves to talk about him, about what a great president he's going to make."

"What about the money? Ortega's campaign has money running out of its ears. I've got people in the Federal Election Commission sniffing the ground. But that fucking Julie Zapruder is a crafty old bitch. Suddenly she's got super PACs lined up like a picket fence. And Tam Bizhenov's people are milking social media and Ortega events like a school of piranhas for whatever the locals will bear."

She ordered a Bud and took a sip from the bottle. "Me? I did a little research on StatNco. Didn't access anything past five years ago to keep from waving a red flag. Just to be safe, I started an article on the history of campaign polling and left it on the computer. Senator, with their resources and know-how they could funnel a billion dollars into the Ortega campaign through a hundred thousand legitimate addresses that couldn't be traced. And that doesn't count the super PACs."

"Someone always makes a mistake."

She pursed her lips, considering, then shook her head. "Given their history—and since they've played this game for years without so much as a taint—StatNco has the system perfected. We've got to operate under the premise that they're smarter than we are."

"So, what's next?"

Her lips quivered in triumph. "You check out this White Coral Clinic. Me, I'm going to run a couple of positive pieces on Ortega. Work my way into the campaign."

"Others have tried that. Ben Mackeson is going to manipulate that press pool like it's a kindergarten."

"Of course, he is. But I've got a date with Trevor on Friday. And I've got what it takes to make him talk." She crossed her long legs and flexed the muscles in her thighs.

CHAPTER EIGHTY

***

MARK LAY ON THE HASSLER HOTEL'S PLUSH BED, HIS ATTENTION FIXED ON THE LAPTOP open before him. Through the window the city-capped hills of Rome were visible. Brenda paced along the opposite wall, a crystal-eyed glare on her face.

"I'm as upset as you are, Brenda. I don't need you here or want you here. I can take this bastard by myself."

"You have no idea what you've gotten yourself into, bro. Chantel plays her own game, and only she knows the rules. We're in trouble. I know it."

Mark sat up. "You can explain all this to me after we take out the son of a bitch who's hurt us. Tell me about this Taylor. Is he really supposed to be the best in the world? Too bad you couldn't get close enough to show him some of your knife know-how. You're the best female I've ever seen with a blade CQB."

Brenda ignored him and opened her computer where it sat on the ornate desk, checked her emails, and found the one she'd been waiting for.

"Got it." She pulled out her notebook, running the simple substitution cipher. "We've got a communication at 18:53. That's less than ten minutes."

She had checked them into the Hassler on Chantel's orders. One of Rome's finest, it stood at the head of the Spanish Steps, and its roof-top restaurant offered stunning views of the eternal city. At least when the weather permitted. It also provided a place where Brenda could employ the special satellite com unit that Jaime Sandoval had supplied. The thing—cooked up in one of Taki Takanabi's labs—didn't even look like a phone.

"Do you think they can find him?"

"Yeah, I do."

Mark examined her icy expression. "I don't get it. You had the world by the balls, making good money in executive protection. Then you throw it all over to run off to the Caribbean and this Chantel Simond? Kind of quick, don't you think?"

Brenda shut down her computer and pulled the battery, ensuring that no one with a wireless device could access it. "You don't have to approve."

"So, who are these people? Drug dealers? I mean, take Chantel. Brenda, there's something about her. Scary and powerful and coldly seductive at the same time. These people could be some serious bad news, and you're working for them?"

"Last best hope of earth."

"That sounds like a cliché."

"Wish it was." She glanced at the aluminum case where it rested on the floor beside her suitcase. Jaime Sandoval had loaned her the equipment it contained. Ultimately, their lives might rely on the device.

"Come on," Mark almost barked. "You get mixed up with them, and suddenly Kelly's dead. Then Mom and Dad. And I'm supposed to believe it's because you pissed off some paid-for-hire sniper?"

"That's pretty much the story."

"Who paid him to go after this Chantel in the first place?"

"Don't know."

"Why aren't you telling me the whole story?"

She swiveled to read his expression. "Because I don't know the whole story. Not yet." She glanced at her watch. "Come on, let's go up on the roof. By now, StatNco's run the data."

"Who's StatNco?"

"Big Brother's Big Brother."

"What's that mean?"

"They spy on the people who spy on everyone else." She stood, pulling her coat on. "Get your shit wired. Whether I like it or not, we're in this together, and we've got a call to make."

Mark followed her, a dubious look on his face as they took the lift to the roof.

Even as Brenda stepped through the doors, her sat phone was vibrating.

"Pepper here." She placed it to her ear.

Chantel's voice, filled with tension, said, *"Devon's in touch. We've got him!"*

CHAPTER EIGHTY-ONE

***

CHANTEL WORE A HEADSET WITH A MIC; SHE AND REGAL CLUSTERED AROUND THE CENTRAL console in the island's operations room. The place was a state-of-the-art communications center buried deep in the villa. From the mountaintop antennae and dish systems, they were tied into every major network on earth. All communications were encrypted through entangled-particle technology ensuring complete security.

On the wall before them the large screen depicted an overhead view of Rome.

Devon's voice came through the speakers as he described what they were seeing. "We identified Taylor on a cafe security monitor off the Piazza Venezia. He was just sitting there, drinking coffee, staring at the camera. If you ask me, he was almost begging to be recognized."

Chantel asked, "Brenda, do you read that?"

"*Affirmative. He was baiting the trap.*"

Devon's voice then added, "He stayed long enough that we were able to task a satellite. We watched him pay the bill, pick up a heavy black bag, and walk down the Via Dei Fori Imperiali."

On the screen, a red dot proceeded along the sidewalk beside the busy street, marking Taylor's route.

Devon continued, "We watched him pitch the black bag over the fence. It dropped down into the Forum, landing behind a wall in the ruins. Taylor paid his entry fee just as they closed, slipped down, and recovered his bag."

"How long ago was this?"

"Twenty minutes."

"Brenda? Did you copy that?"

"*Affirmative. We're approaching the Victor Emmanuel monument.*"

A pause. *"Chantel, it's getting dark. Mark checked his guidebook. The Forum's closed. If that's Taylor, he got in under the bell."*

Devon told them: "Taylor retrieved his bag, walked past the House of the Vestals' and through the arch of Titus. From there he took a walkway up into the Palatine. As soon as he climbed the path, he slipped out of view in the Orti Farnesiani. That's a series of partially excavated ruins amidst a grove of trees. It's a mess up there."

Brenda's voice announced, *"Copy that."*

"Brenda?" Chantel asked, "The plan was that you wouldn't advance until we had his location pinpointed. You're still going in?"

"We are," she replied a little defiantly.

"He's got the advantage."

"Roger that. You've got to hunt snipers where they are."

A long pause.

"Given how we're going to have to play this, we've got a low probability of even making contact, let alone getting a shot."

"I don't understand."

"And I don't get international finance, so we're even. For the moment we need to concentrate on the data Devon is streaming. Any movement on the Palatine? Anything to give us a clue about Taylor's hide?"

"Negative," Devon replied through his link. "We can see people walking, but they look like grounds security. It's eerie, Captain. Taylor just seemed to vanish."

Chantel whispered, "Damn it. We should be getting something on the thermal imaging."

Devon must have heard her. He said, "Perhaps he has some technology? A thermal blanket of some sort?"

"We'll deal," Brenda insisted. *"Just keep Devon's people fixed on that visual."*

Regal was shaking her head. Placing a hand over her mic, she said, "This is like reaching into a basket to grab a cobra. He's going to kill them both."

"Perhaps," Chantel said coolly. "But one way or another, we'll get him when he breaks cover."

When she glanced at Mitch, he was watching her through half-frightened eyes.

CHAPTER EIGHTY-TWO

***

BRENDA SCOWLED AT THE GUIDEBOOK THAT MARK STUDIED IN THE GLOW OF A RED-LENSED flashlight. He'd bought it impulsively. Now, to her disgust, he was using it to plan an op? How much more surreal could this get? First, she finds Mark waiting for her in her hotel room, then Chantel informs her they will be working together, and now this?

For her part, she had an advanced tablet that allowed her to follow the satellite feed in real time, its scale adjustable with a flick of her fingers. She glanced down at the expensive-looking case Jaime had given her.

Her ace in the hole?

Traffic roared past on the *Via del Teatro Marcello*. Exhaust and cold air stung her nose. The huge Victor Emmanuel monument dominated the night, bathed in white light.

Mark crowded close, staring over her shoulder at the tablet and cross-checking his guidebook. His black drag bag was propped on the sidewalk beside the aluminum case.

"Looks to me like going in from the northwest is the smart move." Mark rubbed his nose and sniffed.

"Right across the Capitoline would be the best. Probably pick out a great vantage from the Campidoglio terrace. Problem is...every cop in the place is going to wonder what we're up to."

Mark pointed to the guidebook. "What about this walkway here? Maybe there's some sort of cover we can use? A ledge or terrace?"

"We'll give it a try."

Brenda hoisted her case, glanced at the guarding lions, and started up the Cordonata: the long, widening steps designed by Michelangelo. At the top, beginning to pant, she led the way past the statues of Castor and Pollux and hurried across the irregular cobbles.

Atop his horse, Emperor Marcus Aurelius seemed to reach out, his hand gesturing, as though in a futile effort to slow her headlong rush to confront Taylor.

What does he know that I don't?

Brenda smiled at two Carabinieri who lounged before the Palazzo Senatorio. If they only knew what Mark carried in the drag bag thrown over his shoulder.

Winding between the buildings she led the way onto the terrace. At the rampart she stopped. Mark lowered his bag as they stared out at the Forum below and to the left. Floodlights artfully illuminated the architecture. The whisper of Rome's traffic carried on the early evening.

"So that's what's left of Rome's grandeur?" Mark wondered. "It's just broken rocks, crumbling bricks, and muddy paving stones. What would the Caesars say if they could see it now?"

"Probably the same thing we'd say if we could see Washington D.C. in another five hundred years." She took a deep breath. "Or, if Devon's right, maybe another twenty-five."

Mark reached inside his coat, bringing out binoculars and raising them to his eyes. "You're sure he's not down there?"

"Devon would have seen him leave the Palatine. I think."

"You think?" He paused. "You and this Devon aren't exactly blowing my skirt up."

"My call, brother, is the Palatine. He'll control the avenues of approach, set his own fields of fire and exfiltration routes. He's been here, advanced it, knows exactly where to set his hide."

"You're sure?"

"That's where I'd be."

"Yeah," Mark almost whispered. "Me, too."

He went back to glassing with his binoculars, then asked, "The question is, how do we find him in that mess, and how do we get close? If he knew your buddy Devon was watching, he was damned obvious about laying a trail up from the Forum. That's as good as a 'follow me' sign."

Brenda flipped her tablet open to study the display of the Palatine. She could see the signature of the two night watchmen as they walked along a path. The familiar thrill began to warm her nerves and muscles.

Taylor was up there, somewhere, already set up to kill.

So, which approach has he overlooked? If he's the best in the world: None.

Brenda caught movement behind her. Glancing over her shoulder she saw one of the Carabinieri. He stopped at the corner and fixed on Mark scanning the Forum with his binoculars. The man nodded, apparently reassured as he turned away. Despite her case and Mark's bag, they looked touristy enough to fool a cop.

But they wouldn't fool Taylor.

She turned her attention back to the Palatine where it rose behind the intervening buildings. Taylor was a master. He wouldn't pick a commanding location. He'd choose something off to the side, trading fields of fire for security and ease of exfiltration.

"He knows we won't come from the Forum," Mark thought out loud, "I'd choose the slope behind Santa Anastasia, taking the path up through the trees."

"So would I. Which means it's a death trap."

"That leaves the east, finding a way in from along the Via di San Gregorio."

"The Colosseum allows only two avenues of approach. One on the north, the other on the south.

Mark settled it. "The north. Dad always said, 'Sometimes you just gotta gamble and take your chances.'"

CHAPTER EIGHTY-THREE

***

TOM ORTEGA WASN'T SURE HE LIKED HIS NEWFOUND STATUS AS A CAPITOL HILL CELEBRITY. Trevor led the way through the throngs in the Senate hallways. Before the vote, Bill Garrett, the Republican whip, couldn't have applied more pressure on Ortega if he'd used a vise. Despite Tom's "no" vote on the appropriations bill, it had passed with a wide margin.

Now colleagues scowled at him, with mutters about "political grandstanding" just at the range of his hearing. Nor were the reporters any less bothersome, thrusting their microphones his direction, shouting, "Senator, you bucked your party by voting no. Is this related to your problems with the RNC?"

As the competing cameramen elbowed each other for position, he said, "The country can't afford this kind of spending on top of the COVID debt. And most of it, quite frankly, was bull crap for bloated federal programs."

"Bull crap, sir?"

As soon as it came out of Tom's mouth, he regretted it.

Too damn tired. I'd never have slipped like that back on the teams.

He let Trevor, Seth, and Angie take the lead, calling, "Excuse us. Please, let us pass."

It lightened up when they got to the tunnel, but he still got more than his share of scrutinizing looks.

"Bull crap, huh?" Trevor asked over his shoulder.

"Too many cities, too little sleep."

"Yes, sir."

"What about you, Trev. You're not your usual sharp self."

"Too many nights," Angie murmured, only to draw Trevor's hard-eyed squint.

"What?" Ortega asked as they took the stairs up. "Not making enough? Taken on a night job to cover the bills?"

"Something's getting covered," Angie shot back. "And it's not the bills."

"Shut up," Trevor growled as they started down the hallway to Ortega's office. Just before the door, he turned, jerking his head toward the door. "I want a word with the boss."

Angie and Seth shot smug glances at each other, then entered, leaving them as alone as a person could get in the hall at midday.

"What's up?"

Trevor actually blushed. "I met someone. I know it's affecting my work, Tom, but this might be for real."

"And who's the lucky lady?"

Trevor glanced shyly to the side. "She's a reporter. TNN. Veronica Wolf."

"The saucy, cuts-like-a-knife political—"

"Yeah, yeah, but that's her TV personality. She's not really like that."

"Been seeing a lot of her?"

"It's still so new." He gave a desperate shrug. "It's just been me and the job, and all of a sudden I'm..."

"Discovering you're human after all?"

"You could say that."

"Felt the same way when I met Jen. Listen, it's not such a surprise. I'm amazed you haven't had women beating down your door long before now."

Trevor still looked abashed. "Uh, I'd like to ask a favor. The campaign's just getting started and all, and, well, we were talking the other night. I sort of thought it would be a great story to cover the campaign. You know, like an inside story. What life on the campaign trail's really all about."

Tom nodded. His first instinct had been to say no, but then he'd seen the piece she ran on him two nights ago. It had been a fair shake, the strengths and weaknesses, the challenges in implementing his more radical policies.

"Tell you what. Let me talk to her."

Trevor beamed like a midnight light. "You've got a fifteen-minute gap a half an hour from now."

"Sure. Now, let's get to work."

Tom had forgotten and was halfway through his email when a knock came at the door.

Trevor opened it to admit Veronica Wolf, made a quick and flustered introduction, then closed the door behind him as he left.

"Have a seat."

As she seated herself, he took her measure: composed, professionally dressed, her hair perfect, makeup just right. And no wonder Trevor was smitten, she was a knockout. Her dark eyes had fixed on him, returning his inspection.

"Trev tells me you want to cover the campaign from the inside. Given your reputation for never taking prisoners, I guess I'd want to know why."

She took a moment, then answered, "You're a sensation. No one since Barack Obama has hit the same chord. I've been doing my research. Latino kid from a poor family, you excelled in school. Graduated *summa cum laude*. Enlisted, and your military career was exemplary. You built a successful business from scratch, and you've been a thoughtful and adept politician. Now, as a first-term senator, you've managed to get Ben Mackeson and his team to switch sides. You're suddenly a viable candidate for the presidency right out of the gate. Tell me how that isn't a story worth covering in-depth?"

Tom pushed back in his chair. "What's your take on the country's health as a whole?"

"We're in trouble. The country's fractured on political, regional, and racial lines in ways it hasn't been since 1860. The economy isn't improving, despite the government's manufactured stats. Health care is out of control since the ACA expansion. No one believes anything but confusion is coming out of the Washington insider's game, and both sides are liars. My question is, what makes you different from the rest of the self-serving jackals?"

Tom smiled. "I've been out there, Ms. Wolf. The people fear and distrust government. Bureaucracies are running the whole show. EPA, IRS, Department of Interior, Justice, Commerce, take your pick. Essentially, we've created a *fourth* branch of government. A branch that is alienating the people by 'implementing their mandated responsibilities'. This country's a powder keg, and the professional political class doesn't give a damn." He paused, then added, "But I still do."

She gave him a skeptical glance.

"If the government continues to tighten the noose," he said mildly, "we'll either strangle the country, or something's going to snap."

She seemed genuinely baffled for a moment, then the quickness returned to her eyes. "You must have some powerful backers, Senator, because what you're proposing—"

"Yeah, sounds impossible, doesn't it?" He pointed to the picture of Jessie. "That's my daughter. Out there, beyond the beltway, are three hundred million more Americans who are looking at their kids and feeling just as desperate. Everyone has a breaking point. Will they take their role models from the movies they watch, the video games they play, from the talk show hosts? The media has made mentally deranged gunmen into celebrities. Demonizing the other side makes every problem 'the other party's fault'."

"Moderation isn't a winning ticket."

"My colleagues up here can't seem to grasp the fact that they're playing with dynamite while they're lining their pockets and playing the 'inside' game."

She studied Jessie's photo, as if processing something.

"What makes you think you're the man to do this?"

Ortega looked her hard in the eyes. "Someone has to."

"It's really that simple for you?"

"Telling the truth is always simple. It's the repercussions that will chew you up and spit you out broken and bloody."

She barely smiled at his joke. "But then, the repercussions are the real story, aren't they?"

"Ben will throw a fit, but you're welcome to see just how bloody this thing gets. Maybe someone will learn something from it."

With the slightest narrowing of her eyes, she said, "Count on it."

CHAPTER EIGHTY-FOUR

***

MARK LAY NEXT TO HIS SISTER WHERE THE ANGLE OF TWO RUINED WALLS PROVIDED both concealment and cover. He had his rifle, a black tactical Remington 700 in .308 resting on its bipod. The stems and branches of a winter-bare bush masked their position. Brenda had a thermal scope to her eye as she carefully studied the Palatine's walks, walls, and ornamental trees.

Under her breath, Mark heard her whisper, "Why the hell would you bring us here?"

She was talking to Taylor, of course.

Mark shot her a sidelong glance. Brenda had changed, become a stranger to him. During the war, she'd been focused like a laser, dedicated to the mission with an almost fanatical zeal. At least until Bill Solace was killed. She'd never admitted that she loved the man, not to Mark anyway.

Part of her had died with Bill. In civilian life, she'd been remote, tackling her executive protection business with competent efficiency but not passion.

What the hell happened to you, sis?

This was more than Kelly and Mom and Dad. This new Brenda was hard and unyielding, as if she were facing a demon only she could see. And she seemed bent on protecting him from The Foundation. And that worried him.

Back to the mission, fool.

The Palatine Hill was like a rat's maze filled with partially stabilized ruins, modern construction, hedges, walkways, and grassy open spaces. But wherever Taylor had gone to ground, it was with thermal cover. Something the satellite couldn't penetrate.

With his trained eye, Mark noted every place a sniper should be. Then he turned his attention to places where he shouldn't. That's where Taylor would shoot from.

Time after time, he returned his attention to the Palatine Museum roof. And then there were the towers behind the Domus Flavia, the ancient fountain.

Mark used his night scope as he worked foot by foot, looking for irregularities, any sign of movement, or hint that a sniper lay in wait.

That they were still alive was proof that they'd infiltrated through a route Taylor either hadn't expected or had allowed them to approach.

What are you thinking, damn you? Of all the places on earth, why bring us here? To crouch in the shadow of dead emperors from a vanished world.

In Mark's earpiece Chantel's voice said, *"The night watchmen are headed your way on the path from the House of Augustus."*

"Roger that."

Mark barely shifted his hand to give a thumb's up, his signal to Brenda that he'd heard.

Minutes later the beam of a flashlight announced the watchmen's approach. Brenda focused her thermal scope and watched them walk past. They looked bored out of their skulls, unaware of the deadly game being played around them.

As they departed, scratchy Italian voices could be heard through their two-way radios.

"If we just had an idea," Brenda muttered to herself, glancing at the aluminum case.

Shifting, she pulled the acute directional microphone from her pocket. Bracing it, she focused the delicate piece of equipment and began the slow process of listening, hoping that it would pick up a casual word between Taylor and his spotter. A guy named Bennie if the files could be trusted.

An hour later, they still had nothing.

"Think we ought to reposition?" Mark whispered through his comm.

"I think he's counting on just that," she replied. "Somewhere in here, he's got a long line of sight with an unrestricted field of fire. It's a waiting game. He wants us to move, expose ourselves."

"Yeah, I'd be doing the same thing," Mark whispered.

"Brenda? Our night watchmen are coming back your way."

"Roger that."

Brenda tensed in that old familiar way he'd known since childhood. "Mark, I've got a crazy idea."

CHAPTER EIGHTY-FIVE

***

"YOU'VE LET A SLITHERING VIPER INTO OUR MIDST." BEN MACKESON FIXED HARD EYES ON Tom Ortega. "Veronica Wolf isn't interested in documenting a campaign. She's a human chainsaw who gets her jollies by cutting people down. And the bigger they are when they topple, the more she loves it. I've used her for the purpose myself." An eye narrowed. "Unless, of course, it's something she can dangle like a sword over someone's head for future gain."

Ortega glanced toward the rear of the cabin where Veronica was seating herself in the back row and taking out her laptop.

"What specific sword do you expect her to discover, Ben? Something going on that I don't know about?"

Mackeson shoved hands into his pockets. "You're a real-world guy. I don't have to tell you that everything is compromise. Viewed one way, it's what has to be done for the common good. Spin it another, and you're cutting some deprived baby's throat and throwing a grandma off a cliff."

"That's exactly what I'm telling the people. By fixing the mess we're in, there's going to be positives and negatives. But, say we win? Is it easier to implement policy when you've told the people beforehand that it isn't going to be pretty? Or when you've lied to them, and they think they've been sold a bill of goods?"

Ben ground his teeth, refusing to answer.

"Ben, the country's about to come apart. The whole world is teetering on the precipice of disaster. God alone knows how the Russian problem is going to end. You're a smart guy. You know what has to be done."

Mackeson jerked his head toward Veronica Wolf. "And you think adding a self-serving, grand-standing assassin to the team is going to be a plus?"

Tom glanced thoughtfully to the rear, meeting Veronica Wolf's eyes as she studied him. "If she's a...a human chainsaw? Wasn't that how you put it? I'd say the smart thing is to give her some wood to cut. We just need to point out the trees that need to be toppled."

"I hope to God you know what you're doing."

"The important thing about a chainsaw? You've got to know how to operate it. How it works, and what you have to do to avoid kickback."

"What's kickback?"

"You've never run a saw, have you?"

Ben worked his jaws, thinking. "Tell you what. I've got a call to make. I know just the person who might give us an operator's manual on Ms. Wolf. The kind of information that would give us a handle on our new saw."

"Who's that?"

"Poul Hammond's boss."

"Chantel?"

"No, her brother. And in the meantime, Tom, remember that trying to play with a viper is a good way to get killed."

CHAPTER EIGHTY-SIX

***

BRENDA TENSED, EXPECTING A BULLET AT ANY SECOND AS SHE WALKED, TRYING TO act casual and bored. Even now, Taylor was watching them through his scope, her body fixed in his crosshairs. His finger would be caressing the trigger.

She could *feel* him out there in the night.

The uniforms fit poorly, hers too big, Mark's too small. They strolled casually down the path in front of the Palatine Museum. The cap on Brenda's head barely stayed in place even with her hair piled beneath. It was all she could do to keep from jumping each time the radio on her belt erupted in static-laden chatter.

The guards had been easy. All it had taken was two squirts from Gunnarson's aerosol can, and they'd been out in seconds. They'd be regaining consciousness soon, only to find themselves in their underwear, gagged by their knotted socks, and zip-tied into immobility.

Like any good security guard, Mark stepped to the side, checking the museum door to ensure it was locked.

Still, her nerves were like strung wire, her heart pounding. The bullet could come from anywhere. She'd never feel her ruptured body hit the ground.

These might be my last seconds on earth.

Mark resumed his leisurely pace at her side as they passed aimlessly in front of the oval fountain. She flashed her light this way and that, searching not for Taylor's hide—he'd be too good for that—but for the kind of places a hide or spider hole might be located.

Easy, Brenda. Don't look nervous!

But her skin continued to crawl, and it took effort to make herself breathe. Images kept flashing of Kelly's neck exploding under the impact of a bullet.

"You sure this is a good idea?" Mark's voice was barely audible in her earpiece.

"Too late now." Her mouth dry, and she could barely swallow.

Where is he?

So many dark shadows, ruins, trees, and corners. Taylor's presence hung spider-like and cold in the darkness.

God, Mark's going to die out here, and it will be my fault. First Kelly, then Mom and Dad, and now my brother.

Mark's half-panicked laughter made her jump.

"What?" she hissed.

"He's gonna fucking kill us."

"Then let's turn around and beat feet the hell out of here while we can." And she meant it.

"He killed Kelly...Mom and Dad." His voice held a maniacal edge.

As she searched the ominous dark, memories of Chantel's words echoed within. *No London, Paris, Tokyo, or New York. Just cannibalistic gangs of looters prowling the wreckage.*

So, what was there to live for? From the depths of her heart, she could see Bill Solace giving her that exhausted look.

She chuckled, finding gallows humor in the hopelessness. "*Bene. Ave imperator, morituri te salutant.*"

"Huh?"

"Hail, Caesar. We who are about to die salute you."

"You're a sick fucking bitch."

"Keep your voice down."

The eerie sensation of being watched prickled at the back of her neck as they passed between the Casa di Livia and the villa where Augustus Caesar once lived. Mark flashed his light at the ruins of the Temple of Cybele, then stopped as he flicked the beam toward the arch leading to the Farnese Gardens. He gave her the slight inclination of his head: asking if they should try the gardens?

No, Taylor wanted her in the magnificent ruins. Where he killed her was a statement, a ritual sacrifice to his clients.

She shook her head, walking around the gated ruins of Livia's villa. The woman had been Augustus' wife. The one who'd murdered half of her family to ensure that her son Tiberius followed Augustus as emperor.

A psychopathic woman? Was that what Taylor was telling her?

It didn't seem to fit. Brenda considered herself a protector, not a stealthy poisoner.

Rounding the house, Mark shined his light at the entrance to the Cryptoporticus. The dark tunnel sent shivers down her spine, as if it were an opening to hell. The feeling of threat tightened like a band around her chest.

The interpretive sign told her that the mad emperor Caligula had been murdered in the stygian depths of that covered walkway.

As Mark flicked his light away, he surprised her by yawning deeply, stretching, and turning to head lazily back the way they'd come.

"What?" she whispered when she caught up a couple of steps later.

"Got him."

"Where?"

"That damn tunnel."

"You saw him?"

"Nope. But just the same, he's there."

"And if you're wrong?"

"I'm not. He's got a clear shot at anyone passing between the tunnel entrance and the towers."

"That's why he's not showing up on the thermal scopes. He can't be flanked. He's observing every potential shooting position where we could set up for a counter shot."

"The moment we poked our heads up to range him, he'd have us. And if it goes bad, he's out the other end of the tunnel. Unobserved."

For the first time that night, Brenda smiled. "Time to open Sam Gunnarson's case. Sorry, bro. You're not going to get to shoot him. It's payback time."

CHAPTER EIGHTY-SEVEN

***

IN SIMOND COMMAND, CHANTEL CONSULTED HER MAP AND POINTED AT THE WALL MONITOR. "You heard them. Put everything we've got on that tunnel entrance."

Brenda is staying so cool.

Chantel's eyes narrowed as the computer techs refined the satellite resolution on the dark mouth of the Cryptoporticus.

"We've got a faint thermal reading from the tunnel mouth," one of the techs reported. "Could be human body heat, or it could be that the tunnel is warmer inside than ambient air temperature."

On the monitor, the two figures representing Brenda and Mark had reached their weapons cache. The bodies of the two guards were now wriggling where they lay behind the wall.

Chantel watched Brenda bend over the cool square of her aluminum case.

"What's in the box?" Regal asked.

"An armed drone," Jaime Sandoval said from where he watched with crossed arms.

Mitch straightened. "You didn't clear it with me."

Jaime shrugged. "Brenda asked that I keep it confidential, Chantel concurred."

Chantel turned to Mitch. "Taylor's murdered Janeesh and Dad. If I had to, I'd hit the son of a bitch from the air with hellfire missiles and damn the consequences." She glanced back at the tunnel where it glowed gray in the monitor. "But it would be a shame to ruin such an important piece of history."

"What's the drone armed with?" Mitch asked.

Sandoval told him, "Small, remotely guided infrared heat-seeking missiles. A little bigger than pop-bottle rockets, they explode on contact. While the wound inflicted will no doubt be moderately debilitating, the shrapnel contains a nerve agent."

Chantel smiled thinly, her eyes slitted. "We're going to get them alive. And before they die, we're going to know everything about who hired them, and how to trace the traitor."

"I thought Mark Pepper was going to shoot them." Mitch stuffed his hands into his back pockets.

"He would have, had the opportunity presented," Chantel told him absently. "Instead of a regular bullet, his weapon is loaded with flechettes that would have allowed us to capture Taylor alive."

"You didn't tell me that."

"Mitch, don't get your nose out of joint. No one blames you for Dad's death but you. You're in charge of upgrading the island defense net. That's Dad's plan, and no one, *no one*, is more capable of overseeing the construction."

On the monitor Brenda could be seen as she settled the visored helmet on her head. The holographic display it projected allowed the operator to see what the drone saw, controlling its actions by movements of the hands.

"Devon, can you...? Devon?"

His monitor was blank, and then, a moment later, Devon's face reformed, looking guilty. "Sorry. Must have been a sunspot. All links are reestablished."

Chantel barely noticed the look of irritation that crossed Mitch's face as he pulled his cell phone from his back pocket and squinted at the display, muttering, "Contractors have the worst timing," he pressed an icon and shoved it back into his pocket.

"*Drone's in the air,*" Brenda's voice came through the speakers.

Every eye went to the wall monitor that linked to the drone, allowing them to see what Brenda did. The drone wobbled slightly as it rose, wavered, and steadied.

"Come on, Brenda," Sam Gunnarson growled under his breath. "You were better than this when we were practicing."

Chantel's blood began to race as the view of the Palatine and its ruins refined in the drone's IR cameras. The little flying machine started forward, crossing the remains of the Domus Flavia. The ruined walls and column bases, being heat sinks, glowed white against the cooler winter grass.

The only sound in the room was the faint hum of computer fans.

Chantel's fists were clenched, nails biting into her palms.

The drone veered east, skirting the ruin walls, then passed over trees to the long length of the Cryptoporticus. The tunnel had allowed the emperors to walk to and from the Forum, protected from the elements and observation. As it had once made the perfect place to ambush mad Caligula, it now served the same purpose for Taylor and his spotter.

Brenda's flying had improved, the drone more stable as it dropped low, easing its way along the top of the tunnel.

As the end neared, Chantel rose, heart hammering as if she, herself, were there.

Now it hovered over the tunnel entrance, turning, and slowly lowered.

Good, Brenda. Good. Take your time. Do it right.

"Easy," Gunnarson was whispering. "Easy, Captain."

As the cameras dropped below the lip of the tunnel, two hot-white signatures—men on their bellies, the long shape of a rifle in one's hands—filled the monitor.

"Fire in the hole," Brenda's words came through the speakers.

And then, the display erupted in flashes of white.

Several seconds later, the image cleared to reveal both men, positions altered, and apparently motionless.

"We got them!" Regal cried, leaping to her feet.

Chantel said into her mic, "Val? Extraction please."

"On the way. Congratulations, Captain Pepper."

"Roger that. We'll be ready for dust off."

"Val?" Mitch muttered. "He's there, too?"

Chantel dropped numbly to her chair, a huge sense of relief washing through her. The grinding terror was over. The assassin who'd brought them so much misery and grief was theirs.

"Can't wait to hear those two sing," Regal said as she paced. "All it will take is an injection, stimulating molecules that will trigger every pain response in the body. They'll talk."

On the screen, Brenda and her brother were approaching the tunnel mouth from the side, skirting their way to the opening. Chantel watched

Brenda use a mirror to peek inside, and then step to the opening and pull the grated gate to one side.

Moments later, Val's helicopter landed in the grassy area beside the House of Livia, and Brenda and Mark dragged two senseless bodies to the chopper. Then they were off, the chopper lifting, heading east and out of the monitor's range.

"How are we doing?" Chantel asked.

Val's voice crackled through the speakers. "Don't know who these guys are, Fox, but from the pictures we've got, they're not Taylor and Bennie."

CHAPTER EIGHTY-EIGHT

✳✳✳

THE TRAIN WHISKED ITS WAY SOUTH, WINDING THROUGH ITALIAN HILLS; THE NIGHT BEYOND the window was dotted with lights as they passed towns and farms.

Taylor, fuming, glanced absently at the passing darkness. Bennie sat across from him, arms folded, head down.

"What the hell could have gone wrong?" Bennie asked for the umpteenth time.

"Something."

It's another fucking failure!

It had been perfect. He and Bennie had been waiting in their hide, rifle propped. The night security had obviously changed, the two lackadaisical men replaced by a much more vigilant man and woman. But then people tended to be more alert early in their shift.

The guards hadn't been out of sight more than five minutes before the abort had come through.

"They were there," Bennie muttered. "I could feel them."

"Of course, they were there." Taylor stewed in his rage. "This Pepper woman *had* to be there. We knew they were in Rome, looking for us. She and that brother of hers couldn't have walked away from the challenge any more than we could have."

"Maybe they didn't. Maybe they figured out where we were." Bennie crossed his arms tightly on his chest. "It was an abort, boss. Not our failure. The client called it off, which meant he had his reasons."

"So what went wrong?"

"I don't fucking know. We had all the advantages. Used their satellites against them. With our motion detector, we'd have even had them if they'd tried infiltrating up the tunnel. They should have expected us to be high. In the tower. It should have been obvious.

They should have passed right in front of us to get a shot. It was right there, out in the open."

"Damn that bitch!" Taylor stiffened.

"What?"

Taylor knotted his fist. "You said it yourself. They were right out in the open." He glared hotly at Bennie. "I had them. In my scope. My finger millimeters from the trigger."

"What are you talking about?"

"The shift change? The man and woman? Dressed like security? Did a complete recon, right before our eyes."

"And picked us out like flies on fruit," Bennie groaned. "Fuck!"

"It's the only explanation." Enraged he might have been, but a bitter amusement bent Taylor's lips. He could allow Brenda Pepper this small victory. After all, what good was an unworthy adversary? Yes, she'd spoiled his precious record. But sending Pepper to her grave would be fair compensation.

CHAPTER EIGHTY-NINE

* * *

"SO, IT TURNS OUT THAT WE'RE HOLDING TWO CORRUPT ROMAN CITY BUREAUCRATS THAT Taylor lured to the Cryptoporticus with the promise of receiving bribes?" Regal asked, her arms crossed as she stood on the balcony overlooking the Caribbean.

Brenda—propped on the terrace wall—glanced at Val, then nodded. "Apparently the two were overpowered by Bennie and Taylor, then they were tied up. They tell us they laid there for hours, sweating in fear as Taylor waited behind the rifle and Bennie studied the surroundings through his night-vision gear. Then, all of a sudden, Taylor presses a finger to his earpiece. He mutters something to Bennie. They grab the two guys, jerk them up front, and tell them that if they get up before fifteen minutes pass, it will set off an explosive that will kill them."

Val, his face pensive, added, "They were the fall guys if anything went wrong."

"God," Brenda mused, "these bastards are clever."

"You were better," Regal said evenly. "Posing as the two security officers? A stroke of brilliance."

"But they were tipped off." Val's expression had turned to ice. "How? Who knew?"

"Devon?" Mitch asked where he had been leaning against the wall, listening.

"I trust Devon," Chantel told him.

"Think about it. A 'sunspot' caused him to lose contact the moment Taylor was located."

Chantel shot a disbelieving glance at Mitch, who softly asked, "Do you trust Devon, or just *want* to trust him?"

Chantel rubbed her forehead, as if to soothe a blinding headache.

"Devon's the linchpin holding everything together. He doesn't have to play games with assassins. If he's not with us, it's all lost, and he knows it."

Brenda shrugged. "What about his people? The inner circle running the satellite. Or Rusty Patton for that matter?"

"That's a whole new can of worms," Mitch muttered.

Chantel's green eyes had a pained look.

Brenda straightened, arching her back. She hadn't slept well on the flight back to Simond Island. "You guys will have to ferret that out. My problem is Taylor. My guess is that he's seething."

"Enraged people make mistakes," Val noted.

"True," she countered. "This could very well goad him into the unthinkable and damn the consequences."

Chantel said, "We've already allowed him to distract us. If I'm worrying about Taylor, I could miss something in the markets, or a political nuance that could doom us all. I can't afford a single mistake. So, how do we counter?"

Brenda took a deep breath. "For the moment, I don't have a clue."

CHAPTER NINETY

✴✴✴

WHEN BRENDA WALKED INTO MARK'S APARTMENT, SHE FOUND HIM OUT ON THE BALCONY. With the helmet on, he reminded her of Darth Vader as he bent over the remote-control drone and fiddled with the controls. The muscles that bunched beneath his tee-shirt reminded her of corded rope.

"How you doing?"

"This thing won't fly." He took the helmet off in disgust. "The battery's charged. It whirs when I start it. But when I move my hands, it just sits there."

"The operating frequencies are jammed. You're in one of the most monitored places on earth."

He scowled up at the camera mounted below the roof, grunted to himself, and placed the drone and helmet back in the box before latching it and standing up. "Yeah, so I've noticed. I feel like a caged rat."

"You are."

She stepped up beside him, staring out at the Caribbean, sniffing at the damp vegetation-laden breeze as the night creatures buzzed in the forest around them. "I wish to hell you weren't here."

"Sis, you want to tell me about Simond International? Who they really are? Or am I frozen out? I mean, they just fly us to Italy, hijack a satellite, supply you with tactical gear and intel, and snatch us out of the middle of Rome. And that blond guy, Val, giving you the eye? What's with him? My 'oh-shit-ometer' pegs itself every time he's around. You watch yourself with him."

"How did Chantel convince you to come?"

"She told me I could kill Taylor. She also told me that you needed me."

Brenda massaged her forehead. "My God, I'm standing at the train track with my hand on the lever. Which track do I choose? How many do I sacrifice?"

"Train track?"

"Once you're in, bro, I...I'm not sure you can ever..." She let the sentence hang and studied the cameras.

Mark puffed out a weary exhale. "It's like I fell through the fucking rabbit hole. Kelly, Mom, Dad, and then I'm here? Where the hell have you been for the last three days?"

"Studying intel, planning Chantel's schedule, trying to second guess what Taylor's going to do next." She smiled absently. "You see the news? Platnikov's been relocated 'for reasons of health'?"

"Yeah, I mean wow. I still talk to guys in the teams. Most of them were deployed to Europe. They've been preparing for the big one, training to fight Russians. And blooey, Platnikov goes off his rocker, and civil war breaks out in Russia?"

"International stock markets are up by fifteen percent. Word is that the Kremlin is locked in a power struggle, and Platnikov hasn't been seen since." She stared hard into the distance and saw nothing.

"Okaaay. I know that look. You used to get it after a successful operation where you took out the bad guys. Spill it."

"Chantel and I had some dealings with Platnikov. That's all."

He was watching her like a hawk did a mouse. She'd never been able to fool him.

"You're not telling me everything."

"Nope."

He crossed his arms. "Sis, I don't know who you are anymore. You want to give it to me straight?"

"World's going to shit, Mark, and nothing can stop it: All the nations up to their ears in debt they can never repay. Countries going to war over resources. Climate change affecting agriculture. Eight billion people surviving on a dwindling food supply. You can't count the revolutions and coups, the massacres on the news every night. America's fractured, and states are talking secession. Pick a region and you'll find tinderboxes ready to explode. Platnikov would have been the deal breaker." She paused. "Until the next one comes along."

"So, what's Simond's part in all this?"

"They say they're trying to save something, to stave off the apocalypse for as long as they can."

"They're the good guys? Really?"

"There are no good guys, bro. Just the best of bad choices."

"So you believe them?"

"China's strategic plan is to move on Southeast Asia. Solidify their holdings before India can grab the region. India, in turn, has to deal with Pakistan before they can hope to counter China. Iran is eyeing the Gulf States and Arabian Peninsula for a takeover after they nuke Israel. Europe is expected to collapse of its own weight when energy supplies and trade routes start to falter. They won't be able to feed their people. Russia mistakenly figures it can be self-sustaining once it gets its own people under control. South American economies are going to crash, which will cause old frictions to ignite. Venezuela and Ecuador will turn on Columbia. Argentina will take on Chile, and Brazil is expected to devour itself in civil war."

"What about America?"

"If someone lays a string of nukes across the sky and takes out the computers and electrical grids with EMPs, the east and west coasts turn to barbarism. Urban areas will ignite. Too many people and no way to feed them when the lights go out, the water goes off, and the computers stop working. EMP fries the electronic fuel injection and cars and trucks won't run. The predictive model I've seen expects rural parts of the Midwest, Rocky Mountain West, and South to muddle along on local agriculture."

"Jesus! What are you eating in your Cheerios in the morning?"

She gave him a long, sad look. "Even long-term planners in our own government have been preparing. What do you think gun control, the Affordable Care Act, the NSA spying, the constant growth in government have all been about? Slip-shod for sure, but it's about power and control when things come apart. DoD has several plans for martial law, which is why a lot of the useless bases in strategic parts of the country haven't been closed."

"You've *seen* this?"

She nodded wearily. "Problem is, most government models are based on a slow disintegration that allows them time to implement control 'for the public good'. They don't understand the ramifications of a sudden, catastrophic collapse."

"You sound as crazy as Platnikov."

"I did drink from the same bottle."

"What bottle?"

"Nothing."

At that moment, Chantel knocked, admitting herself at Mark's call. She walked across the room, a familiar-looking bottle of Hennessey Timeless in her hand. Just a friendly reminder that she'd been listening?

Chantel greeted Mark with a smile before handing the bottle to Brenda. "This just arrived. Compliments of Katya."

"What's the verdict?"

Chantel eyed Mark cautiously, as if unsure what she should say. "Katya had to move before she was ready. She expected a whole month to get her ducks in a row, but it looks like Georgi will end up as the number two man in the new government. Some of the more radical players remain a threat. The Gorky Plan, however, is officially dead."

"Katya must be grinning like a cat."

"Katya is Katya." Chantel hesitated, turning her attention to Mark. "Tell me, what do you think of Thomas Ortega? Honestly."

Mark shrugged, but he was eyeing her warily. "He's a politician. Progressive liberals are going to hate him because he's talking about scaling back social programs and cutting taxes and regulations. Social conservatives don't like him because he doesn't give a damn about right to life, who marries who, Draconian immigration reform and doesn't attend the right church. Me, I like the guy. He put his ass on the line and got shot at. And when he talks, it's not full of bullshit."

Chantel considered the words. "He seems to strike a chord with most Americans."

"My boss at the hardware store loved him. Said he was the only politician who understood what it meant to sign a check on the front instead of the back."

She turned back to Brenda. "I need your advice. Robert wants me in Washington. To cement some financial support for Senator Ortega's campaign. It will also give me a chance to spend some face time with some of our accounts."

"Thought we were going to the World Economic Forum in Davos?"

"I'm sending Ricard. Robert made a pretty convincing case."

"Robert made a case?" Brenda shook her head. "For what? Being

Taylor's special target in a shooting gallery? Unless, of course, you take all the meetings on Big Bird."

"You are assuming Taylor knew I was going to be there. So far, this hasn't gone any further than Robert, Regal, and you." She gave Mark a smile. "I believe I can safely assume, Sergeant First Class Pepper, that you're on my side when it comes to Taylor."

"Yes, ma'am. I think you can."

"So, Brenda. If I have to do this, what's the smartest strategy?"

"I talk you out of it, and you don't go."

"Robert seems to think my influence would solidify Senator Ortega's chances of winning in the fall."

"He's one of yours?" Mark asked in surprise.

"I wouldn't say that." She seemed to hesitate. "But we share some common interests. Our data also indicate that if Falco, Brown, or Senator Calloway wins the Republican nomination, they won't have the will to tackle what's coming. And of the five potential Democrats, any of their socialist platforms will precipitate an economic disaster that will drive parts of the country into secession at best, open revolt at worst."

"How would they do that?" Mark demanded.

"By empowering the bureaucracies to seize assets for redistribution in their crusade for racial and social justice. It's a simple formula: Take too much from the producers and you remove their incentive to produce. Why should the producers work twelve hours a day, seven days a week when the government is going to take it all away and give it to someone who's not carrying their weight? Meanwhile, what's left after the bureaucracies take their share is distributed among people who don't have the skills to utilize the wealth as investment capital. For a time, luxury sales increase, but it's a flash in the pan. As that spending decreases, deflation drives the government to seize more assets, which discourages more producers, and the deflationary system cascades downward. The government, simultaneously, is borrowing money to cover the deficit. In that scenario the United States runs out of money within a year and a half."

Mark was staring wide-eyed.

"Ortega's that critical?" Brenda asked.

"That's Devon's prediction based on the metadata. And we're not even sure that Ortega can stave off economic disaster long enough to buy us our five years. Providing we have five years." She gave Brenda a meaningful glance.

Just like with Platnikov. It's happening faster than anyone thought. No one, not even The Foundation, can predict the fallout. Dear God.

"Hold it!" Mark cried. "America's not going to run out of money."

Chantel gave him a sober appraisal. "Sergeant, let's say you have a rich man living at the end of your block. For years you've been loaning him money to expand his businesses with the expectation that he's going to pay you back someday with interest. But during that time, you've noticed that not only are his businesses stagnant, and many are failing, but he's living a life of splendor, hiring lots of household staff, and giving large sums of cash to his cronies who in turn are buying big houses and fancy cars. Now you learn that he's in the hole for more money than his ailing businesses can ever hope to generate. And worse, he's contracted to keep paying his thousands of employees and good friends for years to come."

"I guess I'd get a lawyer and get what I could before he declared bankruptcy."

"When you add the national debt and unfunded mandates together, the United States carries over six trillion in debt and unfunded mandates. At the same time, its gross domestic production is ailing since money that could go into investment is supporting social programs. At this rate, within the next few years, and barring any other disasters, the United States will be unable to even pay interest, let alone a percentage of the principal on its loans. But it's still obligated to keep paying out trillions in entitlements, wages, unemployment, disability, subsidies, and pensions. Not to mention running the government and all of its programs."

"Two years?" Brenda wondered. "How do you know?"

"Because they keep raising the interest rate they'll pay on bonds and treasuries. They have to, as an incentive to investors, since—as I stated in my example—the rest of the 'guys on the block' aren't buying bonds with the enthusiasm they once did."

"Then why isn't someone doing something about it?" Mark demanded.

"For politicians, the mere mention of cutting social security, medicare, or other entitlements, is political suicide."

Chantel turned back to Brenda. "Now, Captain, is there a way to get me to Washington without anyone knowing?"

CHAPTER NINETY-ONE

***

THE PACKED HALL AT RUTGERS UNIVERSITY WAS ALMOST INVISIBLE TO TOM ORTEGA—blinded as he was by the spotlights illuminating the stage where he, Gene Falco, Ed Brown, and Zack Calloway, stood behind podiums for the first Republican debate.

Seated at the desk before them, Jean Masson, public radio's well-known commentator, laced her fingers together. Her attention focused on Governor Falco as he extended a hand toward the audience and declared, "Unlike the good senator from Ohio, I have a totally different perspective on federal employees. These dedicated men and women are the machinery that makes America function.

"To my way of thinking, the good senator is out of line in his demands that we fire half of all the federal employees. Those are jobs! People's lives! What are we going to do? Throw civil servants who've kept this country running into the streets? Not in a Falco administration."

The applause thundered from the audience.

"Governor Brown?" Masson prompted. "You have thirty seconds."

Brown grabbed the lapel of his suit, his hallmark gesture indicating the gravity of his statement. "No one questions that the bureaucracies are too ponderous to function. The Democrats, and yes, Republicans before them, have created a multi-headed monster. The first thing I'd do upon the initiation of a Brown administration is to freeze hiring. Let attrition take its course. No civil servant need lose his job in a bloodbath."

She turned to Ortega. "Senator, it seems your colleagues don't agree with you. If you'd care to rebut, you have thirty seconds.

Ortega laid a hand on the lectern, turning to glance at his opponents.

He waited for a couple of seconds in silence, then calmly said, "We don't have time to wait for attrition. Nor did I ever suggest we ax *half* of the federal workforce. How about this? If the United States is broke, it won't be writing checks. Period."

He looked toward the cameras. "Either we institute a horse-sense-based transition from federal to private-sector jobs and start creating wealth, or this country is headed for an economic disaster like we've never seen."

"Horse sense, Senator?" Masson seemed amused.

He rubbed his chin, giving her a skeptical tilt of the head. "From my experience in politics, sense just never seems to be common."

That brought laughter from the crowd.

He listened to Calloway, Falco, and Brown give their closing statements, and then it was his turn.

Looking at the camera, he said, "My colleagues are good men. The same with the Democrats. They will tell you whatever it takes to get elected. My promise is to give it to you straight, and to ask your help when the heavy lifting comes. Look at the numbers. Think. It. Through. Thank you, and good night."

Applause filled the room.

Ortega shook his opponents' hands, and muttered platitudes.

Then the reporters crowded around, mostly asking inane questions.

"Do you really think that being direct is the right approach, Senator?" an ABC reporter asked.

Ortega smiled slightly. "It's the only hope the country has."

The look she gave him was expectant, the microphone still proffered.

He added, "Pay attention here: The country's in trouble. Let's just see if we can fix the damn thing."

Then Jen walked out from behind the curtain, Jessie, her legs still in braces, grinning from ear to ear.

"Excuse me, my favorite fans are here." And he ran to grab his daughter into his arms and hug his wife.

"Baby? How are you doing?"

"I'm growing new joints, Daddy! It hurts, but you can see it! And I can bend my legs and arms more every day!"

Jen kissed his cheek. "Tom, you were brilliant out there."

He tried to ignore the cameras and microphones pointed in his direction as the press crowded around them. "Yeah, well, we'll see. It's just going to get harder from here. And I'm pissing off a lot of powerful people."

CHAPTER NINETY-TWO

***

ROBERT SIMOND AND POUL HAMMOND RECLINED ON COUCHES FACING THE HUGE TELEVISION. Beside them, on an easy chair, the Republican National Committee chairman, Marcus Dagget, had an irritated expression on his face as he rotated a glass of vodka in his fingers.

Robert chuckled, reaching for his own tumbler of small-batch bourbon. "You gotta hand it to Ortega—he doesn't pull any punches."

"Arrogant prick," Dagget added. "The stupid fuck thinks telling the truth is going to get him the nomination? Back when Romney screwed up by saying the forty-seven percent getting handouts weren't going to vote for him, he was dead damn right. Now it's fifty-five percent."

"People vote for whoever offers them the most free stuff," Robert agreed. Then he added, "Glad you decided to accept our offer to come and watch the debates."

Dagget gave them his best plastic smile. "Wouldn't have missed it, Mr. Simond. Your support over the years has always been appreciated."

"Even when you knew we were throwing our weight behind the Democratic candidates?"

"You had your reasons." Dagget shrugged smoothly. "And I understand that reasons change. Or, at least, that's my hope for the coming election. Gene Falco's a solid man. Reasonable. We'd love to discuss your interests and concerns. I'm sure that some accommodations can be made. Perhaps even in the platform itself."

Robert—expression purposefully thoughtful—glanced at Hammond, who in turn had a serious set to his brow. "You're assuming Falco's going to be the nominee, not to mention the next president."

Dagget spread his hands suggestively. "The country's on the verge of coming apart. The Democratic field doesn't seem to be catching on to that. Ortega's right about one thing: The country's dissatisfied with the way things are going. Gene's got a lot of support, and we're just going to build on that. The fact that you're here? You read the wind just as well as I do, Mr. Simond."

Robert sipped his bourbon, delighted with the taste. Life for whiskey drinkers had improved with the advent of the small-batch distillers.

"It isn't any secret that we control some of the more, um, effective super PACs. Beyond that, we have influence with some other major political donors."

"I'd call that a minor understatement." Dagget leaned forward. "Since we're here among friends, and off the record, let's talk hypothetically. In return for your support, what would you be looking for specifically?"

"We are off the record, Marcus. But we are not talking hypothetically. And as delighted as I am to know that you're not wearing recording equipment, I'm satisfied that nothing said in this room will go beyond it. Isn't that right?"

"You scanned me?"

"The detectors are in the door frame, and they're very sophisticated. We even downloaded your contacts list and the call log from your phone. Oh, and I'd spring for a shielded billfold. You're four thousand and fifty-two dollars from the limit on your VISA. Which you can afford to pay given the one-point-nine million you've got spirited away in that Cayman bank account of yours."

Dagget's smile had turned into a rictus.

"Relax, Marcus," Robert told him genially. "We really don't give a shit. We just thought that mentioning those picky little details would reassure you about our sincerity. Oh, to be sure, we'll be offering support to Democratic candidates in selected races where it suits our purposes, but you're right. For the moment, the wind blows Republican."

Dagget finally remembered to breathe. "So, what do you want Gene to do?"

Poul Hammond's face adopted a placid expression. "Dropping out of the race would look suspicious."

"I don't get it?" Dagget looked from one to the other.

"You're right," Robert said solicitously. "Falco's a good man. And it would be a shame if he had to go down hard, but the Democrats know about his...shall we call them flaws? As you've just discovered, our ability to investigate a person's deepest secrets is unsurpassed. If Falco's skeletons come clattering out of the closet as an 'October surprise'—as I'm sure they will, should he become the nominee—he's unelectable."

Dagget had turned white. "So, you want Brown or Calloway?"

Robert gently shook his head. "Both damaged goods. And I assure you, *I know it.*"

"Who then?"

"It's Thursday night." Robert glanced at Poul Hammond. "The Iowa caucuses are on Tuesday. What do you think? Does Monday give Marcus enough time to deal with Calloway and Brown?"

"I'd think so," Hammond agreed.

"Good." Robert took another sip of his bourbon. "Monday should be plenty of time for the RNC to find a way to throw its entire weight behind Tom Ortega for the Republican nomination."

"That's *insane!*" Dagget was half out of his chair.

"Not at all." Robert stared thoughtfully at the three binders on the table before him. "Each of those reports is comprehensive. One each for Falco, Brown, and Calloway. Far be it for me to tell you how to run your operation, Marcus, but a simple meeting with each of the candidates, allowing them to scan the contents, should provide ample opportunity for them to come to the same conclusion that we have. We do need Falco on the primary ballots so that Ortega can legitimately win the nomination."

"You expect *me* to orchestrate this?"

"Shouldn't be much of a problem for a man talented enough to have skimmed nearly two million, tax-free, from his various enterprises."

CHAPTER NINETY-THREE

***

LIFTING THE COVERS, VERONICA SLIPPED OUT OF TREVOR HUGHES' BED. AT THE DOOR SHE glanced back, assured to see him still in the same position. Not only had the sex been more energetic that night, but she'd added a soporific called Ramelteon to his last drink to ensure his deep slumber.

Collecting her purse, she padded barefoot to his spare-bedroom office and crossed to his desk. A week earlier, she had inserted a device Korkoran had provided into Trevor's USB drive and installed a program that recorded his keystrokes.

Bringing the computer to life, she initiated the program, watching Trevor's passwords appearing as dots. And then it opened the menus.

With nimble fingers she clicked and opened the secure files, Trevor's unit accessing its link to the Ortega campaign. Within minutes she'd downloaded the files. Pressing a key, her spy program inserted itself into the campaign computers.

She slipped her phone from her purse, tapped in a number, and pressed send. "Did you get it?"

"Download's complete. Just a minute." She was mildly surprised that the voice wasn't Korkoran's. *"Okay. Yep. I'm under their skirt and past their panties. It's honey pot all the way!"*

Face expressing her disgust, she ended the call.

Carefully shutting the computer down, she dropped the flash drive and phone into her purse. Returning to Trevor's bedroom, she laid her purse exactly where it had been, climbed into his bed and snuggled herself against Trevor's naked body.

Lips to his ears, she whispered, "Baby, I just can't tell you how much I love you. You're the best thing that's ever happened to me."

CHAPTER NINETY-FOUR

***

THE LINE FOR CUSTOMS AT MIAMI INTERNATIONAL AIRPORT NEVER SEEMED TO END. BRENDA stood beside Chantel as they inched their way forward. Both were dressed in Cancun, Mexico, tee-shirts beneath colorful vacation blouses, the tails knotted at the waist. Each carried an oversized purse, and Chantel wore a floppy straw sun hat to accent her sunglasses. Both had adopted white sail-cloth jeans and sandals.

"So, what do you think?" Brenda asked.

"Depressing."

"Cheer up. We're two housewives on the way back from a girls' Mexican getaway." She glanced ironically at the wedding rings they wore.

"That's not what depresses me. It's riding in the back of that overcrowded airplane, and that obnoxious man who kept trying to hit on you."

"I put you in the window seat for a reason. And that's how real people travel. Which, when I think about it, is a good reason to be depressed. You did good going through security, by the way."

Chantel looked around, expression pinched. "And it's knowing that ten years from now, these peoples' lives are going to be very different. If any of them are still breathing."

"Yeah." Brenda tried not to think about it.

The family just ahead of them walked to the glass cubicle where the customs agent waited.

"You go first, Virginia. You know the story. Five days in a condo, beaches, Carlos and Charley's, great food, and too much tequila."

"Not to mention that I sell insurance in Boca Raton, and my parents live in Cleveland. Yeah, got it."

Chantel was officially Virginia Smith, from Kennesaw, Georgia. Brenda's ID was for Susan Worhouse. Along with passports, they had driver's licenses and credit cards to prove it.

Chantel started forward somewhat uncertainly, smiling at the agent as he took her passport.

Brenda found it amusing that Chantel Simond—tempered steel while facing down Taki and Chicago—would feel insecure confronting something as mundane as passport control.

Brenda fiddled with the wedding ring on her finger, wondering how Devon could have come up with two passports as quickly as he did. She'd inspected the things minutely, seeing all the correct shimmering colors and embedded magnetic strips. Even their photos were appropriately unflattering.

The agent handed Chantel's passport back and waved her through as Brenda stepped forward, extending hers. The old calm had asserted itself. This was just another mission.

"How was the trip?" he asked, running her passport through the machine, eyes on his computer.

"Too short. Ginny and I have been waiting for years for this."

"Welcome home, Ms. Worhouse." He handed the passport back and Brenda hurried to where Chantel was waiting.

"What next?"

"We collect our luggage, customs takes our forms that declare our trinkets and one quart of tequila apiece, then we lug our bags out to the exit where a car is waiting."

She resisted the urge to pet the drug dog as it sniffed her luggage and followed Chantel through the last doors after handing her customs card to the half-asleep agent.

At the curb, they stopped, Chantel glancing around like a true tourist. "Where's the car?"

"Making circles. He'll be here no longer than..." She waved, seeing Happy Gonzales—one of the men she'd employed in Jackson—as he wheeled the Toyota Camry through traffic. As promised, he'd tied a length of yellow flagging tape to the passenger-side windshield wiper.

As he pulled close, Brenda led the way, yanking her suitcase between cars. The trunk popped open, allowing Brenda to toss her bag and Chantel's in before slamming the lid.

She hesitated only long enough to see Chantel seated in the back. Then she yanked the tape from the wiper blade and slid into the passenger seat.

"Any problems?" she asked as Happy eased into traffic and followed the stream toward the airport exit.

"No, ma'am. I was just delighted to get your call." He glanced at the mirror and nodded slightly to Chantel. "Anything you need, whenever you need it."

Brenda smiled wanly. "We really appreciate that. Everything else going to plan?"

"The car's good to go. New tires aired up to spec, oil checked, and freshly serviced. Registration and insurance in the glove box. GPS disabled and black box disconnected. Forty caliber HK Compact loaded and chambered with three loaded magazines in the center compartment. Next to it, you'll find a five-inch Randall stiletto in a down-the-back sheath. Five thousand cash." He reached in his coat pocket and handed her an envelope.

Brenda took it, removed the bills, and placed them in the ridiculous purse. "And the transfer?"

"At a travel center just a ways up I-95. I've got someone to collect me. Then the keys are yours. Give me a call whenever and wherever you leave the vehicle, and I'll have someone pick it up."

"I meant it when I said no one can know. Not a mention on a call, not even an email to any of the guys saying that you saw me."

He met her eyes. "Last time, a woman died in spite of our best efforts. You don't have to tell me the stakes."

"Good, because, Happy, some very bad people will stop at nothing."

"Just be better than they are, Brenda."

Yeah, she thought as they merged into north-bound traffic on I-95. *My bet? He's already out there. Waiting.*

CHAPTER NINETY-FIVE

***

TAYLOR SWAYED AS THE BUS ROCKED AND BOUNCED OVER THE ROUGH STREET. BENNIE had the window seat, watching as Washington D.C. passed slowly by, people on the streets, traffic slowed to a snarl. It was a whole different city from the last time he'd been here, mellower. But that had been before COVID-19.

Again, the client's competence surprised him.

The call had come in Monaco: *"She's headed to Washington. Some secret meeting. We need you there soonest. Get to Paris. Documents will be waiting in your usual hotel room. You and your associate are part of a French tour group. Biographies will be provided for your aliases. Flush them once you've read them. The paper dissolves in water."*

"And kit?" he'd asked.

"Everything you need will be provided. As soon as we have details of the target's location, you will be apprised."

Arriving in Paris, Taylor had discovered he would be traveling as Rene St. Clair, and Bennie was Julian Eppecarte. The backstory was that they ran a modest café in Cannes.

Nor had anyone lifted so much as an eyebrow as they joined the tourist group at Charles de Gaulle International Airport. They'd received their tickets, handy name badges, and boarded the Air France flight to Dulles. There, too, the tour group passed uneventfully through customs and onto this under-heated bus.

Upon arrival at the Holiday Inn, Taylor waited while the tour guide checked his party in one by one. When keys were delivered, he and Bennie recovered their luggage from the stack left in the lobby and made their way up to room 275.

"And here we are," Bennie observed as he peeked past the curtain at the city beyond.

"But where is she?" Taylor tossed his suitcase on the bed before sorting through his clothes to recover the satellite phone.

"If we can trust the client, coming right to us." Bennie walked over and turned on the television. "This time, one way or another, it ends, my friend."

On the television, Tom Ortega was shaking hands at some ubiquitous downtown diner. He was saying, *"Whatever Zack Calloway's reasons for withdrawing from the race, I wish him and his family all the best. Zack's become a good friend of mine, and I know this decision wasn't made lightly."*

"Politicians," Bennie muttered. "Do you believe a single word that comes out of their mouths?"

Taylor narrowed an eye, imagining Chantel Simond in the crosshairs of a high-powered scope. "I only believe in physics, my friend. Let's say one hundred and sixty-five grains of final resolution."

"Assuming the client delivers."

"He always has. And this time, he says it will be different."

"Will it?"

"Of course. This time I'm shooting Brenda Pepper first. Wounding her."

"And what does that gain us?"

"I'm told that she and Chantel have become close. When Pepper falls, Chantel will hesitate in disbelief. Pepper will still be alive. Chantel might even bend down. Which is when I blow her head right off her neck."

"And Pepper?"

"Just the one shot. Low in the guts so the impact breaks her spine, ruptures her bladder and pelvis. Actually, I hope she survives and lives a long life after her numerous reconstructive surgeries."

CHAPTER NINETY-SIX

***

"CAN YOU BELIEVE THIS SHIT?" KORKORAN LEANED BACK IN HIS EXPENSIVE OFFICE CHAIR, one hand on his desk. On the television he watched Tom Ortega gracefully announce his regrets at Ed Brown's withdrawal from the race. The Fox News reporter, stationed inside the Capitol rotunda, then added, *"This was Marcus Dagget's response from Des Moines when the story broke this morning."*

Dagget's face filled the monitor as he said, *"We've always supported Senator Ortega's candidacy. We're an inclusive party, and everyone ought to have a shot at running. And yes, it's a blow to lose Governor Brown, but in the end, this will allow the American people to clearly focus on Tom Ortega, and of course, Governor Falco. The Iowa caucuses are tomorrow, and that's when the rubber really meets the road."*

"Is there any truth to the rumor that both the Calloway and Brown campaigns are going to support Ortega?"

"That is my understanding, and of course, the RNC will back any decisions the campaigns make."

Korkoran lifted his remote and stabbed the off button. "That slimy fucking worm!"

Peggy leaned in the door, having listened to his tirade. But then the entire staff knew how Big Jim felt when it came to Tom Ortega.

"Who?" she asked. "Ortega or Dagget?"

"Both." He narrowed his eyes. "This whole thing stinks like maggot shit."

"Well, Jim, clamp your nose," then she lowered her voice, "because Bill Petroski's in the hall, and I don't think he's had a bath in days."

Korkoran grinned. "Tell the staff to take off for an hour. Then lock the door behind them. I want privacy."

She gave him her two-fingered salute, a knowing twinkle behind her eyes. "Anything to bring that greaser upstart down is fine by me."

"Yeah, 'cause if he wins, you can kiss the upper east side goodbye."

"S-107's not dead yet."

"Nope. Send bilious Bill in."

Korkoran heard his staff leaving their offices, chattering about their good fortune. Then Bill's bluff voice almost overrode the sound of Peggy locking the door.

"Hiya, Jim!" Petroski greeted as his bulk filled the door. "Say, you wouldn't have one of those fancy coffees? I'd really go for—"

"No. Sit." Korkoran reached down for a bottle of scotch he kept behind the privacy screen of his desk. "But if what you've got is good enough, you can take this with you."

"Holy shit! That's a twenty-five-year-old Macallan." Petroski dropped himself in the chair with enough momentum to make the legs squeak.

"So, how'd my girl do?"

Petroski turned his attention from the bottle to Korkoran. "She's what I call a natural. I mean, one minute she's got her cunt cinched so tight around that poor kid's cock that his head's exploding. The next, she's wiggling her way right into Tom Ortega's most holy of holies."

"You monitoring her, Bill?"

His grin exposed fur-yellow teeth. "Just audio. Remote mic that I bounce off the window."

"Destroy it, you idiot." He pointed a finger. "That's an order. And if those recordings ever show up, I'm going to feed you your balls. Am I clear?"

At Korkoran's tone, Bill winced. "Yeah, yeah, I get it. Nothing that could ever be traced back."

"Damn straight. What have you got on Ortega?"

"Almost nothing."

"What the fuck?"

"You asked what I had on Ortega." Bill's expression turned clever again. "Ben Mackeson, however? That's another thing altogether. Once the wily Ms. Wolf got me into the campaign, I let my little worm wiggle its way right into the honey pot, and it's Mackeson and his little group. You want the goods? I got 'em by the balls."

"And how tight can I squeeze those balls?"

"Right up to the attorney general, Jimmy. Julie Zapruder is funneling tens of millions through a series of social media sites and right into the campaign coffers. The program's a marvel. Something put together by StatNco. You drop ten million in on one side, and it gets filtered down to a hundred thousand small donations and then back up through a series of websites into the original ten million. Even if you wanted to trace it, you'd have to work back down to a single five-hundred-buck donation, and sure enough, you find a citizen who kicked in a five-hundred-buck donation. After that it's just a matter of dumb luck—given the volume of data—that you could ever trace a different five-hundred back to that same donor."

"Slick."

"Even better, the big super PACS, they're doing the same thing. One thing's sure: the Ortega campaign isn't running out of bread anytime soon, and we're not even getting close to the election."

"So it looks like grass roots, even if it's coming from the big guys?"

"Better. There's a bootstrapping that goes on at the same time. Joe-Average-Citizen is being swept up in it. I mean people are bragging about their contribution, and it's become the in thing to do. They're generating tens of millions. Legally."

Petroski pointed a finger. "That's just the money side. Tamarland Bizhenov is the wizard behind Twitter, Facebook, Tumblr, Pinterest, and the rest. Every site out there is boosting pro-Ortega posts and comments. Falco and the Democrats can't get close enough to the surface to see sunlight, let alone get a breath."

"It gives Republicans a bad name."

"Hell, Mackeson's team worked all this out with the Democrats first, Jimmy. Moving his team to the Republicans just proves he's an equal-opportunity grafter."

"What about the big donors? Where's the heavy cash coming from?"

"A who's who list of billionaires. And some of them don't make sense. I mean Hal Fierbaugh? The guy's never supported a Republican in his life, and all of a sudden, his dot org is chipping in millions and running pro Ortega ads, saying he's 'A man to get behind'."

"That doesn't make sense."

"A lot of it don't." Bill flashed his teeth again. "Until I started looking into Dot Zhinger Enterprises. She's an old-time Democratic supporter who—"

"Yeah, yeah, the food giant."

"If my guess is right, it's a subsidiary of SimondAg."

Korkoran straightened in his chair. "Bingo!"

"And since we're getting around to Simond. Guess who's on Mackeson's speed dial? Mackeson doesn't wipe his butt after a shit before calling this guy for permission."

"Guy? I figured it for Chantel Simond."

"Sorry. It's her brother."

"What's his name?"

"You know him. Robert Simond. The guy who cages to get invites to all the social galas, the prayer breakfast, the correspondents' dinner, White House soirees."

"Thought he was that screwed-up actress's cousin. That's what he always claims."

"He's Chantel's younger brother. Renaud Simond's only surviving son." Petroski spread his arms wide. "My call is that the buffoon act is just that. The role he plays to stay out of the limelight."

"I'll be damned."

Petroski flashed his brown teeth. "So, do you think you can squeeze those balls hard enough now?"

"I need it all. Put it together for me in a coherent package that I can drop right on the attorney general's desk." Korkoran pointed a finger. "And no goddamn holes, either. I want it so airtight that those bastards in Justice can run it down in days and right into a string of indictments."

"I can have it for you in a week."

"That will work. Give Ortega a chance to savor his success. If the polls are right, he's going to win Iowa, and then take New Hampshire. I want him right on top and rolling for the green when I cut the fucker off at the nuts."

Petroski took two tries to get out of the chair before pulling himself to his feet. "My bill will be in the mail." He gave Korkoran a greasy smile and pointed. "But the bottle goes with me today."

"Works for me."

Almost slapping the Macallan off the desk, Petroski called, "Catch you later, Big Jim."

For long moments, Korkoran stared thoughtfully at his "me" wall with its photos and awards.

"Did that go well?" Peggy asked as she leaned in the door.

"Start looking at real estate brochures for New York, my love. The world is coming up roses."

CHAPTER NINETY-SEVEN

✳ ✳ ✳

POWERLESS IN THE DREAM, BRENDA WINCED AS BILL SOLACE SLID HIS SIDELONG GLANCE her way. His blue gaze burned into her soul. The Afghan sun, mid-summer bright and relentless, cast shadows in the hard lines etched into his face. His tight smile mocked as it thinned his lips.

"What do you think we're doing here, Captain? Saving the world?" His words carried the familiar hard edge.

The grisly scene spread before them: bits of bomb-mutilated human beings scattered on the pale and rocky ground, bloating bodies, blasted rubble.

Beyond the devastated village and torn bodies, the valley rose tan and dusty to the rocky gray slopes below the up-thrust mountains. Their peaks, like teeth, gnawed on the sere blue sky.

She'd wanted to save the world. Now, somehow oddly compressed and distorted, the narrow confines of her world had boiled down to one man: Bill Solace. *If she could just save him...*

She lowered her dream eyes to the strewn dead. Again, she cataloged the bits of mutilated human beings. The familiar torn rags of their clothing flapped in the breeze. The little boy still lay twenty feet to her left, facedown in a pool of his sun-blackened blood. So many children...

"You shouldn't be here, Bill. The area's not secure." Her words echoed as if in a cave.

"We've worked for years. I wanted to see where you finally got him." Solace's crow's-feet deepened as he studied the dead. "Besides, Jim Alexander's people secured the perimeter."

"Glad you trust him."

The familiar sense of horror grew.

The dream! It's just the damned dream!

He gave her that cutting sidelong glance again. A faint smile bent his lips. "Back to the chopper, Captain. You finally got Alahiri. Let's see who's next on the list."

And in that instant, his face changed. Green eyes. Red hair. A woman's face. Kelly's features blending into Chantel's...

Brenda turned from the carnage, knowing what was coming...

No! For God's sake, Brenda, turn. Shout. Do something!

As the terror built, her dream-self walked zombie-like toward the waiting Blackhawk.

Do something!

In the next instant she'd hear the bullet...

***

"*Gaaaa!*" With a scream she bolted upright in the bed, hands clawing at the sheets around her.

The slapping pop of Kelly-Chantel's skull and brains deafened her.

"Brenda?" From the next bed, Chantel's voice intruded.

"Where...where am I?" Brenda stared around the hotel room, illuminated as it was by the tiny blue lights from the TV and microwave clock.

"Brenda. It's just a dream."

"Chantel? Sorry." She gulped for breath, her mouth as dry as a desert stick. "Comfort Inn. Fredericksburg. We're in Virginia just south of DC."

"It was the same dream, wasn't it?"

"Bill," she said before thinking.

"Bill...? Solace? A sniper killed him. He was recommending you for the Silver Star. I've wondered about that. They don't give a Silver Star for good intelligence analysis. It's a combat award, for gallantry under fire. That sort of thing."

Brenda used the sheet to wipe her sweaty face. "I went into Maluf. Wore a burqa and rode in the back of a ratty Toyota pickup. I was supposed to be the wife of a Pashtun arms dealer. We had his wife, kids, and two brothers locked up for leverage. If he'd given me up, I had a pistol to take the bastard out before I shot myself. For three days, I played stupid and took his orders, but I finally got a glimpse of Alahiri."

She rubbed the back of her neck.

"I turned on the beacon in the Toyota, got myself a couple hundred yards down the road, and dove into a ditch just as the entire universe exploded."

"They *let* you take that risk?"

"Bill trusted me." *God, I miss him.*

"The war's over, Captain."

"Yeah."

But when she closed her eyes, it was to see Kelly's neck blown into a red spray, her corpse smacking the pavement. For a moment it lay still. Then the head turned on the shattered neck, and Chantel's horrified eyes stared out of Kelly's face.

Brenda said, "Chantel, why did you go to the cemetery to recruit Mark after I told you I wanted him to lay low someplace safe?"

The silence stretched.

"Captain, you've answered that question yourself a dozen times or more."

"What are you talking about?"

"You killed around one hundred women and children to get Alahiri. How many would you have been willing to kill? Two hundred?"

"My brother is the only family I have left. What does that have to do—"

"Answer the question, please. Two hundred?"

"Yes."

"Two thousand?"

Brenda smoothed her hand over her damp face. "Maybe."

"How about two hundred thousand innocent children?"

Brenda hesitated, seeing the small torn bodies on the ground in Maluf. Two hundred thousand? Even if she'd known for certain that Alahiri himself would have killed that many, could she knowingly slaughter hundreds of thousands of children to get him?

"I...I don't know."

She could see Chantel nod in the dimness. "Somewhere inside you, Brenda, you have a number. There is a bridge you will not cross."

"Maybe."

"Brenda? Listen to me: *I do not.* I will sacrifice anything and anyone. Use any tool I have to. You, your brother, the president of the United States."

Brenda stared up at the over-textured ceiling, remembering Maluf...and train levers, and raw recruits. She asked herself again: DC? Or millions of Americans? Did she really have a number? A line beyond which she absolutely would not go? Most people of good conscience did.

She was no longer sure she was one of them.

"Sure, Chantel. I get it."

But did she?

As she drifted to sleep, she started playing a new game. *"So, Captain, you're in charge of a mission that's going to drop a bomb on a café where your brother is sitting two tables down from the most-wanted terrorist in the world. It's your call. Do you give the order to take him out or not?"*

In the dream, she had lost her voice. Trying to answer, laryngitis left her with nothing more than a hollow whisper.

Replay after replay.

Suddenly mute, she could not physically say the words that would save Mark.

CHAPTER NINETY-EIGHT

***

NO LESS THAN FIVE TELEVISIONS HAD BEEN CARTED INTO THE HILTON SUITE TO COVER the Iowa caucus results as they came in. Beyond the window, the lights of downtown Des Moines glowed against a low-hanging cloud cover. Flakes of snow began to drift down. The storm had held off just long enough, though it had been snowing lightly in the northwestern counties for the last two hours.

Tom Ortega sat in the center of the couch, his left arm around Jen's shoulder, his right patting Jessie where she'd fallen asleep, her head on his lap.

Mackeson, Zapruder, and Tam Bizhenov alternately sat on the second couch that flanked Tom's or stood to walk through the open door to the adjoining war room, where staff monitored the results and tabulated returns.

One by one, Mackeson used remotes to raise the volume on whichever television he chose. Now it was CNN.

Patrick Gaffeney, the political analyst, was saying, *"We've got the latest numbers coming in from Iowa. With two more precincts reporting, and thirty-seven percent of the caucus delegates counted, Senator Tom Ortega, the controversial latecomer to the race for the Republican nominee for president of the United States, has extended his lead over his opponent, Governor Gene Falco. At least in the rural counties, Tom Ortega has come on like a roaring tiger, taking sixty-seven percent of the delegates counted so far."*

"Way to go, Tom." Jen reached up and squeezed his hand.

"It ain't over 'til it's over," Tom reminded.

At that moment, one of Tamarland's people walked in. Dressed in a white shirt, a thin blue tie around his neck, the guy's bald head made him look like a caricature.

"Mr. Bizhenov?" he called, looking down at the tablet he held. "StatNco just texted us. Based on their people actually at the caucuses, Tom's got it. StatNco projects sixty-two percent of the Republican delegates are pledged to Ortega."

Bizhenov, Mackeson, and Zapruder were slapping hands and grinning.

"But that's just a projection," Tom reminded. "We've still got the official—"

"We're there," Ben Mackeson insisted, rising. "StatNco knew the results when the last vote was taken. Sixty-two percent. So does CNN, Fox, and the alphabets. They subscribe to StatNco subsidiaries. But they won't project a winner for another couple of hours to keep their viewers on the hook and their sponsors happy."

"We really start to roll now," Julie Zapruder added. "This is landslide territory. Life gets easier. The donation faucet is turned from a dribble to a gush. We get a bigger airplane, and New Hampshire is looking like another sixty percent."

"Isn't that a bit optimistic?"

Ben Mackeson just gave him a knowing smile. "Falco will be calling to offer his congratulations in about an hour. I expect he'll be remarkably gracious. You'll need to make an appearance downstairs in the ballroom in about an hour and a half, so you might think of how you want to rally the troops and leave them in a state of near ecstasy. Jen, if you and Jessie can—"

"You bet, Ben."

Mackeson barely broke stride. "Then we should be on the plane by one-thirty at the latest, wheels up by two, and on the ground in Manchester by five." He smacked his hands together. "Tom, you've got a Rotary lunch at noon. Sleep on the plane."

"No wonder candidates say such stupid things. They're narcoleptic," Jen muttered.

"They only say stupid things if they don't want to be president," Zapruder growled back. "That's why we have them memorize stump speeches."

"I'll try to be good," Tom promised.

"Excellent. Because, Senator, given the way this is lining out, the only way you will not be president-elect in November, is if you run your mouth before thinking, and personally fuck it up."

CHAPTER NINETY-NINE

***

BRENDA SAT ACROSS FROM CHANTEL IN THE COMFORT INN BREAKFAST ROOM. SHE'D PLACED herself with her back to the wall, the emergency exit immediately to her left. The other guests were mostly either older travelers wearing casual clothing, or younger men—laborers from the look of their scuffed boots and worn jeans.

"This is food?" Chantel murmured as she inspected the waffle Brenda had cooked on the little machine. Then she stabbed the rubbery scrambled eggs with her fork.

"Douse the eggs in Tabasco Sauce," Brenda suggested. "Then slather the waffle with lots of fake butter and use your little plastic knife to cut up the banana. It covers the taste."

Chantel made a face, ignoring the wall-mounted television where the FOX News announcer said, *"Senator Tom Ortega, hot off his landslide in Iowa last night, is already hitting the campaign trail in New Hampshire. His flight was met by cheering throngs who braved near-zero temperatures to greet the candidate as he arrived for the run-down to the New Hampshire primary."*

Brenda gestured with her coffee cup. "You don't seem surprised."

"I'm not." Chantel dropped her fork. "Is there any real food in this country?" At Brenda's lifted eyebrow, Chantel sighed. "Of course, Ortega won. He's going to take New Hampshire and sweep the rest of the primaries with a lock on the nomination by the end of May. Unless he does something really dumb, he'll take the November election with about a thirty-vote margin in the electoral college."

"You *know* that?"

"StatNco does. Twenty-eight percent of the Democrats won't vote for a Republican even if he's Jesus Christ. Neither will eighty-five percent of the federal employees. We're going to lose some of the people wedded to entitlements—even when they know the system is headed for disaster. It's the ones in the middle who will make the difference, and it will give us a seven percent margin in the popular vote."

"In other news," the FOX anchor said, *"Asian markets are taking a beating today, dropping an average of nearly fifteen percent after a false news story about the honor suicide of the Chinese Minister of Finance. The story was followed by reports that several major exchanges were having technical problems and sell-orders were not being processed. The Hang Seng and Tokyo markets are bearing the brunt of the massive, panicked sell-offs."*

Chantel started, jerking around in her chair to stare at the screen.

"Market analysts are anxiously waiting to see if Tom Ortega's stunning upset in Iowa, expected to give the markets a boost, will compensate for the Asian decline."

"I've got to get to a phone." Chantel lurched out of her chair. "Now."

Brenda extended a calming hand. "No. You don't. You call Ricard, and it's the same as lighting a neon sign that tells Taylor, 'Here I am. Come shoot me.'"

"Captain, you don't understand. The perpetrators aren't finished. They're going to use time-outs to pile on more sell orders, then ignore the margin calls. If I can't stop them—"

"It's *you* who doesn't understand. We agreed that we'd do it my way. Now, make a choice: do we keep the meeting in Washington, or head back to your war room on Simond Island?"

Chantel sat back in her chair, eyes still on the television where a high school shooting was being reported. She took a deep breath, closing her eyes. "What went wrong? I was so careful. I know every sleeper hedge fund out there. I've taken precautions. I didn't miss anything."

"How do you know it was you?"

"The predictors didn't even hint at this. Unless it's Taki and Chicago trying to throw a wrench in the works. But they're cutting their own throats unless they're hoping to buy back stock and increase their positions."

"Meaning?"

"If they floated the rumor to scare investors into selling at a loss, they can buy more shares of their companies for cheaper. Increase their percentage of investment in their own holdings. But it's a dangerous move." She paused. "Problem is they don't have the liquidity to cover it. I'd know."

"You think Taki and Chicago are behind this?"

"I've got to call Devon. He'll know."

"Didn't we just have this discussion?"

Chantel had gone rigid, fists clenched. "If Taki and Chicago go too far, we're doomed. You get that, don't you? If the indices plunge across the board, Tokyo, Shanghai, Hong Kong, Shenzhen, and Korea, the other markets will follow, initiating a death spiral. London, Euronext, Frankfurt, BME, and SWX will dive. The New York Stock Exchange and the NASDAQ will be in freefall by the end of trading. We're talking world economic collapse in a matter of days."

Chantel's expression left no doubt about the seriousness of the crisis as Brenda asked, "And the meeting in Washington?"

"Critical. Brenda, you *must* find a way for me to manage both."

Two tables away, a gray-haired woman chortled as she tapped at the keys of her personal computer. She swiveled the machine so her husband could see what she was looking at on Facebook.

Poor woman, Brenda thought. *She has no idea that her world is hanging by a thread.*

CHAPTER ONE HUNDRED

***

WAVING TO THE CROWD, TOM ORTEGA CLIMBED WEARILY ONTO THE CAMPAIGN BUS AS LATE afternoon sunlight slanted across the parking lot and gleamed on automobiles and dirty snow where the plows had piled it.

Some of the old hands in the campaign told stories of other New Hampshire winters and reflected that even global warming seemed to favor Tom Ortega's campaign. This incited some of his more conservative volunteers who still took it on blind faith that climate change was a myth.

He smiled as he passed the seat where Jen slept with Jessie on her lap. If he hadn't loved them before, the sight would have done the trick.

Ben Mackeson sat in the rear with two staffers and rose to meet him at the seat behind Jen.

"Interesting day," Mackeson told him. "You heard about the Asian markets?"

"Something, but no details."

"Asian markets took a bath today but seem to have stabilized. Europe is down, too, but somehow stemmed the flow with only a five percent loss. We barely had a dent in the DOW, and the NASDAQ rose a half point."

Mackeson grinned. "Analysts pin it all on you, Senator. They say the business community has hope for the first time since the Trump election, disaster that it turned out to be after COVID took its toll, and that your win in Iowa hearkens to great things to come."

"Glad they've got the faith," Tom told him, feeling fatigue deep in his bones. It was nothing new—he'd passed the last days of hell week in a semi-conscious state. But he'd been in his late twenties at the time. Doing it in his late forties? That was something different.

"And there's this." Mackeson handed him an Apple tablet and tapped the screen. The photo on internet news showed soldiers running behind a Russian tank, a building burning.

"That's in Tula, a city outside Moscow. Seems all's not rosy in Russia. The story's sketchy so far, but the transition is being contested. A couple of Platnikov's generals were arrested after Platnikov was retired. Someone sprung them, and they've mobilized from a base south of Tula. Apparently, they are taking matters into their own hands."

"Is it just a couple of rogue generals? Or should I be worried?"

"Unknown. But whatever happened to Platnikov, it came down so fast someone is trying to take advantage. Just thought you should know, in case we need to adjust the stump speech. If Russians are fighting, it's better that they're doing it outside Moscow than in the Baltics."

"It's better that they're not doing it at all. Ukraine's been a festering nest of insurgency since Putin stuck his nose into its business. The resistance there is going to seize on this. It's every bit as dangerous when Russia is devouring itself as it is when it's eating someone else."

"I see you've heard the news," Veronica Wolf said as she approached down the aisle and dropped her computer case onto the seat across from them. "More good news, Senator. People shooting at each other makes a military man look better for the big chair."

"I hope they keep a lid on it. Better yet, with all those troops we've positioned in Eastern Europe, the president needs to be reassuring the Russians that we won't be taking advantage."

"Why wouldn't he be reassuring?" Veronica asked.

"Because the guy's not that smart," Tom spoke without thinking.

Changing the subject, Veronica asked. "I heard you were headed to Washington this evening. Mind if I hitch a ride? There's a young man I'm anxious to see."

"I think we've got a seat," Ben told her, a bare glance of disapproval going Tom's way. "But if you miss the six a.m. return, you're on your own."

This, of course, would delight Mackeson to no end. He still didn't trust Veronica Wolf, but to Tom's relief, her reporting had been brutally honest so far.

Nevertheless, as the bus accelerated toward Nashua and the charter that would take him to Washington for the evening, Ortega scrolled through the news on his iPad.

Analysts were calling the stock sell-off a correction and trying to scry out the reason behind it. Something had triggered investor confidence to flag. The consensus was that a disaster was barely averted. For the moment.

And what if it happened all over the world? All the markets dropping? What then?

For the first time in months, he wondered what Chantel Simond would say about it? Or, even, if she were behind the whole thing.

CHAPTER ONE HUNDRED ONE

***

CHANTEL—WEARING A DARK BROWN WIG—LEANED HER HEAD BACK IN THE SEAT AS BRENDA followed a line of cars into downtown Washington. Thankfully, their arrival was late enough that traffic was only a nuisance instead of brutal.

So this was how "average" Americans lived. For two days now, she'd been immersed in their world: lines, traffic, gas stations, convenience stores, and fast food. She had been pressed face-first into their massed humanity, alternately touched, appalled, intrigued, and repulsed. Beneath it all lay the brutal reality that theirs was a dying world.

Nothing I can do will save them.

A slushy rain fell from the sky to briefly spot the windshield before the wipers dispersed it.

"You bought us time, Captain," Chantel said wearily. "I wouldn't have believed it."

"Seeing that happy grandma with her computer was a lucky break." Brenda raised her fingers from the wheel in a gesture. "Ten minutes earlier, ten minutes later, and we'd be on a plane headed for Miami by now."

"It would have been too late," Chantel murmured. "What I managed today? It's a pitiful band aid on a hemorrhaging wound." She turned her thoughtful eyes on Brenda. "Facebook? What on God's earth made you think of that?"

Brenda shrugged as the light turned red. "StatNco monitors everything, right? That gave me the idea to drag you to the hotel computer and establish a Facebook account. Either your key words would raise red flags at StatNco, or they wouldn't."

"Amazing." Chantel shook her head in disbelief. "Fast thinking on your feet, Captain. Although Devon's people must be slipping. I put in the code words, and it took nearly fifteen minutes until Devon was texting me back."

"So, how'd you do it?"

"Ricard and I have developed a shorthand over the years. I turned it into a recipe. Thai pork, Japanese rice, Chinese noodles. Five ounces is five million, a pound is a billion. We worked it out." Chantel smiled grimly. "And no one knows it was me. They think I'm some lady from Richmond staying at the Comfort Inn with three kids. Brilliant, Brenda."

What would I do without her?

Chantel stifled the sudden sense of camaraderie. She couldn't afford emotion—let alone reliance. Since that night in Platnikov's dacha, her relationship with Pepper had evolved into something she'd never experienced. The woman was always there for her, solid, reliable, and capable. The fact that she had her own vulnerabilities and nightmares was another trait in common. They shared so much. Just being in her presence was reassuring.

I am not alone.

The thought hit her like a thrown brick. She swallowed hard, a sudden constriction in her throat.

She didn't dare.

Couldn't.

She'll hurt you in the end.

Chantel—heart racing—forced herself to breathe deeply. That was it. Control. Keep Pepper at arm's length. Remember she is an employee. It will all be fine.

"Hotel's coming up," Pepper said. "Put your glasses on."

Brenda turned into the self-parking at the Marriott garage, rolled down her window and took a ticket. As the arm rose, she took the ramp to P4 before she could find a space close to the elevator.

Chantel watched Brenda reach into the console, retrieve the HK, and do a chamber check. She stuffed the .40 caliber pistol into an IWB holster in her pants.

"Going to war, Captain?" she asked as Brenda slipped the sheathed stiletto over her head and let it drop down the back of her shirt.

"Hope not. Stay put for a minute." Brenda got out, taking a moment to locate the security cameras. Next, she checked around the elevator entrance, familiarizing herself with the garage layout.

Only then did she rap a knuckle on Chantel's window, eyes on the surroundings.

She's as tough and competent in her world as I am in mine. Is that what makes her so attractive? Is that why I just want to enjoy her company? Share some of the burden?

Brenda must have noticed her unease, but misread the reasons for it as she asked, "How does it feel to be a brunette?" They walked toward the elevator. "Think of it as elegant class instead of passionate fire."

"I'll remember that next time we assassinate a Russian president."

"If we were so good at that, why are Russians fighting in Tula? Thought Katya had that under control."

"So did I." Damn it, Brenda was doing it to her again. Reassuring her with that easy camaraderie. Chantel heard herself saying, "We ran the permutations. Platnikov's disintegration forced Katya to move before she was ready."

Brenda kept a hand on Chantel's arm as the elevator opened, ready to pull her back if anyone threatening were inside. Satisfied, she led the way, checking behind to make sure no one was rushing them. As the door closed, Brenda pressed the button for the lobby.

"An envelope should be waiting at the front desk," Chantel told her as the door opened onto the lobby.

As they strode across the polished floor, Brenda noted, "One or more high-value principals are in residence. There's one, and possibly two more, personal security personnel in the lobby."

"Very good, Captain." To her delight Chantel barely received a second glance as the woman at the reception desk handed her an envelope for "Fox".

Back in the elevator, Chantel removed her wig and sunglasses, allowing Brenda to drop them into her oversized purse. Then she extracted a keycard from the envelope and inserted it for the penthouse level.

"Any last things I need to know?" Brenda asked as they rocketed upwards.

"Don't shoot anyone unless you have to." Chantel's lips quirked. "Sorry. It's the lack of sleep."

The elevator slowed, and the doors opened. Brenda stepped forward, her aerosol can in her right hand.

Two men in suits, obviously security, blocked the way. The bigger of the two said, "Sorry, but this is a private floor. We'll have to ask you to—"

"Tell Jerry that Chantel Simond is here and wants to see him," Chantel said in her coldest voice.

Even as the man raised his sleeve mic to his mouth, two more men approached from the sides. Brenda shifted slightly in preparation.

"If you'd follow us, ma'am." The big guy turned, walking down the hall where he rapped two and two on the penthouse door.

An older man, lithe, tall, and eagle-eyed, opened the door.

"Hello, Jerry," Chantel greeted.

He studied Chantel for a moment—hesitated as he took in her clothing—and nodded to the big guy before saying, "Ms. Simond. We weren't expecting you. Please, come in. I'll inform Brian of your arrival. Meanwhile, can I get you anything?"

"I'm fine, thank you." Chantel stepped through the door like a commanding general, Brenda at her heels. The penthouse was all modern glitz and elegance. It was to be expected given that it was normally rented to the über-rich who curried favor among Washington's rulers.

Jerry knocked twice at a double door, leaned his head in, and said, "Excuse me, sir. But Chantel Simond is here, in the next room, and would like to see you."

"*Here?* But she's supposed to be—"

"In the *next* room, sir," Jerry said meaningfully.

Chantel smiled grimly, imagining the consternation.

"Tell her we'll be right with her."

Jerry closed the door, giving Chantel a thin smile. "It's good to see you again, ma'am. You've taken us by surprise."

Chantel's smile was predatory. "My deepest apologies, Jerry. It was last minute, and I happened to be in the area."

Sounds of a heated exchange could be heard beyond the door.

Chantel glanced at Brenda; the woman was inspecting the room with a critical eye while positioning herself to cover Chantel's back. That slight quirk at the corner of Brenda's mouth was now familiar enough that Chantel knew Brenda was enjoying the disruption caused by their arrival.

"Chantel!" Brian Heston announced when he finally opened the double door and stepped out. "What a delight! If we'd known you were coming, we would have made special arrangements."

Chantel gave him a hug and stepped back. "I don't have much time, Brian. If you don't mind, I'd like to get down to business, and then I have a flight to catch at Dulles." She glanced at Brenda. "Captain, you're with me."

"Yes, ma'am."

Brian shot Brenda a worried look as Chantel marched into the meeting room.

At the head of the table sat Inga Simond-Heston, looking like a regal elder in her diamonds and glistening black dress. Robert Simond was at the other end, slouched back, his blond locks flowing over his collar. At his left sat Poul Hammond. Most of the other chairs were filled with older men in tailored suits. And one woman in her 60s, dressed rather frumpily, with short-cut silvering hair, studied Chantel with curious eyes.

Brian Heston extended a hand, saying, "Chantel, I'd like you to meet Ben Mackeson, Julie Zapruder, and Tam Bizhenov. I think you know Samuel Morse, Hal Fierbaugh, and Thad Kayhill."

Brenda took a stance behind as Chantel pulled out a chair and seated herself. "I do indeed."

Morse, a multi-billionaire, was known for his bankrolling of liberal causes. Fierbaugh, if anything, had an even more incendiary reputation. Calloway, just as wealthy, supported ultra-conservative crusades. More than once it had been reported that these men loathed and despised each other. Yet, here they sat, side by side, looking distinctly uncomfortable.

And then there was Inga, who now fixed her displeased gaze on Chantel, opening with, "Chantel, my dear. I see you've found a charming new tailor. How nice that you could join us." Then she glanced at Brenda. "But seriously, I don't think your security need be present. We're harmless." Her eyes hardened. "And we have sensitive matters to discuss."

"The captain stays," Chantel said coldly. "I may need her *expertise* in the near future, and I want her to know what each of you looks like."

Brenda must have taken the cue because everyone at the table but Robert shifted uncomfortably as they turned wary eyes on Brenda.

"I don't understand," Inga raised her hands. "Are you expecting more attempts on your life? Surely, you don't think any of us—"

"Captain Pepper has not only kept me alive during the last months, she ran assassination teams in Iraq and Afghanistan." Chantel gave a flip of the hand. "She eliminated what the Americans called HVTs, or high-value targets. That's a talent one doesn't dismiss frivolously."

Inga shot Brenda a reevaluating glance. "Is that a threat, Chantel?"

"Think of it as more of an explanation."

More furtive glances turned Brenda's way. Something hard, almost seething, had grown behind Brenda's dark eyes. Her jaws clenched.

Robert, still lounging at the far end of the table, had watched with amusement. "Figured you'd be busy with the calamity in the markets. Or was that a planned move on your part to rattle the Asians?"

"Unplanned," Chantel told him. "Devon's ferreting out the party or parties behind it. For the moment, I've stopped the hemorrhaging. My intervention—coupled with Ortega's victory in Iowa—appears to have averted disaster."

Poul Hammond was fiddling with his gold pen, flipping it between his fingers, his gaze vacant, expression preoccupied. He kept shaking his head as if in disbelief.

Brian Heston smiled uncomfortably before saying, "Given the financial crisis, Chantel, we're even more surprised that you can afford the time to join us. And then there's Russia. We congratulate you on your success removing Platnikov but wonder at the news of fighting south of Moscow."

"We thought it was supposed to be a peaceful transition," Inga noted. "Instead, it looks like the ragged beginnings of civil war. I do hope that you and Katya anticipated such a possibility."

"I haven't had time to discuss this with Katya."

Brian Heston added, "Ah, then you *didn't* foresee the possibility of Russia destabilizing."

"They're *not* invading the Baltics," Robert snapped, as if in defense of his sister. "Let it play out, Brian."

Heston shot an irritated glance at Chantel and said, "So, how about we get down to business? First thing. While we've already expressed our sympathies to Robert, we are all deeply sorrowed and disturbed to hear about your father's death. It's a blow to us all."

"Thank you, Brian. If Dad's murder has done anything, it's made it even more important that we act in concert. In the next few days, Devon will be forwarding a preliminary plan for the reorganization of our American assets. We will begin divesting ourselves of advanced technology holdings and using those funds to acquire even larger blocks of agricultural land in the Midwest, South, and central northern Great Plains."

"You're shorting advanced tech?" Morse cried. "Does Taki know about this?"

"He does. Silicon Valley and the Seattle industries can't be maintained when the collapse comes. Our attention has to be directed to sustainable energy production and agriculture. That means defensible refineries and pipelines to support agricultural industries in areas that may benefit as climate change accelerates. I need you to work with Thad Kayhill in the development of simplified ultra-reliable modern technology that can be maintained long-term and locally." She paused. "And EMP protected. The two of you can delegate the talent and manufacturing necessary."

"I don't understand," Kayhill said.

"The challenge is to build a modern kind of Model T that will run forever and can be repaired at the side of the road with parts made in a local machine shop. The same with aircraft. Call it survival technology."

Inga Simond-Heston's eyes had narrowed. "You do not speak for the rest of us. This is a Foundation decision."

Chantel met the woman's challenging eyes. "Taki and Chicago are working on data repositories to store as much electronic media as possible. I want you to work with Devon and Samuel Morse to pick a North American location for such a facility. Working with Chacon, we'll find another in South America, and perhaps a fourth in New Zealand or Australia.

"Thad, in addition to preparing your energy companies for sustainable production in the Great Plains and Rockies, I need you to work with Brian in designing methods to reorganize rural areas for defense."

"Defense?" Brian gaped in surprise. "Against whom?"

"Displaced urban populations desperately fleeing the cities," Chantel told him. "Whether you're a millionaire stockbroker or flip burgers in a fast-food chain for minimum wage doesn't matter. Either way, your job vanishes with the electricity."

"What about the people?" Morse asked. "I mean it's going to be a humanitarian disaster! We need to be stockpiling food, medical and shelter supplies. Emergency—"

"Mr. Morse, I will make you a deal. A trade. The lives of you and your family, out to your first cousins, in exchange for those teeming millions. If you sacrifice yourselves, I will commit the resources to build food dumps and empower Brian to design and stock them."

"I don't understand. What do you mean when you—"

"I mean, *dead.* Will you and your family die to provide those supplies? We're talking what, thirty, maybe forty people? In exchange for as much food, tents, medical kits, and water as we can procure and store before the collapse."

Morse's face filled with disgust. "That's crazy. No one would—"

"Isn't that the Jesus story? When it gets out, you'll be a hero. I'll even have it engraved over the doors of the food repositories. 'Bought with the lives of Samuel Morse and his family'."

Inga slapped a palm to the table. "You're being absurd, Chantel. No one is going—"

"I'm making a *fucking* point!" Chantel stabbed a finger. "We *don't* have the resources, which you damned well know since you developed the theory and helped Devon write the programs. Morse isn't any different than the billions of other human beings out there. He's not going to sacrifice his children, wife, siblings, grandchildren, and great grandchildren for the sake of others."

Morse remained quiet, though his face burned red.

Inga sighed. "Granted, but there's got to be a better way than a descent into barbarism."

"Actually, Inga, I'm hoping we can soften the fall." Chantel turned her attention to Ben Mackeson. "How is Ortega doing?"

Mackeson, a faint glow of perspiration on his face, said, "Very well, ma'am. When Poul approached me about Ortega, I thought you were out of your mind. After working with the guy, he seems to be an outstanding choice."

Chantel asked, "Ms. Zapruder, how are the finances?"

"We're in superb shape. In addition to the funds you've provided, and through Tam's social media and advertising, we're bootstrapping millions from small donors. We'll have a two-billion-dollar campaign by April, perhaps three by October."

"Assuming Ortega doesn't blow it," Mackeson added. "He does tend to speak his mind. So far, each gaff has been spinnable. 'No bull-crap Ortega' and 'Tell it like it is Tom' have a distinct appeal."

"You know him best, Ben. Assume he's elected? When we lay the facts out, along with our strategies for social engineering, will he play ball?"

"Honestly, Ms. Simond, I don't know. The guy really wants what's best for the country. He actually cares about the people. But he's got a no-bullshit pragmatic bent to his personality, and he definitely understands how the real world works."

Ben hesitated. "He knows he has Simond support, and it makes him wary. But when he finds out how he's been elected, and who's behind it?" He shrugged.

Chantel ran fingers through her hair. "What about the Democratic candidates? Who's likely to get the nomination?"

"It's a tossup between Sheila Andrews and Mick Sackerson." Ben frowned. "Mick's another classic narcissist with a nose for the campaign but no managerial skills. Sheila's got a messiah complex. She's ready to lift her shining sword and march her followers headlong into utopia no matter who or what she has to destroy in the process." He paused. "Unless you'd like us to ensure one or the other."

"Neither of them is easily electable in the current environment, I'm afraid," Inga added. "Best bet is Ortega, *if* we can control him."

"We won't control him," Chantel said thoughtfully. "The hope is to convert him."

"You've got the child, Jessie," Robert reminded. "We can always withhold treatment. Maybe infect Ortega's wife with something out of Regal's..."

Chantel raised a hand to cut him off. "If we go to war with Tom Ortega, we all lose." She glanced at Bizhenov. "Where does Ortega poll the strongest? Which demographics?"

"Educated upper middle class, blue-collar conservatives, and business owners. Racially, he's highest with whites, Latinx and Asians. Among males, he's at sixty-five percent. Among women at fifty-three. The big surprise is the eighteen to thirty-four age bracket where he's got a fifty-seven percent approval. His lowest approvals are with federal employees and the liberal-progressive Democratic base."

Chantel paused thoughtfully, then said to Morse and Fierbaugh, "We'll need both of you to blunt the progressive liberal response. Given your clout, keeping the left neutered shouldn't be a problem."

"Ms. Simond!" Fierbaugh cried, "Surely you can't—"

"Mr. Fierbaugh, do I have your support, or do I need to look elsewhere?"

Fierbaugh swallowed hard, a faint sheen of perspiration on his forehead. "I'm with you."

"What are the projections for the Nevada primary, Mr. Mackeson?"

"Ortega by fifteen points."

"And South Carolina?"

"About the same."

"I'd like a meeting with Senator Ortega."

"To do what?" Inga snapped. "It's too soon to put pressure on the man. He'll bolt."

"Pressure? Anything but." She turned. "Mr. Mackeson, tell the senator that I'd like an appointment with him in the morning."

"Yes, ma'am. Where? At his senate office?"

"Here, if you would. I'm sure Brian won't mind."

"Mind? Of course not. Who am *I* to mind?" he asked sarcastically.

"Any other concerns with the campaign?" she asked.

Robert waved a desultory hand. "Just some security issues that we've become aware of."

"Very well. For the moment then, I think we've all got our work cut out." She fixed on Morse, Fierbaugh, and Kayhill. "We'll be forwarding some initial projects and goals. If you would have your people begin implementation, we'd very much appreciate it."

The three men glanced at each other, then at Inga Simond-Heston, who waved a hand, saying, "Oh, go ahead. Do it. The Foundation will deal with Chantel in its own way. You're dismissed. Get out of here."

Three of the most powerful men in the world rose and hurried from the room like scolded children.

"You'd better be right, Chantel," Inga told her. "I haven't decided if I'm on your side or not. If you make a single mistake, or if you've misjudged Ortega, I *will* take you down." A thin smile bent her lips. "Even if it breaks my grandson's heart."

CHAPTER ONE HUNDRED TWO

***

BENNIE SAT IN THE LOBBY, A COPY OF *USA TODAY* OPEN BEFORE HIM. THE TALL CUP OF cappuccino on the table beside him gave him an excuse to set the paper aside and scan the lobby each time he took a sip. According to his watch it was a little after eleven at night. He'd been in position for nearly fifteen minutes.

Taylor was covering the garage, walking around, a cell phone to his ear. It was the best advance they could conceive on the hasty drive from their hotel to the Marriott.

When the call had finally come, Taylor had said nothing, only listened. A faint smile had curled his lips as he hung up, glanced at Bennie, and said: "Marriott. Downtown. The client said hurry."

Bennie flipped to the next page, the action allowing him to catalog the two security agents watching the lobby. They'd given him a once over and dismissed him for the time being.

Bennie reached for his coffee, lifting it to his lips as he asked, "Anything?" into the cuff mic.

"Security guy came by. Asked what I was doing. I said waiting for my wife. You might want to go rent us a room, so we've got a reason to be here."

"Roger that."

Bennie had risen to his feet, stretched, and picked up his coffee when Brenda Pepper stepped out of the elevator and walked over to the registration desk.

Bennie ignored her, reaching up to scratch his chin. "You're not going to believe who just walked right into our lives."

CHAPTER ONE HUNDRED THREE

* * *

THE YOUNG MAN AT THE REGISTRATION DESK RAN BRENDA'S MASTERCARD THROUGH THE scanner. He smiled and handed it back, along with two key cards and her driver's license, saying, "Room fourteen twenty, Ms. Worhouse. The elevators are there. Fourteenth floor and the room will be to your right. Enjoy your stay with us."

She smiled and took the keys, glancing around to see the two security personnel monitoring the lobby. Inga's, she supposed, though one might have been Robert's. A dark-haired man was walking her way, absently scanning a paper, a cup of coffee in his other hand.

Back in the Simond-Heston suite, Brenda had told Chantel: "I'm going down to rent us a room."

"Brian has offered to give us one of the adjoining rooms." Chantel had been frowning at her computer.

"Yeah, I'm sure he has. And let's say something happens that you don't like. Maybe Stephen shows up, and you don't want drool on your sleeve. I need a hole where I can stash you if we can't get out of the hotel—a room registered under Worhouse that anyone checking the register isn't going to recognize."

But partly, she had wanted to get away. Something uncomfortable was scratching at her: Chantel's statement, *"She ran assassination teams in Iraq and Afghanistan. She eliminated what the Americans called HVTs, or high-value targets. That's a talent that one doesn't dismiss frivolously."*

Brenda had no problem with the implied threat. What was the point of being dangerous if no one knew it?

But was the threat only implied? Or a promise?

And if she asks Mark and me to take out someone like Inga?

In the old world—the one she'd grown up in—it would have been unthinkable. But faced with global collapse? If killing Inga meant saving a couple of hundred thousand people from starvation, dying from exposure, or being butchered for cannibalism? How many lives was a bullet worth? Suddenly morality was turned upside down and inside out. Good was no longer good, and evil no longer evil.

When do I reach my number?

Preoccupied, she pressed the up button at the elevator bank.

She'd advance the room, check the location of the stairs, fire extinguisher, and furnishings. And then, by God, she'd empty her nagging bladder!

When the elevator door opened, she stepped in, the man with the newspaper—mid-thirties and fit-looking—slipped through just as the door was closing.

"Fourteen, please," he told her in an accented voice.

She pressed the button and stepped back, key cards in hand. When it came to saving the world, what was her number? A hundred? Thousand? Ten thousand? Or, perhaps, only one?

Am I willing to become Taylor? Is Mark?

But the killing wouldn't just be for money, for personal gain.

Did the dead children she'd blown apart at Maluf care that she'd murdered them to kill a monster? A monster who had smiled at them, perhaps bounced them on his knee?

As the elevator slowed and chimed, the man smiled, and gestured for her to go first.

She turned toward the room, vaguely aware that the guy followed a couple of paces back, fiddling with his newspaper.

So, she asked herself as she stopped at the door, *what if Chantel asks you to shoot someone? Morse, perhaps? Or some politician or reporter who's in the way?*

She slipped the keycard in the lock, opening it after the click.

Are you ready to make those kinds of...

An arm snaked around her throat; the hard muzzle of a gun jammed into her back over her right kidney. As she instinctively thrashed, the chokehold tightened. An accented voice said, "Just step into the room, Captain Pepper. That's right."

She heard the door close. The arm around her neck no longer choked but pulled her against the gun muzzle.

"Hold very still."

Brenda felt her shirt being tugged up, and the HK was plucked from its holster. The man tugged her to the side, shifted, using an elbow on the switch. The lights came on. Then he said, "Turn your head. Let me see into your ears."

She did as he bid, shaking her hair back so he could see she had no earpiece.

"Continue to hold still." The arm disengaged from her neck, but the gun still pressed against her. With his free hand, he efficiently felt her armpits, breasts, and waist, then lowered himself to pat down her legs.

Satisfied he straightened, stepping back and ordering, "Hands behind your head. Take two steps forward. Drop to your knees and cross your legs at the ankles."

She did as he bid. Only then did she see his smiling face. Something familiar about... *Bennie?* Taylor's spotter?

"Thought you liked long distance. Didn't know you worked up close and personal."

"Long range? Close range? The bullet doesn't care."

"Where's your friend?"

"Coming from the parking garage. He's been waiting to meet you. Wants to give you his regards face to face."

Some part of her brain noticed that he held the suppressed pistol with an unwavering grip; his finger rested ever so lightly on the frame above the trigger. Definitely trained and professional.

So how are you going to get out of this one, Brenda?

She glanced at the bathroom. She really needed to...

She made a terrified face, yelped in dismay, and uncrossed her legs as she emptied her bladder.

CHAPTER ONE HUNDRED FOUR

***

BENNIE DROPPED HIS EYES TO STARE AS THE HOT RUSH OF URINE SPREAD AND DARKENED Brenda's white pants. Hands still behind her neck, her fingers tightened on the stiletto's handle where it hung down her back. Bennie's lips had just started to curve into a smile when Brenda whipped her arm forward. The stiletto lanced into Bennie's chest. The blade stopped at an angle, wedged between the ribs.

At the impact, Bennie gasped, disbelieving eyes fixed on the black blade.

Brenda batted the long barrel of the suppressor to one side as she launched herself from the floor. She caught Bennie's wrist, twisted, and curled her body to lever Bennie up and over. He slammed into the floor with a loud thump.

Kicking the pistol away, Brenda leaped high. Using all her weight she drove a knee into his sternum. Ribs cracked. Air burst from Bennie's throat.

As he sucked futilely for breath, she gripped the knife handle, yanked it free, and angling it, drove it deep.

Through the blade Brenda could feel the heart muscle contracting as it was pierced. She jerked the blade sideways. The keen edge sliced through quivering ventricle walls.

Bennie's eyes blinked once, twice; his tongue flicked in his half-open mouth. Then the man's muscles spasmed and went limp.

Taylor's coming!

Brenda scrambled for her pistol, checked it, and then retrieved Bennie's 380 Beretta. A chamber check proved it was loaded, and dropping the magazine, she found it full.

Brenda positioned herself, pistol at the ready, eye to the peephole.

She ignored the urine cooling on her crotch and thighs.

Come on, you shit stinking maggot. Come get me!

Her heartbeat slowed.

She swallowed.

Where the hell are you?

And then she glanced down at Bennie, at the little earpiece that had bounced out of his head when he hit the floor.

"Fuck!" she hissed, dropping down. She found the mic in his sleeve. Putting the earpiece in her own ear, she lifted Bennie's limp hand, asking, "Hey, Taylor? You there?"

"Bennie's dead?"

She heard the voice of her enemy for the first time, and a spear of rage burned inside her. "You're next, you two-footed piece of shit."

"You and me, bitch. Nothing else matters. You'll never fly, never drive, never sleep without wondering when the missile is coming, which door or hallway hides the bomb." And she heard a slight click, as if he'd smashed the transmitter.

She cursed and looked down at Bennie's body. As the adrenaline subsided, the effect was as if her muscles had turned to water. She staggered over to the bed, sat and dropped her head into her hands. Lungs heaving, she sucked one deep breath after another and fought the shakes.

She was in downtown Washington D.C., not some foreign battlefield. And she'd just killed the man who lay on the floor.

What the fuck do I do now?

CHAPTER ONE HUNDRED FIVE

***

IT WAS TOO DAMNED EARLY. TOM ORTEGA SIPPED HIS COFFEE. BEN MACKESON HAD HANDED it to him when the limo picked Tom up at his Georgetown townhouse a little before six.

He'd call Jen after his meeting with Chantel, to tell her his return had been postponed for a couple of hours. Meanwhile, Zapruder and Bizhenov would be winging north in less than an hour to see what could be adjusted in Tom's schedule.

He idly wondered if Veronica Wolf had been notified about the changed plans, or if Mackeson had conveniently forgotten to tell her.

As the limo pulled up in front of the Marriott, Tom's security stepped out and opened the rear door, held it while Tom and Mackeson climbed out.

"Fifteen minutes," Mackeson reminded him. "This Chantel Simond may be important, but so is maintaining momentum in New Hampshire. And you're playing catch up. Gene Falco considered New Hampshire a sure thing. He's spent months up there glad-handing."

"Fifteen minutes," Tom agreed. "Knock on the door when time's up." Not that he minded seeing Chantel again. Something about her had impressed him. Maybe it was the fact that she didn't play games, didn't angle for the advantage. Mostly because she didn't need to.

A neat-looking security agent stood by the elevator, nodded at Mackeson's greeting, then studied Ortega carefully. He pushed an elevator button, saying, "If you'll both accompany me."

They rode to the fifteenth floor in silence; Tom was sorting out details from his meeting with Trevor the night before on pending legislation. His hold on Korkoran Hardy was still bringing protests, but screw it, he *had* read the thing. It *was* a nightmare tangle of contradictory regulations.

On the fifteenth floor, the security guy led the way down the hall to where another agent rose from a chair. He knocked twice, and the suite door opened.

Tom recognized the woman who handled Chantel's security. This time she looked hard eyed with fatigue, her eyes slightly swollen and bloodshot. Nor was she professionally dressed, looking instead like she was prepared for a Kmart shopping spree.

He was tempted to quip "Busy night?" but stopped himself at the last instant. He recognized that hollow, after-action stare.

"This way, please," she told him, leading him to a conference room separated from the suite by double doors.

Inside, Chantel Simond sat at the head of a long conference table, a curious-looking phone to her ear. This time she was dressed like a Florida housewife in white jeans and a flower-pattern blouse. She listened and responded in what Tom recognized as Russian. Then the doors were closed behind him.

The man to his right offered his hand. The guy might have been a Hollywood sex idol with his tanned face and cream-colored suit. Long blond surfer hair hung just over his collar, and he had a devilish smile. Fixing his blue eyes on Tom's, he said. "Robert Simond, Senator. We've actually met at a reception but didn't have a chance to talk."

"My pleasure, Mr. Simond." Chantel's brother? Yes, he could see the resemblance.

A second man, his face familiar, rose and offered his hand. Before he could speak, Tom said, "Mr. Secretary, good to see you."

"Call me Brian, Senator. But the title still has a nice ring to it, don't you think?"

"Yes, sir."

"Have a seat. Can we get you a warm-up on that coffee?"

"No. I'm fine. Thank you. And I've only got fifteen minutes before Ben Mackeson starts pounding on the door and telling me I'm late."

"That's Ben," Robert Simond agreed. "I hear the campaign is coming off brilliantly. Ben and his team are like magic, aren't they?"

"Sometimes I wonder if they aren't too good."

At her end of the table, Chantel rattled off a string of Russian, lowered the phone, and pressed a button that evidently canceled the call. Her face was thoughtful, eyes unfocused where she stared at the notepad before her.

"What news?" Robert Simond asked.

"That was Katya. Things are going to be a bit messier than we had hoped. For the moment, the rebels command two motor-rifle divisions and hold Tula. Devon's in control of communications, allowing only what Georgi and Katya approve. They think they have it contained. We'll know if we're facing a wider war in twenty-four hours."

She raised her eyes to Tom Ortega's, the effect almost electric. "I hope I can count on your discretion, Senator. This meeting is for your information only. What you hear is to be used by you, and only you, as *privileged.* We wanted to give you a heads up concerning what your country, indeed, the world, is facing. Robert, if you would give the senator our précis?"

Robert slid a thin, bound report across the table.

"And what would that be?" Tom picked it up and opened it. There was no title page, just text.

Chantel said, "I assume that you have an understanding of history, Senator. No civilization lasts forever. We have data that indicate ours is on the verge of collapse."

She lifted a hand, stilling his protest. "In the coming months, we'll provide as much documentation as you need. In consultation with us, you may have portions of our data verified by independent peer review."

"The end of the world, Ms. Simond?" He raised an eyebrow.

"Not the world. Just civilization as we know it." Again, she raised her hand. "Yesterday we came within a whisker of disaster when the Asian markets tumbled. We've managed to shore them up, and they've opened higher, recovering enough value to reassure investors. We're not out of the woods, but no one is throwing themselves out of windows, either."

"What do you want, Ms. Simond?" *Payback for Jessie's cure?*

"An ally, Senator." Her commanding eyes bored into his. "Events have made this conversation necessary. Half the world is either at war, or on the verge of conflict. Governments are over-leveraged and bankrupt, including your own. The climate is changing, and both real and perceived feelings of deprivation are increasing among entire populations. Our data indicate we're beyond the point of no return."

"So, what's your goal in all of this?" He crossed his arms, wondering if Chantel Simond was the world's best poker player.

"In the simplest of terms? I don't want to see everything turned into radioactive slag." Her lips quirked. "And neither do you. Nuclear winter doesn't allow much of a future for Jessie. Let alone the rest of the world's children."

"Assuming you're right about the extent of the coming crisis."

"Would that I were not. If you can come up with a way out of this thing, I'll take it and kiss your feet."

"Jen wouldn't like that."

That got a weary smile out of her. "No, I suppose not."

He studied her, trying to get a handle on what she was really after. "Let's get something clear while we're at it. I've given an oath to serve and protect my country against all enemies, foreign and domestic. I will *not* in any manner, shape—"

"If I thought you would, we wouldn't be having this conversation," she almost snapped. Then she smiled, as if amused at herself. "It's been a long night, Senator. I know the kind of man you are. I *think* you will do anything that doesn't compromise your honor when it comes to saving your country and your people. I'm betting the very world on that."

"Why haven't the think tanks, the economists, and the academics who study these things come to the same conclusion?"

"Some have, but their reports are being dismissed as potentially flawed by peer review. To most, however, even the possibility remains unthinkable."

"People have been screaming 'end of the world' for decades now."

She pointed to the report. "You need to gird yourself for the toughest decisions of your life. We're doing everything we can to buy time, to prepare. I think you have three or four years at least before things go critical. But, as events in Russia and Asia prove, that may not be a safe assumption."

He glanced at Brian Heston. "What about you, Mr. Secretary? Why are you here?"

Looking Tom straight in the eye, he said, "I've seen the data, Senator."

Ortega shook his head, aware that Robert was watching him like a hawk. What was his part in all this?

And then his gut sank. "Is that what the campaign is all about? Because if it is, you've made a terrible mistake."

Chantel leaned back, apparently pleased that he'd figured it out. "Gene Falco would be a yes man, happy to accede to our slightest wish. As for the potential Democrats? They think in terms of social appeasement. Draw your own conclusions as to how they will react when shelves are increasingly empty, mile-long lines queue up for the few stations with fuel, and the electricity is failing. You, sir, have been shot at, and shot back." She paused. "'Tell it like it is Tom'? Isn't that what they call you?"

Tom tapped the report. "And you think if I owe you my election and my daughter's health, I'll work for you?"

Chantel considered her words. "Ask yourself this: If we are right, if collapse is inevitable, who the hell else do you want sitting in the Oval Office?"

"So, you've chosen me for the honor?"

"Honor?" she said in deadly earnest. "You win this thing, Senator, and you'll walk into that White House to face a nightmare."

She believed it. But could he trust her?

"Why tell me this now? All it would take is a phone call, and the Justice Department would be all over you."

"This meeting is about character. You can still opt out, buy a cabin in Alaska, and have a pretty good chance of seeing Jessie grow up."

"But that's not going to happen in Chillicothe," Robert added, only to be given a reprimanding glare by Chantel.

"So, let's say I don't turn you in. I win the election and go my own way. I don't play ball with you. Instead, I take my own steps to determine if the country's at risk."

Chantel slapped the table. "Perfect. But do something about EMP vulnerability. We have intelligence assets in Russia, China, and Europe, but Iran, what's left of North Korea, and Pakistan are anyone's guess. Hopefully, we'll have enough advance warning to allow you a preemptive strike."

"Russian aggression is currently the biggest threat to world stability. We might be at war any day."

Again, Chantel gave him that illusive smile. "The Gorky Plan is dead."

"What's the Gorky Plan?"

"Platnikov's top-secret invasion plan for the Baltics. He was going to initiate the operation in June. For the time being you can redeploy your military assets away from the border and relieve tensions."

"That's the president's call," Ortega corrected, wondering if this was bullshit.

Her eerie green eyes seemed to pry at his soul.

"Ms. Simond," he said, rising. "I don't think this is—"

"I don't want your decision today, Senator. I want you back in New Hampshire, looking into the faces of the people, and asking yourself how many of them could survive if the electricity grid were destroyed next week. Or next year. And over the coming months, I'd appreciate it if you'd give some thought to our data. You might even see something we missed. A way out of this."

His gut churning, he stood, taking his coffee. On impulse, he grabbed up the report. "Have a good day, Ms. Simond. The same, Mr. Secretary. And you, too, Mr. Simond."

Bursting from the conference room, he shot mental knives at Ben Mackeson, and started for the door.

"How'd it go?" Mackeson asked as he grabbed his coat and hurried in pursuit.

"Ben, I'm ready to break your neck, you son of a bitch."

CHAPTER ONE HUNDRED SIX

***

VERONICA WOLF—A THICK WOOLEN CAP ON HER HEAD, A MUFFLER AROUND HER NECK, AND oversized sunglasses to hide her eyes—paid the cab driver and hurried into the Marriott.

She stepped through the door just in time to see Tom Ortega and Ben Mackeson as a security agent escorted them into the elevator.

Pausing by the coffee kiosk, she puffed on her hands, as if to warm them. The little lights above the elevator illuminated as the cage rose and stopped. Fifteenth floor.

It was a shot in the dark, against all odds. She walked over to the house phone and hit the button for the operator.

"How can I help you?"

"Connect me to the Simond suite, please. Fifteenth floor."

"One moment. Did you mean Simond-Heston?"

"That's correct."

She waited, her heart beginning to pound, as the phone rang.

"Hello?"

"Jill, please."

"I'm sorry, ma'am. There's no Jill here."

"Sorry, must have dialed the wrong room number."

She replaced the phone in its cradle, a slow smile crossing her lips. "Gotcha!"

CHAPTER ONE HUNDRED SEVEN

***

THE GURNEY WAS ROLLED OUT OF THE MARRIOTT'S SERVICE ENTRANCE AND LIFTED into the back of the ambulance. Brenda watched with crossed arms, jaw muscles knotted.

As the EMT closed the doors, he told her, "He'll be fine. You got to him in time."

The words were said for the benefit of Glen Tanko, the head of hotel security. He stood off to the side, "supervising".

Brenda rubbed the back of her neck as the "EMT", or actor, or whoever the hell he was, climbed into the ambulance, and lights flashing, the thing headed off into the cold Washington winter day.

Brenda checked her watch. Sometime in the next seven hours, Bennie was going to find himself in one of Regal's labs, being used for who knew what.

And I'm in even deeper.

"Thanks for your help," she told Tanko.

"Hope your guy is okay." Tanko gestured for her to precede him into the building. "Never can tell about heart attacks. And he looked so young."

"Maybe we need security for our security, huh?" she joked.

Brian Heston's detail leader had handled all the arrangements. They'd waited until two-thirty in the morning. Two of his guys—obtaining plastic from who knew where—had wrapped the body and carried it up the flight of stairs to the penthouse level. Within minutes of Ortega's departure, the fake ambulance had arrived, the "EMTs" had hurried their gurney and gear into the service elevator, and hotel security had been informed.

By the time Tanko arrived, Bennie was wrapped, strapped, and

CPAPped, and on his way to the ambulance.

The cleanup had been straightforward. The way Brenda had killed him hadn't left much blood, for most of it had pooled in the chest cavity.

Cool as clockwork.

Brenda rode the elevator to the penthouse level, waved at the Heston security team, and made her way to the suite.

Was this how the condemned felt as they stumbled their way through the portals and into hell?

She found Chantel seated by herself in the conference room, her notepad covered with script. The woman's eyes were focused on infinity, and there was tension in the set of her mouth.

Brenda dropped into the chair at Chantel's right, hands between her knees, a sense of desolation in her breast.

Was it killing Bennie? Maybe fatigue from too much stress and no sleep? Or the simple fact that she'd smelled like piss until she had managed to duck down to the parking garage and get a change of clothes?

For the moment, she didn't even want to think. Nothing was going according to plan. The Asian markets, Russia, or the angry Tom Ortega who'd stomped out in obvious rage. Bennie was dead, true. But Taylor had vowed to up the game.

Chantel finally asked, "Are my instincts that bad?"

"Ma'am?"

"I've lost Ortega. And maybe America with him." She sighed. "Damn it, Brenda, it's all falling apart. Instead of saving anything, I'm goading the world into destruction." She placed her hands on her face. "Father would be so disappointed."

"Looks like both of us are striking out. I've arranged a charter out of BWI to Miami. The Gulfstream will meet us there." She glanced around. "Given the row with Ortega, I'm not sure I trust Brian, let alone Inga. We need to get out of here."

Chantel shot her a fragile glance. "Are we that vulnerable?"

"Can you trust Robert to back you, guarantee your safety?"

"Only as long as it benefits him."

"Then let's beat feet before Inga or her son decide to move on you." She hesitated. "Even if it breaks poor Stephen's heart."

Picking up her oversized purse with its wigs, Brenda led the way, her right hand on the butt of her HK where it rested under her shirt.

CHAPTER ONE HUNDRED EIGHT

***

SHOOTING FISH IN A BARREL COULDN'T HAVE BEEN EASIER. ALL SHE NEEDED TO DO WAS watch the elevator. When the cage rose to the fifteenth floor, she had another target.

The first time it had only taken twenty minutes before the elevator had returned to fifteen. When it disgorged at the lobby, Tom Ortega and Ben Mackeson had stepped out. Using her cell phone—held low— she'd had clear shots of both men, videoing them as they crossed the lobby. Ortega's expression dark and angry, Mackeson's worried.

Twenty minutes later, she'd snapped Inga Simond-Heston after she'd descended from fifteen. The woman had passed within five feet of Veronica accompanied by what had to be her security. The aging Nobel laureate, however, had seemed pleased about something, and a catlike smile player on her lipstick-red lips.

Ortega mad, Inga happy? Must have been one hell of a meeting. Maybe good old "I care" Tom was discovering he didn't like being a trout hooked through the lip?

Veronica stepped to the house phone again, punching the operator.

"How may I help you?"

"Brian Heston's room, please."

"One moment."

Again, the phone rang, and this time Veronica hung up before it could be answered. Brian Heston was a registered guest.

"They're lining up like pheasants on a rail fence," she whispered as she returned to her spot next to the coffee kiosk.

Again, the light flickered on fifteen. This time, as the doors opened to the lobby, a brunette woman stepped out, glanced around, and was followed by a second.

Security. Checking for a principal. Had to be.

Veronica snapped shots as they emerged. Zoomed, and took facial shots. But instead of heading for the street, the first woman—an oversize purse dangling from her arm—led the way to the parking garage elevator.

Veronica wrapped her muffler tighter around her throat and followed. Too fucking good to be true. The way they were dressed was just wrong. On the street, Veronica wouldn't have given them a second glance. But here? They were as out of place as housewives from Peoria trying to crash opening night at the Metropolitan Opera.

To Veronica's delight, the parking garage elevator door opened as the woman pushed the button. She was five paces behind when the first woman blocked the door, hand extended, saying, "Please, excuse us. My friend, here, is feeling ill. I'd really appreciate it if you took the next one."

Veronica told her, "Of course." All the while she was snapping shots from the iPhone held low in her hand. The moment the doors closed, she laid on the button.

"Come on. Come on." She watched the floor lights. The cage stopped on P4.

Did she dare try and sprint to the parking garage exit ramp? Try and catch one last photo?

Or would the women be parked far enough from the elevator that she could catch them as they drove by?

Veronica had no idea where the parking garage was, so she waited, literally bouncing on her toes as the cage took its own sweet time getting back to the lobby. Leaping in, she pressed P4, then hit it again and again.

After what seemed an eternity, she pushed through the doors, camera ready as she hurried out. Lines of cars were on all sides, and she could hear a vehicle fading away.

Was that them? Did she finally have a photo of the elusive Chantel as she came from a meeting with Thomas Ortega?

Then, to her right, a car started. She turned, camera ready, as backup lights flashed, and a Jaguar backed out.

Now, that was Chantel Simond's kind of car.

She readied herself, but to her surprise, the Jag slowed, and the driver's window lowered.

Inside, a blond man was smiling at her. "Looking for Chantel? You just missed her."

"Who are you?"

"Oh, I've known Chantel for quite some time, Ms. Wolf. She's headed for the airport. If you'd like, I might be able to get you an interview. I know you're with the Ortega campaign."

Veronica hesitated, sudden unease washing through her.

"Well...another time perhaps," the man said, "Have a good day." He started to roll the window up as the Jaguar rolled forward.

"Wait!" Veronica cried. "You're going to see her? Now?"

"I've got some last-minute business before I meet Tom for the flight back to Manchester."

She almost slipped on the concrete in her hurry to get to the passenger door.

CHAPTER ONE HUNDRED NINE

* * *

TOM ORTEGA PACED THE EXTENT OF THE SUITE. BEYOND THE WINDOW, MANCHESTER, New Hampshire, gleamed in the partly cloudy morning. Patches of sunlight shone across the thin coating of snow that frosted roofs and unshoveled sidewalks.

In the corner, the wide-screen TV, its volume muted, was on CNN.

Tom stopped at the window. "Am I that much of a patsy? I mean, people think they can just use me? Like some fucking puppet?"

Jen sat on the couch, her feet pulled up beneath her. She watched him with worried eyes. The report Chantel had provided lay open to the fifth page. As far as she'd been able to read before Tom had stomped into the room.

"So, the campaign is over?"

"Damn right." He rubbed a hand over his face. "Trouble is how do I handle this? Go straight to the Federal Election Commission? To the attorney general? Or call a press conference and make a public announcement that I've discovered my campaign is illegal. That Mackeson has been violating campaign finance law and foreign money is..." He couldn't finish. "No, that will ruin us all. And there's Jessie to think of."

"How, specifically, did Chantel put it, Tom? They want to dictate your policy?"

"I'm supposed to be an ally. Whatever that means. Are they so incompetent they don't know who I am? I mean, fuck! Did they really think I'd be a stooge for some foreign investment syndicate? I'm going to bring them down, Jen. No one plays me like this. No one."

Jen frowned down at the report. "Did you read this?"

"I flipped through a couple of pages on the plane. Mostly I fought to keep from calling the attorney general. You know I don't make good decisions when I'm mad."

"Then you really didn't *read* this?"

"Not as such, why?"

"Scary stuff, Tom, and I'm just at page five."

"They're using me as a political pawn to influence the American electoral process! Thought Russian meddling in the 2016 election was bad? Or Trump's lawsuits in 2020? If a foreign *company*, not even a government, can dictate who gets elected in this country, we're done!"

"Yes, but what if they're right?"

"Right? Brian Heston, two-term secretary of the Treasury, is *their* man! And how many more? We're talking influence peddling and infiltration at the highest levels! This is bigger than Clinton or Trump, or—"

"Or maybe they're right."

"Right? It's *corruption*, Jen! And I'm part of it!"

"When you were raving a moment ago, you said Chantel compared you to Falco and the Democrats. Tell me what she said."

"Something about how I'd been shot at. That in a real crisis, they could count on me to make the hard decisions. That I should think about Falco, and the potential Democratic candidates, and what they'd do in such a situation."

Jen tapped the report. "This EMP thing scares me. Five bombs detonated in the stratosphere and everything stops. The whole nation is dark, Tom. Phones fried, cars don't run, water doesn't pump, credit cards worthless, bank accounts vanish, the cloud and internet are wiped clean."

"Jen, I'm on the Senate Armed Forces Committee. We went through this with North Korea. Anyone attempting such a strike would suffer annihilation in retaliation."

"So, what if Sheila Andrews is president and news comes that the Islamic Caliphate has five nuclear weapons in the air aboard civilian aircraft and an attack is imminent. What's she going to do?"

"I'd hope she'd order all incoming aircraft to reverse course or land in Canada or Mexico."

"You'd hope? And if she didn't? Or if the planes just kept coming?"

"She'd damned well better shoot them down."

"Tom, you're talking about warm and fuzzy Sheila Andrews who bleeds for the innocent. She'll be worried about the women and children on those planes. What happens to airliners when an atmospheric nuke goes off? They fall out of the sky, right?"

"Unless they've got EMP shielded electronics."

"So, the women and children are dead anyway?"

He stared at her. "What's your point?"

"My point is that Chantel Simond might know you better than you know yourself. Before you terminate this campaign, Thomas Ortega, you decide which candidate you'll give your undivided support to, which of your opponents you want sitting in the Oval Office when this all comes down. But don't even think about answering that question until you've read this." She held up the report.

He frowned at it. Curiosity briefly tempered his rage. He extended a hand. "Give it to me."

CHAPTER ONE HUNDRED TEN

***

"SIR, I SINCERELY APPRECIATE THE FACT THAT YOU'RE WILLING TO TAKE MY CALL," TOM said, glancing to where Jen watched him from the couch. She'd been reading the Simond précis, growing ever more concerned.

It was the second time that day that he'd heard the phrase "Gorky Plan". This time from Jen's lips. To put the issue to bed once and for all, he'd placed a call to the Chairman of the Joint Chiefs of Staff. To his surprise, the call had gone straight through.

"*Senator, I'm just delighted that you're doing so well in the polls. OTR, we're all praying for you, Tom.*" His voice changed. "*Now, what can I help you with, Senator?*"

"Sir? Have you ever heard the term *Gorky Plan*? Something the Russians—"

"*No! And, Senator, you haven't heard it either. Doesn't exist.*"

"Yes, sir. That relieves my concerns."

"*When you're back in town, Tom, I'd be very curious to hear where any such silly rumor might have originated.*"

"Yes, sir. I'll see if I can run it down."

"*Anything else I can do for you, Senator?*"

"No, sir." Tom pushed the end button, eyes on the television. The local news was running.

He looked at Jen. "The Gorky Plan's real. You should have heard General Daniels. Half panicked."

Jen tapped the page. "Says here that they've stopped it for the moment."

"Why are you taking their side?"

"I'm not, babe. I'm taking yours. You know I've got a head for figures. We'd have gone broke more than once if I couldn't have kept an immaculate set of books." Pointing to the report on the table, she said, "All of their figures work. It's scaring me to death."

He was grinding his teeth when Jen grabbed the TV remote and said, "Hey look. It's Gene Falco."

Tom turned as the volume went up. *"Oh, I do wish the good senator well with his 'family emergency'. Got to admire a man who puts his family's needs above New Hampshire's and the country's."*

"What about Russia, Governor? The administration is moving two more divisions to Poland, and yet there are still reports of fighting south of Moscow?"

"Well,"—Falco scratched his nose—*"I'd call that an excellent bit of diversion. Keep us off-balance while they insulate more men through the borders. You know, saboteurs."*

"Insulate?" Tom asked. "Does he mean *insinuate?*"

"What about the international markets, Governor? Some analysts insist we barely dodged a bullet these last couple of days."

Falco waved it away. *"What goes on in those penny-ante Asian markets doesn't affect us here. Besides, it's just rich people who are going to take the hit. Me, I'm in it for the common man. The guy on the end of a shovel or baking a pizza. It's the middle class that counts."*

The picture flashed to a reporter. *"So, there you have it. With the first primary in the nation only hours away, Tom Ortega has taken the day off, apparently figuring that he's got New Hampshire wrapped up. But the people of New England have surprised candidates before."*

Tom's fists were knotted when the station went to a commercial.

Jen was watching him speculatively, one brow arched. "It doesn't matter how you're elected, Tom. All that counts is what you do once you're in office."

"I will not sell my soul, Jen." He took a deep breath. "Not even to save the country."

And that's what it came down to, wasn't it? What was worth more? His honor or the country?

CHAPTER ONE HUNDRED ELEVEN

***

WHEN BILL PETROSKI SLURPED HIS WHIPPED-CREAM-TOPPED LATTE, BIG JIM KORKORAN winced. A glob of white clung to the guy's lip and was about to drop onto his shirt.

Korkoran had already had to lean in close a couple of times as Petroski thumbed through the pages of his report. The guy smelled like rancid sausages. But so far, the report was solid gold.

Sure, there were missing pieces—and quite a bit of speculation—but the attorney general's busy little squirrels needed to discover some of the buried nuts themselves. Otherwise, what was to motivate them?

"So, there it is, boss. Who owes what to who and how they're all linked together."

"It's whom. Who owes what to whom."

"Right." Bill Petroski smiled. The dollop of whipped cream dropped to streak his cheap suit coat with white.

Korkoran sighed, too overjoyed with Petroski's research to care. He could even endure the guy's fuzz-yellow teeth and fetid breath. Little enough to suffer for a triumph like this.

"And you're sure you didn't trip any of The Foundation's triggers?"

The ferret-like eyes narrowed behind Bill Petroski's smudged reading glasses. "If I had, do you think I'd be here today, handing you this? I mean, what you got there? It's a death sentence, man." He fumbled in his pocket, producing a thumb drive. "That paper report and what's in here, those are the only copies. I wiped everything else. If The Foundation tries to follow that back, it dead-ends with you."

Petroski tossed the thumb drive on the table and raised his hands, as if in surrender. "I'm done."

"Campaign fraud, racketeering, manipulating the markets, assassination, my God, the thing reads like a bad novel." He glanced up, jubilation in his breast. "And I'm going to be the guy to bring them down."

Petroski tossed off the last of his latte. "Just make sure I get paid before you hand that to Justice. I want an electronic transfer. No check that can have a stop put to it after you're dead."

Big Jim shot him a triumphant smile. "No way that they're going to fool with a sitting senior senator. Besides, once this is in the AG's lap, it's too late. Like cutting open a sack of marbles, they're going to roll everywhere."

Big Jim punched the intercom. "Peggy? I need an appointment with the attorney general. The sooner, the better."

"*Yes, sir.*"

Petroski rubbed the back of his neck as he stood. The guy looked more sweaty than usual. "Guess I'll call it a day, Big Jim. Might go home and watch some videos. Got some new stuff from Argentina."

Korkoran didn't ask. He didn't employ the guy for his morals.

"I'll have your bank transfer within the hour. But don't get too busy with other projects. I've got someone inside the Ortega campaign."

"Yeah, Veronica Wolf. Nice number, Big Jim. Couldn't have got all that"—he gestured at the report—"without her."

"That's just the thing—I may need a report on her after all. Something to hold over her once she applies the *coup de grace* to Ortega." He grinned. "You never stopped recording her action with Trevor Hughes, did you?"

Bill Petroski looked the other way, pulling at his dirty collar with a finger. Sweat was beading on the guy's face. Big Jim had touched a nerve. "Got video. That good enough for you?"

"I'll be in touch."

CHAPTER ONE HUNDRED TWELVE

***

BRENDA WALKED INTO THE SIMOND ISLAND SECURITY CENTER AND CHECKED THE COMMU-nications log. She'd left Chantel in her office where Ricard was reporting on his meetings in Davos. Chantel had barely changed clothes before she was back at her desk, talking forex, securities, and bonds as she continued to firm up the Asian markets. But even as she was making progress with Asia, Europe was slipping over concerns of Russian strife and the potential for rising interest rates.

That raised the question: were Taki and Chicago on board? Had they bailed at first sign of the crisis? Or had they precipitated it?

It's like leaping onto a tiger's back and grabbing him by the ears. How do you ever let go?

Brenda pulled out a chair, checked the computers, and barely heard Mitch as he padded quietly in.

"Sounds like quite a trip, Captain. Wish to hell you'd let me know when you slip off like that."

"Spur of the moment thing, Mitch. Chantel's orders." She studied the readouts. "Half the island defenses are off-line."

"Yeah." Mitch rubbed his nose as he leaned forward to point at the various sections on the security monitor. "That's to accommodate the new construction. Missile batteries, can you believe? Shore to ship. Something Sonny recommended." He gave her a humorless smile.

"Off-line for how long?"

"Just long enough for the construction crews to tie the steel and pour the concrete."

"End of the world," Brenda said and yawned. "We're really preparing for it. How fucking depressing."

Mitch didn't respond to the obvious. Instead, he said, "Good work with Bennie. I heard he got the jump on you, and you still took him out."

Brenda rubbed her tired eyes. "He'd never have made those mistakes had I been a man. But you need to know, I talked to Taylor through Bennie's comm. He says he's going to missiles and bombs, that it's just him and me."

"And Chantel," Mitch reminded. "If he gets you, he's going after Chantel next."

Brenda stifled another yawn. "You might give Sonny a heads up. If Taylor's buying Stingers, TOWs, or whatever, there's a chance Sonny might hear about it and give us a bit of warning. Meanwhile, we're just going to have to operate as if it's a war zone."

"Devon will run him down," Mitch asserted. "Go get some sleep, Captain. I've got the helm for a while." He paused, a wry twist to his lips. "You can bet I'll never underestimate you again."

"Thanks, Mitch. Keep a lid on things."

She was halfway out the door when he asked, "Captain? By the way, where's your brother?"

"Since he's going active again, I've had him training. He and I, we both need to keep the edge."

She walked as if her hips were dislocated, fatigue dulling her wits. In her quarters, she undressed, finally thankful to be rid of the happy-housewife garb. Pulling back her covers, she placed the HK under her pillow, the sheathed Randall stiletto at her side.

Missile batteries?

There were worse things to have when the world finally blew up.

She had almost drifted off, Mitch's words replaying in her head, when she jerked her eyes open.

Son of a bitch!

CHAPTER ONE HUNDRED THIRTEEN

***

VERONICA WOLF BLINKED; HER VISION HAD GONE SILVER, AND HER EYES WERE SWIMMING with tears. "Please, don't do that again."

"I won't have to as long as you tell me the truth."

She sat in a curiously comfortable chair, though it was unusually shaped.

Nor did Veronica have any idea where she was or how she'd gotten there. One minute, she was buckling herself into the Jaguar's passenger seat, the next she'd awakened in this confined, soundproofed room.

The man who'd introduced himself as Valentine Wiesse sat across the desk from her, a touch pad in his lap, curious thimble-like caps on his fingers. He studied her with neutral eyes.

"When Korkoran explained The Foundation, why did you believe him?"

"I didn't. Not at first."

She tensed, shivering, but no wave of pain followed. How the hell could he tell when she told the truth or made something up? And motherfucker, when she lied, the pain was like nothing she'd ever experienced. The first time, she'd voided every orifice in her body. She'd been left to wallow in it for an hour now.

"And Korkoran called you because he owed you one?"

"I know about his affair."

"Who gave you the technology to penetrate Trevor Hughes' computer?"

"I got that from a guy I used to da—"

Some distant part of her heard herself screaming from somewhere in a sea of agony. When consciousness returned, her body was still spasming. For several seconds she tried to breathe through pain-paralyzed lungs. At the ragged edge of panic—her vision going dark and faint—she was finally able to gulp in cool air.

"Why...are you...doing this?" she whimpered through ragged panting as the world swam back into focus.

"I like it," he said simply. "And just so you know, I've sat in that chair myself. I just *had* to know what it felt like. I mean, son of a bitch, nothing on earth hurts like that."

"Let me die...please?"

He tapped the board with an index finger and her heart jolted from a shock with each touch of his finger. The terror left her mewing like a wounded kitten.

"See, I can start your heart with just a tap. All of your vitals are monitored here. With a couple of strokes, I can kill you and bring you back, over and over again. Then there's pain."

He touched the pad briefly, and her body spasmed as if every nerve were searing on a grill.

"Dear God," she whispered hoarsely after she'd caught her breath.

"That's something, isn't it? Modern electronics interfaced with human neural anatomy? You know, it all came from research on prosthetics. Now, who gave you the tech to compromise Trevor's computer?"

She flinched as he raised his finger, and blurted, "Petroski. Bill Petroski!"

"And he works for Korkoran?"

"Yes. I only met him once. I swear!"

"He's not very good," Val noted absently. "Devon's people thought the guy was kind of an oaf."

"You knew?"

Val shrugged. "Wouldn't be very good at my job if I didn't, now, would I? Can't wait to see what kind of report he delivers to Korkoran."

She clenched her teeth, looking at the foam-and-cork-covered walls.

"What? You just spiked, suddenly full of hope." He gestured at the touch pad. "What gave you hope, Veronica?"

"Noth—" Pain blasted through her.

Her thoughts reeled and scattered as the agony subsided. She glanced down at her body, expecting to see it disfigured with the flesh melted from her bones. Instead, she saw only flushed and healthy skin.

"What gave you hope?" Val repeated easily. "I had hope once. It came from the movies. I wanted to grow up and become a hero. Problem was, my father needed me to work. Can you imagine? I started out smuggling weapons. Bright little tow-headed boy like me?"

He gave her a shy smile. "I didn't learn until years later that Dad used that first trip to get me out of the house so he could murder my mother. Some Russian weapons dealers had latched onto Mom's family. Told her she had to spy on my father. If she didn't, Mom's folks, two sisters, and brother—their families too—were dead."

He pointed an electrode-tipped finger at her. "That's the thing about hope. It always ends up an illusion. So what just gave you hope, Veronica?"

She tried to swallow the bitter taste of vomit that coated her mouth. Her throat was unbearably dry, and her tongue stuck mid-swallow, almost choking her.

As he raised his fingers, she croaked, "No, don't! I'll tell. You're too late anyway. Last I heard Petroski had finished his report on The Foundation. If Korkoran's got it, it's already been delivered to the Department of Justice." She smiled weakly. "And if that's the case... you're all fucked."

"Okay," Val agreed. "That was a good reason for hope. You're actually beginning to interest me, Veronica. That takes a special kind of woman. Outside of getting out of that chair and walking free from this room, what do you want? What's the one thing you'd offer up your body and life to obtain?"

"I..." She struggled for sense. What the hell did she really want? What would she give? "I..."

"It's okay, Veronica. Take your time. People never really have to answer that question. Not truthfully. Even when they ask it of themselves. But today, you have to. And you'll really have to tell me the truth."

He flicked his fingers back and forth suggestively before he said, "Me, I wanted to be a hero. And then I wanted the most beautiful woman in the world to love me with all of her heart. Again, Veronica, I had hope. That first time we made love, I was like a giddy idiot.

She's got scars, you see. They run deeper than the flesh. Poor broken thing. She'd been raped by her brother, and he mutilated her when she told on him."

Veronica shot an uncertain glance his way.

Val shrugged slightly. "That's how I became a hero. By walking away from her when I discovered that she just didn't have it in her heart to love any man after what her brother had done to her."

"You're a sick fuck," she rasped through her swollen throat.

"You'd think, wouldn't you? Especially given all this." He gestured around the room. "Fact is, when I share sex with a woman, I like it slow, gentle, and mutually erotic. I consider the appeasement of a quick orgasm to be crass."

He tapped the screen and her pelvis exploded with an orgasm, wave after wave, which left her twitching and gasping as his finger lingered on the pad.

"How did you do that?" she asked when she caught her breath. Somehow, the reality that he could make her body respond like that was more horrifying than the pain.

"You know how CT scans work? Sort of like that. Converging energy fields in the limbic centers of the brain. Medical imaging technology has so many more uses than just looking inside.

"But we're getting away from the point. So tell me, Veronica, what single thing do you want more than anything in the world? What would you sell your soul to obtain? Money? A man?"

"Anchor's desk. Evening news," she gasped.

"You'd do anything for that?"

"Already have," she murmured.

"I am talking about your soul, Veronica. It's forever. We'll own you, and you'll be one of us. Pick your network and desk."

"You serious? You fucking *tortured me*, you prick!"

"Good solid honest answer. Looking at your profile, Veronica, we've got an eighty percent probability that you'll abide by the deal."

He fixed glacial eyes on hers. "But here's the thing: my mother would be alive today if she'd just gone to my father and said, 'Sonny, they've got my family.' So, when that twenty percent probability starts to rear its ugly head, and you've got doubts? Or if some investigation contacts you about us? Just let us know."

"And then you'll kill me?"

"We only kill people who betray us, Veronica. From your psychological profile, and what I've learned about you in the chair, you've got exactly the kind of personality we need." He paused. "Want to sit in that anchor's chair?"

"Fuck you!" Then she laughed at the insanity of it. "Yeah, I want that damn chair. More than anything."

He pressed down on the pleasure button, watching her gasp and squirm for nearly ten seconds.

CHAPTER ONE HUNDRED FOURTEEN

***

THE LAST MAN IN LINE, TAYLOR FOLLOWED THE QUEUE OF WORKMEN WHO WALKED SINGLE file up the ramp and onto the barge tied at the south end of the island. They were already talking about lunch, and he could smell the frying chicken. A helicopter had borne him from Barbados late last night along with three other new hires.

He'd been pouring concrete all morning, waiting for this opportunity. Ensuring he wasn't observed, he jumped down from the ramp to splash into the ankle-deep water below the low sea wall. In a crouch, he proceeded around the curve until the barge was out of sight, keeping one hand on the cement wall. Sometimes he was wading up to his waist.

As he had been told to expect, maybe a quarter mile from the work barge, a knotted black nylon rope hung down to drift in the low surf.

Taylor took hold and tugged. He climbed quickly, peered over the top of the sea wall, and found a forest a couple of yards beyond a gravel road.

Seconds later, coiling the rope as he went, he slipped into the trees. There lay a Pelican rifle case atop a long wooden crate, netting to make a ghillie suit, and an equipment pack containing food, water, bug spray, binoculars, and night vision gear. BDUs were rolled and tied with a belt that sported a sheathed fighting knife and a compass. In the bottom of the pack, he found tactical boots.

Stripping off his construction clothes, Taylor donned the BDUs and opened the rifle case. A hand-sketched map showed him a route up from the beach, with several camera locations marked by Xs with circles that marked their fields of view.

The rifle was a Remington 700 action in black tactical stock. Chambered in 7.62 NATO it was mounted with his preferred Nightforce

20-power scope and Horus reticle. On the stock was taped a data card indicating that the rifle was zeroed at 300 yards, shooting a 165 grain Sierra Matchking at 2750 feet per second. A separate piece of paper exhibited three holes an inch-and-a-half across with the penciled note: "Three shots, fifteen seconds, at 300 yards from rest."

Taylor checked the rifle, adjusted the sling, and dry fired it several times to learn the trigger. Next, he familiarized himself with the scope's eye relief and set the parallax. Only then did he break open a box of cartridges and load the magazine before chambering a round and setting the safety.

Using the fighting knife, he pried the top off the long wooden crate, finding a vintage RPG-7v launcher and three cased rockets with their grenades.

Taylor lifted the launcher free of the packing and checked the firing pin protrusion. He removed the plastic shipping cap from the first rocket and screwed the booster element in until it was snug.

Next, he took the grenade from its packing and inserted it into the tube, rotating it until the indicator stem locked home. Leaving the safety cap in place, he carefully laid the RPG to the side and prepared an additional rocket. This he carefully arranged in the pack before hoisting it onto his shoulders.

He hated using an untested rifle, but then, sometimes life wanted a person to make lemonade. He slung the rifle and picked up the heavy RPG. Taking another look at the map, he oriented himself, and started up the hill, paralleling an old trail.

The map depicted what looked like a fortification, though it was labeled "Mansion". A raised terrace, or deck, on the south side of the mansion had been highlighted in yellow. Sometime, soon, Brenda Pepper would appear there. And, so, too, would Chantel Simond.

"Gonna send you some company, Bennie. Soon, old buddy. Soon."

CHAPTER ONE HUNDRED FIFTEEN

***

BIG JIM KORKORAN ALMOST BOUNCED ON HIS TOES WHEN THE SECRETARY STOPPED IN front of his chair and said, "The attorney general will see you now."

Korkoran straightened his suit coat, picked up his briefcase, and followed the man through several doors and into the attorney general's palatial office.

As Korkoran entered, Kurt Ramey rose and walked around the imposing desk to offer his hand. "Big Jim, to what do I owe this honor? You planning on filing another Contempt of Congress charge naming me or some of my folks?"

Korkoran barely cracked a smile. "That depends, Kurt. Politics are politics. You and I never really did like each other, but sometimes things crop up that supersede personalities." He reached into his pocket and dropped the thumb drive in Ramey's palm.

"What's this?"

"The digital copy of this." Korkoran unsnapped his briefcase and handed Ramey the Petroski report. "Vince Pacheki was working on this. I saw a draft a week or two before he was killed. Take it and run with it."

"Have a seat, Jim." Ramey walked back to his desk and seated himself before scanning the pages. Not even halfway through, he glanced up over his glasses. "You know what this means?"

"Should be one hell of a story, Kurt. You've had a rocky tenure up here, covering for your guy, shaking down big industry for all you can skin out of them. I've heard that historians are ranking you as the most corrupt AG the country's ever seen. I just handed you a path to redemption among the angels."

"And what do you want out of this?"

"Given what Mackeson and the rest are doing, I think it wouldn't be unreasonable to see Tom Ortega handcuffed and in federal custody. Maybe by tomorrow morning just before the start of voting in New Hampshire. Should make for great ratings on the morning news."

Ramey smiled conspiratorially. He reached into a bottom drawer and pulled out a bottle of what looked like whiskey. "My own special brand," he said. "Made by a little barrelhouse in Tennessee. Have one on me."

Korkoran watched Ramey pour, and took the glass, tossing down two fingers of very nice sour mash.

"You really hate Ortega this much?"

"If he's charged with high crimes, his fucking hold on my bill goes away. You take out Tom Ortega, and you don't even have to mention my assistance in bringing the bastard to justice. The same when you take down Simond International Holdings. The discovery of The Foundation and its illegal actions can be all yours. Savor the moment, Kurt."

Ramey took a deep breath, unable to keep from reading more of the report.

"Don't bother about the spelling and grammar. The guy I had write it is better with code cracking than English."

"Jesus, Jim." Ramey pointed. "They can really do this?"

"Your people are going to have a heyday uncovering The Foundation's dirty little secrets."

"My God." Ramey poured another splash of whiskey into Korkoran's glass. "This is going to shake the country to its very foundations. I won't forget this."

Korkoran grinned, the euphoria of satisfaction, like wings around his heart, seemed to explode in his chest. He tossed off the second glass of whiskey. "You might send me a bottle of that. And now I'm going to get out of your hair and let you get to work. If you need anything, let me know."

"Yeah, a bottle of whiskey. I'll be in touch."

As Big Jim Korkoran walked out the Justice Department main door five minutes later, he fought the urge to throw his arms wide and whoop as he twirled around and around. A curious energy charged his muscles, giving him the feeling he could run like the wind all the way back to the Senate.

Ortega would be in front of a federal judge within twenty-four hours, and Peggy and the kids were headed for the Upper West Side.

He glanced up at the slanting winter sun, the euphoria in his chest starting to burn and tighten like a flame. "You gotta love this job!"

CHAPTER ONE HUNDRED SIXTEEN

***

WHEN POUL HAMMOND OPENED THE SIDE DOOR IN KURT RAMEY'S PRIVATE CHAMBERS, the attorney general was hunched in his chair, chin cradled in his fingers as he finished the report. The bottle of whiskey stood to the side, cork still off.

"You heard?" Ramey asked.

"How does it read?"

"Not that I know much about The Foundation, but it seems like lot of stuff is wrong. Quite a bit is missing, but enough is here that you could be in a lot of trouble." Ramey handed Hammond the report.

"And the thumb drive?" Hammond suggested.

Ramey tossed it to him. "Does this make us even?"

"We're never really even."

Kurt Ramey grunted uncomfortably. "No, I suppose not."

Hammond rolled up Korkoran's report. "You never saw this, and Tom Ortega isn't your concern." He turned to the whiskey, popping the cork in the top. "I'd destroy that glass if I were you. Definitely don't drink out of it again."

Taking the whiskey, Hammond started for the door.

"He said someone else wrote that," Ramey called.

"I know. The guy's got a genetic abnormality. We got to him a couple of weeks ago through his neighborhood coffee shop. Big man with a weight problem like he had? He really should have laid off the whipped-cream-topped lattes."

CHAPTER ONE HUNDRED SEVENTEEN

***

BRENDA WALKED OUT INTO THE MORNING AND STARTED ACROSS THE TERRACE. SHE WORE loose-fitting pants that allowed freedom of movement after having worked out for nearly an hour in the fitness center. She actually felt good, stretching her arms and rolling her shoulders as the cotton shirt she wore rippled with the breeze.

She caught Chantel's eye where the woman sat at a shaded table overlooking the forest to the south and the sea to the west.

"Good morning, Captain," Chantel greeted as Brenda pulled back a chair and seated herself. "You wanted to see me?"

"It's taken a while, Chantel, but I've got it worked out. Funny thing is, it's been right there, in front of me the entire time."

"What might *it* be?"

"The traitor, the reason Taylor's been ahead of us the entire time. It had to be someone close. Someone beyond suspicion."

Chantel stiffened. "Tell me it's not Robert. I couldn't take betrayal by another brother."

"I think Robert's clean."

"Regal?" Chantel said through a tightening voice.

Brenda glanced up as Mitch stepped out the side door and started for them. "I asked Mitch to join us. He's going to want to hear this, too."

Chantel nodded, cold green eyes on Brenda's. "He's probably going to be tasked with the chore of dealing with the traitor. Unless I leave it to Val or Sonny."

"Traitor?" Mitch asked, walking up. "Devon's found him?"

Brenda shifted, raising her left arm to the chair back and rubbed her shoulder with her right. "If I guess correctly, Poul Hammond is the brains behind the assassinations."

"Poul?" Chantel cried.

Brenda glanced up at Mitch. "What do you think? The guy had the means to crash the Asian markets. My bet is that he's got Robert firmly under his thumb, probably been stroking him, talking him up."

"I thought you said Robert wasn't involved," Chantel said worriedly.

"He may not be. But if anything happens to you, my bet is that Poul would be pushing Robert to step into your shoes. You said he doesn't understand finance, but Poul does. If Poul ran Simond International for Robert, he'd become one of the most powerful men in the world. Poof! Overnight."

Mitch was watching her with disengaged eyes, his face expressionless as he said, "We'd want proof before we moved on Poul." He turned his thick glasses Chantel's way. "As head of island security, you want me to go? Until this is cleared up, the captain should really be keeping you out of anyone's line of fire."

Brenda slipped her hand beneath her blouse, making a face as she continued to massage her shoulder. "Too much strain in the gym this morning. Sorry. But to your point, I think we should send Sonny."

"No need to bother him." Mitch glanced again at Chantel. "Your father was my responsibility. If Poul had anything to do with it—"

"You could kill him first," Brenda told him. "All the tracks would be covered. But that would leave me with a big problem. Because Taylor's still out there somewhere, probably drawing a bead on me right now."

Mitch couldn't help it; his eyes flicked anxiously to the forest, his lips trembling.

In that instant, he knew what he'd done. He slapped his right hand at his pants pocket.

Brenda beat him to it, pulling her HK from the shoulder rig beneath her shirt.

"Drop it!" she ordered as Mitch clawed his Glock from his pocket.

"I said drop it," Brenda rose to her feet, front sight on Mitch's sternum.

"Sorry," Mitch muttered through clenched teeth. His Glock was halfway through its arc when Brenda shifted her aim and drove a slug through his right shoulder.

Mitch staggered backward, twisted, and fell, the pistol clattering from nerveless fingers.

CHAPTER ONE HUNDRED EIGHTEEN

***

THERE THEY WERE; THE TWO WOMEN. TAYLOR USED HIS TOES TO PUSH HIMSELF FORWARD under the canopy of giant green leaves.

Clearing a plant stem from his field of view, he lifted the binoculars to his eyes and studied them.

It was Chantel Simond, most likely. The sister, Regal, was supposed to be in Wisconsin overseeing the construction of some factory.

Then he fixed on the brunette. For a long moment he studied her. Brenda Pepper. She'd dressed in a white shirt and pants, her hair teased by the wind as she sat so unconcerned.

How do I want to do this?

The RPG would remove all chances for error.

But, smiling, Taylor pulled the .308 up and into position, winding the sling around his forearm.

And then the man stepped out and walked up to the table, his position partially blocking Taylor's shot.

Damn it! Instructions were clear. The women—and only the women.

Taking deep breaths, Taylor watched through the scope. He didn't have a range finder, but at this distance, he was right at three hundred yards, maybe two seventy-five. He estimated barometric pressure and temperature. The breeze was from the south, following in the direction of the shot.

Even as he watched and planned, he was stunned when Brenda Pepper pulled a gun and stood, obviously covering the man.

An instant later, Taylor watched Pepper shoot the man through the shoulder. As he fell, Mitch's face flashed in the scope.

Taylor bit off a curse and shifted his rifle to the side. Reaching back, he dragged the RPG up, ripping the safety cap from the grenade.

Sighting through the three-hundred-meter aperture, Taylor cocked the hammer with his thumb and pushed the safety off.

His cheek against the insulator, he put the front sight post on Brenda Pepper where she crouched over Mitch, applying pressure to the man's broken shoulder.

"Say goodbye, you fucking bitch!"

He took a deep breath and laid his finger on the trigger.

CHAPTER ONE HUNDRED NINETEEN

***

"HELP ME," BRENDA CALLED AS SHE BENT OVER MITCH, USING A NAPKIN TO PUT PRESSURE on the wound.

Chantel bent down, taking over as Brenda grabbed Mitch's good arm and wrenched it behind him. The man was so shocked he barely resisted.

Mitch's zip ties were in the pocket he normally kept them in, outboard by his right knee.

"You shot Mitch!" Chantel cried. "He's been with us for years! He *couldn't...* He just couldn't. Not to Dad."

Brenda took a deep breath, glancing up at the forest.

"Yeah, well if I'm not mistaken..."

A rifle shot cracked in the morning air, the birds suddenly breaking from the trees.

"What was that?" Chantel looked up, a deep-seated terror behind her eyes.

"Payback," Brenda muttered through clenched teeth. "Now, let's get this piece of shit down to medical. If shock doesn't kill him, he's going to have a whole lot to tell us."

"But somebody shot. Who? Why? And at what?"

Brenda reached into her back pocket and pulled out a radio. "Sit rep?"

"Tagged, sis. And you wouldn't believe what this bastard was about to blow you away with."

"Roger. One tagged, bro. I'll send someone up to help you haul him in."

Chantel, still plugging Mitch's wound with a napkin, said, "Mark's out there, isn't he?"

"He was getting cabin fever. I told him to go train. He's been out in the bush, living off lizards and fish and whatever. When Mitch asked me where Mark was, it hit me like a brick. Half the island security has been turned off during the construction of the missile batteries. Mark should have been pinging sensors all over the island. Instead, Mitch didn't have the foggiest clue where he was."

Brenda met Chantel's worried gaze. "So last night, I radioed Mark. Told him Taylor had infiltrated, and we'd be having breakfast on the south terrace."

"You *used* me for bait?"

"Sometimes you gotta do what you gotta do, Chantel."

CHAPTER ONE HUNDRED TWENTY

***

"HELLO," TOM ORTEGA ANSWERED HIS PHONE.

"I understand you wanted to speak to me, Senator. How's the vote up there?"

"It looks like I'm taking New Hampshire by seven points, but StatNco would have already told you that."

"That sounds about right."

He took a deep breath, watching Ben Mackeson on the television as he smiled and talked to reporters. Questions about Tom Ortega's absence were growing.

"Here's the deal. Jen and I read your précis. We've done a little research in the meantime, but you've no doubt had StatNco monitoring my keystrokes and phone calls."

"And you've decided...?"

"That this country is in trouble. So, I'll run. And if I win, I will do everything in my power to prepare us for what's coming. But I will do it my way. If you try to interfere, you and I will go to war. Is that perfectly understood?"

"Perfectly, Senator. Now, if you will excuse me, you have a victory speech to give in about two hours."

CHAPTER ONE HUNDRED TWENTY-ONE

***

VAL MUNCHED ON CRACKERS TOPPED WITH MELTED CHEESE AS THE EVENING NEWS LOGO flashed on his television. Reaching from his chair, he found the remote and turned up the sound.

"*Good evening from New York. I'm Veronica Wolf, and this is the Evening News. In his stunning primary victory last night, Senator Tom Ortega was gracious in his thanks to the people of New Hampshire. Having covered the campaign myself, I can vouch for Senator Ortega's charm and dedication and his concern for his daughter's health over the last couple of days. It's a delight to report that little Jessie is recovering from her latest setback and will be joining her father on the campaign trail soon.*

"*In other news, the unexpected collapse of Senator Big Jim Korkoran outside the Department of Justice yesterday has been attributed to a heart attack. Doctors at Bethesda Naval Hospital reported the three-term senator from Georgia suffered massive cardiac arrest within moments of his initial complaint of chest pains.*

"*The future of his signature legislation, known as Korkoran-Hardy, the banking reform bill, is currently in doubt.*

"*In other news, the Asian markets seem to have recovered their momentum, making up for losses suffered during the last two days. This information is buoyed by news from Russia that a deal has been brokered with break-away military divisions south of Moscow, and a truce has been declared.*"

"There, you see?" Val crunched another cracker, wiping the crumbs from his shirt. "Isn't ambition a wonderful thing? It placed Veronica in the anchor's chair...and you in mine."

"Val?" the man in the chair groaned. "For God's sake, just get it over with, will you?"

"Over with?" Valentine smiled. "You thought that with Chantel and Renaud out of the way, you'd become a big man. What did they offer you? Must have been good." He paused. "You orchestrated the Asian crash, didn't you?"

"Yes."

"Going to be a big-time player, huh? You sold Mitch on the trading scheme, along with Chantel's old bodyguard. Holding that over his head, you could play Mitch like a violin."

"For God's sake, I was a low man on the totem pole! I don't know anything. Kill me!"

Val seemed not to hear as he continued, "Taylor might have pulled the trigger, but you gave the orders. Killing Renaud? I might have been able to understand. His constant agonizing over right and wrong was incredibly tedious."

Val waved a cautionary finger. "But trying to kill Chantel? The pain and anguish you cost her? That was over the line. Did I ever tell you that I was in love with Chantel once? No? Well, I was."

"I gambled and lost. Fucking kill me, won't you?"

Val fixed cold eyes on the sweating man. "On top of everything else, you came within inches of killing or crippling my father."

"Just...just let me die, Val."

"Eventually." Val smiled. "But I think I can keep you alive for days. Really string this out. Set a new record. Now, let's see what happens if I tap my fingers on all the buttons at once, shall we?"

Poul Hammond's scream was deafening.

CHAPTER ONE HUNDRED TWENTY-TWO

***

BRENDA HAD NEVER BEEN TO THE SIMOND ISLAND HOSPITAL WARD. LIKE THE REST OF THE mansion facilities, the twenty-bed unit appeared to be state-of-the-art with its gleaming white equipment, airy rooms, and immaculate, white-dressed staff.

Dana Riccio and Sam Gunnarson, HK MP5s hanging from slings, stood outside Mitch's door. Each member of Mitch's team had spent a couple of hours in the interrogation chair. In the end it turned out that John Cammack was the only other person on the security team involved with Mitch and Poul Hammond.

"How's the patient?" Brenda asked as she approached.

"Well enough, I guess," Gunnarson replied, conflicting emotions on his face. "I heard you're going to be the new chief." His lips twitched, then he added, "Congratulations."

Brenda nodded to both, wondering at the reservation in Riccio's eyes. But then, she was still an unknown, and the entire island was off-balance.

The head of the bed was elevated allowing Mitch to meet her eyes as she entered the room. A sheet lay tangled at the man's waist, his right shoulder immobilized in a sling and swathed in bandages. He peered at her through his thick glasses.

"So, Captain," he said weakly, "you emerge the victor."

"Poul Hammond's given Val the whole story."

Mitch grunted, his eyes casting about the room and its instruments. "Seems a shame to spend all this time on fixing me up just to kill me, doesn't it?"

"Not my call."

He studied her thoughtfully. "Do I die fast or slow?"

At her silence, he gave her a death-rictus of a smile. "They made me kill Vernie. That really hurt."

"Vernie?"

"Vernard Hall. Your predecessor. I liked him. That was the thing about Vernie. He was always likable. You're hard. Chantel's found her immaculate weapon, and you're it."

"Why'd you sell out Renaud?"

Mitch wet his lips. "These people are like acid, Captain. They'll corrode anything you hold dear, especially your values. Hammond read the signs even before Devon did. It's the end of the world. What's left but to grab the biggest piece that you can as it goes down? The Foundation is going to splinter, turn on itself now that it's down to brass tacks. You were at that meeting, you saw. Chicago and David and Taki are going to fight for everything they can get. They want to form a rival organization to compete with The Foundation."

"I heard that Katya is already taking care of that."

"Maybe, but Katya's priority is saving Russia, and to do that she will turn on Chantel in the end. You'll see. The Foundation is a nest of predatory spiders, and they'll devour each other in the final hours."

Brenda glanced up at the cameras positioned around the room. "Actually, I think Chantel will hold it together."

Mitch paused, then added, "I can almost pity you. Chantel played you. And now you're just as stuck in their web as I was. Chantel doesn't just have you, Captain. She's got your brother for added insurance. She *owns* you now. Body and soul."

"Yeah," Brenda whispered, knowing he was right. Knowing she had only one way out. Would she take it? Or would she play along hoping...

The door opened and Chantel walked in. Dressed in a sky-blue suit with her red hair in a ponytail, she smiled at Mitch. The kind of smile that made a person's blood turn to ice. As she walked forward, she reached into a pocket, removed a syringe and twisted the plastic guard from the needle.

"What's that?"

"Something Regal concocted in one of her labs. She wanted to be here, but she's in the middle of some heavy negotiations on a land deal. In a couple of hours, SimondAg will control most of western Nebraska."

Chantel stepped over, seeing the terror in Mitch's eyes as she inserted the needle in his IV.

Mitch croaked, "The Takanabis aren't going to rest until they've killed you and your whole fam—"

"Felicia was found dead in her bed this morning. Sudden massive stroke. Right about now, Chicago should be feeling the first inexplicable twinges in her muscles. The rest will follow soon," and with that, Chantel pressed the plunger home.

Mitch turned to stare at Brenda, and she could read it in his eyes: *If Chantel can get to Felicia Takanabi in her bed, no one can hide. No one.*

Brenda silently slipped her hand inside her coat and tightened her fingers around the pistol's grips where it rested in her waist holster. Her heart rate kicked up.

Without so much as a glance Mitch's way, Chantel dropped the syringe in the sharps disposal, turned, and stared at the pistol in Brenda's hand.

Three or four seconds passed before Chantel calmly looked up to meet Brenda's eyes. Their gazes held.

"I see you finally came up with a number, Captain."

CHAPTER ONE HUNDRED TWENTY-THREE

***

CHANTEL TRIED TO STILL HER OVERACTIVE BRAIN. GOD, WHAT SHE'D GIVE TO BE A SUPER-computer. Singapore had just collapsed, the economy cratering behind a nosedive triggered by a stock she'd never heard of. Rioting in the streets was threatening to bring down the government. Devon expected the panic to spread to Malaysia, and from there to Thailand.

Australia might hold out.

Her feet whispered on the Saltillo tiles as she followed the hall out onto the patio.

Brenda Pepper sat on a recliner, her gaze fixed on the setting sun as it poured orange-gold across the shining Caribbean. The woman's hair was pulled back, her hands cupped around a tumbler half-full of green liquid.

Chantel seated herself on the cushion beside Brenda's right leg and allowed her mind to empty as she watched the sun slide down behind the sharp ocean horizon. The sky shaded from orange to turquoise before darkening to indigo overhead.

"Brenda, why did you shoot him?"

"What was in the syringe?"

"Water."

"Really?"

"Really."

"I shot him to make a point. He was partially responsible for Kelly, Janeesh, Renaud, my folks, and if he'd succeeded, we'd be dead. The man was a traitor. A fucking serpent. He had to die."

"What's the difference between a bullet and a virus?"

An odd constriction tightened in Chantel's chest. "Felicia's alive. Chicago's fine. I told you that to see how you'd react."

"Did I pass? Or is one of Regal's viruses in my soursop margarita? It would be the ultimate irony. Your father hooked me on these."

Chantel reached out, taking the glass. She lifted it to her lips, savoring a full swallow before handing it back. "No poison...and yes, I know. It could have a virus tailored to your genetics. That was a symbolic gesture."

"Symbolic of what?"

"The last time I drank out of anyone else's glass I was five. And it was Regal's." She turned, suddenly terrified as she fixed on Brenda's hard eyes. "I came here to...I mean, I want you to... Shit! How do I say this?"

"How about just blurting it out?"

"I always had Dad and his insufferable philosophy as a sounding board. Now it's all fallen on my shoulders, and I'm not sure I can bear the load. Not...by myself."

"Maybe, to you, I'm just another weapon. But I won't be a mindless or soulless one. Won't be party to long-term suffering or twisted retribution."

"I see."

"If I'm doing the killing, I need to be part of the decision when it comes to who, why, and especially how. I want my hand on the switch deciding life or death. I have to take responsibility. Otherwise, I'm a robot. Or worse, Taylor."

God, Chantel, you're trembling. She clenched her fists, bracing for rejection. "Fine, anything you want."

Brenda's gaze seemed to burn right through her. Seconds turned into eternity.

A faint quirk of Brenda's lips betrayed her amusement. "Damn, Chantel. Don't crap yourself over it. I'll be your conscience, and as long as I'm part of the decision-making process, I've got your back."

The warm sensation of joy spread through Chantel's gut. "You don't know how hard that was."

"I've seen your scars. I also know what it's like to have someone you can trust beside you. I had that once...with Bill."

Chantel sighed, eyes on the purpling sea. The breeze toyed with her hair. "I'm not sure I could ever feel that way about a man."

"You might. If the right one came along. And what's this 'Fox' that Val calls you?"

"Red hair like a fox. A fast predator. A fox on the run. A foxy lady. Val functions on a lot of levels."

"So noted."

Chantel shared a companionable moment, then asked, "What do you want, Brenda? If you could have one wish?"

Brenda tossed off the last of her drink. "Bill knew, way back then: I think I'm going to save the world."

A LOOK AT: DISSOLUTION BY W. MICHAEL GEAR

***

FROM WESTERN WORD-SLINGER AND ANTHROPOLOGIST W. MICHAEL GEAR, COMES AN ENTIRELY NEW TYPE OF WESTERN – A CONTEMPORARY APOCALYPTIC WESTERN.

For anthropology graduate student Sam Delgado, headed to the wilds of Wyoming, this is his last chance to save his graduate career. He and his urban classmates see this as the adventure of a lifetime: They are going to horse-pack in the wilderness to map and test a high-altitude archaeological site.

Until a cyber attack collapses the American banking system, and an already fractured nation descends into anarchy and chaos. All credit frozen, Sam and his archaeological field school is trapped in their high-altitude camp. With return to the East impossible, Sam, the woman he has come to love, and the rest of the students must rely on hard-bitten Wyoming ranchers for their very survival.

Guided only by an illusive Shoshone spirit helper, Sam will discover the meaning of self-sacrifice. Even at the cost of his life.

Haunting, provoking, frightening and prescient – in the end, all that stands between civilization and barbarism is one young man's courage and belief in himself.

AVAILABLE NOW

ABOUT THE AUTHORS

***

W. Michael Gear and Kathleen O'Neal Gear are *New York Times* bestselling authors and nationally award-winning archaeologists. They have published 75 novels and over 200 non-fiction articles in the fields of archaeology, history, and bison conservation. In 2021, they received the Owen Wister Award for lifetime contributions to western literature and were inducted into the Western Writers Hall of Fame. They live in beautiful Cody, Wyoming.